Lifting her skirts higher, Félicité ran faster and faster. Her breath sobbed in her throat. She did not hear the pursuit until too late.

A great wave of the incoming moontide staggered her. At the same time, she was caught from behind. Thrown off balance, she and her assailant fell, the creaming surf washing over them, wetting them. Félicité struggled, but Morgan pinned her to the washing sand. His mouth tasted of salt and rum and the warm, honeyed sweetness of remorse.

They stripped away their clothing and the flowing, melted turquoise water was warm against their skin. Félicité could feel the pounding of his heart, the pressing of his thighs against her, and the pounding shocks of pleasure that had the same ceaseless rhythm as the tide.

Deep in her eyes as she gazed into the face of the man above her was tangible ecstasy, scintillating and shimmering, the most radiant thing of all. . . .

Fawcett Gold Medal books
by Jennifer Blake

GOLDEN FANCY

THE STORM AND THE SPLENDOR

writing as Patricia Maxwell
NOTORIOUS ANGEL

EMBRACE AND CONQUER

Jennifer Blake

FAWCETT GOLD MEDAL • NEW YORK

A Fawcett Gold Medal Book
Published by Ballantine Books
Copyright © 1981 by Patricia Maxwell

Library of Congress Catalog Card Number: 83-90039

ISBN 0-449-12592-0

Manufactured in the United States of America

First Ballantine Books Edition: October 1983

Part One

Chapter 1

❦

The booming of cannons in salute shook the still, sultry air. The thudding concussion reverberated among the half-timbered houses of New Orleans and rolled over the Mississippi River, bouncing about the hulls of the ships lying at anchor before echoing back from the green tree line of the distant shore. Pigeons startled from their perches flung themselves into wheeling flight with the glaring orange glow of the westerly sun beneath their wings. A mange-ridden mongrel, sniffing in the noisome open gutter that centered the street below the balcony where Félicité Lafargue stood, flinched and cowered, then fled from the sound. Félicité gripped the balcony railing with white-tipped fingers, leaning to stare in the direction of the Place d'Armes. There were distress and scorn in her velvet-brown eyes as she watched the boiling cloud of blue-gray powder smoke that rose to join the heat haze above the rooftops of the town.

Hard on the heels of the salute came an answering roar from O'Reilly's fleet straining at its anchor chains on the river, followed by a fusillade of musket fire. The bells of the Church of St. Louis began to peal with a hard, unmelodious clanging. Plainly there came through it all the deep-voiced cheers of the soldiers, more than two thousand strong, as they shouted in the despised Spanish, *"Viva el rey!"*—"Long live the king!"

The bells stopped. The cheers died away. The pigeons flapped back toward the square. All was quiet.

Félicité drew a deep breath, lifting her chin, squaring her

3

shoulders. The deed was done. The fleur-de-lis of France, the golden lilies on a blue ground, had been lowered, and the lions and castles on a field of scarlet that marked the banner of imperial Spain had taken its place. There was nothing she could do now, nothing anyone could do.

She was glad she had not joined the throng of morbidly curious at the Place d'Armes. Her father, fearing there might be trouble, some demonstration of the townspeople's displeasure, had suggested she stay away, but it had in truth been her own preference. Why should she wish to view the might of Spain brought across the seas to quell their pride, crush their brief independence, and force them to obedience? So long as she did not see the transport ships, the stacked arms and heavy guns, the assemblage of fighting men in numbers to equal, if not surpass, the entire French population, she need not acknowledge their existence. For a few minutes more she could delude herself that this was a nightmare from which she must surely wake.

When had it begun? It must be two, no, three years ago, when the rumors of the secret Treaty of Fontainebleau had begun to stir. Louis XV of France, most glorious of monarchs, had ceded the colony of Louisiana to his Bourbon cousin, Carlos III of Spain, by secret arrangement. The reasons, the machinations behind it, were many, but also meaningless. The people of New Orleans would henceforth, no matter how they protested, be forced to regard themselves as Spaniards.

Protest they had, by letter, by public proclamation, by special deputation to France. The king would hear none of their pleas. And yet hope of a reconciliation with their mother country, the land from which they had come and that had ruled over them for the seventy-odd years since the founding of the colony, would not die.

The hope was kept alive, in the main, because of the long, weary months Spain had dallied, neglecting to take up the burden of financing and governing this remote and poor outpost of her vast domain. Was it any wonder that the French in New Orleans had grown impatient, had begun to talk of refusing the Spanish yoke and, if France would not have them, setting up an independent republic and governing themselves? Could they be blamed for thinking that with such a show of loyalty the king might relent, and even if he did not, things could be no worse?

Félicité sighed, taking a turn about the small, shadowed balcony. The soft lavender light could not conceal the gleam, like old gold coins, of her hair, which seemed almost too heavy in its piled curls. It revealed also the delicate pearl sheen of her skin stretching over the oval bone structure of her face, the straight nose, the dark brows and lashes that were so unusual with her blondness. She wore a day gown of India calico in a pale gold stripe with a basque, or stomacher of gold-embroidered white silk; holding back her flounced petticoats in front, and at the elbow-length sleeves, were shining knots of champagne ribbon. She came to a halt, pressing finely molded lips together, dark remembrance in her eyes.

The trouble had escalated with the arrival of the first Spanish governor, Ulloa. A scholarly man of great pride and little understanding of people, he had been more interested in the flora and fauna of the new land than the problems of those who inhabited it. He had held himself aloof, taking a bride from South America in a private, almost secret ceremony, denying the townspeople any share in the merrymaking.

Perhaps in order not to inflame a trying situation, he had never formally taken possession of the colony for Spain, had allowed the French flag to continue flying over the town, had kept the French commandant in office. It was no wonder that everyone was annoyed and confused.

As the grumbling, the marching, the plotting in coffee houses and posting of placards had become more forthright, Ulloa had taken alarm. With his bride, he had gone on board his ship tied up at the river levee, preparing for a fast escape should it become necessary. This show of timidity only encouraged the conspirators, who had come to count among their numbers nearly every able-bodied man in the town, if not in the entire colony. Within the week, a group of young men, exuberant with wine and the joy of a different type of wedding from that of the Spanish governor, had gathered on the levee to taunt that haughty and invalorous man. A wag had suggested they set the ship adrift, and in seconds the lines holding it were cut. Ulloa, instead of ordering the ship resecured, had let himself be carried downstream, then with the dawn had upped canvas and set sail for Spain, there to pour the tale of his mistreatment and daring escape from dangerous insurgents into the king's ears.

Carlos III, enraged at the flouting of his authority, had sent for one of his most able commanders, Captain-General Alexander O'Reilly. Elevating him to the rank of governor-general, he had charged him with the responsibility of putting down this rebellion in Louisiana. The Irishman had arrived at the mouth of the Mississippi River near a month ago, where he had met with a delegation from the town that had included the French commandant, Director-General Aubry, still in office, plus several men of substance, and the Spanish officials left behind when Ulloa had decamped.

With a courtier's smiling, meaningless phrases, he had sought to allay the fears of the townspeople, but the sight of twenty-odd transport ships laden to the gunwales with men and arms, in addition to O'Reilly's frigate mounting one hundred guns, had not, somehow, been reassuring.

In the street below, a man appeared, tripping along on red-heeled shoes with the skirt of his satin *frac* coat swinging about his knees. Unconsciously, the lines of Félicité's features tightened to guardedness.

Glancing up, her adoptive brother, Valcour Murat, doffed his tricorne in a mocking greeting, then passed beneath the balcony to enter the house.

He had given his hat and cane to the maid and was unencumbered when he strolled into the room behind her. Félicité turned in a silken swirl of panniered skirts to step through the open doorway, moving toward him.

"Where is Papa?" she asked, her voice low and musical.

"I left him awed by the spectacle of O'Reilly being received by the dignitaries of the church, bowing his head for the chanting of a *Te Deum* and accepting the benediction of the host. The smell of incense being disagreeable in connection with such a cause, I came away."

"Yes," Félicité said in complete understanding. "So. Now we are Spaniards."

"Not I." Valcour lounged out onto the balcony and, sweeping aside his coat skirts, dropped onto one of a pair of straight chairs that sat on either side of a small table. "I will always be a Frenchman."

"Try telling that to Don Alejandro O'Reilly!" She sent a smoldering glance after her brother.

"With pleasure, *ma chère*, with pleasure."

She swung back out onto the narrow ledge that hung above the street. "Valcour, you wouldn't—"

"Wouldn't I?"

"It's far too dangerous. This man is no Ulloa. He'll not be frightened by a few broadsides tacked to trees, or a mob drunk with wedding champagne and shouts of *liberté*."

A sneer moved over Valcour's expressive face, and he made a negligent movement of his shoulders. "What can he do?"

"What can he do?" Félicité tilted her head, one winged brow lifted in disbelief. "He is an Irish mercenary, a hired killer in the service of Spain with an army at his back. He can do what he pleases!"

"A Frenchman is the equal of any ten Spaniards, or an uncivilized bog Irishman for that matter. Do not excite yourself. It is doubtful it will come to that. We will prevail without force, just as we triumphed over the other long-nosed Iberian sent to lord it over us."

Félicité stared at him. There were anger and spite in his words, and yet they held also a hint of steely purpose at odds with his appearance. Valcour Murat was of no more than medium height, with a thin frame and a pale, rather sallow complexion. To make up for the deficiencies of nature, he had adopted the mode of dress and languid airs of an exquisite. On this day he wore a close-fitting bagwig heavily powdered and tied at the back with an enormous black bow known as a solitaire, the ends of which were wrapped around his neck and tucked into his snowy stock. Froths of fine lace appeared at his shirtfront and fell over his wrists. His coat was of celestial blue silk heavily embroidered in silver thread. His waistcoat of lavender-gray satin was also stiff with embroidery, as were the bands at the knees of his breeches. His clocked stockings were without a wrinkle. His face had been lightly dusted with cornstarch powder, and on one cheek, hiding the ravages of a childhood bout with smallpox, he had placed a gummed patch of black velvet cut in the shape of a cabriolet carriage complete with a miniature horse. The only incongruous note was the rapier that hung from his side with the chased silver scabbard pushing through a vent in his coat skirt.

Félicité moved once more to the railing of the small balcony. "I'm not so sure."

"Have you no faith in me, or in your father's judgment of which side in this matter deserves his allegiance?"

"It isn't that," she said over her shoulder. "When we set ourselves up as an independent country we are challenging the might of Spain, threatening its power and prestige. They dare not let us succeed for fear of losing their other colonies in the New World."

"Both France and Spain are giving away colonies right and left—witness the passing of Canada by Louis XV to the British and the ceding of Florida to the same by our would-be master. What should the loss of a few arpents more matter?"

"What a man, or a country, may give away or lose through carelessness and the fortunes of war is different from that which he will allow to be wrested from him."

"You are an expert then on men, *ma chère*, as well as the colonial policies of France and Spain?"

She sent him a darkling look from the corner of her eye. "You know very well I am not."

"You relieve my mind. It would be a great pity if I were forced to turn my attention to avenging your honor in the midst of this most fascinating crisis." He shook out the lace at his wrist, adjusting its fall.

Despite appearances, it was no idle threat. Valcour had taken it upon himself more than once to discourage the ardor of men attracted to her, or depress the pretensions of those who aspired to her hand. He had no small measure of skill with the rapier he wore, and a temper notorious for its uncertainty. He could, when the occasion arose, inflict devastating wounds upon his opponents while smiling in enjoyment.

It was not as if he had any right to stand between her and matrimony; Félicité's father was well able to direct her in that undertaking. Monsieur Lafargue had not as yet seen fit to approve a husband for her, did not seem to notice, in his absorption with his own affairs of business and politics, that she required one. His daughter was far too dear to him and necessary for his comfort for him to part with her, though she would soon, at the venerable age of nineteen, have passed beyond the first fragile bloom of youth to something perilously near spinsterhood.

For herself, having formed no lasting attachment to any of the young men of the town who had presented themselves to her, she was not anxious to leave her father's house. She was all too well aware that when the time came for her to wed, considerations such as wealth and family background would be given more weight than her preferences. There were among her friends, the girls with whom she had attended the convent school of the Ursuline nuns, many who had been wives these four years past, and were now mothers two and three times over. She did not begrudge their superior standing, though she was often curious about the physical duties, the transports of joy and pain, that had become their lot.

These mysteries had exercised her mind much of late. She had begun to wonder if she was destined ever to come close to them, or if she would continue as she was, acting as housekeeper for her father and brother, pampered and protected by them for the rest of her life.

It was also becoming a trifle embarrassing to be escorted everywhere by Valcour. He was an attentive gallant, as proficient on the dance floor as on the dueling field, as ready to lend his presence to an outing to the market on the levee for fresh fish and vegetables as to the most elegant soirée. And yet, he was no substitute for a proper *parti*. It was a question of pride. As little as she relished the idea of marriage, she disliked the appearance of an inability to attract a husband.

Valcour's interference was his own choice, an assumed responsibility. Nearly ten years Félicité's senior, he had been taken in by her father when she was no more than a few months old. His parents had succumbed to the same cholera epidemic that had taken her mother's life. The age difference between them had been too great for them to be truly close as they were growing up, but still, as she had developed into adolescence he had begun to take special notice of her. He had always been there, someone to turn to when her father became immersed in his books and radical ideas of freedom and equality. The blood that ran in their veins was not the same, but there was a bond between them made up on Valcour's side of pride and possessiveness amounting almost to jealousy, and on Félicité's of trust and an uneasy relief that her unpredictable adoptive brother never turned the vicious edge of his nature to her.

"Valcour," she said, her voice quiet as she clasped her hands together at her waist, "I am afraid."

"Don't talk nonsense, *chère*," he said, his tone threaded with impatience. "Be a good girl and ring for refreshments, will you? I am parched with thirst after my exertions in this heat."

She stepped inside and called for the young maidservant, Marie. She arrived breathless and anxious. Félicité ordered ratafia, a cordial flavored with almonds and peaches, for herself, and wine for Valcour.

"I will have cognac," her brother corrected, eyeing the maid without favor. "And you may send Dom to me with my fan."

The maidservant curtsied and went away. After a moment Félicité returned to the balcony and the subject that troubled her. "I mean it, Valcour, I'm frightened."

He sighed, pushing erect, taking a stance beside her and picking up her hand to fondle it in his cool, dry fingers. "How can this be? You forget, I know your courage."

"Courage? I have none."

"Was it cowardice then that made you brave the current of the river a few years ago, learning to swim like an eel, or that allows you to ride now with all the grace of a Valkyrie? And what was it made you swagger through the gaming hells at my side in breeches, coat, and sword like the most cocksure, beardless gallant, and even to challenge the man unwise enough to slight you?''

''Madness, I think,'' she answered with some asperity, ''though the last is hardly true. You were much too quick with your own demand for a meeting to allow me to issue mine.''

''Well, perhaps. As I have tried to impress upon you before, acting as my fencing partner with buttoned epées is one thing, swordplay with naked blades is something quite other. There are some to whom dueling scars would be an asset, a definite improvement, but you, *ma petite*, are not one of them.''

''Unfair, as always.''

''Right, as always.''

''And with your usual deviousness, trying to distract me. It won't work. A certain boldness I may have for myself, but I possess very little where you and my father are concerned.''

''Yes, but—listen!''

From the Place d'Armes there came the roll of snare drums. The beat fell into the measured cadence of a field march, signaling vast numbers of men on the move.

Valcour cocked his head to one side, a cynical smile tightening his narrow lips. ''It appears we are to have the honor of seeing the troops of his Spanish majesty marching in review. Aren't you overcome with the thrill of it?''

''The threat of it, you mean!'' she answered, her tone grim. ''No doubt we are meant to be cowed into submission by a display of force.''

''Thrown into veritable paroxysms of fear,'' he agreed. ''Will such a tactic succeed, do you think?''

Félicité flushed under his coolly questioning gaze. ''Surely such arrogance can only anger the people of New Orleans, encouraging open revolt?''

Valcour nodded. ''I knew you were laboring under a simple irritation of the nerves. You could not be so chickenhearted as to shiver in your silk slippers at the mere thought of the Spanish dons.''

''It was more than that.''

"I know. Your papa's involvement in this plotting in court-yards is a worry."

"And yours also. It is treason, or so some say."

"Ridiculous. How can we betray a country that has not officially possessed itself of the colony?"

Félicité did not answer. The sharp, steady rattle of snare drums was coming closer, and they could hear the muffled tramp of marching feet.

Behind them, the maid appeared with a tray bearing their refreshments, and with Valcour's manservant, Dom, close on her heels. Félicité took her glass, watching as Dom bowed, presenting a fan of painted chicken skin to her brother before stepping back out of the way so Marie could serve his master's cognac.

The Negro man, strong, well-proportioned, had said nothing. He could not speak, though that had not been his condition when Monsieur Lafargue had bought him at auction five years before. A few months after he had been brought into the house to be trained in his duties as valet for the older man and Valcour, Félicité had asked Dom the whereabouts of her brother. The manservant had replied that he had gone to a cockfight and from there meant to visit the house of a certain mademoiselle. The woman mentioned was a quadroon, a free woman of color, though Félicité had not realized it at the time. When she had spoken of the matter to Valcour, he had been coldly angry, forbidding her to question his comings and goings again, or to speak of the woman. That same night Dom had suffered an accident, falling from a second-floor window into the court at the rear of the house. His tongue was bitten in two, so evenly it might almost have been severed by a knife.

Now the maid flitted from the room, but as the manservant turned to go, Valcour stopped him with an upraised hand. His yellow-brown gaze scanning the street below, one of the main thoroughfares down which the Spanish must come, he said, "I wonder if there could be found an unemptied *pot de chambre* in the house?"

"What?" Félicité stared at him in sudden mistrust.

"Are you so strict a housekeeper that you require the

12

servants to sling the contents of such into the gutter more than once a day?''

''Valcour, you can't mean—'' Félicité stopped, staring at him with dismay in her eyes, unable to put her terrible suspicion into words.

''Can't I?''

''It would be insanity, an unforgivable insult!''

''I'm not sure our garlic-eating friends would notice the additional stench.'' Valcour allowed himself a thin smile for his witticism as he unfurled his fan and plied it with languid strokes.

''Think of the attention it will focus upon us! You may as well post a sign on the front of the house declaring our leanings toward independence.'' Reason, she had discovered, was the only way of reaching Valcour when he embarked on one of his mad starts.

''You think they don't know already? O'Reilly will be well aware of who has been plotting here. Our good and brave commandant, Aubry, will have made certain of it.''

''There's no need to invite trouble.''

''I have a feeling it will come whether we invite it or not, rather like the Spanish, wouldn't you say? Dom, procure for me a chamber pot, as full as may be found. Quickly!''

With set face, the manservant bowed and went quietly from the room to do as he was bid. At the far end of the street, the Spanish soldiers had appeared, stepping through alternating bands of deep shadow and bright, slanting wedges of sunlight falling between the houses. They advanced with relentless precision, a wall of red now fading, now washed with blinding color. The dust raised by their measured tread rose to hang like a pall in the air above them.

''Valcour, I beg of you, don't do this.''

''A most affecting plea; I wonder how I resist it,'' he mused, contemplating the Fragonard scene depicted on his fan.

''By consulting nothing except your own whims!'' she said bitterly.

''Unjust. You will enjoy the spectacle. Come, admit it.''

13

She gave a quick shake of her head. "Only think of the consequences."

"Too late, *ma chère.*"

Dom had arrived with a pot of rough earthenware stenciled with a floral design, its malodorous contents sloshing halfway to the rim. At the same time, the first of the soldiers, their faces red and beaded with perspiration from their exercise in the stiflingly hot summer afternoon, compounded by dress uniforms heavy with gold braid, were beginning to pass below. An officer on horseback rode at their head, his glittering epaulets catching the dying rays of the sun, the ramrod straightness of his seat in the saddle holding all the assurance of a conqueror.

"Valcour," she tried again.

Her brother ignored the protest, making a flicking motion with his fingers toward the railing in a wordless command.

Dom shifted uneasily, his skin taking on an ashen hue. Félicité looked from the Negro servant to his master. "But consider. Dom will be blamed. They will never believe it was not meant as an insult, that he only happened to be emptying the chamber pots at this time of day, on this occasion. They may flog him, put him in the stocks, or worse."

"How distressing," Valcour said with a mock shudder. "But I fear you are right. The Spanish are known for their severity in matters of this sort, are they not? Still, it must be done. Now, Dom."

"You can't mean it," Félicité began.

"Dom?"

The soft note in Valcour's voice held an unmistakable undercurrent of menace, one the servants of the house had long been accustomed to obeying without question. The manservant's face tightened, then with a hopeless look in his eyes he lifted the earthenware pot and flung the liquid over the railing into the street.

"Faugh!" Valcour exclaimed, jerking a scented handkerchief from his sleeve and waving it in the air against the smell. You nearly splashed me."

From below came angry cries, followed by a hubbub of shuffling feet and shouted orders. Félicité spared no more than a glance for what was happening with the column of soldiers before coming to Dom's defense. "He would most certainly have been recognized if he had stood closer to the edge to throw."

"What difference would that make?" Valcour demanded, still waving his handkerchief.

He stopped abruptly, a cold smile lighting his eyes as the sound of pounding came at the entrance to the house on the lower floor. Félicité had time to do no more than set her ratafia down on the table beside her brother's empty cognac glass before footsteps were heard on the stairs. As she turned to stand beside Valcour, Marie led a detail of scarlet-clad soldiers into the room that connected to the balcony. At their head was an officer, the man who had been on horseback at the forefront of the column.

She stood still, clenching her hands into fists among the folds of her skirts, while Dom did his best to melt into the gathering shadows of the portieres that framed the doorway. Valcour trod forward with his handkerchief held in a graceful, arrested gesture that might have been taken for surprise. "I protest," he drawled. "What is the meaning of this intrusion?"

The officer sketched a bow, dividing it between Félicité and Valcour in a manner so perfunctory as to be an affront. "I am investigating an insult to the troops of his majesty King Carlos of Spain, which just issued from this house. In his name, I demand an instant and complete explanation."

Valcour glanced at his insignia. "And your name, *mon colonel*?"

"Lieutenant Colonel Morgan McCormack." The reply was hard and uncompromising.

Valcour sent Félicité a small smile before turning back to the other man. "That explains it, then."

The height, the breadth of shoulder, the russet-brown hair worn unpowdered and tied in a queue, and the green eyes of the officer marked him as being Irish, undoubtedly one of several of O'Reilly's countrymen said to be serving also as mercenaries in his entourage.

The colonel ignored the comment. "The explanation, if you please."

Raising a thin brow, Valcour said, "We are all eagerness to serve you, and of course the Spanish crown, *mon colonel*, but first it might be well if my sister and I could be informed as to the nature of this grievous insult?"

"That must be obvious." Lieutenant Colonel Morgan McCormack's face tightened with suppressed anger and the recognition of the irony that laced Valcour's tone.

Valcour sniffed, then had recourse to his perfumed handkerchief. "Even so," he murmured. "It appears, however, that you achieved a miraculous escape from the—deluge?"

"As you say. The men with me were not so lucky." The patience of the other man was growing visibly thinner. His command of the French language was excellent, though his accent was less than perfect.

"Obviously." Valcour flipped his handkerchief once more, a pained look in his eyes as he surveyed the drawn-up detail.

"The source of the odor which you find so objectionable came from this house, let me remind you," the colonel ground out. "Three people were observed on the balcony just prior to the incident, the three of you gathered here. The only question is which of you is the guilty party."

"I fear my sister and I must claim ignorance." Valcour held out his hand to Félicité, and with muscles stiff with reluctance, she moved to his side.

"You will forgive me, but that hardly seems possible."

Valcour frowned. "Are you saying I lie?"

"I am saying I am determined to find the culprit, no matter who stands in the way." The hard gaze of the colonel moved beyond Valcour's shoulder to where Dom stood.

"For such a small—accident, Colonel McCormack? These things happen every day."

"Not to soldiers of the Spanish crown. You know as well as I this was no accident. Will you cooperate, or must I place everyone in this house under arrest while I get to the bottom of it?"

The maid, Marie, listening beyond the open doorway, clapped her hand over her mouth to stifle a gasp. Valcour stiffened, then shrugged with an airy wave. "To a man of sense and breeding, the answer must be plain. It is the menials who empty the slops.''

Dom shrank as from a blow, his face twisting and his mouth opening and closing as he tried to speak. The guttural sounds he produced bore no resemblance to words in their pitiful desperation.

The colonel gave a nod. His face like a mask, he rapped out an order that brought his men to attention with muskets leveled while two of their number prepared to place the manservant under arrest.

Abruptly, Félicité could bear it no longer. She stepped forward, placing her fingers on the rigid strength of the colonel's forearm. ''No, wait. I cannot let Dom pay for my action. It was I, Colonel McCormack, who—who treated your men to the unexpected shower.''

The thick brows of the officer snapped together as he stared down at her. ''You?''

It was as if he had only at that moment allowed himself to acknowledge her existence, despite his first formal greeting. His green gaze had seemed to pass over her with stern regard, and yet she had the illogical conviction that he had missed no detail of her appearance. Now he took a more thorough inventory, noting the golden hair that was the legacy of her Norman forebears by way of ancient Viking coastal marauders, the finely molded perfection of her features, her creamy shoulders and slender form covered by the richness of her clothing.

Félicité flushed under that deliberate, sweeping stare, coloring also for the vulgarity of the crime to which she had laid claim. Still, she refused to lower her dark-brown gaze or to permit the angry confusion she felt to be revealed in her expression.

''There is no need, *chère*,'' Valcour protested, red spots appearing under the powder on his face as the officer's attention remained upon her. ''No need at all for you to sacrifice your reputation for so worthless a creature as my man Dom. Nothing whatever in this situation demands it.''

She turned on her brother. ''Doesn't it? When he is no more than a pawn in this game?''

"But one of so little worth," he suggested.

"That isn't true!"

The colonel broke in then. "Enough. The two of you may resume your quarrel another time. For now, the king's business takes precedence. Young woman, you must realize—"

"Lieutenant Colonel McCormack," Valcour broke in, his tone rising, "I really must ask you not to use that tone of voice toward my sister, especially as she is the most innocent of females."

"Meaning?" The word was spoken with dangerous calm.

"I fear I am the culprit you seek," Valcour answered, his smile wry as he lifted his shoulders.

Colonel McCormack flicked a hard glance over the other man. "That hardly seems likely."

Valcour bowed. "I extend you my compliments also, *mon colonel,* and my deepest sympathy in addition. It seems you now have three guilty parties. What are you going to do?"

"Three of you there undoubtedly are; three guilty persons, no. As you so obligingly pointed out a few minutes ago, m'sieu, it is obvious who the most likely suspect must be. Ladies and gentlemen with the means to hold their fellow men in bondage do not stoop to do their own dirty work. It follows, then, that the servant is the one who acted. It is unlikely he did so of his own choice, a conclusion proved by his appearance of fear. Someone ordered him to act."

"How astute of you," Valcour sneered.

"The colonel inclined his head. "Thank you."

"The only question is, which one, since we have both confessed?"

"I think that you, m'sieu, are a deal too fastidious for such a course, but that you might claim credit to protect your sister. That being the case, the guilty party, as much as it pains me to say it, must indeed be you, mademoiselle."

As he finished speaking, the officer looked to Félicité. Though she had admitted the deed, had fully expected to take the punishment for it regardless of the form it might take, to find herself accused in all seriousness of it was galling beyond endurance.

"Yes," she cried, "and why not? It may help you to

understand how little welcome Spaniards are in New Orleans, to say nothing of O'Reilly and his hired Irish cutthroats!''

McCormack's eyes narrowed to an emerald glitter. "As of this day, mademoiselle, you are living in Spanish Louisiana; you are a Spanish citizen, and the uniform you saw fit to desecrate is that of the defenders of your own country. I trust you acted heedlessly, with more patriotism than malice. Bear this in mind, however. A repeat of this offense, or anything like it, will not be tolerated. The fact that you are a female will not protect you from swift and severe penalty.''

He did not wait for a reply, but turned on the heel of his jackboot and, with a barked order, preceded his men from the room. Félicité stared after him with the heated flush of chagrin and outrage blazing across her cheekbones.

"Arrogant, overbearing—'' she breathed when she could speak.

"Dangerous," Valcour supplied.

"What do you mean?''

"He has a quick intelligence, and is without conceit.''

"How can you say so?'' Félicité demanded. "His stock was so white it was blinding, and his boots shone like satin.''

"The effect of pride and self-discipline, not vanity, my dear sister.''

"If all the Irish with O'Reilly are like him, life will be insupportable!'' She swung around in a flurry of skirts to stride out onto the balcony once more.

"You may be right,'' Valcour agreed, though his tone had the sound of preoccupation, and he stood frowning as he pulled his lace-edged handkerchief through his hands.

In the street below, the soldiers still filed past, now the infantry units in their uniforms of white with blue collars and cuffs.

"*Bella, bella,*'' came the shout from their ranks as her presence was discovered, alone on the balcony without male guardian or duenna. "*Blanco y oro! Señorita* of white and gold,'' ran the murmur, and more than one face was turned upward toward where she stood.

Félicité stepped back, but not before she heard the harsh

sound of a command that sent every pair of eyes staring straight ahead once more, nor before she saw Lieutenant Colonel Morgan McCormack mount his bay stallion standing under the overhang of the balcony. Setting his officer's tricorne upon his head, he rode away down the street without looking back.

Chapter 2

urry, Ashanti!''
"I do the best I can, mam'selle."
The maidservant settled the knee-length chemise with its deep, lace-edged décolletage about Félicité, smoothed the soft batiste material around the waist, and tightened the strings of the whaleboned stays, pulling them up snug. Gasping for breath, Félicité clung to the footboard of the great cypress bed as the other woman, a tall, magnificent Negress of the Ashanti tribe, mercilessly closed the small gap that remained in the stays at her back. Dressing in such haste was a trial. Félicité had not dreamed that her father and Valcour would wish to attend the soirée being given tonight, on this third day of Spanish occupation, in honor of the new governor-general, O'Reilly. To give her the news that they would present themselves there within the hour while she was still supervising the removal of the dessert plates from dinner was just like Olivier Lafargue. He had no conception of the time necessary to have her hair put up and powdered in the formal style, to struggle into her largest panniers and heaviest, most elegant robe *à la Française*, to powder and rouge her face, or apply her patches.

"Your stockings, mam'selle."

Félicité moved to sit down on the side of the bed, allowing Ashanti to slip the tubes of silk up over her legs, fastening the garters above her knees. Over these went her slippers of embroidered satin, the high heels covered in the same material. Next came the panniers, half-circle hoops of wood woven together with leather straps in a basket arrangement, and fastened around the waist with a belt. Over these went the petticoats, stiffened with starch and hemmed with ruffles of lace. The top one was of gold silk with deep lace flounces on the front panel that would show beneath the open panel of her overskirt.

The heat inside the bedchamber that served also as her dressing room was oppressive. The night coolness hovering beyond the second-floor windows with their shutters set ajar could not dispel the warmth caused by the candles burning on either side of the dressing table where Félicité had sat to have her hair done. As she returned now to the dressing table to attend to her face, Félicité picked up a fan of woven palmetto and plied it vigorously.

"Take care, mam'selle. You will disarrange your hair."

"What do I care, Ashanti? I cannot imagine what possessed Papa to decide to attend this soirée."

"To stay away from the party would be to call attention to yourselves," the maid said, her voice soft.

"And we must not do that." Félicité's tone was weary.

"It would not be wise."

It was a sentiment much repeated in these last few days, especially since the landing of the Spanish troops. It was as if the brief flurry of rebellion had been no more than a game, a childish threat to persuade Louis XV of France to take them back under his wing. Now the game was over and prudence dictated caution. The people were quiet, remaining in their houses for the most part. There had been disquieting rumors that O'Reilly had drawn up a list of names of the men who had actively conspired to set up a republican form of government, that he meant to deport all involved after stripping them of their belongings. Other reports had him preparing a stockade on Cat Island in the gulf off the coast near the

21

settlement of Biloxi, where they would be left to the mercy of the sun, sand flies, and salt water. Most scoffed at such tales, preferring to believe in Commandant Aubry's assurances of clemency, maintaining that a proper show of humility would convince the Spaniards of their resignation to the change of government. Still, everyone was uneasy. Even Félicité's father had become subdued. There was about him a look of gray defeat she did not like. To see him take the prudent course, being forced to compromise his principles in the face of such overwhelming odds, was enough to make her long to do something reckless.

"You are pale, mam'selle. Perhaps a touch more rouge?"

Félicité dipped the hare's foot into the pot of rose-red powder and stroked it once more across the high ridges of her cheekbones. "They say the Spanish don't approve of women aiding nature in this way."

"That may be, but it hasn't kept them from wailing like love-starved cats under your window for two nights past."

Félicité smiled as she met the eyes of the maid in the mirror where Ashanti stood just behind her at the dressing table. "It's an old Spanish custom, the gentlemen serenading the ladies they admire. I suppose I should be complimented."

"They think so, these soldiers with their twanging guitars."

"There was one who sang rather nicely." Félicité picked up a patch in the shape of a lyre, and after a moment's consideration, placed it just below the corner of her mouth to emphasize its tender curves.

"Perfect, mam'selle," Ashanti said of the patch, then went on, "It was wise of you not to appear in your window. M'sieu Valcour was livid enough without that."

A shadow came and went in Félicité's brown eyes. "Yes. My gown, now."

The robe *à la Française* was of yellow silk embroidered with a pattern of green leaves and vines and edged with lace touched with gold thread. It fastened with hooks to a tightly fitting embroidered basque that ended in a point, falling open over the petticoats. The low neckline was edged also by the lace ruffle of her chemise, and the ruffles edging the sleeves of her chemise fluttered too under the tightly fitted falling sleeves of the gown for a fuller effect. The skirts that swept over the panniers were full and spreading, ending in a train in the back that fell from loose Watteau pleats at the shoulders of the gown.

Ashanti slipped the last of the hooks into their loops, adjusted the set of the pleats, and stepped back. "You look fit to appear at the court of the Sun King himself, mam'selle."

Félicité glanced at herself in the mirror. The whiteness of her hair under its powder gave her a regal, sophisticated appearance, while making her eyes seem darker and more mysterious than usual. One had to endure such trivialities for the sake of fashion. "Does it seem to you, Ashanti, that my bosom is just a little bare?"

"This gown is a trifle lower in that area than you usually wear. You could wear a neck ruff of lace as a distraction, if you like, or insert a *tâtez-y*."

The last-mentioned item was a pleated frill artfully called a "touch here." Félicité shook her head, then stepped to the dressing table and took up a square of lace. She twisted it deftly in her hands, then, with a small smile, tucked it into her bodice.

"Mam'selle, no," Ashanti breathed.

"I think yes." The lace, pleated in the shape of a small fan, was a good imitation of a white cockade, the symbol of Bourbon France.

"Take it out, mam'selle," the maid pleaded.

Félicité hesitated, knowing the foolhardiness of such a gesture full well. At that moment there came a call from beyond the door. "Félicité, we are waiting."

"There is no time to find a substitute. More than likely the stupid Spanish will never notice. I must go. My pattens, Ashanti."

With her face set in lines of severe disapproval, the maid moved to do her bidding.

Pattens were wooden clogs that slipped over her shoes to lift her above the ground. The extra height would keep her skirts from trailing in the filth and dirt of the street, during the walk to the house where the soirée was being held. Carriages were the exception rather than the rule in the town. It was no great distance inside the walls of the fortified settlement to any place a person might wish to go; moreover, the wet climate where the streets ran with water more often than not, combined with the soft alluvial soil that made paving stones sink out of sight the moment they were laid, made wheeled vehicles impractical. In truly inclement weather, entertainments were postponed, though Félicité had seen the time when the mud was so deep that pattens were useless and the ladies had taken off shoes and stockings and waded. On arrival they had dipped their feet in a pan of water, dried them, donned stockings and shoes again, and danced the night away.

The French regime had been a casual one, with great friendliness and camaraderie, with a distinct feeling of being kindred souls in the wilderness fighting to maintain the elegances of life. Many were the homes of rough, split lumber with crystal chandeliers hanging from the rafters and Persian carpets on the puncheons. What did it matter as long as the lusters sparkled, the wine flowed, and the conversation kept one's wits nimble?

No doubt all that would be changed now that the Spanish had come. All would be form and formality. It was said that Navarro, one of the Spanish officials who had come with Ulloa and stayed behind when he was expelled, was building a house with a gallery across the entire upper floor; that he had ordered intricately wrought iron as fine as lace in the way of railings for it and rich fabrics to cover the walls. So sheeplike had the French inhabitants become, no doubt before long everyone would be pulling down the half-timbered houses and building galleried mansions for themselves.

There were flambeaux in metal holders burning on either side of the door of the house where the soirée was being held. Candlelight shone from the windows, and through the openings with their shutters thrown wide could be seen a press of people in their finest clothing. The smell of hot myrtle wax from the candles made of the native shrub vied in the air with the scent of perfume in which most of those gathered had bathed, the use of water for either drinking or cleansing of the person being deadly dangerous. Félicité's father had always decried the superstition, at least as it touched on personal ablutions, enjoying daily submersion in warm water and vigorous scrubbing with soap. Félicité had naturally gained the same habit, plus a strong wish that more would do the same.

She glanced at her father with a slight wrinkling of her nose as she paused just inside the doorway to allow Ashanti, who had, of course, accompanied her, to divest her of her pattens.

Monsieur Lafargue only shook his head, his lips curving in a smile before he handed his *chapeau bras* to Valcour's manservant and nodded a dismissal so that their attendants could go in search of the refreshment and music provided for them in the rear of the house. He had lost weight in the last weeks, Félicité thought. His powdered wig concealed his thinning hair with its gradually increasing gray streaks, but it brought the grayish cast of his skin into relief. He did not trouble himself overly much with his appearance. His satin coat, once sky-blue, had turned lavender in the creases and was longer than the current mode. In addition, his perpetual stoop, caused by his forever being crouched over a book, did not help the once fine fit. For no good reason, Félicité, watching him, felt the ache of tears in her throat. If anything should happen to him, she did not know what she would do.

With her father on one side and Valcour, resplendent in silver brocade and sparkling paste buttons, on the other, Félicité swept forward to join the throng. Immediately she was drawn into the chatter, the exchange of greetings, the inspecting of the toilettes of the other women, and having her own inspected. A few of the older men and women sat on chairs on one wall, but most moved freely about, doing their best to drown out the music being provided by a string quartet in one corner. There was no dancing as yet; that would not have been *comme il faut*, since the guest of honor had not yet put in an appearance. The canopied armchair at the end of the room provided for O'Reilly's comfort was unoccupied.

The event was not long delayed. Abruptly the music stopped. A fanfare of trumpets sounded. A Spanish official stationed near the rear door of the room stepped forward, threw back his shoulders, and announced: "By the will of his most august and Catholic majesty King Carlos III of Spain, Governor-General Don Alejandro O'Reilly!"

Hard on the words appeared a pair of men in the scarlet uniform of Spain carrying heavy silver maces. Behind them came an armed honor guard in double file. They halted, and between them a man entered the room. As he strode forward the musicians struck up the national anthem of Spain.

Tall, with an erect military bearing, O'Reilly was dressed in white satin of severe cut decorated with wide, gold-embroidered braid, slashed by his red ribbon of office and covered with glittering orders. His features were strong, with a long nose and firm lips. Though many looked close, there was little warmth to be seen in his blue eyes. His progress was slowed by a decided limp.

The instant he had gained his chair, the mace bearers moved to position themselves one on either side of the governor-general, while the guards ranged themselves behind him. Immediately afterward, his officers began to file into the room in a river of scarlet uniforms, flowing down one side as the French guests recoiled to the other.

As the last strains of the anthem died away, silence descended. There was the rustle of clothing as people turned to stare at each other, but no one spoke. The hostess of the gathering stood twisting her hands together in indecision, trying to catch the eye of her husband.

It was then that O'Reilly spoke, a low-voiced order carried by one of the men near him to the musicians in the corner. They nodded, then, with verve, struck up the anthem of France.

All over the room people relaxed, allowed themselves to smile, to sigh, to move their lips to the familiar words. It was a grand gesture, was it not? He must be a sympathetic man, this O'Reilly.

The moment the officers filed into the room, Félicité recognized Lieutenant Colonel Morgan McCormack. How could one not, when he was so tall, topping even his cold-faced general? He lounged with his broad shoulders propped against the wall, at ease and yet alert, his green gaze moving over the crowd, observant, watchful. Félicité glanced away, noticing Valcour. He was watching O'Reilly, a curl to his thin lips. When she flicked a quick look at the colonel once more, he was staring at her, probing the mass of her powdered hair as if to find a hint of gold to be certain of recognition. Velvet brown and brilliant green, their eyes clashed. It was Félicité who looked away, the color rising beneath the traces of rouge on her cheeks.

The French anthem came to an end. O'Reilly, signaling for the general dancing to start, made his apologies. "You must excuse me from commencing the festivities, if you please," he said, his voice carrying effortlessly to every corner of the large room as he gestured briefly toward one of his limbs. "My infirmity makes me an unlovely sight upon the floor. I would prefer to wait until I can become lost among the crowd. Pray do not stand on ceremony, but enjoy yourselves."

It seemed to Félicité that as the governor-general finished speaking he looked with particular significance toward his officers. There was a stirring along the scarlet line, and one by one the men detached themselves and moved across the width that separated the two groups. The faces of a few mirrored eagerness, others embarrassed reluctance, while still others appeared grimly determined. None, however, hung back.

Tension was suddenly a palpable thing in the room. The musicians faltered into a minuet. Young French girls, with Spanish officers bowing before them, cast agonized glances at their mothers. A few of these matrons gave slow nods, and a number turned their backs, pulling their female offspring away to safety, though some had the presence of mind to claim a prior promise while commanding with imperious glances the instant attendance of older sons, nephews, or the sons of bosom friends. Slowly the floor filled, though the proportion of red uniforms was not large.

A man with a thin mustache and dancing black eyes came bearing down upon Félicité. He was, she thought, one of the soldiers who had stood in the street to serenade her. It was difficult to be certain, of course, since she had only had a brief glimpse of him through the louvers of the shutters.

There was no necessity to make her excuses or insult the

man. Valcour took her hand and, holding it high over the wide width of her panniers, led her out onto the floor beneath the nose of the crestfallen officer.

They bowed and postured through the graceful minuet, with Félicité's skirts sweeping the crude rubbed boards of the floor and their faces set in the prescribed expressions of polite boredom. From the corner of her eye as she pointed one satin slipper, Félicité caught the movement of a messenger between O'Reilly and the musicians. When the minuet came to an end, the string quartet, without pausing, began a stately pavane, the dance of the Spanish court.

A second pavane followed the first. Félicité and Valcour joined Monsieur Lafargue at the refreshment table, where a wine punch was being ladled out by a liveried servant.

"You and Valcour make a handsome couple, *ma chère,*" the older man said, saluting them with his glass. "Easily the most accomplished on the floor."

"La, that is no great compliment," Valcour said with an airy gesture, "when clumsy Spanish officers in their jack-boots are the competition." From the pocket of his coat he took a snuffbox shaped like a coffin, with a skull and cross-bones enameled in black and silver on the lid. His movements precise, he flipped open the lid with one hand, took a small pinch, and lifted it to his nostrils. On a long, slow breath, he put the box away, took out his handkerchief, and only then gave a quiet sneeze into its snowy, perfumed, lace-edged folds.

It was at that moment a man Félicité recognized as Braud, the court printer of documents, spoke to her father in a low voice, drawing him off to one side. After a moment, Monsieur Lafargue turned to beckon to Valcour. A feeling of disquiet assailed Félicité. It was well known that Braud was involved in the activities of the revolution. It had been he who had printed the broadsides handed out on street corners and the placards that had gone up everywhere stating the aims of the rebels. He had also inked the documents entitled *Decree of the Council,* circulated the year before in October of 1768, and the *Memorial of the Inhabitants of Louisiana on the Event of October 1768,* both of which had put forth the grievances of the population and the means the conspirators meant to use to redress them. If Braud wished to speak to her father, it must be concerning the business of the conspiracy.

"Mademoiselle, we meet again."

Félicité whirled to face Lieutenant Colonel Morgan McCormack. She had not seen his approach in her concern for what was happening with her father, and she was caught off guard. That he realizd her dilemma and knew she had until now sought to avoid contact with the Spanish officers was obvious from the mockery that glinted in the depths of his green eyes. Under the circumstances, there was no point in being gracious.

"Not," Félicité said plainly, "by my design."

"It seemed best not to wait on that event." He inclined his head.

"I am happy you understand that much." His hair was powdered for this formal evening, the queue covered by the usual black satin bag. Félicité surprised herself by entertaining the thought that he was better without that stark white contrast to his bronzed, almost swarthy coloring.

"Regardless, our acquaintance must be pursued, Mademoiselle Lafargue."

"I don't remember giving you my name."

"An oversight, I'm sure, one I made it my business to correct."

"Why so?" Félicité spread the fan that dangled from a silken cord at her wrist, using it to cool her heated cheeks.

"For the purpose of furthering our acquaintance."

He was not going to allow her to ignore the opening he sought to create. "There can be no point. We are of two different nationalities. Moreover, you serve a master I cannot like!"

"My master is now yours also, something you would do well to remember." His voice was quiet with an undertone of steel. Reaching out with a smooth, controlled gesture, he twitched the lace handkerchief, the white cockade of Bourbon France, from the low bodice of her gown. It fluttered from his fingers to the floor, and he bent swiftly to retrieve it, presenting the bit of white lace. "Your handkerchief, mademoiselle. I believe you dropped it."

29

It happened so quickly it was unbelievable. No one else seemed to have noticed. If it were not for the hard impudence that gleamed in Morgan McCormack's eyes, she might almost have thought it an accident, that he had brushed against her, dislodging the cockade. It would not be wise to create a scene, but the effort it cost her to accept the handkerchief, to speak a few frigid words of gratitude, was a drain on her composure.

"Where was I?" he went on. "Yes, I was speaking of my reasons for seeking you out. My commanding officer, the representative of Spain in Louisiana, has decreed that there will be pleasant social interchange between his men and the community. It is my duty to carry out his orders."

"That is certainly complimentary, colonel!" Félicité snapped her fan shut, and with fingers that trembled with the anger that gripped her, tucked the handkerchief into the elbow-length sleeve of her gown.

"Is it my compliments you want? I was sure you would disdain them, but it is not always possible to judge these matters." His grave words were shaded with irony.

"You deliberately mistake my meaning. That being so, you will not be surprised if I hold myself excused from this conversation." With a proud tilt to her head, Félicité swept around, preparing to depart.

He put out a hand to catch her arm. "I think not, Mademoiselle Lafargue."

There was something in his voice and in the emerald glitter of his eyes that held her. His touch, the warm firmness of his grasp with its hint of much greater strength than he cared to exert, was oddly disturbing. Her tone as cold as she could make it, she said, "I am not accustomed to being manhandled, Colonel McCormack."

"Nor am I accustomed to having ladies turn their backs while I am requesting the honor of their presence on the floor."

"Is that what you were doing? Your technique could use improvement." She looked pointedly at his strong brown fingers still closed around her forearm, but he did not release her.

"I doubt my technique has any bearing on your answer.

Perhaps you would be more reasonable if an inquiry was to be opened into the incident of the chamber pot?''

His expression did not waver as she stared at him. There could be no doubt that he had the power to do exactly as he said. ''You—you would do that, simply because I am unwilling to dance with you?''

''I am vindictive by nature, it seems. Lamentable, but true.''

''I don't believe you.'' The words were defiant, as was the look in her eyes, but her tone was not as strong as she would have liked.

''Shall we put it to the test? Or will you swallow your spleen and admit that taking the floor with me is preferable to a day in the stocks?''

The prospect of being forced to stand bent over at the waist with her neck and arms clamped rigidly between the wooden boards and her face and posterior unprotected targets for the mud and filth flung by every street urchin was not something Félicité could contemplate with equanimity. The stocks in the Place d'Armes were temptingly close to the levee markets, and missiles of rotted fruit and fish entrails were too often the lot of the unfortunates sentenced to them. There was every likelihood that she could find herself in that position. It would probably be considered a light punishment for the crime she was supposed to have committed.

A bitter smile curved Félicité's lips. ''Is this an example of the magnanimity of the Spanish crown O'Reilly promised—to grant reprieves, then snatch them away when it suits the purpose of those in power?''

''Magnanimity is for those who earn it, those who accept their fate without waiting to have it forced upon them,'' he answered, a shadow of grimness on his features.

His words were ominous, but there was no time to consider their import. His grip was slowly tightening. The feeling had left her fingers, and she was being drawn irresistibly toward the dance floor. ''Why me, Colonel McCormack?'' she demanded, trying to pull back. ''There are other, more compliant ladies in the room.''

He sent her a quick, encompassing glance from under thick, rust-tipped lashes. ''None who look as you do, none

31

whom it would give me so much pleasure to annoy with my attentions.''

The compliment, if it was one, was oblique, and yet she had caught the glint of admiration in his eyes. ''At least you realize their effect!''

He inclined his head without answering, indicating an open space in the shifting, posturing dancers with a gesture of one hand. She had the clear choice of defying him, of jerking free, and causing a stir that might well fan the tensions of the gathering to a fever pitch, even bring on an official investigation of the chamber-pot affair that could embroil Valcour and her father; or she could capitulate, appearing to support her part in the dance with willingness, if not pleasure. It was only as she made her decision, lifting her chin and moving easily beside the officer into the pavane, that she glanced to where Valcour and her father stood. Her brother was staring at her with stunned disbelief on his face and the dawning of fury in his eyes.

It was some few minutes before Félicité could collect her composure. The movements of the dance separated them, then brought them back together. She glanced at the set face of the man leading her through the figures. As they came closer, their shoulders touching as they met beneath their raised hands, she could not resist a soft gibe.

''You are a ruthless man, colonel, but I suppose that is no more than is to be expected of a mercenary.''

''You say the word as if you find the profession distasteful,'' he answered in a direct challenge.

''Fighting the battles of others for pay instead of personal conviction, regardless of who is right or wrong? That doesn't sound like something to be proud of.''

''And yet it is an honorable road to advancement.''

''That is your purpose then, advancement? And under a foreign king? That appears to make you in some sense an adventurer.'' Félicité sent him a look of limpid inquiry from under her lashes as she delivered this additional insult.

''Is that supposed to be worse?'' A muscle tightened in his jaw, but there was no other sign he was aware of her intent.

She pretended to consider. "Why, I don't know. I suppose it depends on your motive."

"Would poverty and virtual enslavement help my desperate case?"

Did he dare to laugh at her low opinion of him? It was difficult to be certain as they were parted once more. "Louisiana has been plagued by more than her share of men who come to make their fortunes and get out rather than staying and building their lives here."

He lifted a brow at her serious tone. "They have until now been French adventurers, of course—doubtless a more noble breed?"

"Their manners were better, certainly," she said with vinegary sweetness, and dropped a brief curtsy as the pavane came to an end.

"Wait," Lieutenant Colonel McCormack said as she started to turn away. "There will be another dance in this set."

"If I remain on the floor with you overlong, colonel, you might find yourself leg-shackled to me." The asperity of her reply was caused as much by resentment of the easy command in his tone as from reluctance to do as he bid. It was true, however, that in ordinary times two dances in succession could be tantamount to the announcement of an engagement between a couple.

"That would be social interchange with a vengeance, would it not?" he answered, a smile curving his firmly chiseled lips. "Though I don't doubt O'Reilly would be pleased at the establishment of such friendly relations."

"I would not have thought that would be an object with him," Félicité said tartly.

"I assure you it is, among other things."

The words were nearly lost in the beginning strains of yet another pavane. Glancing at the musicians, Félicité said in clear tones, "If I must dance with you, colonel, would it be too much to ask that the music be something more spritely, perhaps a French *contredanse?*"

Her voice was more carrying than she realized, for on either side of her the suggestion was taken up. "But yes, *mais oui! A contredanse!* French music! French!"

Whether out of loyalty or obstinacy, or simply because the officers were unfamiliar with the steps of the French dance suggested, the men in red set up a shout of "Pavane! Pavane! Spanish! Spanish!"

The voices rose to a babble. An irate Frenchman pushed a Spaniard. The Spaniard pushed him back. A woman screamed. There were shouts, and blows, and the sound of silver maces thumping on the floor for order. The crowd surged first one way, then another, swept by a sense of impending panic. Félicité was shoved aside by a portly man in wine satin with perspiration oozing from under his periwig. The next moment she was sheltered in the iron curve of Colonel McCormack's arm. He stared down at her, a hard glitter of accusation in his emerald eyes. Suddenly the thunderous crash of muskets going off in the enclosed room reverberated against the walls. Splinters flew from the ceiling, and the chandeliers swung crazily with a tinkling of crystal lusters that was loud in the abrupt silence.

The crowd turned toward the canopied chair where O'Reilly had been sitting. Wreathed in the blue-gray smoke of discharged gunpowder, he stood facing them, flanked on either side by soldiers holding muskets that still smoked.

"The evening," the new governor-general of Louisiana said deliberately, "is over. I bid you all goodnight."

Chapter 3

❦

The market was a hive of activity. As far as the eye could see, people were strung out on the ground in front of the earthen levee. Men and women were talking, gesticulating, shouting, and singing their wares that were displayed in carts, barrows, woven baskets, crates, and barrels, or strung up on poles. Germans from up the coast hawked fresh milk, butter, and cheese, as well as live poultry, root vegetables, and pickled cabbage. Indian squaws in beaded leather sold fresh-dressed venison, squirrel, and rabbit, as well as woven baskets of cane or split ash, and the powdered root of the sassafras used to thicken ragout and bouillabaisse. Acadians, newly arrived refugees expelled by the British from Nova Scotia, sold dainty embroidery, items of carved wood from spoons to carefully crafted cradles, also fresh-dressed frog legs, young pigeon squabs, the meaty tails of alligators, and fresh greens, scallions, and mushrooms gathered in the wild meadowlands, anything that might be had with few resources other than the use of their hands. From in and around the city there were figs, pears, and pomegranates as well as pineapples and bananas from the ships just in from Havana. Usually there were ample supplies of oranges and lemons, but the hard freeze two winters before had killed the trees to the ground and they had not yet recovered.

Félicité was interested in none of these things, nor in the hogheads of molasses, the snail-shaped jars of olive oil, or the admittedly appetizing confections made with the native pecans by the free women of color. Her goal was the fresh

35

seafood, and with Ashanti close behind her carrying a shopping basket, she threaded her way through the strolling shoppers toward the area where the fishermen always displayed their catch.

At one point she paused to inspect a shipment of laces, ribbons, and bolts of cloth boldly laid out by a British seaman. The merchandise was contraband, and subject to confiscation, since official Spanish policy dictated that the colony could trade only with vessels of Spain. Much the same policy had been in effect during the French regime also, but the arrangement had never been workable. It was impossible for the French or Spanish governments, so far away, to supply all their needs at prices they could afford. Trading with the British merchant vessels, as they sailed up the river to supply the English post at Natchez, had become a practice so much winked at that the ships had begun to tie up regularly for business at a certain spot near the city. Since the British territory actually began at Bayou Manchac above New Orleans, going to trade for the contraband was called "going to Little Manchac." The conditions had also encouraged the operations of pirates in the gulf. These men who preyed on the shipping of other nations could always find a market for their stolen goods in New Orleans, where the need for everything was so great. Merchants did not scruple to take anything they could get, and without asking embarrassing questions. As a result, scarcely a month passed without some new atrocity committed by the pirates coming to light—women and children being set adrift in skiffs without food or water; young girls and nuns raped and carried off to the pirates' island strongholds; boys horribly molested; men passengers keelhauled, tied to ropes and dragged again and again under the ship, or else tied to the anchor chains and left there while the great hook was cast overboard. It did not do to dwell on such things, however. It was a cruel world. People must eat and clothe themselves.

The heat of the day was growing as the sun advanced overhead. It brought forth ripe odors from kegs of rum and butts of wine, from half-eaten fruits and vegetable refuse that lay around the stalls, and also from the green animal skins that were tied in bundles or hung on willow stretchers. A small boy with mud between his bare toes and his shirt hanging out played with a crayfish, leading it on a string. A quadroon, dressed in blue lutestring and protecting her complexion with an enormous fan painted with gaming symbols, tripped by on the arm of a Spanish soldier wearing a quilted leather jerkin and a wide-brimmed hat of black beaver banded in red.

Ashanti touched Félicité's arm. "If we are going to have the *maître*'s noon meal ready by the time he and M'sieu Valcour return from the house of the governor, we had best hurry."

Félicité took the reminder in good part, giving an absent nod. Ashanti was right, though it had been difficult to tell, from the way the invitation that had come this morning was worded, whether the men would be invited to dine. It had been decided between Ashanti and herself to make a bouillabaisse. If the men returned to eat, fine; if not, it would not spoil and they could have it for their dinner.

They bought fresh oysters, a few crabs, a handful of shrimp, and two nice pompano. With these nestled in wet leaves, they turned homeward. Félicité had paused to smooth the silken yellow feathers of a parrot at the bird stall when a commotion arose at the far end of the market. People were gathering around a man who had come from the direction of the center of town. A few cried out as he spoke. Others looked stunned or turned to their neighbors with grim faces.

Apprehension touched Félicité. She glanced at Ashanti and saw her own fears mirrored in the dark eyes of the maid. Without speaking, they picked up their skirts and moved swiftly toward the growing mass of people.

"What is it? What has occurred?" Félicité asked a woman on the edge of the gathering.

"It is said by Reynard the tailor that all those men who went today to the house of the governor have been arrested, that they were lured there for that purpose. They say Spanish soldiers marched these men through the streets at the point of bayonets. He saw this with his own eyes, and followed to see what was to be done with them."

The blood drained from Félicité's face, but she had no time for weakness. As the old woman paused she said, "Yes, yes, go on."

"You are the daughter of the merchant Lafargue, are you not? My heart overflows with pity for you, my dear. These men, the finest flower of the colony, the *crème de la crème,* were taken to the old barracks near the convent of the Ursulines. What happened to them then, no one knows."

"Dear God," Félicité breathed. Her father and Valcour, arrested. "I—we must go home. There may be a message."

They hurried through streets that had abruptly emptied of people, echoing only with the sound of slamming doors, banding shutters, and the worried hushing of children. The half-timbered house with its jutting balcony was silent, however. There was no activity, no messenger, no missive delivered, though Félicité questioned the young upstairs maid until she was in tears. Of Dom, Valcour's manservant, there was no sign. He had been sent on an errand by his master and had not returned.

The hours crept past. The items bought in the market were delivered to the cook in the kitchen in the rear courtyard. Soon the savory aroma of seafood soup wafted through the house, along with the smell of the long crusty loaves of bread that would be served with it. Noontime came and went and still there was no word. After a while, Félicité tried to eat, but it was impossible. Pushing her plate away, she sat staring at a fly that buzzed around it, seeing nothing.

Toward the middle of the afternoon, Félicité could bear it no longer. She sent Ashanti to the barracks to discover what information she might as to what was happening with the imprisoned men. The maid was not gone long. The barracks were heavily guarded. No one was allowed inside for any reason. Messages, for the time being, could be neither sent nor delivered. None could be certain exactly how many men had been taken by the soldiers at the governor's house, but a number of others had been arrested in their homes, among them Braud, the printer, and Attorney General Lafrénière. Since facilities for prisoners were limited at the barracks, already overstrained with the influx of Spanish soldiers, several of the prisoners had been rowed out to the Spanish frigate, the vessel on which O'Reilly had arrived, now anchored in the river before the town.

Darkness settled over the streets. The green myrtle-wax candles burned late. Now and then a neighbor would come with a whispered rumor. Villeré, a planter from one of the outlying plantations, had been lured into town by a letter from Director-General Aubry and put into chains as he passed through the gate in the palisade. His wife, hearing of the arrest, had hastened to town. Learning he was aboard the frigate, she had herself rowed out to the ship, where she had pleaded to be allowed to see her husband. Villeré, hearing his wife's voice, had tried to go to her, fearing she would be offered insult by the rough seamen. Struggling with his guards, he had been pierced by their bayonets. His bloodied shirt had then been thrown down into the skiff to Madame Villeré with the derisive comment that she was now a widow. Other, no less disturbing, tales had the prisoners undergoing torture during their interrogation, being stretched upon the rack or delivered to the thumbscrews.

It was impossible to sleep. Félicité and Ashanti bolted the doors and shutters and extinguished all candles save one in Félicité's bedchamber. Félicité readied herself for bed; removing her clothing, bathing, donning a nightrail and dressing saque before she permitted Ashanti to brush out the long, shimmering strands of her hair. She could not bring herself to climb up on the feather mattress, however. This was the first time in her memory that she had been without male protection in the house when night deepened. Sometimes Valcour and her father were both out until quite late, but her father, at least, had always returned before she retired for the night.

Mending, setting fine, tiny stitches into the ruffles of one of her father's shirts, or in a three-cornered tear in a tablecloth, occupied a length of time. The art of stitchery was something she had been taught by the sisters at the convent, something that required only a small part of her attention after so many hours spent perfecting the technique. Ashanti also plied her needle on the other side of the candle, though they did not exchange more than a half-dozen words.

The maid was of an age with Félicité; they had, in fact, been born in the same month. Ashanti's mother had been Félicité's mother's own personal maid, brought with her as a part of her dowry on her marriage. The two children had grown up together; playing, learning, eating together, even sleeping in the same room until Félicité had gone to the convent. Closer than sisters in some ways, Félicité worried at times that the other girl had no real life aside from her duties. Ashanti did not seem to mind. She had been taught a number of things by her mother that the older woman had not seen fit to impart to Félicité, things of nature and the earth handed down from her African ancestors, or learned during her mother's journey to the New World by way of the tropical island of Santo Domingo. She was content.

The death of Ashanti's mother when the two girls were in their teens had caused a change in their relationship, since it was then that Félicité had assumed her role as housekeeper. The necessity of giving orders and seeing that they were carried out had solidified their positions as mistress and servant. Still, Félicité depended greatly on Ashanti. Without her quiet good sense and strength of will, the house would not have run with anything near its accustomed smoothness.

Félicité could remember only one occasion when Ashanti had been visibly upset. For the past several years she had slept on the lower floor of the house, in a small chamber facing the court. One hot summer night two years previously, Valcour had come home late from a night with friends on the town. More than a little the worse for drink, he had stepped through to the court for water from the clay jar in which it was kept, to cool his aching head. Seeing Ashanti's door open to the night air, he had become intrigued. He had looked in to see the maid lying on her cornshuck mattress asleep, clothed only in her short shift. What happened next had never been entirely clear. Ashanti said Valcour had thrown himself upon her meaning to ravish her, and would have succeeded if she had not fought back, using the secrets her mother had told her to send him howling in pain from the chamber, clutching at his lower parts. According to Valcour, the maid had awakened when she saw him passing in the moonlight. She had started to scream, and when he went toward her to tell her who he was, and that she was in no danger, he had tripped and fallen across her bed. She had then become hysterical and most disagreeably violent.

Regardless of who was correct, the dislike they had for each other now bordered on hatred. Valcour reserved for the maid an attitude of malicious disdain, while Ashanti avoided him as much as was possible, only remaining in the same room with him if Félicité was present also. She ignored his commands unless they were channeled through her mistress, a daring thing indeed considering the awe and fear in which he was held by the other servants. Ashanti gave no sign of being afraid of him, but still her mistrust was plain. Her manner toward him was always wary, and the glances she threw at him from the corners of her black eyes were shaded with uneasy contempt.

At a small sound from the street before the house, Félicité looked up, her velvet-brown eyes meeting her maid's dark gaze. Ashanti put aside her sewing and left the bedchamber. She returned a few moments later with the news that Dom had returned. He knew nothing of the men who had been arrested. His errand had been entirely different, a personal message delivered by Valcour's orders, though he would not even attempt to make known by his usual gestures the name of the man who had received it.

Félicité sighed, rubbing her hand over her eyes, raking her hair back so that it fell behind her shoulders in a thick, shimmering curtain. "You had best go to bed, Ashanti. There is nothing to be gained by sitting here. It is unlikely we will hear anything before morning."

"If you will try to rest also, mam'selle."

"I will try." Félicité made a last stitch in the cloth she was mending, made a quick knot, and broke off the thread. She pushed her needle into a pincushion, folded the cloth with quick competence, laid it aside, and stood up. Ashanti helped her remove her dressing saque, then hung it away in the armoire, releasing the smells of rose petals and vetiver as she opened and closed the carved door.

Félicité moved to the bed and climbed up on the mattress.

On her knees, she carefully drew the mosquito *baire* that draped from a hook in the ceiling around the bed, closing the folds so she could not be plagued by the flying, stinging insects. As Ashanti bade her a quiet goodnight and took up the candle before slipping from the room, Félicité lay down and closed her eyes.

Sleep did not come. She stared up into the darkness, thinking of the events of the past few days. Ever since she had heard of the arrest, she had been haunted by a fear that she had not been able to face. What if she, by her antagonism toward Lieutenant Colonel Morgan McCormack, her impulsive claiming of responsibility for the insult with a chamber pot perpetrated on the Spanish soldiers, her incitement of the crowd to opposition at the soirée over the matter of the dance music, was to blame for the arrest today of her father and Valcour?

It was true that Valcour had instigated the chamber-pot affair, but apparently he had expected the reaction to be slight, or else for it to seem no more than the carelessness of a household servant that might be lightly punished. Certainly he had never intended for it to be recognized as the studied insolence it was, or for it to be connected directly to Félicité, her father, or himself. Too, at the soirée, Félicité's comment on the music had not been intended to disrupt the evening or provoke the violence that had ensued. It was those who had taken up her words with such virulent anger who had brought about the near riot. Félicité was certain she had heard Valcour's voice among their number, as well as the tones of certain other hotheads and young men about town who resented seeing Frenchwomen in the arms of the Spanish officers.

On the other hand, her clashes with McCormack had been no one's fault but her own. He was arrogant and officious, with an attitude of superiority in strength and force of arms that was no less irritating because it was unconscious. The way in which he had used that admittedly superior position to blackmail her, bending her to his will, still had the power to make her seethe with indignation. At the same time, the threat he had issued then was, she recognized, the basis for the fears that gripped her now.

As the gray-blue light of dawn sifted through the shutters, Félicité dropped into a fitful and dream-wracked slumber. It was midmorning when she woke. Donning a gown of soft, much-worn cotton in a *toile de Jouy* print, and with a lawn fichu at the neckline, she left her room. Her intention was to pack a basket of food to take to the barracks, since the fare usually provided for prisoners was uniformly bad. While she was about it, she might also discover news of her father and Valcour, and the reasons for their being jailed.

Monsieur Lafargue, Félicité's father, was a merchant. His house, like many of those in New Orleans, was built on a style brought from countless medieval French villages. It was constructed of *bousillage*, a plaster made of mud held together with gray moss and deer hair packed between upright timbers. Its lower floor facing the street was occupied by a draper's shop and warehouse, while the small back rooms facing the court were used for servants' quarters, laundry, and storage. The family quarters were on the second floor. Entrance to these was achieved through a tunnel-like portal that passed from the street under the house straight back to the court, with a staircase rising in the rear portion. On the second floor were six fairly commodious rooms; four bedchambers, a *salle,* or sitting room, and the rear stair hall that was also used as a dining room.

Félicité had started down the stairs on her way to the kitchen in the courtyard when she heard the tapping of heels on the banquette. She drew in her breath as a thin figure came into view wearing a tricorne with an enormous floating plume draped over one shoulder, and carrying a long knobbed walking cane decked with ribbons.

"Valcour!" she cried, starting forward.

"In the flesh," he replied, his tone grimly jaunty as he swept off his hat in a bow of greeting.

"Where is Papa?"

A grave look smoothed her adoptive brother's features. "He is still, unfortunately, the guest of our Spanish masters."

"You mean—he is still being held? But then, how does it come about that you are here free?"

"Why," he said, veiling his eyes with his lashes and

43

conjuring up a simpering tone, "you must know, *ma chère* Félicité, that a frippery fellow like myself is far too vain and lacking in wit to be guilty of fomenting a revolution. Such ideas are so bourgeois and boring. I yawned through one or two meetings because it was what passed in New Orleans as the fashionable thing to do at the time, but I would so much rather have been elsewhere."

"They were fooled by such addlepated nonsense?"

"I can be quite giddy and extravagantly foolish when it pleases me," Valcour said, tilting his head. "I am not sure our Colonel McCormack was taken in completely, but his handsome countenance was so thoroughly expressive of stern disapproval that I must suppose he considers me no danger."

"He was there?" Félicité had to force the words past the knot in her throat.

"Yesterday morning, yes. He is, it seems, second in command during this period of martial subjugation, answerable only to O'Reilly himself. He was not on the scene when I took my leave a few moments ago, by the mercy of *le bon Dieu*."

The note of tightly held anger in Valcour's voice was both an indication of how galling he had found his interview with the Spanish and a warning of the dangerous effects it had had on his temper. "If you would like to go and change," Félicité said, "I will have croissants and chocolate sent up for both of us."

"I am touched by your thoughtfulness," he said, his narrow lips twisting into a smile. "I do desire above all things to remove the prison stench. Be so good as to send Dom up to me also, if you please, as soon as it may be arranged."

Over chocolate and warm crusty rolls, Valcour told Félicité what had happened the day before at the house of the governor-general. The men who had been invited to O'Reilly's levée had been greeted with all cordiality. After some little time had passed and refreshments had been served, they were requested to step into an adjacent apartment. Inside, O'Reilly had addressed them in chiding tones while Aubry, the director-general, stood by looking red-faced and flustered. He said that Louisiana was deficient in the respect it showed to Spain, that King Carlos was much displeased at the violence which had been lately exercised in the province, and at the offense which was committed against his governor, Ulloa, and his officers and troops. His majesty was irritated by the writings which had been printed and which reviled his government and the great nation of Spain. That being the case, O'Reilly said, he had been ordered by his king to arrest and have tried, according to the laws of the kingdom, the authors of these excesses and deeds of violence.

The governor-general had then proceeded to read the orders of his Catholic majesty which prescribed to him the course he was pursuing. He had added: "Gentlemen, I regret to say that you are accused of being the authors of the late insurrection. I therefore arrest you in the king's name."

During the reading of his orders, a number of Spanish officers and a body of grenadiers had filed into the room with fixed bayonets, surrounding the men. O'Reilly had then informed the men that their property, according to the custom of Spain with regard to prisoners of state, would be seized and inventoried. If they were found guilty, it would be sold, and after providing for amounts owed to creditors and sums for the support of wives and children, the remainder would become the property of the state.

Félicité stared at Valcour. "You mean this house will be seized?"

"And every stick of furniture in it, every ornament, every gown you own and pair of shoes, every trinket and shoe buckle and inch of lace."

"They can't do that!"

"They can, they have." Valcour drank the last of his chocolate and set the porcelain cup painted with roses and violets in its saucer.

"I can't believe it," Félicité whispered. This disaster had come so suddenly, after they had been given reason to think themselves safe, that she could not accept its magnitude.

"Nor could I," Valcour agreed, his face grim. "For a man to be asked—no, ordered—to deliver up his sword, all the while encircled by the points of dull but deadly bayonets—it is not an experience I care to repeat."

"No. At the barracks, Valcour, were you mistreated?"

"Not physically, if that is what you mean," he answered, "but there was no doubt in our minds that the Spaniards guarding us looked upon us as doomed men."

"I thought O'Reilly told you there would be a trial."

"A mockery, *ma chère*, Spanish justice. King Carlos has demanded recompense for the slur upon his name and reign; moreover, it has been decided that it will be best for the good of Spain's other foreign provinces if an example is made of the men who dared to defy the rule of his Catholic majesty. That being the case, twelve men have been chosen for the honor—two officers of the French army, two lawyers, four planters, and four merchants."

Félicité stared at him. "What are you saying?"

"That is how we were designated by the Spanish guards, not by name, but by occupation. We were, you see, a representative sample of the men in the colony. Who we were, what part we had played in the rebellion against the crown, made little difference."

"That's terrible. It—it means that the trial will be a farce, that O'Reilly has already decided the guilt of the men arrested."

"Quite true. And since I did not fit into any of the convenient categories, nor have the look of a raving revolutionary, I was spared."

"But my father—"

Valcour reached out to take her hand, squeezing it until her fingers were numb. "Your father is Lafargue, the merchant, a prominent man, a freethinker, wealthier than most. That makes him the guiltiest of them all."

Tears welled up into Félicité's eyes, overflowing, pouring down her cheeks. She pulled her hand free, raising trembling fingers to her lips. Valcour's words stripped her fears bare, leaving them stark and trembling inside her.

"Félicité," he said, his eyes darkening with an uneasy concern, "forgive me if I was abrupt, if I cause you distress, but the truth must be faced."

She took a deep breath, striving for composure. "I—I suppose you have had time to become used to the idea. I have not."

"I should not have brought it out so boldly. I have much to do, however, and there may be little time for arrangements."

Félicité gave little heed to the portentous sound of the last. "There must be something we can do to save Papa. I cannot stop thinking that he may have been arrested because of me, because of the unpleasantness between Colonel McCormack and myself. Perhaps if I went to O'Reilly and explained, or even to the colonel himself—"

"No! It would be useless. Already O'Reilly is being besieged by women begging for the lives of their men."

"This man McCormack must have influence. Surely if he was approached in the correct manner he could be persuaded to use it."

Valcour stared at her, his eyes narrowing to slits. "And what, dear sister, do you consider the correct manner?"

"Why, I'm not sure. With apologies for past behavior and a plea for mercy, for him to reconsider this punishment of my father for my deeds." Félicité spoke disjointedly, flinging a hand out in passionate despair. "I could beg, cry, anything that may be necessary to secure my father's release."

"Anything?" Valcour queried softly.

Félicité lifted her lashes to meet her brother's hard gaze, a flush rising to her cheeks as she realized his meaning. "I did not mean that literally. Such a thought never occurred to me!"

"That does not mean it will not occur to Colonel McCormack."

"He wouldn't—he couldn't."

"No? He is the conqueror, though he has yet to draw his sword." Valcour's tone was bitter, the lines around his mouth curving downward in a sneer. The coat of puce-colored broadcloth he had changed into was a poor choice for his sallow skin and the shadows of sleeplessness that lay beneath his eyes. Such inattention to matters of dress was a sign of how agitated he was over the situation.

"Such a thing is impossible, it must be," she whispered.

"The women of a subjugated people are always fair game."

"Among barbarians, perhaps, but Spain and France are

47

civilized countries. Our rulers are cousins; we speak languages based on the same Latin roots.''

''O'Reilly and McCormack, if you will remember, are Irishmen.''

''That doesn't make them uncivilized!''

Valcour leaned toward her, bringing his fist down on the table with a crash. ''Forget hopeless measures! Believe me, it would be madness. There is only one thing to be done now, and that is to make ready to leave.''

''Félicité's brows drew together in a frown of puzzled consternation. ''Leave? What do you mean?''

''What could I mean?'' he snapped. ''Go, depart, take ship! We must gather up everything of value we can carry before they come to inventory your father's possessions, before they come to confiscate everything you own and set you out, like a pauper, in the street.''

''If I did that, it would make me a criminal, a thief who had taken state property, would it not? Where could I go that they would not find me?''

''You could go to the British at Manchac, or you could come with me, to France.''

''You are going to France?'' There was both disbelief and an accusation in her voice.

''It seems the most intelligent thing to do. Why should I stay and risk the chance that after interrogating the others O'Reilly may decide to make an example of a *bon vivant* or two?''

''How will you go?''

''I have friends who will take me as far as Havana, where I can book passage to Le Havre.''

''Friends?'' She had been aware that Valcour had acquaintances neither she nor her father knew. He had on occasion disappeared with them for days, even weeks, at a time. Usually, questions concerning them were met with cold and discouraging anger. Now, he merely shrugged.

''Is that where Dom was yesterday, making these arrangements for you?''

''What if he was? I have not trusted these Spaniards from

the first, when we were given such soft assurances of O'Reilly's friendship and regard.''

"And will the Spanish soldiers allow you to leave, just like that?''

"They will not be able to prevent me if I go by way of the bayous.'' Valcour's face held a grim triumph as he made this announcement.

"The only men who are that familiar with the back door to New Orleans, the bayou passages, are the smugglers.''

"They can be convenient people to know, these men. They will bring me to Balize at the mouth of the river, where a ship will be waiting. What does it matter how I go, as long as I remove myself from the grasp of the Spaniards and reach the shores of France? Come with me, Félicité.''

"I can't leave Papa, you must see that.'' That he could imagine she would was more than she could understand.

"You can't help him. He would be the first to tell you to go, to put yourself beyond danger and certain penury.''

"You make it sound as if he has been condemned already. Despite what you say, there is every chance the men imprisoned will be proved innocent when they are brought to trial. Haven't I heard you and my father argue that to object to becoming Spanish subjects could not be considered a crime while the Spanish governor, Ulloa, had not presented his official commission, and while the flag of France still flew over the Place d'Armes? That, indeed, until those conditions changed we were still under the protection of France? That being the case, how can they be guilty?''

"The Spanish will find a way to twist the truth to their advantage. I tell you, Félicité, that their purpose is not to mete out justice, but to frighten the people of New Orleans into obedience.''

"Obedience, or flight?''

The words were out before she considered how they sounded. In dread, she watched as Valcour came slowly to his feet with his eyes blazing and his nostrils white and pinched with rage. He moved to stand over her, one hand resting on the back of her chair.

"Are you suggesting, *ma chère*, that I am afraid?''

"Not in the way you mean, Valcour," she said, lifting her chin, meeting his gaze squarely. "I was distraught. You must see that. You must realize also that I cannot leave my father. Who would take him food, or clean clothing? Go if you must, but do not ask me to do the same. It is impossible."

It was long moments before he moved or spoke. A fly buzzed in at the shutter that stood half open with the morning sun lying in a golden pool on the window sill. Abruptly he pushed away from her, moving toward the door. "*Mon Dieu*, what a fool I am! Let us hope, my dear sister, that you do not regret this decision."

Félicité did not speak to Valcour again. He left the house a short time later, after giving Dom detailed instructions about the packing of his clothing, wigs, and other necessary items of his wardrobe. Toward dark, Félicité questioned the manservant and learned that he had been ordered to take his master's baggage to a certain house under cover of night. For himself, there would be no need of a portmanteau; Dom was not going to France with his master.

There was little time to trouble with such matters as what would be done with the manservant. Félicité carried a laden basket of food and clean linens to her father at the barracks. The Spanish officer on duty accepted it from her, searching through it with careless hands that allowed the ruffles of her father's clean shirt to trail across the butter for his bread. The man would not listen to her request to see him. Such visits were strictly forbidden. The officer himself was grieved that he must disappoint so lovely and gracious a lady, but orders were orders. He was even more desolated when she repeated her request later that evening when she fetched her father's supper, though the answer remained the same.

The night passed. Félicité rose early, since she could not rest in any case. It was as well. To the disasters that had befallen were added others. The first of these was discovered by Ashanti. As she was airing out the master's bedchamber, she discovered that the flat, narrow brass box that usually rested upon the top of the armoire, behind the pediment, was not in place. This box was where Monsieur Lafargue kept his small hoard of gold coins. It was found at last, pushed into the back of the armoire in Valcour's bedchamber. Unsurprisingly, it was empty.

That Valcour would take this cache belonging to her father, without a word or offer to divide it, was so beyond belief that for long moments, Félicité could not bring herself to accept the evidence of her own eyes. It was equally unlikely that Dom would have stolen it. Still, she sent for the manservant to question him. In this way she discovered that Dom had not returned to the house after delivering Valcour's baggage to him. A search of the small room he occupied off the court revealed nothing taken, no sign of a hasty departure. It was the upstairs maid, sent to hang out a basket of wash, who brought them the answer to the mystery. Falling into gossip with a servant girl from next door who had ventured forth to shake out a dust mop, she learned that Dom had been sold to a nephew of the other girl's master. A fine bargain he had gotten too, since Monsieur Valcour Murat had seemed anxious to close the sale, agreeing to the first price offered.

Her father in prison, her adopted brother gone, her father's emergency reserve of money taken. Dom, who had, strictly speaking, belonged to her father, since he had been purchased in Monsieur Lafargue's name and did double duty as manservant for both men, sold for a pittance. Surely nothing else could happen?

It could. Scarcely had the dishes from her solitary breakfast been cleared away when a loud knocking was heard on the portal of the lower floor. Ashanti went to answer the summons, returning to conduct a group of officials into the sitting room, where Félicité waited. They were the delegation sent to inventory the possessions and papers of one Olivier Lafargue, prisoner of state.

"You are Félicité Marie Isabel Catherine Lafargue?"

"I am." Félicité gave the answer with as much composure as she could manage as she stood stiffly before them for this visitation.

"You are the only child of the prisoner?"

"That is true, although he has an adopted son."

"May we know the whereabouts of this person?"

Félicité lifted her chin. "I do not know."

The man asking the questions, a newly appointed alcalde, frowned. "He resides in this house?"

"He did until his arrest the day before yesterday. He has not slept here since then. I understood that he had been released from prison, however. Is there some problem?"

"We will ask the questions, señorita, if you don't mind," the alcalde said in pompous dismissal. "All we require is your cooperation in the listing of your father's belongings for his majesty's government."

There followed an exhaustive enumeration of every item in the house. With pettifogging exactness, the alcalde and his assistants listed lengths of cloth and spools of ribbon in the draper's shop and warehouse on the lower floor. Ascending the stairs, they counted beds, armoires, settees, cushions, bed linens, lengths of toweling, clothing and its buttons, silver, china and crystal, basins and ewers, pots, pans, skewers, spits, and even foodstuffs, down to the last crock of preserves. They did not, of course, forget to list the three slaves that were left, Ashanti, the upstairs maid, and the cook. With a sealed box of her father's papers under one arm, the officials left at last, the alcalde pausing at the foot of the stairs.

"You realize, señorita, that you are now enjoined from disposing of anything in the house and its environs? To do so before the case of Lafargue comes to trial would constitute theft from his most Christian majesty King Carlos."

"I understand," Félicité replied, and watched with hard eyes as the strutting official bowed and took his leave. What she did not understand, and no one had seen fit to explain, was how she was to live in the meantime.

Ashanti had come to stand behind her. "Mam'selle Félicité," she said, her voice low, "what are we going to do?"

The question from the maid, usually so self-assured, was an indication of how disturbed she was, and why not? If Monsieur Lafargue was found guilty, she would be taken away from the house she considered home and the people she thought of as family to be sold to a new master. In the meantime, the house was without a protective male in a town swarming with Spanish soldiers and mercenaries, and there were four women, including the young maid, the cook, Ashanti, and herself, who must somehow be kept safe, and fed from the meager supplies in store.

Félicité turned slowly to face Ashanti. "I think I will have to visit Colonel McCormack after all."

Chapter 4

It might have been thought odd by some to place the barracks of the soldiers of France in the same rather isolated section of the town as the convent of the Ursuline nuns. To the French it made perfect sense, having the men sent by the crown to protect their persons and the *religieuses* sent to protect their souls quartered in the same area. If the good sisters needed help in spading their gardens, digging drainage ditches, patching the roof, or other such tasks, there were the soldiers near at hand to come to their aid. When the convent bakehouse occasionally turned out more cakes or loaves of bread than the good sisters could eat, the always hungry men were appreciative. On the arrival forty years before, of the "casket girls," the young females sent out by the French crown as wives for the colonists with their worldly goods contained in a single box, or casket, the soldiers were on hand to keep the overardent suitors from storming the convent where they were lodged. At the time the Natchez Indians had risen in force and massacred the French colonists at Fort Rosalie on the Natchez bluff, the surviving orphans had been sent to the convent, and the soldiers had built cribs and made toys out of bits of wood and string. And both events, the presence of women and homeless children, had encouraged the men who had come to the colony with muskets and swords in their hands to put them down and pick up plows and other tools to forge for themselves a place in this New World.

For the French soldiers, the convent with its constantly ringing prayer bells was thought to be a softening, positive influence; for the Spanish there was some doubt. Their God was so much more stern and unforgiving, He in Whose name the Holy Inquisition still held sway in Spain.

With the change of flags, there was also a change of jurisdiction within the church. Spanish priests, with their austere outlooks, hair shirts, and scourges, would soon be directing the worship of the people of New Orleans. Who could say what terrors might be in store if they brought that most secret and holy office of the Inquisition with them?

And now, though there was a prison near the Church of St. Louis on the Place d'Armes that had been good enough for the French, citizens of the colony were being held at the barracks by the new Spanish masters, guarded by the vast contingent of soldiers encamped around it. The prayer bells rang with a more urgent sound now from the convent, and over the walls came the constant murmur of voices. There were many reasons for prayer in New Orleans.

Félicité moved along beside the convent wall with Ashanti at her side, her face set as she retraced her footsteps, heading back toward town. She had left her father's noon meal at the barracks and inquired after him. The report was the same; he was well, but could see no one, not the other prisoners, his family, a legal representative, no one. The myrtle candle would be taken in to him, as would the books Félicité had brought from his library and the food, but no messages could be passed. As to the whereabouts of Lieutenant Colonel Morgan McCormack, he was at the house of the governor. It could not be guaranteed that he would see Señorita Lafargue. He was a busy man, the colonel, though he must surely be the man of iron his men sometimes called him if he was able to turn away so beautiful a young lady.

The Spanish soldiers had grown bolder in the last few days, or so it seemed. They were everywhere, lounging in every dim spot of shade, leaning against the walls of houses, sitting in the open-air restaurants watching, making quick, liquid comments among themselves as she passed. Or maybe they only seemed more in evidence because so few of the other residents of the town dared to venture abroad. People were frightened to draw attention to themselves. Moreover, the men who had been arrested, some of the most prominent in the colony, were interrelated, the uncles, cousins, godfathers, if not some more intimate connection, of nearly everyone in the close-knit community. The atmosphere was, therefore, one of unexpected family tragedy.

A few blocks from the governor's house a pair of Spaniards in the red uniforms of officers fell in behind her and Ashanti. Though they did not attempt to overtake them, the officers matched their paces to theirs. Félicité had paid no particular attention to them as she passed. Not only was she intent on the interview that was to come, but she had kept her eyes turned straight ahead so as to give no possible encouragement. Ashanti had glanced at them, she thought, but made no comment.

Félicité quickened her footsteps slightly. Ashanti did the same. Behind them the two men did likewise. They were in no real danger, not in the open street in broad daylight, and yet the fact that the officers dared to annoy her in such a way was both infuriating and frightening. It was a relief when she saw the governor's house near the river looming up before her.

They were within a few yards of their destination when a cart, coming from a side street leading toward the levee, drew up before the house beside that of the governor. It was piled high with leather-bound trunks and boxes, all of which appeared scuffed and worn, though not enough so to obliterate the gold-embossed coronet with which they were stamped. A man in livery jumped to the ground, then handed down a woman. Dressed in a traveling costume of jet black plentifully decorated with lace, she was a striking figure. Of average height, she appeared taller because of her regal bearing. Her face was memorable, with strong bones, wide-set eyes under dark brows, and a firm but generous mouth. Her hair of midnight black was marked at the temples with bands of silver-white that swept back into her elaborately piled coiffure like wings. She carried nestled in the wide sleeve of her gown a small dog that put out his head and barked with a sharp yapping as Félicité and Ashanti approached. The woman turned her head with a smiling apology, warm amusement crinkling the corners of astonishing blue eyes, before she passed into the house.

What was a Spanish noblewoman doing in New Orleans? As intriguing as the question might be, Félicité did not have time to dwell upon it. She dismissed the incident the moment she was past the house.

There was a crowd in the street outside the building O'Reilly had taken for himself. The people gathered in knots, talking in low voices, their faces pinched and worried as they waited for an opportunity to speak to the governor-general. The missions on which they had come seemed unlikely to be crowned with success. In a large anteroom just inside the door, a harassed-looking young officer with his wig askew shuffled papers and explained over and over in execrable French that the honored gentleman was seeing no one.

Admiration ousted the exasperation in the officer's eyes for an instant as Félicité, in her gown of cool white muslin sprigged with violets topped by a lace-edged lawn fichu and apron, came to a halt in front of him. It did not enliven the weariness of his tone, however, as he began his litany once more. "I am sorry, señorita. The governor-general has matters of great weight to occupy him this morning. He cannot see you."

Félicité was becoming used to being addressed in the Spanish form. She ignored it, summoning a smile. "It is not the illustrious governor-general I wish to see. Can you tell me, please, if Lieutenant Colonel Morgan McCormack is at this place?"

"Yes, señorita." The man did not trouble to hide his curiosity.

"Could I be permitted to see him?"

"The colonel is busy, busier even than Governor-General O'Reilly himself, if such a thing is possible. He has given strict orders that he not be disturbed."

"It would be for a few moments only, the merest sliver of his time."

"I am desolate that I must disappoint you, señorita, but it would be as much as my life is worth to show anyone into his presence just now."

"Oh, but please, you must! It is vitally important." Félicité leaned toward him in entreaty, placing one slender white hand on his desk. The dim light in the room moved with a soft sheen across her shoulders and the gentle planes of her face, giving her a look both sensitive and seductive.

The young officer on the other side of the desk swallowed visibly. "Indeed, señorita, I would help you if I dared."

There was a stir behind Félicité, and an officer stepped to her side. It did not need Ashanti's small start of surprise to alert her mistress to the fact that he was one of those who had followed them to the governor's house. He sketched a small bow. "Forgive this intrusion," he said in her native tongue, "but I could not help noticing that you are troubled. It may be that I, Lieutenant Juan Sebastian Unzaga, can be of service."

As much as she despised the necessity of coming here, it went against the grain for Félicité to be unable to carry out her objective. It would be foolhardy to refuse aid, regardless of the source. Turning, she considered the slim, dark-haired Spaniard with the audacious black eyes and pencil-thin mustache who had presented himself. Without surprise, she realized the lieutenant was the man who on several occasions had risked the displeasure of her neighbors, her father, and Valcour by his serenades beneath her window. She summoned a smile, and with a small helpless shrug, told this Lieutenant Unzaga of her problem.

"A simple matter, surely?" he said, lifting a brow at his fellow officer. "I see no reason why the request of this lady should not be granted."

The man behind the desk remonstrated, and there followed a heated discussion in quick-fire Spanish. The officer on duty was, apparently, overruled. Turning back to Félicité, Lieutenant Unzaga bowed once more, and indicated she might accompany him while her maid waited outside.

There were low mutterings from the crowd as Félicité

moved deeper inside the house with the officer. Flinging a quick glance over her shoulder, she saw more than one dark and suspicious look turned in her direction. The obvious resentment troubled her; still, it could not be helped.

The lieutenant tapped on the door that opened from the far side of the anteroom, then stepped aside to permit Félicité to enter. She moved into a large chamber with two tall windows that opened onto a view of a small, unkempt garden. These windows faced the southeast, and the air inside the room was warm and sluggish with the heat of late summer. Because of it, the man seated at the graceful though sturdy desk had removed his uniform jacket and placed it over the back of a chair. In shirtsleeves, he sat behind piles of papers, lists, and ledgers, his strong brown hand driving a quill across a sheet of parchment. He looked up with a frown as Félicité and the other officer came forward, then threw down the pen, leaning back in his chair.

"Bast, what is the meaning of this intrusion?" he inquired in hard tones.

Lieutenant Juan Sebastian Unzaga seemed undaunted by such a cool welcome. "I found this lovely creature outside being barred from your company, and I thought, Morgan, my friend, what a pity it would be if you missed seeing her through ignorance of her presence."

"I am obliged to you," the colonel drawled, "especially since I am certain you had only my welfare in mind."

"What else?" The lieutenant gave the other man a smile of elaborate innocence.

"Your own, for a start, if I know you. I fear you will be disappointed, however, if you expect to win the gratitude of Mademoiselle Lafargue. She has had no liking for the Spanish regime from the first day of our arrival, and has even less reason for affection now."

"Mademoiselle Lafargue, of course! What an idiot I am. It was you, Morgan, was it not, who stole her from beneath my nose at that ill-fated dance three days ago, you she left standing, looking very foolish, when the soirée came to a sudden end?"

"As you say." Colonel McCormack gave a slow nod, his

dark-green gaze resting on Félicité's face. "She is also the daughter of the merchant Lafargue now lodged at the barracks."

"*Por Dios!* I had not realized." The Spanish officer turned to Félicité, the handsome lines of his face set in an expression of sober concern. "Accept my condolences for your misfortune, Mademoiselle Lafargue."

She lifted her chin. "Condolences are not in order, lieutenant. My father is not dead—at least, not yet."

"Mademoiselle—"

The colonel made an impatient gesture. "Since she is here, Bast, it will be as well if the young lady could be allowed to state her purpose."

Lieutenant Unzaga inclined his head, unabashed. "Of course. Mademoiselle?"

Félicité glanced from the smiling Spaniard to the Irish mercenary colonel. Because of the light falling from the windows behind him, his face was in shadow, while she herself felt exposed, with every nuance of expression revealed. She moistened her lips with the tip of her tongue. "I—if I might speak privately, colonel?"

Morgan McCormack glanced at the lieutenant, who sighed, said a graceful farewell, and withdrew.

Quiet descended. Now that she had gained the colonel's attention, she was at a loss. He surveyed her through narrowed eyes that missed nothing, neither the care she had taken with her appearance this morning, nor the quick rise and fall of her breasts beneath her fichu as she strove to contain her agitation. His chestnut hair was damp at the temples with perspiration in the overwarm atmosphere, curling slightly despite being severely clubbed back. There was an inkstain on one finger of his right hand as it lay on a stack of papers. The ruffles of his sleeves and at the neckline of his shirt were mere pleatings of linen unadorned with lace, a detail that made him seem austere, unapproachable. Félicité wished suddenly that she had not come. Speaking with this man would avail her nothing except embarrassment, and it might well make the situation in which she and her father found themselves worse, if such a thing were possible.

"Well, Mademoiselle Lafargue?"

"As you must have guessed, colonel," she began, her voice husky and her hands clasped before her, "I have come because of my father. For him to be imprisoned, for any of the men to be put behind bars, is unjust and unjustifiable."

"Are you saying your father and the others are not guilty of conspiring against the Spanish crown?" Despite her accusation, there was no heat in the question he put to her.

"How can they have conspired against the crown when the king's representative had not officially taken possession of the colony? They were men without a country, repudiated by France, not yet claimed by Spain."

"That is not true. The Treaty of Fontainebleau had been signed, the Spanish representative was in residence. If Ulloa did not present his credentials, it was because he was reluctant to further inflame the feelings of the populace against him. But no man of those who marched and shouted revolutionary refrains could have doubted that Louisiana had become the property of Spain. Therefore, the things they did brand them as guilty."

"I don't concede that," Félicité said, "but even if it were true, why these men and no others? Why not round up every able-bodied man in the colony, every person who spoke or whispered, or even dared to think of governing themselves instead of submitting to a king who cared nothing for their welfare, a ruler thousands of miles away? If this is conspiracy, then nearly every person in the colony is equally guilty. It is a travesty to arrest a few for the crimes of the many."

"There are many who commit murder, but the ones who are imprisoned are either those who are caught in their crime, or those whose probable guilt can be proven."

"My father is not a murderer! He is only a draper, a dealer in silks and cottons who likes to concern himself with ideas and ideals in his leisure time. There is no reason for him to be singled out unless it is a matter of petty vengeance!"

He came to his feet, pushing back his chair and moving around to stand with one hand braced on the corner of his desk. "Could it be," he said in grim query, "that we are now coming to the crux of the matter?"

Félicité resisted the urge to step back away from him.

"Yes, I think we are. You are a high-ranking officer in O'Reilly's entourage. You were incensed when your parade of force through the streets was made ridiculous by the traditional offering of scorn flung by a servant from my father's house. Then later at the dance—"

"An insult that you ordered, I believe, mademoiselle?"

She bit her lip, vexation and an odd shame she had not felt at the time bringing the heat of a flush to her face. The urge to clear her name, in the hope that it might influence the treatment of her father, vied in her mind with loyalty to Valcour. Though he had left the city, he could not be out of the reach of the arm of Spain should O'Reilly decide to question him more closely about his political convictions.

"You did, didn't you?" the colonel queried with a lifted brow.

"Yes, yes, I did," she agreed, transferring her gaze to the landscape of the Loire Valley done in dark oils that covered the wall behind him.

"It has puzzled me that your brother, who was also present at the time, did nothing to stop you. Could it be that he shares your rebellious leanings?"

This was dangerous ground. "Who can say what he thinks, unless it is a question of the merits of one sort of snuff over another, or some such thing? More likely than not, it was sheer indolence that kept him from interfering. You spoke to him yourself while he was detained at your pleasure. Surely you were satisfied that he is not a revolutionary, or you would not have authorized his release."

"I did not sign any such order."

"But someone must have."

Colonel McCormack moved to the front of his desk, where he leaned against it, folding his arms. There was a grating sound in his voice as he answered, "Not to my knowledge."

"What are you saying? That he escaped?" Félicité flicked him a wide-eyed glance, trying to make sense of the colonel's attitude, trying to see how this new development might affect her father.

"It appears that he simply walked out, vanished, while the guards were occupied with the women besieging the place, trying to see their men. How the door came to be so conveniently unlocked is a matter still under investigation.''

She hesitated, then took the plunge. "If—if such a thing could happen once, it might happen again."

"No, it could not. The men now on guard at the barracks were hand-picked, the most reliable from my own company."

"Oh, yes," she cried, disappointment making her reckless, "no one else must be spared! The full complement of lawyers, planters, and merchants must be made to suffer as an example to the rest of us! Neither you nor O'Reilly will be satisfied otherwise."

"The orders to seek out and punish the leaders of the insurgency came from King Carlos himself. The governor-general and I had nothing, personally, to do with the arrest of those unfortunate men. My only connection with this affair has been to obey the direct orders given to me by my commander, dictated from his written instructions brought with him from Spain."

"Orders," she said scornfully, "the excuse of all those who preside over actions they know to be wrong. You don't really expect me to accept that, do you?"

"It's the truth."

The strain, the worry and impotent anger of the past few days, pressed in upon Félicité in a great wave, swamping caution. "What do you know of the truth, a paid soldier used to smooth and plausible answers that relieve you of responsibility while you condemn men to death?"

"Are you saying I lie?"

He stared at her, the expression in his eyes grimly shadowed, though there was steel in his tone. She had gone too far. She lowered her lashes, putting her hand to her face. "I don't know what I am saying. It's just that—things have happened so quickly, and that I am so afraid for my father. Why? Why must it be him? Why should he be chosen to suffer? He's no fanatic, no rabble-rouser. He has always been such a quiet, peaceful man. He is a scholar, a man of ideas, not a revolutionary."

"Sometimes those are the most dangerous kind," Colonel McCormack said, a softer note entering his voice. "You must not despair, mademoiselle. The men who have been arrested will be tried in all fairness for their deeds. If your father is as blameless as you say, then the court will discover it, and he will be sentenced accordingly. It is possible he could be released, or spend a few years at most in prison.''

''A few years, plus the confiscation of everything he owns, everything he has worked for his life long. I suppose I must be grateful, also, for this small mercy? May I ask, since so much depends on it, who will be the judge with this power over my father's life?''

For the first time, the colonel glanced beyond her, the lines of his face stiff. ''He will be tried before a panel of judges, in the presence of the governor-general and several officers of rank.''

Félicité allowed herself a bitter smile. ''Spanish judges, and Spanish officers, too, I make no doubt. Will you, colonel, be among them?''

''That will be my duty, yes.''

''And what,'' she said, drawing a deep, uneven breath, ''will it take to assure that my father will receive a fair and impartial trial, that he will be given the lightest possible sentence?''

His brows snapped together, and he came erect, towering over her. ''Forgive me, mademoiselle, if I misunderstand you, but are you offering me a bribe?''

The idea was not as unsound as it might appear. Corruption and venality, the exchange of favors, of money and goodwill under the table, had become the accepted way of getting things done in the colony, where the laws designed to benefit a country on the other side of the ocean strangled commerce on this shore. In addition, previous governors sent by the court of France had been much more interested in lining their pockets, or building a base from which to advance to larger things in the service of Louis XV, than they had been in honest and correct administration. Under the French, a probe of the sort she had made, even one so crudely put, would all too likely have been met with playful disclaimers, gracious denials, but eventual smiling accommodation. The colonel was not smiling.

"I meant no insult," she said hurriedly. "I was merely trying to discover the most promising method of helping my father."

His features did not relax. "Believe me, mademoiselle, there is none. Though the court may decide the degree of innocence or guilt, the sentences meted out will be decided by the governor-general as the supreme authority in Louisiana. There is no way you, or I, or anyone else, can influence that decision."

"You can't actually expect me to believe that you, his fellow countryman, a man guided by him to promotion in the Spanish army, hand-picked to come here as his second-in-command, has no influence, nothing to say in counsel with the governor-general?"

He frowned. "The gossips have been busy."

"Knowledge can sometimes mean the difference between life and death. Why should we not talk among ourselves of the men sent to rule over us?" He had not denied that O'Reilly might listen to his opinions. Could it be that his denials before had been nothing more than the rhetoric of pride, mere words to increase her desperation and also the amount she and her father would be willing to expend? Félicité studied the man before her, ready to use any advantage. It was disconcerting to discover that he was watching her with equal intentness.

"I am a colonial officer, a mercenary," he answered, bitterness etching his tone.

"You are second-in-command with the authority to dismiss an incident such as that of the chamber pot, or, as you claimed, carry it further. That much being true, you could surely arrange leniency for my father."

"That privilege belongs to Don Alejandro O'Reilly, and to him only, as administrator for the colony."

"And what of you, Colonel McCormack? Have you no ambition to achieve a similar post, to make your own mark on the New World? If my father were freed, his gratitude would be such that he would be happy to arrange trading concessions, or other access to goods that would bring income useful in your future advancement."

"Access to goods? I assume you are suggesting smuggling activity, or maybe even the outfitting of a privateer?"

"If that is your preference."

"Tell me," he said, his tone colorless, "is your father aware of your promises on his behalf?"

Félicité felt a small thrill of triumph at this expression of interest. "No, he isn't, but I am certain he would cooperate in any way necessary."

"I wasn't aware that the possibilities you outline were within his power to arrange. It occurs to me that it might benefit the crown if a more diligent investigation were made into the affairs of Monsieur Lafargue, perhaps even a reevaluation of his estate!"

There was a glitter of emerald hardness in the sudden, piercing look he sent her from narrowed eyes. With a tightening of her nerves, Félicité recognized that he really was indifferent to the prospect of personal gain. It was an attitude as unfortunate as it was incredible. Through stiff lips she said, "As you please, colonel, since it seems you are determined on your revenge."

He stared at her for long moments, his gaze drifting from the honey-gold curls confined beneath a muslin cap edged with lace, down over the curve of her cheek to the roundness of her breasts beneath her bodice, then to the slim span of her waist and the fashionable fullness of her skirts. It was a thorough appraisal, one that left her trembling with rage and something more she could not have named.

"As I please? Not quite, mademoiselle. If you are so certain your father is being held because of your behavior, it puzzles me that you offer recompense in such terms that only he can pay. Are you so unwilling to sacrifice your pride for your father's sake?"

"What do you mean?" The expression in her brown eyes was wary, her tone uncertain.

"I mean, there is a commodity of value that has so far gone unmentioned, one that only you can offer."

"I don't think I understand." She was afraid she did, but she refused to commit herself for fear she was wrong.

"I think you do. I am speaking, Mademoiselle Lafargue, of the pleasure of your company."

Anger boiled up inside her. The worst thing about his suggestion was that she could not afford to reject it out of hand, could not risk the retaliation that might be directed toward her father. "You—you can't mean it!"

"Why would you think so? You are a beautiful woman. I am alone in a foreign country, surrounded by people who, to put it mildly, are less than friendly. I find myself growing tired of cold shoulders from the females I meet. A warmer relationship would be most welcome."

His manner was odd, almost as though he mocked himself instead of her, as though he expected her to take to her heels at any moment, leaving his insolent proposal only half broached. "It's preposterous! Valcour tried to tell me how it would be. I should have listened to him!"

"And just what did Valcour Murat say?" he inquired in hard tones.

"That you would expect me to—that it would be necessary for me—that—"

He lifted a brow as she stumbled to a halt. "Yes, Mademoiselle Lafargue?"

Embarrassed rage came to her aid. "He said that as a woman I would be fair game, especially to a man like you, that—that the taking of such personal favors was one of the rewards of war."

"And you are unwilling?"

It was impossible to read his expression behind the screen of his lashes. Félicité lifted her chin. "How could I be anything else?"

A tight smile curled one corner of his mouth. "There was always the possibility of an unexpected boon. But let it go. As fascinating as the idea might be, that was not my meaning."

"It wasn't?" She was relieved, of course she was, and yet she was also aware of a confused sense of pique. She thrust it from her with determination, trying to concentrate on what he was saying.

"I believe I mentioned to you the governor-general's interest in improving relations with the community? It is his goal to deal with the punishment of the leaders of the insurgency as soon as possible, then put the unpleasantness behind us so that the day-to-day administration of the colony can proceed on a normal footing. It is his contention that the easiest way to make our presence in the town acceptable is by encouraging his officers to behave naturally, though with all gallantry, toward the female population. If this results in numbers of his men settling down here, then that will not displease either him or the Spanish crown. Insufficient population has always been one of the problems of the Louisiana colony.''

"Colonel McCormack, do you mean—?"

"Any officer who is seen riding with a Frenchwoman, strolling in the Place d'Armes with one on his arm, or dancing at the various assemblies, is certain of commendation. Likewise, the lady in question might reasonably expect a favorable response to any request she might make. Especially one who steps out first as a pattern card of behavior for her sex in the town.''

"And that is all?" Félicité asked, the tone of her voice blank.

He smiled, his green gaze meeting her brown eyes in a direct clash. "That was the original intention. I will be happy to take your brother's suggestion under consideration if you prefer.''

She drew in her breath as a rush of heat suffused her, followed by the chill of dismay. The brief glimpse of controlled ardor she had caught in his expression brought the rise of something near panic to her chest. "If this is your idea of gallantry—''

"I am offering you the opportunity to aid your father in the only way possible. Isn't that what you wanted?''

"No! No, it's impossible!" The words were spoken before she could think, before there was time to soften them or make them less final.

"Decisions taken in haste are often regretted, mademoiselle. I will give you time to consider before I require an answer.''

The tone of his voice was assured, faintly mocking. It was a dismissal of sorts, one Félicité was not loath to take. Fearful of what she might say if she stayed, she whirled in a flurry of skirts. Snatching open the door, she stepped through and slammed it behind her.

Chapter 5

❦

Félicité was given less than seven hours to consider the colonel's proposition. She spent the time in agitated reflection, going over the scene between herself and the Irish mercenary again and again. Half the time she was assailed by the fear that she might have harmed her father's case instead of aiding it, by the wish that she had spoken more diplomatically. The other half, she paced the floor in flaming outrage at his confident manner, railing that she had not given him a final refusal in virulent and emphatic words. Ashanti, when she had listened to the tale of the colonel's perfidy, counseled cautious accommodation up to a point. What choice had she, after all, when brave men of wealth and resource were bowing the Spaniards into their shops, girding themselves to take the oath of allegiance required by O'Reilly? It could not hurt to be on terms with McCormack, and might actually help. At any rate, her situation was too precarious to make an enemy of him.

Ashanti was not the only person who feared for Félicité. An hour after Félicité's return from the governor's house, she had received a call from a neighbor woman. A motherly soul with a penchant for gossip, she was all sympathy over the arrest of poor Monsieur Lafargue and concern that Félicité was alone. She had noticed that Valcour did not go in and out these last few days, and wondered what was the reason. Her husband had seen the dear boy on Bayou St. John in company with a set of men of reputations most unsavory; smugglers, *chère*, veritable pirates, if the truth were known. It was a pity to wring the heart of *le bon Dieu* himself how families were being torn apart by the cruel orders of this devil O'Reilly. The man was made of stone; everyone said it was so. He could not be moved by the tears of a mother or the pleas of a young and gentle bride. Did Félicité know that Jean Baptiste Noyan, the very nephew of the great Bienville himself, founder of the colony, was among those arrested, dragged from the side of his new wife? A mere boy, he was, son-in-law to Lafrénière, also taken up by the soldiers. How evil could such a one, scarcely a man yet, be? And poor little Madame Noyan, to be bereft of father and husband at once! Life was a great sadness, nothing more, nothing less.

The neighbor heaved a sigh from the depths of a comfortably padded bosom, and returned her thoughts to Félicité. Her situation was grim, a young girl alone with nothing more than a trio of female servants in the house to protect her. What Valcour could be thinking of to leave her so was a puzzle, with the Spanish soldiers loose in the town. How long their officers could control them was anybody's guess, though the officers, especially the paid Irish hooligans, might well be worse than the men. It would not be surprising if every woman in New Orleans was raped in her bed! Would it not be best if Félicité removed next door as her guest, or at least sought refuge with the good sisters at the convent?

Such a course did not recommend itself to Félicité, any more than did the idea of resigned and prayerful acceptance of the events gathering around them. What did that leave, however? She could protect herself with pistol and sword, but she could not secure the release of her father by marching in and brandishing such weapons. The odds against success were overwhelming. It was possible, then, that her best chance of improving his chances was through Lieutenant Colonel Morgan McCormack.

It was a calculated risk; she knew that. Though there had been some sign that her cooperation, as outlined by the colonel, would result in the lightest practicable sentence for her father, there was no guarantee. The colonel, very carefully, had not put what he was offering into words, any more than he had said precisely what he expected in return. In such a situation, it would be fatally easy to read too much into what he said, or not enough.

Noon came and went. Movements slowed to a standstill as the heat grew, and breathing became an effort. The sky overhead washed out to a faded blue without a sign of clouds. A heat haze shimmered over the cypress shingle rooftops of the houses, and people retreated inside, closing the shutters against the silver-white glare of the day. Only as the sun began to settle toward the west did they come out again, moving at a lethargic tempo that would not increase until the coolness of the evening made itself felt.

The walls of the houses held the accumulated warmth until well after dark, however, and it was the custom to venture out of doors in the twilight, to sit on the steps or balconies. The more energetic walked slowly along the streets to the river levee, or strolled around the Place d'Armes, the dusty parade ground before the Church of St. Louis.

The levee was Félicité's favorite promenade. Scorning to be deterred by the presence of the Spanish, she set out with Ashanti to take the air. It was possible the soft and peaceful air of the evening and the breezes off the river would banish the dull headache that had formed behind her eyes and quiet the turmoil that gripped her.

It was a vain hope. Hardly had she reached the area of the river-front when she saw a uniformed officer detach himself from a group beneath the sycamore trees that edged the parade square and come toward her. There was a challenge gleaming in the emerald depths of Colonel McCormack's eyes, though his bronzed features were stiff as he stopped before her. "Mademoiselle Lafargue, an unexpected pleasure," he said, executing a perfunctory bow.

"I suspect that is something less than an accurate statement," she returned in cool tones.

His smile was ironic. "I assure you, I am most pleased to see you."

She was not certain enough that he had been waiting there on the chance that she might put in an appearance to charge him with it. Instead she murmured, "It is a pity I cannot say the same."

"So it is, especially since we will be spending much time together in the future."

She stared at him, hardly aware of the light warning touch of her maid's fingers on her arm. "What makes you think we will, colonel?"

"I may be wrong, of course, mademoiselle, but since you have not yet twitched your skirts and walked away from me, I am encouraged to think you have decided to favor the plan I outlined this morning."

It had come without warning, this moment of decision. In an effort to gain time, she said, "I cannot believe you were serious."

"I was never more so." The timbre of his voice was low and deep, his expression watchful.

"Why me?" she asked abruptly.

"You are a beautiful young woman," he answered. "Besides which, if you will remember, it was you who brought yourself to my attention."

"Not for this purpose!"

"That much is certainly true, though it scarcely matters now. Tell me, Mademoiselle Lafargue, will you walk with me, or will you not?"

His words seemed to indicate that he expected no more of her than this public show of cordiality, as he had suggested that morning. Félicité took a deep breath. "It seems, Colonel McCormack, that I have little choice."

"Regrettable," he said, the word clipped for all the quietness of his voice. "However, it is not I who compels you."

"No, you are merely using the situation to your advantage, are you not, colonel?" There was a shadow in her clear brown eyes.

He made no attempt to avoid her gaze as he turned, offering his arm, indicating the direction they would take. "Quite true, I am."

The agreement had been made; it would be useless to quibble over how it was carried out. With no more than the barest instant of hesitation, Félicité placed her fingers on the broadcloth-clad arm of the colonel, and they moved off together.

Ashanti, with a sigh that might have been of relief or pained acceptance, fell in behind them.

Félicité was more aware than she cared to be of the man beside her, of his height, the lithe grace of his stride, the muscles beneath the sleeve of his uniform, and his sheer male presence. For long moments these things were so overwhelming, so at odds with the unreality of what she had done, that she failed to notice the covert glances cast in their direction, or the manner in which people gave way before them. As she recognized how it must look, Monsieur Lafargue's daughter walking out with a red-coated soldier, one of O'Reilly's Irish henchmen, while her father lay behind bars, a wash of color rose to her hairline. Then she lifted her chin. Her conduct was no one's concern except her own. The wisdom of what she was doing would one day be evident, and in the meantime she would stroll with the devil himself if it would benefit her father.

They reached the levee and climbed the rickety wooden steps that led to the top of that long, curving bulwark of earth. More than ten feet across on top, slanting to nearer twenty at its base, it had been thrown up as a not always adequate protection against the Mississippi River at flood stage. Now, in late August, the river was at its lowest level of the year, but so wide and mighty still that its far bank was indistinct in the evening distance. It smelled of fish and mud and rotting vegetation, and yet the breeze that rippled its surface was fresh and cooling.

Colonel McCormack slanted her a look of grim amusement. "Are you always so silent, or am I to assume you are having trouble finding a topic suitable for the occasion?"

"I wasn't aware that I was supposed to entertain you."

"You aren't," he answered, the warmth dying out of his eyes, "but an appearance of common politeness does seem in order."

"By all means, if that is your wish," she answered, and had the pleasure of seeing a frown of annoyance appear between his brows.

"My wish," he said, stressing the last word, "is to be treated as you would treat any other man of your acquaintance."

"But you are not any other man," she pointed out, a clouded expression in her eyes. "My father's fate may depend on your goodwill."

"If you follow that idea to its logical conclusion, then politeness would seem mandatory."

"Is that a threat, colonel?"

"If you mean bread and water for your father if you displease me, no. Everyone, man or woman, should pay for his own misdeeds."

For some reason she could not have named, his words were more chilling to Félicité than an outright intent to make her father suffer for her uncooperative attitude. It was not so much the thought that she might be in jeopardy as it was the implacable manner in which the words had been delivered. Her voice cold, she said, "Am I to understand then, Colonel McCormack, that your presence here may be as much because of the affair of the chamber pot as for my pleas on my father's behalf?"

An expression impossible to decipher flitted across his face. "The reasons, mademoiselle, are many and varied, but since the fact has been accomplished, they need no longer concern us."

"Very well," Félicité replied after a long moment. To follow his lead seemed easier, and possibly safer, than delving into that question any further.

He smiled with a touch of mockery. "While you are in so agreeable a mood, I will request that you address me as Morgan, that being my given name."

Félicité inclined her head in acquiescence, carefully refraining from extending the freedom of her name to him. That did not deter him, however.

"Thank you, Félicité," he said, his manner grave, though his expression was expectant.

She sent him a fulminating glance, but did not protest.

They turned south along the levee, he fitting his long strides to her slower pace. After a few moments she said with vinegary sweetness, "Tell me, how do you like Louisiana?"

"It's an incredible place," he answered with no more than a flash of dry humor for the commonplace nature of the topic.

"I've never seen anything like the way things grow here. They seem to spring up overnight. I've seen weeds and vines that measure a foot or more of increased length or height overnight. Between the rich soil and the warm climate, it wouldn't surprise me if three different crops could be produced in a year's time."

"You sound almost like a farmer."

"And why not? One way and another, I come from a long line of farmers." Bitterness like an acid etched his tone for a moment, then was gone.

Félicité decided to ignore the lead he had given her. "The heat doesn't trouble you?"

"I've served in the Caribbean, in the Mediterranean, and in Spain almost constantly since my eighteenth birthday. Hot weather is nothing new, though I can't say I enjoy the flies and mosquitoes that seem to go with it. I've never seen them quite so bad anywhere else."

"It's the swampland that surrounds us; they breed in stagnant water. I'll admit they are a nuisance, but I don't suppose they have ever killed anyone. By serving, though, colonel, I take it you mean with the army?"

He glanced at her with a lifted brow, saying nothing.

"I—mean Morgan, of course," she corrected with a small stammer.

"If you refer to the Spanish army, no," he answered, taking up her question. "I was apprenticed at the age of fifteen to a lawyer. Slightly less than two years later, I was caught on the street by an English press gang. They knocked me senseless after a short but bloody struggle, and I was trundled to the coast in a wagon. When I woke up, I was bound hand and foot and was being carried on board a ship."

"A lawyer's apprentice?" she asked, flinging a quick frown at his hard, martial features. "Somehow I can't see you in that profession."

"Nor could I," he said with one of his brief, almost reluctant smiles. "It was considered a good position by my father. If I learned the ways of the English law, I might be able to prevent them taking any more of our land. It would have been more practical to have bound me over to a baker.

At least we could have eaten, something not too many people were doing in Ireland just then, or now for that matter.''

"You became an English sailor, then. Was that more to your liking?'' Despite herself, Félicité felt a stir of interest in Morgan McCormack's tale.

"If you can ask such a question, then you know nothing about the life of a deckhand before the mast, especially one on an English ship. It was nothing except unremitting toil in all kinds of weather, food seasoned with maggots and weevils, and the constant lash of the cat-o'-nine-tails.''

"But you escaped.''

"The frigate we were sailing in had the good luck to be taken by pirates in the Caribbean.''

"Good luck!'' she exclaimed.

"As it turned out, yes. The men who are willing to go to sea for long months at a time are few. Pirate ships, like those of the English navy, are always short of men. Knowing that most of the crew on English ships have been pressed against their wills, the better pirate captains give the seamen the chance to change their allegiance and improve their fortunes. Since the alternative is to be set adrift in a small boat at the very best, most take it.''

She could not resist a touch of spite as she said, "And was that occupation more to your taste?''

"It had its compensations.'' The glint in his green eyes was a hint that he was aware of her belittling attitude, though he made no comment.

"Such as?''

"The pirate ship made port more often, the food was better, and in most cases, any ship attacked was well armed, so in most cases the capturing of a prize was a fair fight with the outcome depending on the quickness, skill, and daring of the captain. The man I served under was interested in spoils, nothing more; money, jewelry, cargo. He got no pleasure from watching men die, and was content to allow the ships and their passengers to go on their way, spreading his fame, and perhaps reloading to be preyed on another day.''

"A paragon!''

"So he was, until he was pinned to the deck by a falling mast in an engagement off the island of Puerto Rico."

"A pirate ship without a captain? Sounds like chaos."

"It is," he said grimly, "but the position has to be filled for the good of everyone involved. Sometimes a new captain is elected, sometimes he elects himself by defeating all other comers."

"Don't tell me," she said in mock respect, "that you were chosen?"

"After several of the other contenders had carved each other up to the point of anemia, yes."

"Then how does it happen that you aren't a pirate still?"

He shrugged, a quick movement of broad shoulders. "The pirate's creed is simple: a short life but a merry one. I found I had too much farmer's blood in my veins to appreciate it. I weighed the risks against the rewards, and decided the former outweighed the latter. I was already branded an outlaw by the English; I had nothing to lose by capturing British merchantmen. But it looked as though it would be better to throw in my lot with another country before I had pounced on the shipping of all, doing myself completely out of a refuge."

"How did you come to choose Spain? Why not France, for instance?

"I was in a Spanish port when the decision was taken."

They walked on a little way without speaking, passing a milch cow staked out on the slope of the levee, placidly cropping the grass. A group of young boys pushed past them laughing and calling in high spirits, shirtless, barefooted, carefree. They stepped aside for a Negro woman balancing an enormous load of laundry in a basket on top of her head. She spoke to Ashanti, and Félicité's maid paused to exchange a few words with her as Félicité and the colonel moved on a few steps.

"Your brother," Morgan McCormack said as their way cleared once more, "I understand, is no longer staying with you."

"No." She slanted him a quick, inquiring glance.

"On the occasions when I have met him, he seemed—an interesting man."

"Interesting? In what way?"

"He is not, in my opinion, what he seems on the surface."

This was dangerous ground. "Valcour? Surely you mistake. He calls himself a fashionable fribble; that should tell you something."

"A fashionable fribble with a reputation as a dangerous man with whom to cross swords? An unusual combination in my experience."

"The quickness and coordination that a swordsman requires are gifts of nature."

"Granted, but not so the skill and accuracy that makes a man a formidable opponent. These things take work and dedication, plus something more, usually a willingness to use the blade, or else the necessity."

"You sound as if you have some personal knowledge of the subject."

"Most soldiers do," he answered, his tone dry.

"And most pirates?"

"As you say."

"Valcour is neither," she pointed out with an air of reasonableness.

"Nonetheless, you will tell him," he said with heavy irony, "should you see him, that I would like a word with him. The matter of his unauthorized departure from prison remains. It would be unfortunate if we were forced to put out a flier on him like a common criminal."

At that moment, Ashanti rejoined them. Without giving Félicité a chance to answer, Colonel McCormack made a brief adieu with the excuse of the press of responsibility, bowed, and walked away. Watching him go, Félicité was aware of a hollow feeling beneath her ribs. It was caused by the suspicion that he had sought her out not because of their agreement, but specifically to give her the message for Valcour. If that was indeed the case, then she should not be troubled by him again. But was it?

"What is it, mam'selle? Why do you look so?" Ashanti asked, her smooth, fine-boned face with its high cheekbones and flaring nostrils creasing with anxiety.

Félicité told her in a few short sentences, including what

the neighbor woman had said concerning her brother's whereabouts.

"It may be," Ashanti said, a faraway look in her eyes, "that it would be better if this man, this colonel, should find M'sieu Valcour and put him back in prison."

"What are you saying, Ashanti?" Félicité exclaimed.

"He is an animal, M'sieu Valcour, one who caters always to his appetites, who enjoys rending and tearing the flesh of others."

"Ashanti, please." The maid had not been rational about Valcour since the night when he, as she claimed, tried to violate her.

"Very well, mam'selle. But what of the colonel? He is much of a man. You walk with him before the town, something that is allowed among your people only if the couple is to be wed."

"I don't intend to marry him, if that's what you are thinking!"

"But would it not be better to entice him into the church for vows than to allow him to share your bed without them?"

"Sharing my bed is not part of the bargain, Ashanti!"

"Are you sure, mam'selle?" Taking Félicité's silence as an answer, she went on, "The idea is there. Even if he does not speak of it now, he will someday. When he does, you must have your answer ready."

Félicité frowned. "Must I? What makes you think so?"

"It is in the way he looks at you, mam'selle, and in the air when he comes close, a quiet thunder, like the beat of a distant drum."

Gooseflesh rose uncomfortably on Félicité's arms, running with a chill down her spine. "He will have nothing of me, Ashanti, nothing. I will see to that."

"Guard yourself well, then, mam'selle. Give soft answers and gentle smiles. And don't cross him. Never cross him, mam'selle."

Despite the colonel's abrupt leave-taking, that was not the end of their pact. He arrived in the street outside the Lafargue ménage early the next morning. Mounted on a superb bay stallion, he led a dappled gray filly with the proud neck and

78

fine bone structure that spoke of Arabian bloodlines. Where he had found such good stock was a mystery until Félicité remembered a vague rumor brought on the servants' grapevine of a transport ship given over entirely to the mounts of the Spanish officers. To refuse to test the mettle of the mount brought for her pleasure was unthinkable, not only because of her agreement with Morgan McCormack, but because she could not resist the prospect of a gallop. With Ashanti's help, she struggled into her riding habit and descended to the street.

Félicité returned from the outing perhaps a shade more in charity with the colonel. No hint of the reason for her accompanying him had intruded. The man had set himself to please, to gain her confidence and put her at ease. Though suspicious of such tactics, Félicité could not but own that he had a certain hard-bitten attraction when he cared to use it.

They had ridden along the river, leaving the stale miasma of night odors from the town behind them, plunging into the freshness of the morning. It was only as the sun climbed higher, pouring its molten heat down upon them, forcing them to turn back, that active animosity had arisen between them again. It came when Morgan introduced the subject of Valcour once more. He had learned of Dom, her brother's body servant, and wanted to speak to the man. The information that the servant could neither speak nor read and write was not to his liking; still, he insisted on seeing Dom. Since the name of his new master was something the colonel could learn from anyone, Félicité had no choice except to tell him.

There was a problem with Valcour that Félicité had not yet faced. If he was anywhere near New Orleans, if he came and went in the town, then he must eventually learn of her association with the Spanish-Irish officer. He had disapproved, sometimes violently, of any interest taken in her by men of her own social and national background; what would be his reaction to her seeming preference for the company of the mercenary?

It had crossed Félicité's mind more than once that if Morgan McCormack was aware of Valcour's attitude he might well be using the situation to entice her brother out of hiding. It was unlikely such a plan would succeed, even if she was correct in her suspicions. When she had refused to go with Valcour, to leave her father and flee for France, he had more or less washed his hands of her; it was unlikely he would put his head into a noose for her sake. And yet, he had not departed for France, had not even left the vicinity, though he had certainly made preparations to do so, as witnessed by his sale of the body servant. What he was doing she could not imagine, nor could she help being apprehensive.

There was another evening stroll with Colonel McCormack, made bearable by the light, if strained, conversation. This time he came for her at her house, and returned her to the foot of the stairs at the entrance passage. She did not invite him inside, nor did he suggest it, though there was a moment when he stood waiting, almost expectant. Her fears had been allayed somewhat, since at no time had he indicated by word or deed that he expected more from her than their formal meetings. It was simply a reluctance to allow him to enter the private precincts of her life, to bid an enemy to enter her father's house while he himself resided in prison at the behest of that man's government, that made her bar his entrance.

There was a shuttered look about the colonel's face as he bowed, ready to take his leave. "I have matters to attend to in the morning," he said, "which will make a ride impossible. There is a masque arranged for the evening, however. Will you do me the honor of accepting my escort?"

Félicité sent him a straight look, appreciative, suddenly, of the fact that the request for her presence was not couched in the form of an order, as it well might have been. Gravely she replied, "It is I who shall be honored."

Levées, soirées, *bals masques*, such entertainments were not unusual for the town, but they were normally reserved for the winter season from November until after Easter in imitation of Paris, whence came the rules of polite society. That they were being given now was but a symptom of the consternation that had swept the town. To make the new masters welcome, to disarm them with frivolous amusement and an air of gaiety, was a technique ingrained through ages of seeing conquerors come and go in their homeland of France.

No one understood this more thoroughly than the women of the town—the hostesses, the fearful wives and mothers.

Regardless, Félicité could not think that her arrival at such an affair as the *bal masque* on the arm of the colonel would be looked on with favor. Knowing that she would be the object of many stares and much censure, she dressed with care, but also with a certain proud defiance.

The night was sultry and oppressive. Not a breath of air filtered through the shutters of Félicité's bedroom. The heat of the candle flames around the dressing table, combined with that of the curling tongs Ashanti wielded, brought a flush of hectic color to her face, though it might well have been augmented by the appearance of the costume she was wearing.

Of softly draped muslin edged with gold-embroidered blue satin braid, it was a copy of the Greek chiton made popular by Madame Du Barry, official mistress to the King of France since April. The blond courtesan had been involved in a liaison with Louis XV for some years previous, and the fashion doll on which the ensemble had appeared had arrived in New Orleans the past winter. Du Barry, a commoner by birth, was not much emulated. Moreover, the simple style and material seemed no substitute for the richness of brocades and silks and the stiff formality of panniers, high-piled hair, and powder. Still, the chiton was eminently suitable for the masque held in the caldron warmth of a late summer night.

The one thing not apparent on the miniature version displayed by the fashion doll was the extreme low cut of the neckline, a most revealing plunge that was repeated in the back, and the lack of sleeves, which left her arms and shoulders virtually bare. While admittedly cooler, such a lavish display of her charms might well give rise to speculation Félicité would as soon avoid, such as in what other particular she might be seeking to copy the king's mistress.

It was too late to fret over it. If she had thought her reputation could withstand the wearing of such a gown weeks before, then surely it could do so now.

"There, mam'selle," Ashanti said, setting the curling tongs back on their frame erected over the candlestick. "It is done."

Félicité rose to her feet, shaking out the folds of white,

unstarched muslin. The soft material draped around her, molding itself to the slender, pliant lines of her body. A gold cord looped and tied into a girdle encircled her waist. On her feet were soft leather sandals without heels, the fastenings of which crisscrossed up the calves of her legs, which were nude of stockings. In keeping with the simplicity of the effect she sought to create, she had washed all traces of powder from her hair, then Ashanti had drawn the shining golden mass into a knot at the crown of her head, from which fell a cascade of soft, gleaming curls.

"You are most beautiful, mam'selle, even if it does look as if you are wearing your nightrail."

It was an apt description, since the gown was worn without undergarments of any kind beyond a thin underdress. Lacking the confinement of stays or the bulkiness of panniers, minus her chemise that with its long tail drawn between her thighs and tucked into her petticoat tapes in front constituted her drawers, her body appeared unfettered to the point of abandon. And yet there was also a look of purity, of passionless allure seen in portraits of the Holy Virgin in her flowing robes. The impression was one of angelic, unknowing wantonness.

"Perhaps I had best send my excuses?" Félicité suggested doubtfully.

"How can you, mam'selle? The colonel will not allow it."

"I could plead illness, if it were not such a coward's trick."

"You have never been that, mam'selle." At the sound of a firm knock, the maid tilted her head. "That will be the colonel now. Shall I send him away?"

Could the maid manage it? Félicité doubted it. "No," she said, gesturing toward the demi-mask of white satin edged with braid and the shawl of Norwich silk that lay close to hand. "I will go."

The streets were dark, making the linkboy Morgan had hired a necessity in order for them to pick their way along the rutted thoroughfare. Gazing down one dark-shadowed way, Félicité saw the flash of heat lightning along the horizon beyond the dark open space of the river.

The pine-pitch torches that burned outside the house where

the masque was being held were welcome beacons as they burned with a yellow-orange flare in the still, heavy air. Inside, however, it was scarcely more bright than without, as was the custom with such entertainments, where a major part of the amusement depended on keeping identities concealed until the unmasking at the stroke of midnight. As might be expected, the atmosphere was lively, and a trifle free, though not to excess. Still, the masque was not considered an appropriate occasion for the appearance of *jeunes filles.* Most of the women present were young matrons bent on discreet flirtations, or widows. Their hostess, a woman who often spoke of her *cousine* who was a companion of the mesdames of France, the daughters of King Louis, enjoyed a marriage in the aristocratic style with both her and her husband turning a bland eye to each other's little indiscretions.

Félicité's costume, therefore, was not as *outré* as she had feared. There was not another Greek chiton to be seen, but at a single glance one could see a Circe in a skimpy gown without petticoats that featured green spangles on sarcenet, and a lady from the Court of Love in a slim gown with wide, flowing sleeves and a pointed cap from which was suspended a veil. Yet another costume appeared to be constructed of feathers attached to a black gauze underdress fully as décolleté as her own, if not more so. Though the wearer was masked, her unpowdered hair gave her away. It was the Spanish lady, the noblewoman Félicité had seen near the governor-general's house. The white wings in her dark hair revealed her identity, though she seemed as careless of the fact as she did of the glimpses of her charms revealed by her floating gown. Those females who had worn the heavy court fashion were already looking wilted, fanning themselves with vigor as they dabbed with scented handkerchiefs at the perspiration making tracks in their maquillage, and casting glances both scathing and longing at the gowns of the others. Nonetheless, when Félicité slipped her silk shawl from her shoulders, handing it to an attendant, the man at her side drew in his breath. She sent him a quick glance from under her lashes. He was staring at her, a trace of disapproval stamped on his hard features, though his green eyes through the slits of the scarlet domino he wore over his uniform appeared luminous with something that might have been desire.

"Morgan, my friend, you have captured a goddess, a veritable Diana, an Hebe—no! A Venus!"

Those liquid, admiring tones could only belong to Juan Sebastian. He had not put in an appearance outside her window for several days, not since she had met him in the office of the colonel, in fact.

"So it seems," Morgan answered.

"I am consumed with jealousy. I swear upon my honor, no other lady in this room, nay, in New Orleans, can compare to Mademoiselle Lafargue!"

"You are too kind," Félicité said in conventional reply, though there was a crinkle of amusement around her eyes for his obvious flattery.

"Not so kind as I would surely be if you did not have this surly Irishman at your elbow, who is, lamentably, my superior."

"I see," Morgan drawled, "that I am going to have to do something about the lack of discipline and respect in the ranks. A few weeks on duty aboard the frigate in the harbor should serve to instill an appreciation for those virtues."

"You jest, my friend! Don't you?" Juan Sebastian, also in a red domino, bent a look of comical inquiry upon the other man.

Morgan's chiseled mouth curved into a deliberately enigmatic smile.

"Ah, I think you jest, but in case you do not, I will beg a dance from the beautiful one on your arm, the memory of which will sustain me should the worst befall. I realize this is the opposite of what you intended, *compadre,* but the fault is your own for failing to take into account the fatalism in the Iberian character."

"Approach at your own risk," Morgan drawled.

The Spaniard laughed, and with a flourish of his capelike domino, moved away. The room was full of dominos, it seemed, most of them scarlet, though there was a sprinkling of black and gray ones. In every case there was a scabbard point nudging at the material in the back, as the gentlemen kept their swords at their sides. With the powdered wigs and black demi-masks, it had the effect of making most of the males in the room look alike, a vast concord of brothers.

Félicité's quick gaze fastened on a slim gentleman in the corner, talking to a lady whose coiffure was shaped like a beehive, complete with silken bees perched upon the mass. Because of the dim light and the fact that he was half turned from her, she could not be certain it was Valcour; still, she was almost positive it was he.

Without haste, she allowed her gaze to wander to the next couple, and the next. Her voice deliberately casual, she said to Morgan McCormack, "Do you suppose the governor-general is here?"

"He is supposed to put in a brief appearance. He is not fond of masquerades, however. I suspect it will be after midnight before he makes an entrance."

Félicité was saved from having to discover another subject for conversation by the arrival behind them of a giggling friend from convent days. She had in tow her plump, curly-haired, olive-skinned husband. Her manner exquisitely polite, Félicité presented the couple to Morgan, and the four of them stood chatting until the music began.

They took the floor together, she and the Irish colonel. It seemed to Félicité that every eye in the room was riveted upon their performance as they went through the figures. Glancing once at Morgan from under her lashes, she found him watching her, his expression speculative, absorbed.

"You are very quiet this evening," she ventured.

"The better to concentrate on you."

"A boring exercise, surely?"

"You would not think so," he answered with a sudden flashing smile, "if you could read my thoughts."

It would not do to discourage such passages between them completely, and yet her position must be made plain. "I'm sure I am more comfortable without that ability."

The evening crept onward. Félicité danced with Juan Sebastian. Afterward he left her sitting beside a window alcove while he fought his way to the punch bowl to bring her a cooling drink. Scarcely had he vanished into the growing press of people when there was a movement at her shoulder.

"Well met, my dear sister," Valcour said in a sibilant undertone.

Félicité flashed a startled glance upward in time to see her brother's ironic bow and the jerk of his head that indicated that they move deeper into the alcove. Immediately she glanced to where Morgan, easily recognizable for his height, stood on the other side of the crowded dance floor in close conversation with a pair of his fellow officers and, curiously enough, the Spanish noblewoman. He was paying no attention to her. When she swung back, Valcour had disappeared. Her manner casual, she came to her feet, and, plying the fan that hung from her wrist, she stepped into the shadowed recess also.

"You are in looks," Valcour said.

"Never mind that! What are you thinking of, coming here? In fact, why are you in New Orleans? I thought it was your intention to fly for France."

He shrugged. "I am in no hurry."

"It might be well if you could bestir yourself. Did you know the Spanish are watching for you, that Colonel McCormack means to lay you by the heels again so he can continue his interrogation? It seems your release was a mistake."

"Careless of them, wasn't it? I don't believe I should encourage such slack habits by turning myself in. Besides, the Spanish are such petty bureaucrats, writing endless reports about the least little thing. Why should I cause them more work?" He took out his coffin-shaped snuffbox, used it, and put it away, plying his handkerchief in a careless gesture.

Félicité sent him a glance of exasperation. "If Colonel McCormack discovers you are here, he may count the trouble well worth the pleasure of recapturing you."

"Ah, the good colonel. I saw him arrive, the entrance of a conqueror, with you like a captive on his arm. I had meant to do no more than pay my respects to my hostess this evening, but seeing that nauseating performance, I felt it behooved me to find out the meaning of it."

"The cause is not hard to find," she answered, her tone dry as she recounted the circumstances that had led to her appearance this evening with the colonel. As she spoke she grew aware of the rush of the wind that stirred the drapes, and the blue-white gleam of lightning beyond the window opening, coming steadily nearer.

Valcour drew a deep breath, his dark eyes glittering, when she had finished. "That he should dare to use such tactics to force his company upon you surpasses belief, or bearing. Having succeeded thus far, how much more will he require of you?"

"He has acted the gentleman when we are together."

"Oh, has he indeed?" he sneered, cutting her words short. "A fine cover for his real purpose, I make no doubt."

"There—there has been no suggestion of anything more," Félicité said, snapping her fan shut.

"Nor will there be, until one fine night you will find yourself in his bed, wondering how it happened."

"He wouldn't dare!"

Valcour sent her a veiled look that included a sweeping appraisal of the gown she wore. "For all your years, Félicité, you are an innocent. If proof were needed, it would only be necessary to look at you. That costume you are wearing is an invitation to be bedded. Why, and how, the colonel has refrained until now is a mystery to me."

The words, so near to her own misgivings, touched her on the raw. She raised a brow. "Not at all. Like most of what women wear, it is an invitation only for men to contemplate that pleasure while keeping their distance."

"The colonel had best keep his," Valcour grated. "The man is beginning to annoy me. It might be well to ensure that he causes no more distress for you, or me for that matter."

"What do you mean?"

"Why, nothing that need alarm you, *ma chère*, unless you are forming a *tendre* for the man?" Valcour's face was illuminated by the crackle of a lightning streak that flickered with a yellow glow in his eyes.

"Don't be ridiculous!" she snapped.

"Well, then, forget I spoke. Forget, in fact, that you saw me this evening."

"No, Valcour," she began, but it was too late. He was

gone, melting away into the crowd. She stood staring after him with her teeth set in her bottom lip. Long seconds passed before she realized she was not alone in her interest in her brother's progress. With a swift intake of breath, she turned to face Morgan.

He transferred his gaze to her face without hurry. Putting the glass of lemon-scented punch he held into her hand, he said, "Bast sent me with this for you. He told me I would find you over here, but until I caught sight of you in the alcove I thought I had misunderstood. The gentleman to whom you were talking left rather abruptly, didn't he?"

Despite the casual tone of his voice, Félicité's nerves tightened. "He must needs find a more accommodating partner before the next set forms."

"Oh? You had no wish to be partnered by your brother, then?"

Félicité laughed, an automatic response, a protective gesture for her companion since childhood. "You thought he was Valcour? He would not be pleased, I assure you. The man was quite dowdily rigged out, a provincial from the country, I do swear. To the best of my knowledge, I have never laid eyes on him before."

"My mistake," Morgan said, but his eyes were like green glass as his gaze returned to where Valcour was bidding his hostess goodnight, preparing to depart.

Chapter 6

The slowly gathering storm had not yet broken when Félicité and the colonel left the masque, though the night sky was rent by silver shafts of lightning, and thunder rumbled unceasingly overhead. They had come away soon after the unmasking. Félicité, a prey to nameless fears and megrims, would have requested that she be taken home much earlier if Morgan had not been certain to see it as a disinclination for his company or a sign of disturbance over her suspected meeting with Valcour. How wearing it was to be forced always to pretend, to watch every word and gesture. Félicité was so tired, her nerves so on edge, that she flinched at every flash overhead, hardly knowing whether she wished to hurry homeward, putting an end to this interminable evening, or to slow her footsteps to conserve her energy.

The rising wind swept along the street, stinging their faces with the fine grit it carried, fluttering the flame inside the pierced-tin lantern the linkboy held and molding Félicité's gown against her. There was dampness in its breath, and the dank smell of the river. Somewhere down a side street, a shutter swung on creaking hinges, banging to and fro with a monotonous, echoing sound. A dog barked a muffled warning. The voices and lights from the house they had left died away, and they were engulfed in the darkness of the overcast night.

Félicité had ignored the offer of Morgan's arm. Now as she stumbled on the uneven banquette made of ship's gunwales laid end to end, he reached out to catch her elbow, drawing her close beside him.

89

"I heard a strange tale this evening," he said, his voice low so as not to be heard by Ashanti, following along behind, or the linkboy, a mere youngster this time with an Italian look about him.

The hard grip that held her was disturbing, as was the sense of force that seemed to emanate from the man at her side. "How so?"

"It concerns you, and Ulloa's nightshirt."

"Oh." The monosyllable was flat.

"As I said, a strange tale, and also an interesting one. I can't picture you sneaking into a man's bedchamber, rifling his armoire in the dead of night; you, who will not take a step without your maid trailing along behind you."

Félicité glanced up at him. "It—it was a wager."

"So I understand, one taken by your brother, though he apparently persuaded you to execute this daring theft for him."

"That isn't true. We did it together."

"It was you who actually crept into the governor's bedchamber while he slept, was it not? You who were chased by the guards for three blocks before you lost them?"

"Who told you?"

"I'm not quite sure. A female in the guise of Queen Isabella, complete with a huge cartwheel ruff, seemed to think I would be amused. She took pains to assure me that the story was common knowledge among your friends."

"That may be, I don't know," Félicité said shortly. "It was a childish escapade, one I would as soon forget."

"Possibly, though you certainly seem to have a penchant for venturing into lions' dens."

His bland tone gave little away; still, Félicité sent him a sharp glance. There was no time for more. They were nearing the Lafargue house, and the linkboy had paused, stepping aside to allow them to enter the arched entranceway that led under the upper floor to the stairs.

Ashanti, with a murmured apology, slipped ahead to rouse the maid left on watch so the girl would unbar the door. As the colonel turned to press a small *pourboire* into the hand of the linkboy and bid him wait, Félicité stared ahead down the dark passage in irritation. She had left orders for torches to be lit against their return, but either they had not been obeyed, or else the rising wind, funneling down the entrance, had blown them out.

Morgan swung toward her. She moved forward, expecting to see light blossom at any moment from the direction of the stairs, aiding the faint glow from the linkboy's lantern.

There came a thud, as of a slammed door, followed by a cry, a muffled sound that might have come from Ashanti's throat somewhere ahead in the darkness. Suddenly the night was alive with moving shapes made horrible by the hiss of drawn swords in that enclosed space. Lightning flashed, and in that brief blue-white instant, the figures of three men could be seen hurtling down upon them.

Morgan shifted, unsheathing his sword with a rasp as he whirled the domino he carried around his left arm as a buffer. Behind them the linkboy gave a strangled gasp, then whirled and took to his heels, leaving them in darkness.

Hard hands caught Félicité, and she was flung headlong. She stumbled to her knees, scraping her hands on the rough stone of the passage floor, striking her head on the railing of the stairs. Pain exploded in her brain. Dizzy, half blinded, she pulled herself up, calling for Ashanti and the other maid. Behind her came muffled grunts and curses as the men clashed with Morgan. The shuffling of their footsteps as they jockeyed for position was loud in the windy blackness.

"Imbecile! You nearly ran me through," came a snarl from the shifting men.

Valcour! Félicité had feared that it was he, though she had not wanted to believe it. This was no vengeance, this cowardly attack in the dark with odds of three to one, no gentlemanly chastisement such as that meted out upon the dueling ground. This was murder, planned with all the deliberation of an assassin. There could be no justification for such a base attack, and no honor in it.

"Ashanti!" she cried. "A light! Bring a light!" If Valcour was in danger of being recognized, he might desist, if it was not too late—

There was no answer. Whirling, Félicité scrambled up the

steps. She did not dare think of what had happened to her maid and the others. There would be time enough for that later. She flung herself against the door that led into the rooms she shared with her father. The latch moved under her hand. It was not locked, only pulled to in order to block the light of the single candle that burned in the *salle*. Snatching up the brass holder, shielding the taper, she threw herself from the room, pounding down the stairs.

Suddenly she halted. At the turn of the staircase stood Lieutenant Colonel Morgan McCormack with a bloodied sword in his hand. There was a tear across the breast and sleeve of his uniform coat surrounded by a dark spreading stain. His face was like a mask, stiff and sinister.

"You won't need that," he said, the words falling softly from his lips, "though I don't doubt it would have been a great help to my assailants. They might have found me with their blades, instead of each other."

"What do you mean?" she whispered. "Where are they?"

"They could not wait. When your accomplices discovered the contest less unequal than they imagined, they broke ranks and fled, leaving you behind—with me."

"Accomplices?"

"Your brother and his friends, if you prefer."

"Oh, but they aren't—I'm not it—"

He made a quick, slashing motion with his sword that set the candle flame to wavering. "Do you take me for a fool? I saw the two of you with your heads together tonight. No doubt if he had had more time to plan, Valcour Murat would have chosen his ambuscade more carefully. A single man always has the advantage against two or more in close quarters, especially when the light is dim. For him all are foes, none friends."

He took a step forward, and involuntarily Félicité retreated. "I'm glad you were—unhurt."

"Spare me the pretense. You hold in your hand the only thing that could have aided your brother, a light. That would condemn you if there were nothing else."

"I knew nothing. I swear." His slow steps as he mounted the stairs sent a shaft of fear through her. She backed away, aware with every taut nerve in her body of the open rectangle of the doorway behind her.

"You don't expect me to believe that, you with your honeyed concern for your father, your half-promises dangled like a carrot before the donkey, all sweet and gentle allure. You beguiled me until I was ready to believe you were exactly as you appeared on the surface, until I was ready to follow you anywhere, even into a death-trap! If you are going to use yourself as bait, you will have to learn to take the consequences."

There was self-derision mixed with the contempt that blazed in his emerald eyes as they raked over her. A sense of peril vibrated in the air, ringing through her mind with the clamor of a warning bell. As her sandaled foot touched the top stair, she whirled, diving for the door. She wrenched it shut behind her, throwing her shoulder against it as she fumbled for the bar.

Before she could drop it home, she was hurled backward. The candle flew from her grasp, snuffing itself in the pile of the rug as the brass holder hit with a clang, rolling, skittering on the wood floor beyond the rug to fetch up against the wall. It was followed by yet another metallic, ringing clatter as Morgan dropped his sword.

Then he was upon her in the darkness, his hands biting into her shoulders as he dragged her to him. His mouth came down on hers in a fury of possession and punishment. She turned her head, twisting, straining away from him. He jerked her closer, crushing her to him so she felt the muscular strength of his lean frame, taut with anger, and the board-hardness of his chest.

"No—you don't understand—" she gasped, but the words were smothered on her lips as his mouth bruised hers once more. His hands, smoothing across her back, encountered the deep opening of her gown. His fingers closed upon the braided edges, slipping also beneath the linen underdress, and with a wrench, he pulled them apart. The soft muslin tore with the rending sound of a small scream.

Félicité felt the rush of the night air against her bare back, knew the moment when the rent bodice was dragged down over her arms, exposing her upper body to the waist. For an instant she stood stunned, then rage swept in upon her with a rush, throbbing in her brain with a sickening ache, fueled by the acid rise of fear she dared not face. In that brief flicker of time, Morgan bent and slipped an arm under her knees, swinging her high against his chest. He strode toward the open doorway of the nearest bedchamber, Félicité's own.

She fought then, kicking, arching her back, jackknifing, trying to claw despite the confinement of her arms. It did no good. She was swung dizzyingly and dropped upon the bed.

Lightning flashed, streaking into the room in an unearthly glow. Morgan McCormack stood above her, a terrible being, godlike, with the bronzed planes of his face gleaming like sculptured metal and the emerald fire of desire in his eyes. He was stripping the buttons of his waistcoat from their holes, shrugging from his jacket. Félicité rolled, scrambling across the wide, soft surface of the bed, sliding with her gown riding above her knees, reaching for the other side. He dived after her, clamping his arm around her waist, hauling her backward. His hand swept over her naked thighs as he lifted her, dragging her toward him. The pins slipped from her hair, allowing the silken mass to spill across her shoulders in a gilded skein, cascading over the corded sinews of his arm as he pulled her beneath him.

She writhed, panting, pushing at him, gasping in triumph as she freed one arm. In desperate wrath she struck for his eyes with her fingers curved into talons. His head snapped back out of range, but she had the satisfaction of feeling her nails rake along his neck and chest before her wrist was caught and imprisoned in an iron grasp.

Her girdling belt loosened as they struggled; she felt it fall from her waist. His mouth seared the tender curve of her neck, trailing a fiery path along her shoulder. She braced her feet, heaving under him. He shifted his weight, stilling her movements, forcing her to straining quiescence. Her breast tingled as his lips found one trembling mound. He tugged at the flimsy muslin of her gown, pushing it lower over the taut flatness of her abdomen.

''No,'' she whispered, that rasping word a plea and a

denial. This could not be. It could not. It was wrong, impossible, unbelievable.

The protest seemed to inflame him, fueling his rage. He kicked off his boots and divested himself of his cothing in a few quick movements. With merciless strength he stripped the tatter of her gown from her, forestalling her attempt to bring up her knees by sliding his own heavier leg across them. With one wrist fastened beside her face by the iron grip of the hand that passed under her neck, and the other pinned under him, he held her immobile. He cupped her breast, brushing his thumb over the rose peak that was contracted in anguished apprehension. As his hand moved lower, smoothing the slender curve of her waist, tracing the tautness of her stomach and down along her flank, a shiver ran over her. His traveling touch drifted over the marbled whiteness of her thighs, slipping between in a caress of startling, unbearable intimacy.

Convulsively, Félicité lunged away, trying to roll, wrenching her arm in its socket until a red mist of pain rose to cloud her vision. She managed to push one ankle from under him before she recognized her error. He thrust a knee between her opened thighs, raising himself above her. She felt the heated firmness of his manhood against her, knew in shafting horror the tender vulnerability of her own body. In frenzy, she arched away from him, her nerves and muscles shuddering with the force of her resistance. By slow degrees he pressed her against the waiting, unyielding rigidity poised for the relentless entry.

With burning abruptness it came. Félicité drew a ragged, agonized breath that lodged in her chest. Maddened, feverish, lost in the sensation of wounding fullness, she turned her head from side to side. She was scarcely aware of the moment when the man above her hesitated, the air leaving his lungs as if he had received a body blow. A soft imprecation rustled on the air, nearly drowned in the rumble of thunder overhead. Morgan's grip loosened, though he did not release her. The tension inside Félicité ebbed infinitesimally. She sensed the slow surfacing of a curious expectation. Pain receded, became a tingling awareness of the hard, naked body against her and the sultry dew of perspiration that seemed to melt them together. She allowed her tightly closed eyelids to relax, permitted her lashes to sweep slowly upward.

Morgan was a warm and heavy shadow, constricting movement, until lightning gleamed across his features. There was a grim shadow of doubt in his eyes until he looked into hers, seeing the glitter of tears and the accusing, bewildered fury. His expression hardened as dark descended once more.

"A high price, I will admit, my darling Félicité," he said, his breath warm against her cheek, "but not nearly as high as I would have paid if you could have had your way."

"I—I never meant—"

"I'm sure you didn't," he cut across her words. "Nor did I. But fool though I may have been, I am not one to argue with the hand of fate."

Words, biting, blistering, explaining, pleading, tumbled into her mind. They never reached her lips. Morgan eased deep inside her, submerging her once more in pain and the tumult of the senses. He drew back, thrusting again and again, his movement quickening. He released her wrists, levering himself higher. Caught in the rending storm of his ardor, crazed by the inescapable violation of her innermost being, Félicité clutched at his chest, digging her nails into him in her extremity. She raked across the edge of ragged flesh, felt the liquid slide of blood. At the edge of her mind, she heard his swift, indrawn breath of pain, but was powerless to stop herself. Locked together in torment and the heated essences of their bodies, they strove in immortal combat. Fear had left Félicité. She would survive, though nothing would be the same, she would never be the same. She would never be so certain of her strength, or of her right to remain inviolate, nor would she be so righteous in her anger, positive that she was free of blame. For there was within her the corrosive knowledge that in this attack upon Morgan McCormack she was not without guilt. Beyond the windows the storm broke with a roar and the rain came hissing down.

Some time later, Morgan eased from her. The bed frame creaked as he rolled to the edge and came to his feet. He moved to the window with swift strides and swung back the shutter, filling the room with the wet rush of the rain. Thunder rumbled, a distant mutter. The minutes ticked past. Félicité lay without moving, her wide gaze on the dark shape of the man at the window, standing with his arms braced on the sill.

Morgan took a deep breath, letting it out slowly before he turned back toward the bed. He sat down on the side, reaching to curl his warm fingers around her shoulder. "Are you all right?"

She jerked away from him, pulling the coverlet over her. Though she ached in body and mind, pride dictated only one answer. "Yes," she snapped.

"I could apologize, but it might ring a bit false."

"I don't require anything from you—except your absence! I would like you to leave my house, now. Get out!"

"That may be what you want," he said slowly, "but I don't think it would suit me at all."

"What—do you mean?"

"Staying here in this house might have certain advantages. I can think of several without half trying."

"You can't," she began.

"Oh, but I can," he answered, deliberately misunderstanding her. "To begin with, if your brother puts in an appearance anywhere in New Orleans in the next few days it will be here, to check on your welfare. It would be only sound tactics to await his return. Secondly, housing is scarce; the governor-general has been considering commandeering quarters for his officers, mostly to get them out of his own hair. It would be a relief to him, I'm sure, if I arranged my own domicile. And thirdly, there is your condition. Ravishing virgins has never had any appeal to me. If I had known—but I did not. It is a burdensome responsibility."

"Hah!" Félicité ejaculated in bitter scorn. Clutching the coverlet to her, she sat up higher in bed.

"Your opinion of my principles notwithstanding, I feel a most inconvenient need to offer reparation."

His tone was dry and slightly ironic. Félicité wished suddenly that she could see his face. "Are you suggesting—"

"It had occurred to me, yes, that an offer of marriage would be in order."

"You cannot be serious. One moment you accuse me of conspiring to murder you, the next you offer me your name. It's ridiculous!"

"Nevertheless, I mean every word."

"Why?" she flung at him. "To curry favor with O'Reilly? This would be improving relations with a vengeance!"

There was a trace of grim amusement in his tone as he replied, "Would it not?"

"Aren't you afraid of giving me even more reason to be willing to rid myself of you?" she asked in waspish tones.

"You were, I think, an inexperienced conspirator. That being the case, I will undertake to protect myself from anything else you might devise."

"I was no conspirator of any kind!" she cried, clenching her fists in front of her. "I had no idea there was anyone waiting, none at all."

"You expect me to believe that, after seeing you with your brother?"

"That had nothing to do with you. I never dreamed—"

"So you do admit it was Valcour?"

"But I didn't know what he meant to do, I swear."

He got to his feet, bending to take up his coat where it lay on the floor before he moved into the *salle*. She heard the striking of flint, saw the yellow flare of cotton in a tinderbox, one he must have taken from his own pocket. It was followed a few seconds later by the spreading glow of a lighted candle. Its brightness grew as Morgan returned, striding in splendid nakedness to set the bronze candlestick he had found upon her dressing table. Hastily, Félicité averted her gaze, staring at the black square of the window, where rain spattered in, splashing with a quiet and oddly musical sound upon the floor.

Morgan stepped to the foot of the bed and leaned one shoulder against its hand-hewn cypress post. "If I believe what you are saying," he drawled, "it would make it all the more imperative that you become my wife."

Félicité swung to face him, her brown eyes hard and her voice low and vibrant. "Never, never in this life."

"Never," he said, his green eyes holding hers with a

steady regard, "is a long time. I trust you won't come to regret that decision."

Any answer she might have made was routed from her brain as she really looked at Morgan for the first time in the candlelight. Blood crept in twisting rivulets down his chest and one arm, dripping slowly from the tips of his fingers. It streaked his body, smearing it with drying, rust-brown smudges. Her widened gaze moved to the coverlet she held. It was so stained, so covered with splotches and smears of blood, it was impossible to tell which was Morgan's and which her own.

"*Mon Dieu,*" she breathed, and spread one hand before her, staring at her bloodstained fingers with the nails rimmed with red.

Morgan glanced down at himself. With a grimace of irritation, he clamped his hand to the long gouge that was cut into the flat muscles of his upper chest, running across his arm. "Sorry, I didn't realize."

Sickness moved over Félicité. She could not think what to say, what to do with this man who had invaded her life so thoroughly. Confused and deathly tired, she felt the need to weep, but knew she was past the relief of tears. The rain slackened, its fall muted to a soft drumming. Above it came the sound of a distant banging, as if someone was beating at a door. The noise was insistent, catching at her attention. She turned her head to listen.

Abruptly, she remembered. "Ashanti," she whispered.

"Your maid?"

"I don't know what they did to her, or to the other women."

"We had better go see." Morgan frowned.

"No, I'll go," she said hastily, her brown gaze flicking to the blood that seeped through the brown fingers he held over his wound. "You had better sit down."

He lifted a brow, his tone caustic as he answered, "Your concern is touching, but this is nothing. It's been like this for some time now. A little longer isn't going to hurt."

"I—I don't need you," she said.

"As you please."

Félicité glanced at his face as she slid from the bed, dragging the coverlet with her. His features were set, closed in. Swooping to the armoire, she took down her dressing saque, draping its voluminous folds around her before she dropped the stained coverlet and stepped away from it. It was only then that she noticed she wore her soft leather sandals with their ribbons still laced up the calves of her legs. For no reason that she could think of, the discovery brought the heat of a flush to her face. Without looking in Morgan's direction, she hurried from the room.

In the *salle,* there was a blanket chest where rags were kept. She paused and lifted the heavy lid, drawing out a roll of bandaging made from the worn center of a clean sheet. Her fingers tightened upon it, then with her lips pressed together in a straight line, she whirled back into the bedroom, tossed the roll onto the bed beside Morgan, then hurried out once more.

The thumping noise she had heard was louder as she ran down the stairs. It seemed to be coming from the court, possibly even from Ashanti's sleeping quarters. She was right, she found as she emerged into the damp night. Ducking her head against the streams of rain still falling from the roof, she slipped along beneath its protective overhang. Outside the maid's door, she lifted the wooden bar that held it in place, the usual method of restraining slaves at night, though it had not been used at her father's house for years.

The panel swung inward. Ashanti hung back, outlined in the glow of a tallow candle, until she recognized Félicité.

"Mam'selle!" she cried, throwing herself forward to take Félicité's hand, clinging to it. "I have been out of my mind with worry."

"It's all right," Félicité said, a catch in her voice.

"Those men, they set upon me in the dark, threw me in here and shut the door. I heard you call, but could do nothing. Tell me what has happened. What has M'sieu Valcour done now?"

In a few short phrases Félicité told her, not even stopping to feel surprise that the maid should guess the attack was her brother's doing.

"You say the colonel was injured? Was it bad?"

"He says not," Félicité answered in a suffocated tone, "but there is a great deal of blood."

"Where is he? We must see to him." The maid slipped past Félicité, glancing back as she did not follow at once. Her face changed then. "Why, mam'selle, you are wearing your dressing saque, and your hair—your hands—"

"It—it was a mistake." The words were unplanned. Why she should attempt in any way to exonerate Morgan she could not have said.

"Are you hurt?" Ashanti demanded, searching her face, her eyes dark with concern. "Tell me what that one has done to you, that monster of cruel pleasures? What has he dared to do?"

"The colonel thought that I was a part of the attack against him. He—"

"The colonel, not M'sieu Valcour, has made you look so?" The maid came close, a frown drawing her brows together.

Félicité lifted a hand, rubbing at her face in distress, massaging the bruised place on her temple where she had struck the staircase earlier. As difficult as it was to find the words, her maid would have to know. She sighed, letting her hand fall. With a slow nod, she began to tell Ashanti what had happened.

The maid touched her arm in a gesture of sympathy when she understood. "Come then, mam'selle, and let us go upstairs. I will make a tisane for you and put you to bed."

"But the colonel is there."

"If it is as you say, he will not harm you," Ashanti said soothingly.

Félicité sent her a swift glance. "I am not afraid of him! I only want him to go, and he will not."

"Perhaps—" the maid began, then paused before going on with a rush, "Perhaps it would be better if he stayed?"

"Why? What are you saying?" Félicité demanded, staring at the other girl in the dim light of the wavering candle in the room behind them.

"Never mind. Come, let me tend you."

She was so weary, so sore. The splattering of the blowing

rain was slowly wetting her dressing saque. The wind through the thin material was cool to her fevered flesh, and she shivered, drawing it around her. "All I want is a bath."

"You shall have it," Ashanti promised, and, turning, led the way back toward the stairs, waiting there to allow Félicité to ascend them before her.

Morgan had donned his breeches, though nothing else. He stood scowling before the mirror of the dressing table with one hand holding a pad of cloth to his wound while with the other he tried to wrap the trailing ends of the roll of bandaging around his shoulder. He was not having much success. As Félicité came to a halt in the doorway, he threw her a glance, but did not speak. She moved a few feet into the room, permitting Ashanti to enter.

The maid sent Morgan a long stare, then lowered her eyes. Her face shuttered, she went to the curtained recess where the small copper-lined bathing tub was kept and drew it out into the room. From the washstand she took a linen cloth, a small, precious cake of soap, and a glass box containing scented starch. Placing these on a ledge molded in the tub, she turned to the bed. With a few quick movements, she stripped the soiled sheets from it and, bundling them under her arm, left the room again.

Félicité hesitated where she stood just inside the door, torn between the need to repossess her own private quarters and the urge to turn and flee, leaving them to Morgan McCormack. How strange it felt to see him there, to see his boots lying beside her bed and his waistcoat and shirt thrown across a chair, as if he had a perfect right to strew his things about. It was irritating, and at the same time disquieting, especially when coupled with his refusal to leave, his hint that he might take up residence.

The dressing saque she wore had a ribbon tie at the neckline, but the edges of the front opening merely came together without lapping. Catching them close in one hand, Félicité moved to the window. The rain had nearly stopped. In the courtyard below, Ashanti had appeared to fling the sheets she carried into the laundry room. She must have released the young maid and the cook from the room they shared, for they came from the kitchen, talking, waving their hands, as Ashanti moved into that room to stoke the fire, preparing to put water on to heat. The maid was taking the change in her mistress's circumstances very calmly. There was no point in hysterics, of course; still, such fatalistic acceptance was not quite what Félicité had expected. It was almost as if the girl had no objection, as long as the man was Colonel McCormack.

Ashanti had tried to warn her. Félicité could not quite bring her words to mind, but she had stressed a need for caution, almost as if she had a presentiment of what might happen. That was all well enough, but given the situation, Félicité did not see how she could have behaved any differently. Her eyes bleak, she leaned out to catch the shutter, pulling it in to latch it.

Behind her, Morgan cursed under his breath and tossed the roll of bandaging to the top of the dressing table. As she turned he was holding the blood-soaked pad he had taken from his shoulder in his hand, looking for a place to dispose of it.

"There in the bowl," she said, indicating the china ewer and matching washbowl that sat on the washstand.

He stepped to cast the pad into the bowl, sending her a dark glance from the corner of his eye as he moved back. "I don't suppose you would have a needle and thread close to hand?"

"Why, yes."

"This damned gash needs something to hold it together. Every time I raise my arm it parts and starts bleeding again."

"You mean to sew it up?" she asked, her gaze flicking to the oozing cut across his chest before flicking away again.

"No, my sweet, I mean for you to sew it."

Her startled brown eyes met his bright green gaze. "I couldn't."

"Oh, come," he mocked, "I would have thought the prospect of poking a needle in me would have delighted you."

"You have a strange idea of my character, colonel."

"I am willing to be enlightened," he said, his tone soft.

103

She lifted her chin. "Are you now, when you refuse to believe a word I say?"

"Deeds, they say, speak louder than words."

"So they do," she answered, allowing herself a small smile. "What then do yours say of you, Morgan McCormack?"

"I did offer an *amende honorable,*" he reminded her.

"You cannot have wished, or expected, me to take it!"

"You think not?" he queried.

The emerald brilliance of his stare was difficult to sustain. She dropped her gaze to his chest. "You are bleeding all over everything," she snapped. "I'll get the sewing box."

When she returned, she set the basket on the dressing table, but did not remove her hands from the handle. "Don't you have a surgeon who came with you from Spain to deal with things such as this?"

"A man came with us, yes, but I would as soon have a gravedigger attend me. So far, nearly every man he has touched has died with gangrene. Besides, he never bathes."

"That is another thing—do you think you should cleanse your wound?"

"Sword cuts are usually clean. More than that, it has bled enough to purify anything. I once knew a one-legged pirate who recommended treating injuries with applications of brandy both inside and out, however."

"Would you like a dram to bolster your courage?" she inquired in dulcet tones.

"Not I," he said easily, "but I have no objection to waiting until you have fortified yourself."

"That won't be necessary." Her face cold, Félicité released the basket and stepped to the washstand, where she tipped water from the ewer into the bowl to wash her hands. The liquid was soon red, though more from the pad Morgan had discarded than from the stains on her hands. Emptying the contents of the bowl into the slop jar, she rinsed her hands, then turned back to the sewing basket.

"You will need to sit down," she said over her shoulder.

"I would as soon stand."

"Possibly, but though it may give you satisfaction to show

how stalwart you are, I won't be able to reach the sword cut without standing on my toes."

The asperity of her tone seemed to amuse him. She could have sworn there was a smile curving his lips as he swung toward the only chair, removed his clothing from the seat, and sat down with one leg thrust out before him. "I am at your service," he drawled.

With black upholstery silk, the strongest thread she possessed, threaded in her needle, Félicité stepped into the *salle*. There was cognac in a decanter on a side table in that room. Splashing a little into a glass, she dropped her needle and thread into it, then carried it back into the bedchamber. At the dressing table she took up a pair of embroidery scissors and the candle. The shadows in the room wheeled around the walls as she turned toward the man in the chair.

"Can you take this?" she asked, pushing the brass candle holder at him. "I will need the light."

For an answer, he held out his hand. She approached warily, surrendering the holder, stepping around to his right side. This close to him, with the light falling directly on his chest, she could see the long angry red streaks where she had raked him with her nails. The sight gave her no joy; if anything it made her slightly ill. She turned her attention with determination to the deep slash torn in his chest.

"Look out." He shot out his hand to catch a golden strand of her hair that spilled over her shoulder as she leaned toward him. She started, recoiling, before she saw that he had only been trying to prevent her from getting singed by the candle flame. He did not release her hair. She was held by its shimmering length. His green eyes were dark as he watched her, gently sliding the silken tress he held between his fingers.

By slow degrees Félicité neared him once more. His steady regard was so unnerving that she lowered her lashes. "Are you certain you want me to do this?"

"Positive."

"It will hurt."

"Undoubtedly."

She was not sure she could, not for him, not now. She was aware of a faint trembling that seemed to come from inside her, growing more obvious as it traveled along her limbs, becoming its worst when it reached her fingers. She felt both hot and cold at the same time. Compounding her problems was the fact that it was impossible to keep the front of her dressing sáque closed as she bent over Morgan, if she had to use both her hands for the task she must perform.

"Only think," he recommended, his voice soft, "of how you felt toward me half an hour ago."

She sent him a look of loathing, drew in her breath, and fished her threaded needle from the cognac.

The first stitch was the hardest. The tough resilience of his skin was a surprise, as was the difficulty of judging the thickness of it. Morgan, his gaze on her face, did not flinch, gave no sign that he could feel the piercing thrust of her stitches. She flicked a glance at him after a time to see that his attention had wandered, drifting downward to the parted edges of her dressing saque. Her lips tightened, but there was nothing she could do; she needed both hands just then to cut the thread from the last knotted stitch.

The instant it was done, she stepped back, straightening, turning. The cut was still oozing blood, and she moved to place her needle and scissors on the dressing table, picking up the bandaging and forming a pad. She was just pressing this, moistened with cognac, to the wound when Ashanti returned. The maid glanced at what she was doing, then, her face impassive, poured the cans of water she carried into the tub.

"Your bath is ready, mam'selle."

There was an awkward pause. Félicité, holding the bandage with one hand and the front of her saque with the other, stared from her maid to the man who had invaded her room. As much as she longed for cleanliness, she could not remove her clothing and step into the tub in the presence of Morgan McCormack.

Morgan surveyed her, his green gaze resting on her pale face for a long instant, before he looked at Ashanti standing stiffly to attention beside the steaming bath. His features hardened, then abruptly he heaved himself to his feet. "I will wait in the other room."

Gratitude was a strange thing to feel just then. Félicité

pushed it from her. He was halfway to the door when she realized she still held the bandage pad in her hand. "Wait. Your shoulder, I—I will bind it."

"Allow me, mam'selle," Ashanti said, gliding forward.

"Yes, perhaps that will be better." Félicité came to a halt. Ashanti was good with illnesses and injuries.

The maid took the candle from Morgan and set it beside the tub. Touching him lightly on the arm, she indicated the *salle,* where a candelabrum, lighted moments before, showed a steady glow. Morgan stepped into the other room.

And yet somehow, as the maid picked up the roll of linen and followed the colonel from the room, closing the door behind her, Félicité was not pleased with the arrangement.

Chapter 7

F*élicité soaped herself* slowly, frowning at a point on the whitewashed plaster of the opposite wall. The tepid water was soothing, a balm to the aches and bruises of her body. Other than such physical reminders, she did not feel different. Nothing had changed; she was still the same person. The trembling inside her had died away. She felt exhausted but calm, ready for her bed.

However much she might pretend to normalcy, things were not as they had been. Lieutenant Colonel Morgan McCormack waited beyond the door of her room, a man who thought she had wronged him, who felt he had some authority over her, some right to her company, as a result. That he was able to enforce his opinion with both coercion and main strength was doubly galling.

What was she going to do? What could she do? With her father in prison and Valcour a hunted man, she had no one to protect her. Her father's friends had been arrested with him. Her mother's people were dead, her father's family left behind in France. The French director-general was not only powerless under the new regime, but was a sycophant, accused of collaborating with the Spanish for his own gain. The only man who outranked Colonel McCormack in Louisiana was O'Reilly, and it was useless to think he might interfere in the private affairs of his second-in-command over a mere woman, and she the daughter of a Frenchman to be tried for treason.

She was at the mercy of Morgan McCormack, then. It might be said that she had brought it on herself, though she could not see how she might have acted otherwise. Very well. If there was none to stand between her and the colonel she must see to her own preservation—and let the colonel look to himself!

Ashanti entered the room. Over her arm she carried fresh linens with which to remake the bed, and in her hand was a cup of steaming tea. It smelled of herbs and spices, one of the African maid's tisanes. Ashanti set it on the floor beside the tub, in reach of Félicité, then moved to unfold a sheet, spreading it on the feather mattress.

Félicité raised herself, reaching for the hot drink. She took a sip. "What is this? I don't think you've ever made it for me before."

"There was never the need before, mam'selle. This tisane will prevent you from conceiving a child after this night's work."

There had been no time to think of such things for Félicité, or at least no inclination. She stared at the dark brew, a bleak expression in her eyes.

"Drink, mam'selle. It will be best, as long as you remain unwed."

"Yes," she sighed, and obediently drank. "Is—is Colonel McCormack still—"

"He is still in the outer room. I wrapped his wound well; it will not bleed any more."

108

"I hope he appreciated it," Félicité commented, her tone tinged with bitterness.

"I think so, mam'selle, he did thank me. I wonder if you saw this man's back?"

"His back?"

"Yes, mam'selle. It is a thing of horror, scars on top of scars. I saw as I tended him."

"He spoke once of being a sailor on an English ship. Flogging with a whip with nine strands is much practiced on board such vessels, I believe."

"It is terrible," the maid said as she tucked the top sheet tightly under the mattress, sending Félicité a fleeting glance. "Scars of shame."

"Shame? Why?"

"That men should treat other men so."

"Men are capable of much cruelty," Félicité said, staring into her teacup. "Why it should be so, I don't know."

"He—does not go, this colonel?" Ashanti went on, her tone puzzled, and also curious.

"He has refused," Félicité said shortly.

"For this night?"

"For this night, and the next, and the next. He means to live here!"

"Ah, that is good, mam'selle."

"Good?" she exclaimed. "You don't know what you are saying!"

"He will protect you, and keep you safe."

"And who will save me from him?" Félicité set down her cup and, catching the rim of the tub, came to her feet so violently that water splashed out onto the cypress floor.

"You will, mam'selle," Ashanti said, moving to fetch a towel, holding it for Félicité as she stepped from the tub, her frank gaze holding certainty as it slanted over the slender curves, glistening with water, of her mistress. "The question is, who will save him—from us?"

What the maid was suggesting so subtly was that as long as Morgan was domiciled in her house, he was on her ground. There was much that could be done to make him uncomfortable in such a case, much to cause him to wish that he had never set eyes on her.

There was no time to consider the possibilities. Félicité was dusting herself with the starch scented with violets and Ashanti was holding her nightrail, ready to slip it over her head, when the door opened. In a flurry of movement, Félicité dropped the lamb's-wool puff she held and dived into the nightrail, letting it slide down over her as she thrust her arms into the armholes outlined with cap sleeves. Jerking the ribbon tie at the neckline into a bow, she swung to face the man in the doorway.

"What do you want?" she asked, her fury heightened by the flush of embarrassment that colored her cheeks.

"I thought if you were through with the tub, I might take advantage of the water that's left." There was an odd light, almost like amusement, at the back of his eyes as he watched her.

It was a moment before Félicité realized she was standing in front of the candle, that it outlined her body in its bright-yellow nimbus. She stepped quickly to one side, her features set in lines of hauteur that dared him to comment. "You wish to bathe?"

"Is that so strange?"

"For most people, yes," she answered in all frankness.

"It's a habit I picked up in the Indies. I was used to swimming and saltwater bathing on ship. Do you object to my use of your tub?"

There seemed no point in that. "You know you shouldn't get your shoulder wrappings wet?"

"I think I can undertake not to do that."

"I will call the upstairs maid, and she and Ashanti can move the tub into one of the other bedchambers for you," she said with as much graciousness as she could summon.

"There will be no need."

She stared at him, a suspicious look coming into her velvet brown eyes. "What do you mean?"

"I mean," he answered quietly, "that I would as soon have it right here—that is, if your maid has finished?"

"I am done, colonel," Ashanti said, and dropping a curtsy, moved toward the door.

Félicité took a step forward. "Ashanti, no—"

"Yes, mam'selle?" The maid came to a stop, her gaze questioning, and yet touching with compassion.

"Nothing. You may go."

The door closed behind the slim black woman. Morgan began to unbutton the side flaps of his uniform breeches. Félicité stood undecided in the middle of the floor. The urge to go, to leave the colonel in undisputed possession of the bedchamber, was strong, but stronger still was her pride. She would not have it appear that she was running away.

To run away, to snatch open the door and go racing into the night, was a great temptation. But where could she go, how could she live? She had no money, no means of paying her fare to another place, and as long as she stayed in New Orleans, there was no one who could save her from the might of Spain, and its representative in the colony, Lieutenant Colonel Morgan McCormack. Beyond that, there was her father. What would become of him if she deserted him? While he was held in a Spanish prison he was a hostage for her good behavior. The events of the night might already have prejudiced the colonel against helping him. It would be best if she could put aside her grievances and do what she might to convince Morgan McCormack she had no part in the attempt against his life. In that way she might prevent her loss this evening from becoming total.

Behind her, the colonel was stepping into the tub. Her movements jerky, Félicité moved to the dressing table and took up the hairbrush that lay on its surface. She pulled it through the soft mass of her hair, working the tangles from the shining, honey-blond strands that fell to below her hips. After a time, she glanced at the mirror, and found that it reflected the scene behind her where Morgan sat in the small graveyboat-shaped tub with his knees beneath his chin, scrubbing gingerly at his ribcage just under his bindings. That view made him seem more human, less the overpowering, vengeful figure of authority.

There was a pin caught in her hair, one that had been

loosened in their struggle. Félicité slipped it free, then turned, drawing the long tresses over her shoulder as she smoothed them. She sent the colonel a quick glance from under her lashes. "You take a great deal on yourself, don't you?"

"What makes you think so?" He squeezed water from the linen cloth and ran it over his face and around the back of his neck.

"Everything you have done since the moment we met," she answered plainly.

"You mean my methods of assuring that events turn out the way I want?"

"Something like that," she agreed.

"One thing you learn quickly as a sailor, pirate, or mercenary—if you don't control events, they will control you."

"That's all very well if you have the strength or the power to prevail."

His green eyes narrowed as he watched her. "What are you getting at?"

"I suppose," she said carefully, "that I am trying to ask what you mean to do now, about my father."

"I've told you before, his fate doesn't lie in my hands alone."

"You also said that under the right circumstances, O'Reilly might be disposed to leniency," she reminded him, her voice sharpening in her anxiety.

Deliberately, he squeezed water from the cloth, draped it over the edge of the tub, and stood up. "The situation has changed."

"It hasn't, not really. If you would only believe me—"

She averted her gaze as he reached for the towel left lying on a chair, but the subject was too important for her to turn her back on him.

"Why should I believe you? What cause have you given me to accept anything you say as the truth?"

"If it's causes that matter, what cause had I to wish you dead? My father's only hope for justice lies in you."

"No doubt you discovered that I had already put in my report on your father's case, stating my views on his lack of active involvement and my recommendation of pardon or a token sentence. If that was the case, there would be nothing more to be gained by continuing our agreement. It would only be good tactics to rid yourself of a possible threat.''

She stared at him, shaking her head. ''No,'' she whispered.

''Not that I blame you, the situation being what it was,'' he went on as if she had not spoken. ''On the other hand, I see no reason to throw away my present advantage because of your lack of success.''

''Meaning?'' She raised her head, her brown eyes clouded with doubt.

''I think you can guess.''

Despite the soft timbre of his voice, the words were implacable. ''You—you expect me—my compliance, now that you will be staying under this roof.''

''It seems only reasonable to me.''

''There are no words strong enough to tell you how it seems to me!''

''Oh, I'm sure there are,'' he countered, leisurely wiping the droplets of water from the lean, muscular length of his legs and tossing the toweling aside.

She sent him an annihilating glance, then looked hastily away again as he made no move to cover himself. ''If—if I agree, what then?''

''What?'' He stretched his right arm as if testing it for soreness, then raked a hand through his hair where it had become loosened from its queue.

''I mean,'' she said, holding hard to her rising temper, ''will you let things remain as before, or will you find it necessary to report what happened here tonight?''

He frowned. ''A report will have to be made; how am I to explain this little nick of mine otherwise? As to what, exactly, the wording of it will be, that depends.''

''On what?'' she snapped.

''On you.''

He moved toward her, looming over her. There was darkness in the depths of her eyes as she stared up at him. ''This is wrong. You will regret what you are doing someday.''

"Threats?" he queried, a musing tone in his low voice.

"A prophecy," she answered, "unless you are incapable of feeling anything."

"There was a time when I would have forfeited that point. I'm not sure that's true any longer." He reached to pick up a lustrous strand of her hair, letting it drift from his fingers in a shimmer of soft golden highlights. "Come to bed."

A suffocating tightness rose in Félicité's throat at that simple command. Her heartbeat quickened, and her fingers curled slowly into fists. "I can't."

"You are tired," he said, taking the hairbrush from her hand and putting it on the dressing table, holding her wrist in a loose grasp as he scanned the pale oval of her face, noting the dark circles like bruises under her eyes. "Come on."

At the roughness of those last words, Félicité allowed herself to be led a few steps before she drew back. "Colonel McCormack—"

"I've told you before. My name is Morgan, something you would do well to remember. Are you going to get into bed, or am I going to have to put you there?"

"Your wound—"

"To hell with it! At this moment I have the firm intention of letting you rest unmolested, but if you force me to lay hands on you, I can't answer for the consequences!"

Félicité snatched her wrist free. With a glowering glance from under her lashes, she set her foot on the stool that sat beside the bed and mounted to the high mattress. Sinking into its comfort, she reached for the sheet, drawing it up over her knees. She would have liked to draw it higher, but despite the cooling effects of the rain, it was still warm in the room. That prospect of discomfort was one more thing to be laid at Morgan's door. She watched him balefully as he moved to snuff the candle, then open the shutter for air.

Surefooted, quiet-moving in the dark, he approached the bed. The bed ropes creaked as they accepted his weight. The ceiling hook jangled as he took down the looped-up mosquito *baire*, drawing it around the bed, enclosing them in its gauzy folds. He lay down, and all was quiet.

Félicité eased down against her pillow, stretching to full

length. She lay still, listening to the steady breathing of the man beside her, aware of the thud of her heart against her ribs. Her nerves tingled with the urge to jump up and fling herself off the mattress, to scream her hatred and her refusal to carry this game a single step further. She could do no such thing. She had to accept this. It was her penance for ever becoming involved with this man, for being her father's daughter.

Abruptly, he stretched out his arm across the width of the mattress that divided them, pulling her toward him, turning her to fit her body to the curve of his own. She lay stiff and unyielding, staring into the dark, waiting for the marauding hands, the violation of her senses.

"Go to sleep," he said, his breath warm against the back of her neck. "Morning will come before you know it."

Félicité came awake by slow degrees. There was a disturbed feeling at the back of her mind, a sensation of distress that was allied to an odd excitement. Daylight, dim but unmistakable, seeped under her eyelids. Her nightrail had worked upward with her twistings and turnings during the night nearly to her waist. There was a weight across her chest as she lay on her back. The warm globe of one breast felt confined, cupped in a gentle yet firm hold.

Her eyes flew open. Morgan leaned above her, resting on one elbow. His green eyes held a curious, questioning light while a wry smile flickered over his mouth.

"Good morning."

She closed her eyes, and opened them again. He was still there. "Good morning," she said, her tone far from gracious.

"It is indeed."

She sent him a venomous glance. "For you, maybe."

"It does depend on your point of view," he agreed as he slowly tightened his hold on her breast.

Like a recoiling spring, she caught his hand and flung it off, rolling away. He lunged for her, clamping an arm across her waist despite the wince of pain that passed over his features. It was the glimpse she caught of that fleeting grimace that stilled Félicité's movements. He took instant advantage of that weakness, hefting himself closer, lowering his head to cover her warm lips with his own. Félicité felt the touch of his tongue, the press of his naked body against her own bare thighs. Resistance now was futile, since her purity was forever gone, and for so many reasons she must steel herself to surrender eventually. It would be less hurtful, less likely to arouse Morgan's anger, if she permitted him to do as he pleased, if she accepted the treacherous languor that hovered at the edge of her consciousness, allowing it to sap her strength and make submission bearable.

A knock came on the bedchamber door. Hard upon it, Ashanti called, "Your morning chocolate, mam'selle, M'sieu Colonel!"

Morgan raised his head, a frown drawing his brows together. "Chocolate? By your orders?"

"My maid always wakes me at this hour with chocolate," Félicité said, her tone a trifle defensive. There was confusion in the depths of her brown eyes as she tried to free herself from the self-induced lassitude that gripped her.

He gave a soft grunt, staring down at her, his green gaze clashing with the velvet of her own. Abruptly, he pushed away from her, levering himself to one elbow. "It's just as well. I need to report for duty at the governor's house anyway."

"Your sword cut—"

"I doubt it will interfere with paperwork, all that I spend my time doing these days."

Félicité called to Ashanti to come in, then sat up, pushing her hair over her shoulder as she watched him stretch, flexing the muscles of his right arm that had also been injured as the sword had sliced across it. "What about your uniform? It will need repairs, cleaning and pressing."

He shook his head. "It will do until I reach my quarters, where I can change."

Ashanti, pushing aside the mosquito *baire*, cleared her throat. "I found the coat of M'sieu Colonel in the *salle* last night. It has been sewn up, sponged, and brushed already. I would be happy to attend to the rest also."

"That was considerate, but my man will see to anything

more that may be necessary." The expression on his face was arrested, thoughtful.

"As you wish, M'sieu Colonel." The girl brought the chocolate tray to Félicité and placed it across her lap, meeting her eyes with such a limpid gaze that Félicité was at once certain the colonel had reason to be wary. Turning with her quiet grace, Ashanti left the room, though she failed to close the door.

Morgan glanced from the open portal to Félicité, pouring chocolate from the china pot, her lashes lowered. Whipping back the covers, he strode to the door and slammed it shut. Returning to stand beside the bed, he accepted the cup she offered.

"It strikes me your servants are well trained, in most things," he drawled. "This should be a comfortable bivouac."

Rage at the reminder of his decision the night before washed over Félicité, then receded. "I trust you will continue to think so."

He sent her a long glance, his gaze lingering over the shining, tumbled glory of her hair, the creamy perfection of her skin with its tint of angry pink, and the proud, thrusting outlines of her breasts under her soft nightrail. "So do I."

He sipped at his chocolate, then, finding it none too hot, drank it down in a few swallows. As he brushed aside the *baire*, leaning across the bed, she flinched, but he only set his cup on her lap tray. His face grim, he drew back and turned.

Through slitted eyelids, Félicité watched as he moved away. He seemed unconscious of his nakedness in her presence. Was he so used to appearing in that guise before women, then? Perhaps he often frequented the rooms of the *filles de joie*, the daughters of joy, the harlots of the seaport towns and the garrison towns that were a part of his life? It was more likely than not, no matter how distasteful the idea might be. Soldiers, common adventurers, were not the sort of *partis* fathers looked for when casting about for a husband for their daughters; their chances of advancement were slim and the prospect of an early demise great. What other type of feminine companionship was there for them except the public women?

Morgan McCormack was a man who exuded power despite his state of undress. The morning light, increasing at the windows, sculpted the muscles of his back in light, outlining in harsh clarity the paler strips of old scourge marks in the sun-bronzed darkness of his skin. As it slipped along his tapering waist to the flat hardness of his flanks, it brought forth the contrast in shading between his upper and lower body in a sharp demarcation line, as if he was accustomed to going without a shirt. Though she had little to go by, to Félicité he appeared more rampantly male than any other man of her acquaintance. There was about him a quiet assurance that she had never come in contact with before. The discovery was unsettling. It would have been much more satisfactory if there had been some obvious weakness which might have been exploited.

It was as Morgan found his breeches, pushing one leg into them, that the door opened. Ashanti paused on the threshold, then, ignoring the colonel with determination, spoke to Félicité.

"Breakfast will be no more than a few minutes in preparation, mam'selle. Shall I serve it in here?"

Félicité slanted a quick look at Morgan unhurriedly pulling up his breeches, fastening their side buttons. "I—yes, please, Ashanti."

The maid signified her understanding, then, tilting her head in the direction of the copper tub with its cold, soap-scum-coated water, asked, "Shall I remove the bath now?"

Félicité was about to agree when Morgan answered for her. "Later. And never mind breakfast for me. I won't be staying."

"Yes, M'sieu Colonel," Ashanti said, dropping a smart curtsy before she departed once more in obedience to the tone of dismissal in his voice.

It did not sit too well with Félicité to have him order her servants for her, especially Ashanti. The prospect of his early departure was too welcome for her to risk saying anything that might make him alter his plans, however. She pressed her lips together.

Morgan picked up his shirt, pulling it on over his head, breathing a soft imprecation as he stretched his wound trying to push his right arm into the sleeve. If she had not been at such odds with him, Félicité might have been tempted to help. As it was, she sat unmoving, sipping at her cold chocolate.

When he had begun to push the tail of the blood-splotched shirt into his breeches, she finally spoke. "When will you return?"

"Why?" He straightened the pleated ruffle of his shirtfront and picked up his waistcoat, sliding it carefully up his arm.

"I only wondered if you would be here for dinner—so I could decide what to tell the cook to prepare."

"Don't worry about a meal for me. Anything will do."

She supposed from that she was to assume he would be back by that time. His attitude was not a familiar one. Oh, Valcour was often vague as to the hour of his return; regardless, he demanded the richest and most time-consuming foods be prepared against the eventuality that he might decide to put in an appearance. Even her father had been deeply interested in the dishes that were to be set before him at the table.

Thinking of her father, Félicité felt a deep chill settle over her. She bit the side of her lip, then, with a hard set to her mouth, glanced at the man now buckling on his sword belt. "Colonel—Morgan?"

"Yes?" He flicked her a quick look as he adjusted the hang of his rapier.

"What will happen now? In the matter of our agreement, I mean."

"You want to know if I will honor it, even though you tried to cut your part in it short?"

"I told you, I did no such thing!"

"The question is, can I afford to believe you?"

"The question is," she corrected him, "do you want to, or would you rather pretend I am at fault so you won't have to face what you have done!"

"There is that possibility," he agreed, and looked up from the search for his boots with a grim smile for her astonishment. "It is a minute one, but because of it, I am prepared to let the previous arrangement stand."

"You will use your influence to see that my father receives his freedom?"

"That was never assured. I will see that the sentence is as

light as possible. More than that is beyond my ability to guarantee.''

It was so little, so small a concession, and yet if it meant the difference between life and death, so great a one. Could her contact with Morgan really change the punishment to be meted out to Olivier Lafargue in the Spanish court? Would it? She did not know; therefore she had no way of telling if the price she was now paying was too high.

''And what of me?'' she asked, forcing the words past the hard knot in her throat.

''You?'' He lifted a brow, fully dressed now, raking his hair back, confining the waving strands with the black tie that held his queue.

Félicité pushed the gauzy folds of the mosquito *baire* aside, her eyes dark as she searched his face. ''What will I do? What will I be to you in the meantime, your *chère amie?*''

''If it pleases you to style yourself that way.''

The quiet mockery of his words fanned her sense of helplessness. ''It doesn't! You may think you have the upper hand, but I won't tolerate this a day, an hour, a second longer than I must to save my father!''

''The trial is likely to be a long one. It may go on six weeks, even two months, before a verdict is reached.''

''A travesty,'' she scoffed. ''You know well enough O'Reilly would find these men guilty and hang them tomorrow if it wasn't for the public outcry it would cause.''

''I haven't the time to argue the issue with you now.'' He moved to place his hand on the knob before he turned back. ''I will point out, however, that you are in your present plight because you connived with your brother to seek my death. For that crime, I don't believe you can complain that justice has been either slow or unsure.''

''No,'' she said, ''not if I am guilty. But what if I am innocent?''

He stared at her a long moment, the green of his eyes as dark as jade, then, without answering, he opened the door and went out, closing it quietly behind him.

*   *   *

It was midafternoon when Morgan's manservant arrived. A small man with the lined and worried face of one of the monkeys brought by seamen from the African continent, he introduced himself as Pepe. He carried with him a portmanteau which, he said, contained the uniforms of Colonel McCormack. When he was shown into Félicité's presence he was at the head of a procession of three husky soldiers, each burdened with trunks, boxes, and oddly shaped parcels.

His bow a masterpiece of respect and homage, he said, "Señorita Lafargue, I have been told by my colonel to report to you. Since you have had the kindness of heart and soul to accept us under your roof, it is our wish to disturb you as little as possible. You need only tell me, Pepe, where the colonel is to be established, and I will do all else."

Where indeed? Félicité stood frowning in indecision. What would Morgan expect from this arrangement? Would he wish to share her bed at all times? Or only to enter it at his convenience? Was this request made by his servant a delicate way of allowing her to make the decision of where he would sleep, or was it a mere courtesy, a means of creating the pleasant fiction that she was to be nothing more than his hostess?

"Señorita?"

She was his hostess, wasn't she? Why should she not arrange matters to suit herself, and let him complain if they were not to his liking?

"Marie," she said to the young maid hovering in the doorway, "show Pepe to M'sieu Valcour's room, since my brother will not be needing it. You will then remain to see that he has everything he desires."

"*Gracias, señorita*," the little man said, his eyes lowered as he bowed then turned to follow the girl.

Félicité said impulsively, "There is also a connecting room facing the street on that side of the house which the colonel may find useful. It was my father's study, but I will clear it of his papers."

Pepe turned back to incline his head once more. "You are all goodness, all thoughtfulness, señorita. I am certain my colonel will be grateful."

Would he? Félicité was not so positive.

The remainder of the day sped by in a flurry of activity. The tramp of booted feet was a constant sound up and down the stairs. Pepe was everywhere, directing the removal of what was left of Valcour's possessions, seeing to their storage in a room off the courtyard, rearranging the furnishing, laying out the colonel's razor and ivory-backed brushes, bestowing his clothing in the armoire with many a careful pat and adjustment. Dismissing the soldiers, he descended to the laundry room with a handful of soiled garments, among them the shirt and breeches Morgan had worn the night before. From there he nipped into the kitchen to check on the progress of the preparations for dinner, making so many suggestions and disparaging remarks that the cook rounded on him with an upraised iron spoon, threatening to brain him.

The food was not of the best; the cook knew it, as did Félicité and everyone else in the house. How could it be when there was no money to purchase fresh vegetables and meats in the market? It was due solely to the charity of neighbors, who sent their servants to the back door with a loaf of bread, a few crabs, a fistful of scallions, and a young chicken, that they were able to scratch together a meal of any kind. It was a good thing such matters were unimportant to Morgan, for the situation was likely to get worse.

Morgan returned when night was falling. His footsteps as he climbed the stairs and crossed the entrance hall were slow. Félicité's fingers tightened on the piece of embroidery work that lay in her lap as she sat in the *salle,* sewing in the dim light that fell through the doors that stood open to the balcony. She did not look up until Morgan came to a halt in the doorway.

He stood framed in the opening, staring at her with overbright eyes, almost as if he had not expected to find her there. His face was flushed beneath the bronze of his skin, and he held his right arm clamped across his abdomen with his fingers thrust into his sword belt while his tricorne hat hung from the other hand. His gaze fastened upon her, moving from the shining, honey-blond curls arranged in a crown upon her head, down over the pale oval of her face, avoiding the dark apprehension of her eyes to probe the soft folds of her fichu tucked into the square neckline of her floral print gown of cream silk.

"Mademoiselle Félicité," he said, inclining his head with what appeared to be extreme care. "I bid you good evening."

"Good evening," Félicité returned. She looked away with an effort, folding her sewing and placing it in the basket that sat on the table beside her chair.

"Did Pepe put in an appearance?"

It was at that moment that the small manservant came hurrying from the rooms that had been given over to Morgan's use. "I am here, my colonel, you need not worry. Your chamber is prepared, your bath—"

"I should have known," Morgan said, a flicker of what might have been amusement crossing his stern features.

The manservant sent him a sharp glance that missed nothing as he reached to take the tricorne from Morgan's unresisting fingers. "Indeed you should! Will you change before dinner, perhaps bathe, take a glass of wine? The maid, Ashanti, has told me it will be fully half an hour before the meal is ready."

"For now the wine will suffice."

"If you will permit me, I will remove your boots that you may lie upon your bed."

"Thank you, no."

"But my colonel, I am persuaded your head aches; and your wound, it should be looked after."

Morgan lifted a brow. His voice soft, he said, "I am not an invalid, Pepe. I will have the wine here, with Mademoiselle Lafargue."

"Yes, colonel, at once, colonel." In breathless haste, the small man scampered from the room.

Félicité, watching Morgan's advance from under her lashes, could see well enough what had caused the manservant's concern. The shoulder of his uniform appeared stretched and strutted, not merely from the bandage beneath it, but from swelling. Moreover, he had all the signs of being in a raging fever. To point out his condition seemed unnecessary; he could hardly be unaware of it. Likewise, any offer of aid,

123

judging from his response to Pepe, would be both unappreciated and of uncertain safety.

She waited until he had thrown himself into the armchair across the table from her and thrust his long legs out, crossing his mudcaked boots one over the other, before she ventured a question. "Did you make your report—on the attack against you, I mean?"

"I did."

"I suppose Valcour is now a wanted man?"

"He was wanted before, for treason, and still is. A charge of attempted murder, on further consideration, seemed unnecessary."

There was an edge to his tone that sounded a warning, but she could not heed it. "He—he hasn't been caught?"

"Not yet," he said deliberately, "and if you are fretting about what character I gave you, let me put your mind at ease. The official version reads that I saw no evidence to indicate you were involved."

"But you said—"

"What I said, and what I know to be the facts, are two different things."

"Oh."

"Yes," he drawled. "I have been wondering about my sanity all this day. What I should have done was given evidence and let you take the consequences for your misdeeds."

"But you didn't." Her words were tentative, almost an inquiry.

"No, and I have a feeling that is something I am going to regret." He sent her a long, burning glance. "I have always said no woman is worth being cashiered for. The question is, my sweet Félicité, will I be proved right or wrong?"

Félicité met his fevered gaze with coldness. Her tones brittle, she said, "I doubt it will come to that. You have only to say that you were mistaken, that you overlooked the evidence that pointed toward my guilt."

"The governor-general doesn't permit mistakes, not in his officers."

"It seems then," she answered, "that it will be to your

advantage if the question of my guilt or innocence doesn't arise."

It was a moment before he spoke. "It strikes me that my position as an officer has been extremely useful to you, first to protect your father, now to do the same for you. I might even go so far as to say that you are dependent upon my goodwill."

"You might." Félicité forced the words past the sudden constriction in her throat. "What of it?"

His expression was difficult to discern in the encroaching shadows of the room, but his voice held an abrupt note of grim satisfaction. "That fact is the only thing that makes this situation worthwhile."

"Why?" Félicité flung at him as she came to her feet. "Because you anticipate what I will do to keep it? I wouldn't count on it! You are here, and that is enough!"

"For you, maybe, but not for me."

There was no time to reply, even if she could have thought of something to say. Pepe came into the room then, bearing a decanter of claret and a pair of glasses on a wooden salver. As the manservant poured the wine, Morgan watched Félicité with narrowed eyes. Her challenge and its answer lay between them like a flimsy barrier that had been felled with a single blow, leaving behind debris that must be cleared away.

"Shall I light a candle, my colonel?" the manservant asked.

Morgan looked up at him. "You must ask Mademoiselle Lafargue. This is her home."

"Of course, forgive me," Pepe said in tones of chagrin. "Shall I, señorita?"

Félicité gave her assent with a wave of her hand. The servant moved to kindle a flame and touch it to the tapers in a candelabrum on a floor stand. She swung away, her trailing skirts held out by panniers sweeping over the floor as she walked to the open doorway leading out onto the balcony. A gray moth fluttered past her, wafted on the fitful breeze that stirred the portieres. The darkening sky had a lavender tint that was reflected in the puddles lying in the still street below. A cat, half grown, half starved, came picking its way along the muddy thoroughfare, then dropped into a crouch before pouncing on a crayfish, carrying it off in triumph.

It was a little cooler since the rain, though a humid stickiness hung in the air. It was this, combined with tight stays, that made it difficult to breathe evenly. Her hands were trembling, and she clasped them together, staring with unseeing eyes at the house on the opposite side of the narrow way. If it were not for her father, she would pick up her skirts and walk out the door, down the stairs, and into the street. She would throw herself on the mercy of some neighbor, some merchant who had done business with her father. If she pleaded hard enough they might lend her the means to join Valcour at Balize, where she could take a ship for France. If it wasn't for her father—

"Come drink your wine."

Félicité let out her breath in a soundless sigh. Turning with reluctant obedience, she moved toward the table, skirting Morgan's outstretched legs to take up her wineglass. She cast the man in the chair a quick glance. He had loosened the buttons of his waistcoat and removed his stock. Now he drank his wine as though he were parched with thirst, and leaned to refill his glass. Lifting his right arm to tilt the decanter must have been an effort, for when he leaned back, the candle flame that shone in the russet waves of his hair caught a sheen of perspiration across his upper lip.

Pepe had effaced himself, though he had retreated only as far as the entrance hall. Through the open doorway, he could be seen hovering over the table in that large open space, getting in Ashanti's way as she checked the setting for dinner. His presence and that of her maid prevented a return to the subject they had been discussing. It was just as well.

Félicité drank from her glass. The claret was from a cask her father had put down two years before, one of his favorites. She swallowed, clearing her throat. "When Ashanti took my father's meal to him this evening, the guard told her he thought the trials for the men under arrest would begin soon."

"Very likely they will. As far as O'Reilly is concerned, the sooner the better."

"What are they waiting for? Why don't they begin tomorrow?"

He shrugged. "Evidence has to be gathered, depositions taken from anyone who might have knowledge of the insurrection; witnesses must be found, two per man, who are willing to swear to personal information concerning their guilt."

"From men like Director-General Aubry, I suppose?" she said, her tone heavy with scorn.

"And from Father Dagobert, and others like him. Every effort will be made to discover the exact truth."

Père Dagobert was the French Capuchin friar who was the religious leader of the community. If anyone could give an unbiased accounting of the happenings of the past month, it was he. A generous and kindly man, beloved, well known for his tolerance of human foibles, he could be depended upon to do everything in his power to aid the prisoners.

Félicité moistened her lips with wine once more. "Ashanti also heard on the street that Foucault has been arrested."

"That's right." Morgan did not look at her as he spoke.

"But it's absurd. The man was the commissary-general under the French, little more than a keeper of the king's stores."

"Among which were the weapons supplied to the men who attacked Ulloa's ship."

"Such an attack, cutting the lines that held the vessel to the levee!"

"There was a force of four hundred armed men present at the time. It was only Ulloa's good fortune that they decided he wasn't worth more drastic measures of ensuring his departure."

"Armed men?" she scoffed. "They were guests in high spirits returning from a wedding. I seriously doubt their numbers would have come to two hundred, much less four."

"That is one of the things the trial must discover."

"First Lafrénière and Braud, now Foucault, all men of rank under the French regime, men with the king's commission. This grows more unbelievable every day."

"I suppose it must, and yet the list of men arrested is not

long in comparison to similar incidents elsewhere. In the provinces of Mexico two years ago, eighty-two men were executed for insurrection, and with much less evidence against them.''

''That may be, but they were Spaniards, one supposes. I speak of Frenchmen. Why should they answer to Spain?''

''The instigating of rebellion after the transfer of the colony to Spain makes theirs a double crime, against both their own government and mine.''

Félicité set her glass down with a sharp thud. ''You are all mad! What does it matter if a man disagrees with the policies of a government, no matter which one? Why should it become a thing of life or death?''

''A man may think what he pleases, but he may not persuade others to think the same. The moment he does, he puts himself in opposition to authority. If enough join him, then the country is divided, and therefore weakened. Strife causes uncertainties that interfere with the basic rights of all men; the right to raise food for their families, to work to better themselves, to learn, to create, to enjoy. And in this state of chaos, it becomes easier for a stronger, more determined country to move in its armies and conquer those in disarray.''

''And yet sometimes that happens,'' Félicité said bitterly, ''when there is peace and all men are in agreement.''

From the doorway to the combined entrance and dining hall there came a cough. Pepe bowed when he had their attention. ''Dinner is served.''

The first course was a small bowl each of crab bisque. This was followed by *coq au vin,* along with a few spears of unadorned asparagus as a side dish. There was plenty of bread, but no other vegetable, no red meat course, no rich sauces, no gelatins. For dessert there would be only a custard to round out a menu that might well have been prepared for someone who was ill. That was, in any case, not far from the mark. Morgan picked at his food, drinking a few spoonfuls of the bisque, taking a mouthful of chicken.

As the meal progressed, Pepe cast several anxious glances at his master. He was in and out often, pouring the wine to complement the food, removing the crumbs that fell from the bread as they broke it, taking away the used utensils.

Pausing at Morgan's elbow to refill his wineglass, the manservant said, "Was the chicken not to your liking, my colonel?"

"It was fine," Morgan replied.

"But you eat so little. I would offer you a sliver of ham or some such thing as a substitute, but there is no other food in the house. None."

Morgan glanced up at the man. "What are you saying?"

The manservant made a small movement of his thin shoulders. "Other than a bit of flour and chocolate, and a small pot of wild honey, there is not another morsel in the kitchen. Half of what was cooked this night was taken to the prison, at that. According to the woman who presides in the kitchen, there is no money for more."

Morgan turned to Félicité, a frown drawing his brows together. "Is this true?"

"What of it?" Félicité answered, a flush of angry humiliation lying across her cheekbones.

"I find it hard to believe, especially in view of your offer of riches not too long ago."

"That was a matter of commissions and privileges, not—not hard currency. Even then, I had been warned not to try to sell any of my father's property that had been listed for confiscation, and of course the draper's shop has been closed since his arrest. You would have had to wait on his release, his vindication, before you could have received the reward I was offering. I could not venture to sell even my own wearables, it being assumed, and quite rightly, that even these belonged to my father."

His scowl deepened. "But surely your father has something put by, a ready reserve that might have been used for food? No one could object to your taking it for that purpose."

"There was a small amount, but it—is gone." She lowered her lashes, staring at the chicken congealing on her plate.

"Gone?"

"Taken, by Valcour."

He leaned back. "Why didn't you tell me?"

"To what purpose?" she inquired, her tone hard.

"I would have given you money."

Her head came up. "I want nothing from you!"

"That may be, but you have to eat. And though I have no particular preferences in food, I believe I would notice if there was none at all on the table."

There was no answer to that. When he saw she was not going to reply, Morgan turned on Pepe, making him jump with the suddenness of the attack. "You had funds, did you not?"

"Yes, my colonel."

"Why is it you didn't go to the market when you noticed the need?"

"I would have, my colonel," the manservant said in doleful tones, "but by the time I realized the lack, it was too late. The people of the market had closed their stalls and gone home for the day."

Silence descended. Morgan stared from his manservant to Félicité. He closed his eyes, putting a hand up to rub over them, then downward to rasp over the day's growth of stubble on his chin. Lowering it, he grasped the arms of his chair and pushed to his feet. He swayed a little as he said, "I believe I will have that bath now."

His voice had been steady, and his movements were well controlled as he moved around the end of the table, and yet there was an unnatural set to his shoulders, as if he was exerting greater than normal strength to keep himself erect. Almost against her will, Félicité rose, watching as his strides took him through the door and into the *salle*. She was only a few steps away, with Pepe close beside her, when he turned in the direction of the bedchamber he had used the night before, her own.

"This way, my colonel," Pepe said, gliding forward to touch his arm, indicating the chamber that opened on the far side of the *salle*. "I was directed to establish your quarters on this side of the house."

Morgan swung slowly around. "Were you?" he asked. "Were you indeed?"

"But yes. Two rooms have been given over to your

convenience, one for sleeping, the other for your work, should you care to do it here.''

What Morgan might have done if he had commanded his full strength Félicité did not care to consider. As it was, he sent her a glittering glance with a threat in its depths.

''How gratifying,'' he drawled. ''I can't wait to see them.''

Chapter 8

❧

The hour was late when the stirring from the rooms allotted the colonel finally died away. Before it was over nearly everyone in the house had been involved—Marie, the upstairs maid, to bring extra hot water as far as the outer door and to find quilts for a pallet for Pepe to be put down in the connecting room; Ashanti to search out fresh bandaging; and the cook to simmer the collection of leaves and herbs Ashanti insisted was necessary for a fomentation for the inflamed wound. Only Félicité was not pressed into service.

She did not offer to help, but neither did she interfere. Morgan had more than enough people taking care of him, or trying to do so. No one would expect her to show concern, least of all he. He was in no danger, according to Ashanti; a man of M'sieu Colonel's great strength would recover in a day or two, with her aid, from such a thing as a slight poisoning of the blood.

After a time, Félicité sent the maid to retrieve the copper tub Pepe had appropriated. She took her own bath at leisure, soaking in the scented water. Finished, she donned her nightrail, brushed and braided her hair, then blew out the candle and lay down upon her bed.

131

Sleep was impossible. The turmoil and disturbance of the day, combined with the distress of the night before, had left her nerve-strung. The residue of fearful anger ran like acid in her veins, churning in her mind with all the cutting things she might have said if only she had thought of them. With bright, stinging eyes, she stared up into the darkness of the mosquito *baire* enclosing the bed. She did not see how she could have behaved differently, and yet the situation in which she found herself lay upon her conscience and her pride with an intolerable weight.

The hours passed. Félicité closed her eyes and dozed, only to wake once, twice, three times. The fourth time that she was jerked into awareness, she heard the crowing of a cock. Before the sound had died away, there came the tramping of the dawn patrol passing, the squad of stiff Spanish marionettes whose duty it was to keep the town quiet.

They did their job well. So still was the fading night when they had gone by that Félicité could hear the thudding of her own heartbeat. There also came from the room across the *salle* the creak of the bed ropes and the rustle of the cornshuck mattress as Morgan flounced and turned. Was he in pain? Had his fever worsened?

It made no difference to her, of course, except she could not bear to think of a human being in need. Moreover, her father's case would not be helped if the Spanish mercenary was allowed to die in the Lafargue house.

Pepe was nearby, sleeping in the room that had been her father's study. Surely he would awake and see to his colonel? It was his duty, after all, one he seemed to enjoy. How could he sleep through such a racket of shifting bedclothes and wincing sighs? Still, some men were heavy sleepers, especially when they were tired, as the manservant had every right to be.

For long moments, Félicité could hear nothing. Had Morgan stopped breathing, or had he merely fallen into the quiet and even respiration of sleep? The last was much more likely. There was also the possibility that Ashanti's warm poultice had done its work, that his fever had broken. That was not a comfortable phase of any illness, but Morgan should be able to see to some things for himself, to throw off his cover or reach a carafe of water. The man was not helpless. At least he had not been the last time she had seen him.

With her lips pressed in a stiff line, Félicité slid from the bed and padded to the armoire to take out her dressing saque. She swung it around her, pushing her arms into the sleeves with impatience. She would just go to the door, she told herself as she drew her long braid out, letting it dangle over her shoulder; there could be no harm in that.

Félicité's window and the balcony doors leading from the *salle* had, despite the heat, been closed against the miasmas of the night. The shutters of Morgan's chamber stood ajar, however, as did the door. A pale light seeped into the room, outlining his long length in the bed. The sheet made a diagonal line across the flatness of his abdomen, leaving his upper torso bare. His right arm was stretched out stiff and straight, but his left was flung above his head. The bandaging that covered the top part of his chest on the right side was an indistinct contrast to his skin in the dimness. She could not tell if it was overtight with swelling from where she stood, but she did not think so. Seconds ticked by. He did not move. Apparently he was asleep, though he might also be unconscious. The *baire* had been let down from its ceiling hook and pulled about the bed, but he must have pushed it open on one side, perhaps for air from the window on the left. It was a wonder he had not been devoured by mosquitoes.

On tiptoe, Félicité crept toward the bed, holding her breath against the squeak of an uneven board or the scrape of an unwary step that might betray her. Her gaze fastened on his face. She thought he did not seem as flushed as before. In repose, he was, in a bold way, attractive. His forehead was broad and the bones of his face strong and well defined. The shape of his nose and the chiseled outline of his lips were classical, as was the jutting firmness of his chin. Some women might be taken in by such a face, but not she. From the first she had seen his arrogance, his overbearing certainty of right.

He had tucked the edge of the mosquito *baire* beneath his pillow to keep it back. In this as in all else, he had to make things difficult. Félicité hesitated, of half a mind to leave him to be bitten as he deserved. Then, with a sigh of exasperation, she reached toward the edge of the *baire*.

With the swiftness of a cat, the man on the bed pounced, catching her wrist. A long arm coiled around her waist, and she was jerked forward and dragged up on the bed. She gave a gasping cry as she fell on her shoulder, a cry that was cut off as Morgan pushed her to her back, reaching across her thighs to pull her feet onto the bed also.

"What are you doing?" she demanded, though the words lacked the fierceness she had intended.

"Putting you in my bed, since you object to letting me share yours."

"I thought you were sick!" She tried to raise herself, but was prevented by the tightness of his hold.

"I think I must be," he answered, the hand of his good left arm moving upward to clasp her waist once more, "though the poison in my blood has nothing to do with the cut of a sword, and much with the one who stitched it."

"I did nothing! You watched me ply the needle yourself!" she protested.

"I watched you, yes, and with as much pleasure as pain, but the damage was done before then, long before." He lowered his mouth to hers then, tasting, exploring, forcing her lips to part as he probed deeper. His fingers spread, he slid his hand upward, pushing aside the edges of her dressing saque, cupping the firm mound of her breast.

His touch was searing, even through the soft linen of her nightrail. His fever might have abated, but it had not left him entirely. Félicité put her free hand on his shoulder, pushing at him as she moved her head a fraction. Against his mouth she said, "You will hurt yourself."

His grip tightened. "Not if you don't fight me. Nor, in that case, will I hurt you."

What choice did she have? From this situation of her own making there could be no rescue, no succor. By slow degrees, she allowed her resistance to ebb, steeling herself to accept whatever came.

He turned her to him, sweeping the dressing saque aside, pressing her against the long length of his body until her breasts were flattened against his chest and the nightrail that separated them seemed on fire with the heat of their bodies. He found the thick braid of her hair and loosened the plaiting, working the strands free so that it spread in a waving cloak around her. The better to veil her in its shimmering length, he stripped the nightrail over her head and drew the tresses forward to cover her. With burning lips he kissed her eyelids then, scorching the curve of her cheek and the hollow of her throat, scalding the trembling peak of her breast through the fragrant, iridescent cascade of her hair. He spanned her waist with his hand, smoothing downward over her stomach that was taut with apprehension, sliding with gentle insistence between her thighs.

Félicité felt a quickening inside her, a rising warmth that she sought to deny in her unwillingness to respond to the man beside her. It was impossible. She could not evade his touch, his presence, his sure caresses that refused to recognize her defenses. They captured her senses, turning them against her. She was suffused with glowing heat that ran along her veins with the flicker of flame, flushing her skin, though she was beyond embarrassment. She brought her hand up, spreading the fingers over the muscles of his shoulder, aware of a need to be held closer. There was an aching emptiness deep inside her, allied to a distress-tinged darkness in her mind. Her chest felt tight, and her breath came in uneven gasps. She turned her head from side to side, caught in a pervading despair. It seemed to communicate itself to Morgan, for he went still. Then with abrupt decision, he eased over her open thighs and pressed into her.

A small cry escaped Félicité at that smooth, sliding entry. As his movements increased, she knew a dissolving sensation. It spread through her like the bursting of a levee. Her pent breath left her. Her hands fell away, the fingers uncurling, and she felt the hot trace of tears gliding from the corners of her eyes.

He gathered her closer. Covering her lips with his, he plundered their sweetness. As hesitantly she touched his tongue with her own, his grasp grew more fierce. Held fast, she plunged with him into the cauterizing fire of unhallowed desire. With her eyes tightly closed, she felt the singe of its passing, and, watching its dying flare against the darkness of her eyelids, was forced to wonder if she would have to bear the scars.

Félicité was scarcely conscious when she heard the opening of a door and the scuffle of footsteps. Morgan, still lying over her, reached to snatch at the sheet, covering them both.

"For—forgive me, my colonel, I thought I heard a call."

"Get out," the man beside Félicité growled, "and stay out."

The footsteps retreated in haste. Morgan slipped from her, drawing her against him in the circle of his arm. An instant later, Félicité slept.

The sun was high, striking its rays of molten gold into the room, when Félicité opened her eyes again. The heat was a living, smothering thing. She could feel the slow trickle of perspiration along her hairline, sense its dampness under her cheek, while along one side of her body it seemed as though she were being burned by living coals. She brought up a hand to push at the sheet that covered her.

Abruptly Morgan stiffened, as though her movement, slight though it was, had brought him awake. Her rigid muscles protesting, Félicité turned to stare at him. There was wariness and a shadow of what might have been apprehension in her brown eyes. He returned her gaze a long moment before he relaxed, one corner of his mouth tugging in a smile.

"I thought last night," he said softly, "that I must be delirious. It seems I wasn't."

Her mouth tightened. "I'm not so certain about that. Besides, it wasn't last night but daybreak this morning."

"It seems longer than that," he murmured, allowing his green glance to wander over the pink-and-cream hills of her breasts, uncovered as she sought coolness.

His eyes were clear, his skin tone normal, but his hair was wet and his body gleamed with perspiration. Both the sheet on which he lay and that which covered him were drenched. It was this, more than the warmth of the morning, that had caused her own discomfort.

In sudden discovery she said, "You—your fever has broken."

"And why not, considering the excellent care I have had—and the potent medicine."

"You mean—" she began, then stopped, lifting her chin as the gleam in his eyes told all too plainly to what he alluded. "That was certainly not my intention!"

"No? Then why did you come? Just what were you doing in my room?"

"I wasn't planning to murder you in your bed, if that's what you think. In fact, it crossed my mind the questions from Spanish officialdom would be exceedingly tedious if you should die!"

"I see," he said, grimness moving over his face. "I think I can safely promise to save you from such ennui."

She sent him a suspicious glance as she shifted away from him, pushing herself up in the bed. "Thank you. It would be a pity if I could no longer be dependent upon you!"

"Wouldn't it," he agreed with a lifted brow. Noticing her attempt to avoid touching him, he looked down at himself. "Good God, I'm sweating like a horse. Where in the devil is Pepe? Any other time he would have been in and out a dozen times."

"To the best of my recollection, you ordered him to stay out," she informed him.

"So I did, but it isn't like him to take me quite so literally."

"No doubt he was shocked out of his wits."

"That seems unlikely," he returned, his tone dry.

"Oh?" Did he mean that his servant was not easily shocked, or that it was not too uncommon for him to find his colonel in bed with a female? The thought was somehow disconcerting.

Morgan ignored the opening. "What of that girl of yours? How does it happen that she hasn't deluged us with chocolate yet?"

"Perhaps she thinks that a man as sick as you were supposed to be needs his rest."

"I have always been swift to recover," he murmured, his tone apologetic, though amusement danced in his eyes.

"Or perhaps," Félicité persevered, "Ashanti was afraid she would get her head bitten off."

"That's probably it," he said, deliberately misunderstanding. "There can't be many women as ill-tempered as you are proving to be in the morning."

"Ill-tempered? I?"

He only sent her a bland smile, sitting up as he gave a shout. "Pepe! Damn you, Pepe, come here!"

That sent her diving under the sheet as the connecting door between Morgan's bedchamber and the next room swung open.

"Yes, my colonel?"

"Where have you been? And where is mademoiselle's chocolate?"

"I was waiting for you to awake and call," the manservant said with an injured air. "I also told Ashanti it would be best if she did the same."

"Well, we are awake now," Morgan pointed out. "Bring the chocolate, and I want a bath."

"A bath! But, my colonel, so much immersion in water will make you as weak as a newborn."

"I'm that already," Morgan said, and overrode Félicité's unladylike snort of disbelief with ease. "I am also hungry, so I suggest you rattle your bones, Pepe, and find something substantial to break our fast."

Pepe coughed. "There is a matter of funds—for the market?"

"You know where they are kept. Take what you need!"

When Pepe had bowed himself out, Morgan flung back the sheet, fanning it to give Félicité air. She snatched at an edge to pull it over the lower part of her body. She was fast becoming used to having him see her from the waist up, however, and some concession had to be made to the heat. In any case, she was able to conceal herself most effectively, as she sat up again, by drawing a pair of honey-colored tresses forward over her shoulders.

He slanted a jaundiced look at the silken screen of her hair, then glanced at the shutter standing open at the window. He nodded in that direction. "It would be cooler in here if that were closed."

"Yes, undoubtedly." Félicité gave the opening no more than a fleeting inspection.

Tilting his head, he went on, "I would shut it, but I am not feeling quite up to the exertion."

He wanted her to step naked out of bed so he could have the pleasure of watching her. She had no intention of obliging him. "No, you mustn't waste your strength. Ashanti can attend to it when she brings the chocolate."

"But in the meantime, we expire."

She scanned his face. He certainly seemed to be overheated. She glanced around her, spying her nightrail where it was rolled, half hidden in a fold in the bedclothes. "Very well, I'll do it."

Following her glance, he leaned to snap up the nightrail just before she reached it. He wadded it in his left hand, and she lunged for it, only to find herself lying across his chest. Recoiling in haste, she scrambled away from him, sliding out of bed on the other side as he heaved himself after her. Her foot touched soft material. Even as a grin of triumph began to curve his lips, she bent to scoop up her discarded saque, whirling it around her. Backing to the window, she slammed the shutter and pushed the wooden bolt into place. That done, she stood irresolute in the sudden dimness, glancing from the man in the bed to the door that led into the *salle*.

Morgan levered himself back into a sitting position. "Thank you. You may come back to bed now."

"I think not," she said, flinging her hair back.

"Why? What else is there for you to do?"

"There is the marketing, the housekeeping, my—my father's meals and clean clothing—"

"All things Pepe and Ashanti can take care of between them without your help. I thought you had decided it would be to your advantage to see to my continued good health."

"There's nothing wrong with you!"

"Oh, but there is. I think, in fact, that I am deathly ill, so ill I am going to have to send a message to the governor-general saying I am not able to leave my bed today."

"What?"

"Or, possibly, tomorrow. Only think how pleased O'Reilly

will be when you restore his second-in-command to him, fully recovered.''

"It will be no doing of mine!''

"Not so. You are without doubt strong enough medicine to put any man on his feet, though I am not certain that, like the elixir of the Turkish poppy seed, you may not be addictive.''

She cast him a doubtful look. "But we cannot stay in bed all day today.''

"Can we not? If that is what I want?'' The faint smile with which he regarded her remained the same, but there was an implacable note in his voice.

If it had been a question of wills, she might have withstood him, but it was more than that, much more. Weighting the scale of Morgan's desire for her company was the fate of her father. The design and fabric of her future, and her own freedom to weave it as she pleased, had become nebulous, something to be set aside indefinitely.

"You—take an unfair advantage,'' she said through stiff lips.

"That may be. But if I am to have you, what other choice is there?'' He held out his hand. Moving with slow reluctance, Félicité went toward him and allowed her fingers to be caught in his warm grasp.

Morgan's threat to remain with her was not idle. Immediately after breakfast he sent Pepe with a message to O'Reilly's headquarters. The governor-general would not be surprised to receive it, he said; he had suggested several times the day before that his second officer would be better off for a few days of recuperation in bed. Until now, Morgan had not appreciated how well O'Reilly understood these matters!

In the dimness of the shuttered room they napped through the morning, rousing to wakefulness from time to time before drowsing again. They partook of a light luncheon while sitting propped up by pillows, then settled again to pass the torpid, overheated hours of the afternoon. Morgan was demanding, and yet his need of repose was real. While he lay relaxed in slumber, Félicité was able to collect her thoughts, to sort through her emotions. That she could feel anything approaching passion in his arms was debasing. She knew that this assault upon her senses need not necessarily have anything to do with love; still, she would have preferred to remain unmoved. She could not. And yet, insofar as she could prevent it, she would not let Morgan see how he affected her. His hold upon her was strong enough; there was no need to add to it.

Still, for the first time in days, Félicité was able to relax. As the time spent in bed with Morgan lengthened, the darkened room began to take on the aspect of a retreat. Here she could drift, unmindful of what might be occurring beyond these four walls, unheeding of events she could not change. Let it go, then. As long as she must bow her will to Morgan's wishes, what use was it to look beyond this moment, this circumstance? She might as well close her eyes and seek the soothing opiate of dreams.

It was just before dinner when a messenger delivered a packet of close-written sheets for Morgan, along with a three-page letter of instructions and questions. The second officer in charge of the Spanish army of occupation was, apparently, indispensable. There were limits to the time he would be allowed to absent himself from duty.

Morgan looked over the papers, then tossed them to one side. When the evening meal was over, however, he climbed out of bed, donned his breeches, and spread the sheets out over the desk in the study. Félicité watched through the doorway for a time as in the light of a branch of flickering candles he sent a quill slashing over page after page of parchment. Now and then he would lean back, checking a list with his lips pursed, or rake his fingers through his hair in frowning concentration as he came to a decision. He seemed engrossed, oblivious of his surroundings, though now and then his green gaze wandered to the white-draped bed and her shape beneath the sheet.

Restlessness crept in upon Félicité. She felt peculiar sitting, waiting. The house was quiet as Ashanti and the others had their meal in the kitchen. It was well after dark, a late dinner hour being the custom in this semitropical land where appetites stirred only fitfully until the cool of the evening. Soon the moon would be rising.

Félicité slipped from bed, finding her saque, drawing it around her. She let herself out of the bedchamber and moved across the *salle* to her own room. There on the dressing table she found her brush and used it to bring some order to the tangled mass of her hair. Running water into a bowl from the lavabo fastened to one wall, she bathed her face and neck for coolness. On impulse, she added more water to the bowl and sponged her entire body. She had bathed that morning before Morgan, but she relished the sensation of freshness.

Dusting herself with violet-scented cornstarch, she took another clean linen nightrail from her armoire. Its well-washed softness felt good against her skin. At the same time, with it covering her nakedness beneath her dressing saque, she felt less vulnerable within herself.

She had picked up her hairbrush, trying to decide what would be Morgan's reaction if she braided the long length of her hair for the night ahead, when she heard the strains of the guitar. The sound came from the street, a soft and haunting air tinged with melancholy. It drew closer. As Félicité stood listening, the musician paused in the street outside the house and lifted his voice, a soft, clear baritone, in the words of an old Spanish love song.

Juan Sebastian Unzaga. The voice could belong to no other. Embarrassment and dread gripped Félicité, along with an odd sadness. She cared nothing for the Spanish soldier, but still his persistence and his willingness to make his feelings plain by this public salute were touching. He could not know of her recent change of status, or he would not have come. No doubt he would learn of it soon enough; such things could not be kept a secret in so closely knit a community. In the meantime, what was she to do?

She put down the brush and glided from the room with the skirts and shoulder capelet of her saque billowing around her. At the doors that opened out onto the balcony, she paused, glancing toward the study. The door to that room from the *salle* was closed. She could hear no movement inside. Perhaps Morgan had not noticed the serenade, or, noticing, had not realized the Lafargue house was its object. There was one other possibility; that he realized, but did not care.

It was not that Morgan had any right to object, and of course she didn't mind one way or the other. It would be best, however, if there was no confrontation, nothing to draw attention to the house and its new occupant. The best way to ensure that might well be to do nothing, to ignore the man in the street below, letting him finish his song and move on without acknowledgment.

The only trouble with that resolve was that Juan Sebastian seemed disinclined to curtail his performance. As soon as he finished one song his nimble fingers began to draw forth another melody from his guitar. The music soared upward, pouring in through the doors that stood open to the evening breezes. He could not see Félicité where she stood, she was sure of that. Regardless, it was as though he sensed her presence, so full and resonant with longing was his voice. It caught at her imagination, vibrating through her, stirring the impulse to see him, to step out onto the balcony and accept the homage he offered, knowing full well that such humble supplication was the creation of the night and the music, nothing more.

At a slight sound behind her, she turned. Morgan stood with his hands on his hips, his dark-green gaze raking her where she stood in the shadow of the portieres. His tones tight with sarcasm, he said, "How much longer is this caterwauling going to go on?"

"I—I couldn't say."

"I can," he grated, and walked past her out onto the balcony.

"No!" Félicité cried, moving swiftly after him to clutch his arm, to draw him back. It was too late. They were caught in the silver-white gleam of the halfmoon just swinging above the rooftops of the town.

"Félicité," Juan Sebastian breathed as he caught sight of the white shimmer of her nightclothes and the golden cape of her hair about her shoulders. "How beautiful you—"

He stopped short as he saw the dark shape of the man beside her. For long seconds no one spoke, no one moved.

Morgan stepped to brace his arms on the railing. "Well, Bast?"

"I—I did not know. I never dreamed—" On the upturned face of the Spaniard the brief delight was replaced by confused disappointment.

The tableau they presented was damning. A gentleman did not remove his coat, much less his waistcoat and shirt, in the presence of a lady unless they were on terms of intimacy. And although the ladies of the French court and the *haut ton* received both male and female callers in déshabille, enjoying tidbits of gossip while being dressed by their maids, that was an amusement for married women, not young girls, and for the daylight hours only. By appearing as they had, they could not have made their relationship more plain.

"Now you do know," Morgan said quietly.

"Yes." Juan Sebastian drew himself up with all the pride of a grandee, which indeed he was by birth if the gossips were right. "I will bid you goodnight."

The disillusion in his tone, and the bitterness, struck Félicité like a blow. She wanted to call after him as he turned away, to explain. With the realization that she could not came some small recognition of how the days ahead were going to be. Her face set, she swung back into the house.

Morgan entered behind her. His features impassive, he watched as she moved about the room in agitation, avoiding the doors that led to either bedchamber.

"Am I to take it," he drawled, "that you would rather I had not sent Bast away?"

She sent him a venomous glance. "I would rather you hadn't made it so obvious that you were staying here."

"I can't see that it matters."

"Oh, no, I'm sure you can't. You weren't the one who was branded a harlot."

"Nor were you. Bast is unlikely to spread the news of my presence to all and sundry." His tones were laden with rigidly contained patience.

"He won't have to. It wouldn't surprise me if half the town knows already."

"If that is so, there is nothing we can do about it. It strikes me that you weren't overly concerned until Bast came on the scene. Can it be it's not your loss of honor and respectability that troubles you so much as the loss of a suitor?"

She stared at him, a cold sparkle in her brown eyes. "How can I expect you to understand my feelings? You a mercenary who traded honor for gain so long ago you have forgotten how it feels to be without it."

"You haven't answered my question," he reminded her, his face taking on a metallic hardness.

"Why should I? You have taken from me my chastity, my character. You have seen to it that I will be reviled and despised as a traitor and an immoral woman. Because of you and what you represent, my father has been imprisoned, shut away from all contact as though he were already dead before the eyes of the world. My brother has fled, my home and everything I possess have been listed for confiscation and will almost certainly be taken. By what right do you question me about anything? By what right do you dare?"

"I did offer recompense," he reminded her, "and future security."

"Recompense? Security? As well to offer the innocent man held in custody the compensation and safety of prison walls!"

"It is a pity you feel that way."

"What else can you expect?"

"Gratitude?" he suggested.

"Gratitude?" She almost spat the word. "For what?"

"For risking my career and my future prospects to intervene for Olivier Lafargue."

"That you did, if indeed you did so bestir yourself, as a part of a bargain in which I was to be seen in your presence, though you seem to have carried it a great deal further than was intended."

"You are not entirely without blame in that last instance, if I remember correctly," he countered, an emerald glitter in his eyes.

"I may have told Valcour of your attendance, and even let

145

fall the fact that you would be escorting me home that evening, but as I tried to tell you before, I never plotted to have you killed. I could not have done such a thing, any more than I could have ordered a chamber pot emptied on your soldiers from yonder balcony.''

He lifted his head, a blank look descending over his features. ''If you didn't order the chamber pot emptied, then who? —Valcour. I might have known.''

''Yes, Valcour! Since he has gone beyond your reach, there can be no harm in admitting it.''

''It seems I must readjust my thinking,'' he said, his voice silken as he moved toward her. ''A closer examination of your—thought processes may be in order.''

The expression in his eyes was anything but detached. Hastily, Félicité said, ''I see no necessity. You have only to believe me.''

''I am afraid I have become too cynical, too dishonorable, for that. I require to be shown.''

''How—how can I do any such thing?'' Félicité queried, a trifle breathless as she retreated before his advance.

He reached to slide his arm around her waist, drawing her against him. ''I leave that,'' he said softly, ''entirely to your imagination.''

Chapter 9

*F*élicité's misgivings concerning the attitude of the town toward her fall from grace were well founded. In the next few days, as she went back and forth from her house to the prison or the market, hardly a soul spoke to her. Her neighbor from next door who had brought her news on the day her father was arrested came no more. The gifts of food that had temporarily sustained them ceased. On the day when, with the rest of the inhabitants of the town, she put in a reluctant appearance at O'Reilly's headquarters for the swearing of the oath of fealty to Spain, she caught sight of her giggling friend from convent days. The young woman spared not even a smile. Stiff-backed, she and her husband turned away, cutting Félicité dead, leaving her isolated among the people who shared her birthright. Compared with the abusive taunts that were sometimes whispered after her in the streets, or called in louder tones in the market, this snub was nothing, and yet it hurt her more than anything she had yet endured.

Greater than the pain of ostracism, however, was her growing fear that some rumor of the fact that she was living with a Spanish officer would reach her father. Though he could not have visitors, he could speak to the guards, could sometimes receive a note if the officer in charge was in a lenient mood, even if he could not send one. The state of mind that must overtake him in such a case, the torment without knowing the reasons for it, was something she did not dare contemplate. To add this burden to the fears and oppression of the spirit he must already be supporting was unthinkable.

Her father was not of a robust constitution. He had also an introspective and pessimistic frame of mind. The only thing worse than having him discover her circumstances would be if he should learn that they had come about in her attempt to save him. He would be appalled. His pride and honor would be extinguished by such a sacrifice for his sake. Situated as he was, helpless to exercise his parental obligation to protect her, he might well make himself ill.

At last she hit on a means of deflecting some of the damage of any rumors that might reach him. In a note of forced cheerfulness, delivered with his food tray, she told him with perfect truth that a number of Spanish officers had been quartered upon the townspeople, and that the Lafargue house had been honored with the person of the second-in-command under O'Reilly, one Lieutenant Colonel McCormack. With great care, she stressed the advantages in the situation, those of extra food and the addition of the colonel's manservant to make the work easier and serve as an escort for Ashanti and herself when they walked out on the streets. She did not, of course, mention the fact that Valcour was not in residence. In fact, some small reference she made to her brother might be taken to indicate that he was still there, going about his usual pursuits. Valcour had not bothered to apprise the imprisoned man of his previous disappearance; it seemed safe to conclude that he would neglect to send word of this last. As distasteful as was the subterfuge, it was the only way she could think of to protect her father.

What she would do when Olivier Lafargue discovered the truth on his release, if he was released, she did not know. It would have to wait upon that time.

It was more than a week after Morgan had set up his quarters in the Lafargue house. Félicité, with Pepe close beside her, was returning homeward after delivering her father's meal. She was in no hurry; preparations for Morgan's dinner were well in hand, and in any case, he seldom made his way to the house from O'Reilly's headquarters before dusk. Walking in the evening air was pleasant. She considered making a circuit of the Place d'Armes as she had in other times, but decided against it. There would be too many opportunities there for her to be humiliated. It would be much better if she turned her footsteps back toward the center of town.

The streets had been laid out by a military surveyor when New Orleans was founded nearly seventy years before. They ran straight and true to the river, with the side streets cutting across them in precise right angles, instead of winding like European thoroughfares. It would be easy enough for her to make her own square walkway, returning at its end to the Lafargue house.

She skirted the parish Church of St. Louis, intending to traverse the garden behind it to reach the next side street. Across the way, she caught sight of the flash of a red uniform and the golden glitter of officer's braid. Without thinking, she came to a halt, pausing in the deep shade of a moss-draped live oak. Pepe froze into immobility beside her, sucking in his breath with an audible sound. It was only then that

Félicité was certain the officer was Morgan, only then that she noticed the woman on his arm.

Dark, dressed in black silk overlaid with a skirt of gold lace, her hair dressed high with its distinctive white wings threading the shining blackness and gold combs supporting a mantilla, it was the woman Félicité had seen arriving that memorable day she had gone to see Morgan at the government house. She strolled beside the colonel, her bearing regal, her manner gracious and assured. For his part, Morgan gazed down at her as though she held him fascinated, one brown hand covering the slim white fingers that lay upon his sleeve.

That Pepe knew something more of the situation than she was obvious. Félicité slanted him a quick glance. "What a charming-looking lady. I wonder who she can be?"

"I believe, mademoiselle," the manservant said carefully, "that it is the Marquesa de Talavera."

"How interesting. A Spanish title, I presume?"

"This is so. It comes to her from her husband, the marqués, a fine man who, regrettably, is no more."

"She is most attractive."

Pepe inclined his head. "La Paloma is considered to be one of the most beautiful women in the Old World, or the New."

The name he had given the woman meant "The Dove." It seemed an unlikely title for such a personage, conjuring up as it did mental images of soiled doves, the name often applied to public prostitutes. Sending Pepe a look of frowning inquiry, Félicité repeated, "La Paloma?"

"She is called so because of her hair, mademoiselle," he said, his face impassive, "and because the reference amuses her."

"I see," Félicité said, though she was not certain that she did. It would not do for the manservant to think that she was overly interested, however. It was no concern of hers if Morgan McCormack wanted to flaunt members of the Spanish peerage around the town. She sincerely hoped that the lady was able to keep him entertained for the remainder of the evening.

If it had not been for seeing Morgan with the other woman,

however, Félicité might have been less polite when she met Juan Sebastian Unzaga a few yards from home. He stepped from a doorway to bar her passage, sweeping the ground with his hat as he made a leg before her. She returned his greeting with as much aplomb as she could muster while ignoring the flush of embarrassment that rose to her cheekbones.

"Mademoiselle Lafargue—Félicité! I had to see you, to speak to you."

"For what purpose?" She gave a small shake of her head as she tried to smile.

"To make certain that you are happy, that this—arrangement between you and my friend Morgan is what you want."

Félicité glanced at Pepe. "Your concern is flattering, but I hardly see how I am to answer such a question."

"By telling the truth! May I not ask that much? And that you give me a few precious moments of private conversation with you."

Before she could form an answer, Pepe inclined his head. "Your pardon, mademoiselle, I will leave you. You have only to call if you need me."

The man Morgan called Bast waited until the manservant was out of earshot, though not out of sight as he took up a vigil in the open doorway that led to the staircase of the Lafargue house. Juan Sebastian, his thin face earnest, turned to Félicité. "This *volte-face* you have made, from despising my countrymen to allowing one to share your bed, is unbelievable to me. I can only suppose you have been coerced in some way."

"Oh, come," she said, essaying a small laugh. "You are too absurd."

"That may be, but I have felt that you were too fine, too full of grace, to—"

"Please," she interrupted with a small, abrupt gesture, at the same time turning her face away.

"I will say no more, since it distresses you. Whatever your reasons, I will respect them. Only tell me if there is any way that I may aid you."

"I appreciate your concern, but I think not."

"Very well, then. I know that you are alone, without a

male relative to see after you. I beg you will come to me if anything happens to cause you pain, if you ever need a protector.''

"A protector?'' She turned to stare at him.

"You may be assured, Félicité, that my protection shall always be extended to you with love and devotion.''

"This is—most irregular, most unconventional. I don't know what to say.''

"Say only that you agree.''

"But Lieutenant Unzaga, it seems in the highest degree unlikely that I will require to change my protector.''

"One never knows. Some say the fates, like justice, are blind.''

He bowed then once more and walked quickly away. Félicité watched him go, a troubled frown between her eyes. His last words, nay, the whole tenor of his conversation, echoed in her mind with a disturbing ring. Did it indicate that he had some inkling of how matters stood between Morgan and herself? Or was it only that he refused to believe she was a willing party in her association with Morgan out of some exalted idea of her character? It made no great difference, and yet it might be best to be wary of Juan Sebastian Unzaga.

Morgan returned to the house earlier than usual. With Pepe in attendance, he removed his coat, waistcoat, and sword belt and splashed water over his face before he joined her in the *salle*. Over a glass of wine they engaged in stilted conversation. Félicité made a great play with the palmetto fan she held, using it to screen her face and to keep her hands busy, as well as to stir the muggy stillness of the air. She thought Morgan sent her a penetrating glance more than once, but his comments were general, concerning the unloading of a shipment of arms and ammunition, reports of increased pirate activity in the gulf, and the robbery of a party of colonists from an outlying parish who had been returning home after making the trip into town to swear allegiance. It was, all in all, a relief when dinner was announced.

The food set upon the table was plentiful and delicious. Still, Félicité could display little appetite. The sense of strain between Morgan and herself grew more pronounced with every passing moment. A brooding expression descended over the features of the man across the table, and he waved away the dessert Pepe offered. Toying with the last few swallows of wine left in his glass, he watched as Félicité tried to do justice to the custard that the cook had prepared. Under the circumstances, it was all she could do to choke down the sweet concoction. Finished at last, she pushed aside her dish. As if on signal, Pepe entered to remove it.

"Would you care for coffee in the *salle?*" he inquired.

Félicité shook her head. "It's much too hot."

"As you wish, mademoiselle. And you, my colonel?"

"Thank you, no." Morgan's tone was dismissive. He waited until the manservant had whisked from the room before he reached up to massage his shoulder.

Félicité watched him for a moment. Pepe had been tending the wound. As a result, she had not seen it at close quarters without the bandaging for several days. Morgan seemed to consider it an inconvenience best ignored, as though it was less a weakness if it remained unacknowledged. She had assumed it was healing satisfactorily, but she could not be sure. Before she could think better of the impulse, she asked, "Is your cut paining you?"

There was surprise bordering on amazement in his eyes as he glanced up at her. A slow smile curved his mouth. "No, but the twice-damned thing itches. I think it's time your sewing stitches came out."

"That should be no problem."

"No, except that such tasks make Pepe nervous, and then he can be confoundedly cow-handed."

"I suppose I could do it for you." Immediately regretting the offer, she added, "I will understand if you would rather I didn't."

He shook his head, his green gaze holding hers. "I can think of no one I would prefer."

Félicité went to fetch her sewing box, and they repaired to his bedchamber. He stripped off his shirt, then took a seat in a low chair. Félicité brought the scissors. Stationing herself in front of him, she took a deep breath and leaned to cut away the bandaging. She started a little as she felt his hands at her waist, but he only drew her nearer, between his long legs.

She clipped the strips of cloth with slow, even strokes, slipping the needle nose of her embroidery scissors under them with care so as not to scratch the skin. The pad came away in her hand at last, revealing the long, pink line of the slash. It was well healed, covered with a clean scab in which the black thread of the stitches was plainly visible. With one hand on Morgan's good shoulder, she stretched to place the bandaging on a side table. The rounded shape of her breast beneath her bodice brushed his cheek, and she drew back sharply.

The upward glance he sent her was bright, and also speculative. His thumbs smoothed the narrowness of her waist, rubbing over the whalebone stays that constricted it, before he spread his fingers out over the exaggerated width of the panniers supporting her skirts at the hips.

"Why," he asked, his tone musing, "do women wear these things?"

"Because it's the fashion."

"You mean, because some royal lady with an enormous backside decreed that all other women should look no better than she, like a horse with carrying baskets on each side?"

"Such a gallant description. I must thank you for it."

"Oh, I know well enough that your shape is slimmer by far," he assured her, with laughter threading his voice. "I only wonder that you would change it so drastically."

"Perhaps you would prefer it if I wore my nightrail? Or even breeches like a man?"

"That might be interesting. I rather liked that gown you wore to the masquerade ball. But as to what I would prefer—"

"I know well enough," she interrupted, her tones scathing. "You would be happiest if I went naked."

He flicked his thumbs once more over the stays that compressed her ribcage. "I would admit it would be more— convenient."

His touch, the tenor of his words, sent a tremor of something like anticipation along her nerves. She tried to ignore it, concentrating on slipping the point of her scissors under the embedded silk thread that bound the wound, cutting it, catching the knot, and pulling the stitch free.

He watched her deft movements for long moments. When she had only two stitches left, he slanted her a quick look. "I understand you spoke to Bast this afternoon."

"Pepe told you, I suppose?" She snipped a stitch with a sudden sharp movement.

"As it happens, he did." He cast a doubtful glance at her fingers where they tightened on his shoulder as she reached for the knotted thread.

"As it happens," she said, her tones hardening, "I don't like being spied upon."

"No one was spying on you. The encounter seemed a little unusual to Pepe, and he assumed I would be interested."

"Did he also tell you I met Père Dagobert walking with the Jesuit priest, Père Antonio, in the street near the infirmary, and that I spoke to them both?"

"He didn't mention it, nor did he tell me what Bast had to say to you that was so important he had to accost you in the street instead of paying a call like a civilized person."

"Oh, it was most respectable, I assure you! Probably much more so than your conversation with the dashing La Paloma during the same hour."

It was admirable the way he sat unflinching as with growing recklessness she yanked out the last stitch with a section of dried scab still clinging to its knot. "Who told you about that?"

"No one. I saw you myself."

"Who spied on whom now?"

"Not I," she cried, flinging down the scissors with a clatter. "I was walking home from the prison when I chanced to see you with that woman."

They stared at each other in tight-lipped anger. Félicité made a small movement, as though she would pull away from him, but his grip became more rigid, holding her in place. Rather than begin an undignified struggle, she stood still, though the enmity in her brown eyes deepened.

Abruptly he gave a nod. "All right, I take your point. If I

tell you about Isabella, will you return the favor by explaining what Bast wanted?''

"Whom you speak to, man or woman, is immaterial to me."

"I am sure of it. Very well, then—"

"But," she added hastily, "I will listen, since this woman seems out of the ordinary."

"She is that," he answered, smiling a little though his tone was dry. His hold relaxed a fraction as he went on. "She was born Maureen Elizabeth O'Connell in Ireland. Her father was a farmer, a breeder of horses, prize stud stock. When Maureen was thirteen, a middle-aged Spaniard came looking for mares. He bought one or two, and also bought the horse breeder's daughter. He took her to Madrid, where he kept her in seclusion for five years, calling her his little dove, educating her in various ways, some of which were beneficial to a young girl, some not. When his wife died, he married young Maureen, and she became Isabella de Herrara, the Marquesa de Talavera. Eight years later, the marqués died. There being no other heirs, no children of his previous marriage, she inherited his fortune."

"She doesn't look Irish," Félicité commented when he came to a halt.

"No more does she. If anything she appears every inch the Spanish noblewoman; which, let it be understood, she is. The marqués forced her acceptance at court. He took her everywhere with him, taught her how to manage his estates, to ride, to shoot, to use a sword. Unknowingly, he also prepared her for a life of independence after his death. For La Paloma there are no rules except those she makes herself."

"Are you saying she is—above the conventions, even immoral?"

"In a strict sense, no. I have never known her to do a base or an evil thing, and I have been acquainted with her since we were children together, playing in our fathers' fields that lay side by side. On the other hand, she has been many things to many men in many places, none of which would qualify her to be canonized as a saint."

Félicité glanced at him through her lashes. There was nothing in what he had said to indicate what the woman might have been to him in the past, or what she was at the present. Her interest sprang from mere curiosity, of course. "I see," she said. "What I witnessed was no more than a meeting of childhood playmates?"

"You might say so. And now, it is your turn."

She looked beyond him. With great reluctance she said, "Bast was only concerned for my happiness. He seemed to think that you—that we had become close in a very short time, and under the present circumstances, particularly my father's imprisonment, it had a strange look to him. I tried to reassure him, but I'm not certain he believed what I had to say."

"Why? What makes you think so?"

"He—he was kind enough to offer me his protection should it happen that I decide to leave yours."

Morgan swore softly. The pressure of his fingers about her waist increased until she gave a small gasp for breath. Immediately he released her. "Sorry," he said, his voice brusque. "I'm also sorry that you had to endure such an insult."

"I wasn't insulted," Félicité said, lifting her chin. "If anything, I was touched by his thoughtfulness."

"Is that so? It begins to look as if I will have to do something about Lieutenant Unzaga."

"What do you mean?"

"I believe a job can be found for him chasing smugglers in the bayous below the town."

"You wouldn't," she said uncertainly as she met his dark-green gaze.

"Why not? He might as well make himself useful there as anywhere else."

"But—but he is your friend!"

"So he is. But there are limits to everything. I will not share you with any man, Félicité, either physically or mentally."

"You cannot control my thoughts," she snapped, swinging away from him.

His hand shot out to close around her waist, jerking her off balance so that she fell across his lap. He cupped her face in his hand, his emerald gaze raking the parted softness of her lips before it stabbed into her wide brown eyes. "Can't I?" he said quietly, before he set his mouth to hers.

The trial of the conspirators began in late September. The presiding judges visited the prisoners in their cells, questioning them minutely. They went over and over every detail of their behavior, attitude, and actions from the time of Ulloa's arrival in New Orleans until the infamous day of revolution on October 28, 1768, and recorded every word they uttered. Satisfied at last, the learned gentlemen departed. Thereafter, in secret chambers, they heard the testimony of witnesses against the indicted men. Two witnesses each were brought forward to lodge accusations against Nicholas Chauvin de Lafrénière, the attorney general under the French; Jean Baptiste Noyan, the nephew of Bienville and son-in-law of the first man; Pierre Caresse and Pierre Marquis, both planters; and Joseph Milhet, a wealthy merchant. Witnesses were also rounded up to testify concerning the actions of Joseph Petit, Balthasar Masan, Julien Jerome Doucat, Pierre Hardy de Boisblanc, Jean Milhet, Pierre Poupet, and finally, Olivier Lafargue.

Never at any time during this period did the prisoners appear in court, never did they see the men who gave testimony against them. It made no great difference. The actions of those involved had been so public, so widely known, that to deny them was useless. Most of the twelve proudly admitted the part they had played. For their defense, they relied upon the contention that at the time when the crimes with which they were charged were alleged to have been committed they were Frenchmen, and therefore not bound by the laws of Spain. To bolster their case, they pointed out that Ulloa had not taken possession of the colony in official ceremony, had not presented his credentials during his tenure; that they themselves had not sworn fealty to the King of Spain; and that they had remained bound by their oath to the King of France until they had been absolved from it by the solemn ceremony that had taken place shortly after the arrival of O'Reilly.

The ease with which Morgan had demolished these arguments when Félicité had presented them to him brought now a slowly growing apprehension. No matter what they might claim, the prisoners were now in the hands of the Spanish court, and if the authorities refused to recognize the validity of their defense, preferring to condemn them under their own laws, who was there to gainsay them?

The prosecuting attorney general on behalf of the King of Spain was Don Felix del Rey, a man who had practiced before the royal courts of Santo Domingo and Mexico. He was a formidable man, according to all reports. It was said that he meant to set the charge against the twelve men as high treason, grounding the prosecution on the statute of Alfonso XI, which was the first law of seventh title of the first Partida. This statute pronounced the punishment of death and confiscation of property against those who incited any insurrection against the king or the state, or took up arms under pretense of extending their liberty or rights, and against those giving them aid or comfort. Justice, the attorney proclaimed, would be swift and sure.

Nevertheless, the days dragged past, turning into weeks. Some hope for the fate of the prisoners was felt when Braud, the court printer, swearing that he had acted under orders from Foucault, the commissary-general, in printing the proclamation of rebellion, was able to produce the signed order, and was freed. As for Foucault himself, he steadfastly refused to answer questions put to him by the judges, Director-General Aubry, or O'Reilly, demanding instead to be tried in France. Rumors had it that he was to be granted his wish, and even now awaited a ship to transport him to his mother country. If such leniency was also shown to the other men, all might yet be well.

It was a stormy time in more ways than one. Black clouds boiled up day after day from the gulf, and the warm rain descended, turning the streets into quagmires and lowering the spirits of the entire population. A number of ships failed to make port. Many of the losses were blamed on the treacherous winds and currents of the Caribbean, but from the men on the ships who were lucky enough to make port came tales of marauders in those warm, blue waters. One ship in particular seemed to capture their imagination. Sailing under a red flag showing a bird in flight with a skull in its claws, it was called the *Raven*. Hardened freebooters from tropical ports, it was said, blanched when they spoke of it. Its captain showed no quarter. The men who sailed with him did not say much of what they had seen when this corsair captured a ship, but there were whispers of women brutally raped, children torn from their mother's arms, and men cut to pieces for fish bait.

Félicité stepped from the low doorway of the outside kitchen and looked up at the overcast sky. A gust of wind brought a shower of heavy drops down from the black gum tree that spread its limbs overhead. Among them were a few bright-red leaves. The autumn was advancing. The mornings were cooler now even without the dampness of the continual rain, though it was warm by the middle of the day. There would be no need for a fire yet for several weeks, unless it was to discourage the gray mold that grew on every piece of leather, or the mildew that spotted the linen.

The rain had stopped as evening began to close in. It was a welcome respite, though the gray-white look of the sky did not give much hope that it would be a long one. Letting out her breath in a silent sigh, Félicité began to pick her way toward the door opening that led to the stairwell.

"Mam'selle, your tisane."

Ashanti came hurrying after her, offering a cup filled with dark steaming liquid. Félicité took it with a grimace. The concoction made by her maid, taken daily, had so far been effective. Her monthly courses had come with thankful regularity.

The maid watched in satisfaction as Félicité began to drink from her cup. "The colonel should return soon."

She nodded without enthusiasm.

"He should like the filet of beef we are preparing, also the shrimp bisque and oyster pie."

"I should certainly hope so, since we have been in the kitchen the best part of the afternoon."

"Have you decided what you will discuss with him after dinner?"

"It grows harder and harder to find a subject that will not cause an argument. French art, French wine, and French literature have been exhausted. French theater he dismisses as frivolous, French opera he admits as passable, but—''

''*Mon Dieu*,'' Ashanti said with a wry shake of her head. ''And yet more often than not, you speak in your tongue instead of his adopted Spanish.''

''That's so,'' Félicité agreed.

''Then we are making progress.''

''Of a sort, but I wonder more every day if this—this campaign of ours isn't pointless.''

''How can that be, mam'selle, if the man second only to O'Reilly himself is becoming more admiring of things French every day?''

''He may appreciate the ease and charm of our way of life, but I am doubtful it will affect his judgment, or his attitude toward what he conceives to be his duty.''

''You may be right, mam'selle, but we can only try. For most men, the pleasures of the stomach, the mind, and the flesh are more important than all else.''

''But the colonel is not most men.''

''In that you speak truly,'' Ashanti agreed.

''At any rate,'' Félicité went on, ''I already have his promise to do what he can for my father.''

''And yet, how much more willingly might he not carry out his promise, and with how much better effect, if he is grateful for the satisfying of his senses? Besides, there are many days, many months and years ahead when we must come to terms with these Spanish masters. Will it not be much easier for everyone if they learn to take life slowly, to stay out of the heat of the sun, to enjoy instead of trying to force us to endure endless toil at midday for the sake of our souls, and approach heaven with our lips turned down in a frown?''

From inside, the cook called to Ashanti, and the maid dropped a curtsy before turning to answer the summons. Félicité lingered for a moment, taking small swallows of her tisane. Sometimes Ashanti spoke as though the relationship between her mistress and Morgan McCormack would go on forever. That was impossible, even if she had desired it. Soon now the trial would be over and her father's fate made known. Regardless of what that might be, there was little hope that he would be able to keep his property. It would be sold to the highest bidder. She would have to move, leave this house where she had been born, where she had spent all the years of her life. More than likely, Morgan would have tired of the arrangement by then and would be just as happy to see her go. What she would do then, how she would live, where she would find the money to buy food for herself and her father, were questions for which there were no answers. For the most part, she tried not to think about it, tried not to look beyond the end of the trial. In her more optimistic moments, it seemed possible that Morgan might be able to secure her father's release, to have his name cleared of all charges. Olivier Lafargue would return home then, Morgan would depart, and things would be as they were. It was a comforting vision, though seldom long-lived.

She glanced down at the cup in her hand. At least with Ashanti's brew taken at this time, when Morgan was not present, she had some small control over the functions of her body that spelled her destiny. There would be no child forced to serve as a hostage to the future. With an abrupt movement, she drained the cup and stepped to set it on the corner of the kitchen table just inside the door, before swinging back and continuing along the walkway.

It was dim inside the upstairs rooms with the onrush of the cloudy evening. At the movement of a dark shadow blending with the portieres at the end of the *salle*, Félicité came to a halt, her heart jerking against her ribs. Faint crimson light flowed across the front of a uniform coat as Morgan turned.

"Oh, it's you," she said, lifting her hand to her throat.

"Whom else were you expecting?" His tones were flat, without their usual raillery.

"No one. I just didn't—know that you were home."

"You were busy below, and I saw no reason to disturb you. But what is this of home? A slip of the tongue, surely? This may be yours, but I am certain you don't consider it mine."

"I—I thought your home was in Ireland?"

He moved his broad shoulders. "Not any more. My mother has been dead these many years; my father was forced to sell the land our family had held for generations, and the sight of an English overlord riding over our acres sent him to his grave a few months later. I have a brother and a sister someplace; God knows where. They may be dead too, for all I can tell.''

"I didn't know.''

His voice bright-edged, he said, "There is a great deal you don't know about me.''

"That may be, but I assume that as a professional soldier your stay in this house, or in Louisiana for that matter, will not be long.'' She tried to see his face as he stood half turned from her, but his features were no more than a bronze outline against the gray gloom.

"What makes you think so?''

"Governor-General O'Reilly has done such a thorough job of subduing the people of New Orleans, of reorganizing our legal system, sending out census takers to count our numbers, and establishing the system of Spanish magistrates, that a civilian governor can now safely fill the position he holds. No doubt the King of Spain will have other work elsewhere for him to do, and for you.''

"What you say may be true, but I am not sure I will follow O'Reilly when he goes.''

"Not follow him? But why?''

"The governor-general has been authorized to grant parcels of virgin land from a thousand to five thousand arpents, the equivalent of the same in acres more or less, to anyone willing to build, to clear and cultivate it as a Louisianan. The provision was made before he left Spain. That prospect was what brought me here in the first place.''

"This land is to go to anyone?''

"To anyone he deems worthy.''

"Which is to say, any one of his followers, any Spaniard, any man with the money to—prove his worthiness?''

"The land is not for sale, if that's what you mean," he answered, his tone hardening.

She turned sharply away. "Of course not. Such corruption is only for the French regime.''

"I didn't say that," he objected, his voice soft.

"You didn't have to. To the stern and pious Spanish, all

criminals are French, oh yes, and especially all smugglers and pirates. What you fail to consider is that it is Spanish laws and arrogant Spanish misunderstanding of what living in Louisiana is like that makes it so.''

"You are right."

Caught in mid-tirade, Félicité swung to stare at him. "What did you say?"

"I said you were right, at least as concerns smuggling and piracy. The laws of Spain that require the trade of its colonies to be restricted to Spanish goods brought in on Spanish ships are short-sighted. Because of the monopoly, the colonists pay high prices for inferior goods and receive unnaturally low prices for their exports of furs, raw wood, indigo, and dyestuffs. France had the same policies, but they were never strictly imposed, and so were livable. Spain has begun in the last three or four years to relax its grip on trade in its other colonies, but it will be some time before the situation in Louisiana will be stable enough to do the same here. In the meantime, the success that O'Reilly has had in shutting off the routes of illicit trade has caused the recent rise in piracy, and the smuggling that goes with it."

"You are actually criticizing the great O'Reilly! I can't believe it." That he was repeating what she already knew was not so important as this fact.

"I'm not criticizing his actions; as I've pointed out before, he is only following orders. But I can't agree with the result."

"Surely all the man has to do is call in a few patrols, be less vigilant."

"Unfortunately, that is not in his code. To him, an order is something to be carried out as quickly and completely as possible."

"So I perceive," she said with bitterness etching her tone. "And it makes no difference if human lives are at stake."

Silence encroached, thickening, clogging the air. Morgan drew a deep breath and let it out slowly. "Attorney General Don Felix del Rey made his summation for the prosecution today."

"Does that mean," Félicité asked, her voice sounding strange to her own ears, "that the trial is over?"

"As nearly as makes no difference. The judges will hear the final arguments by the attorneys for the defense. Since it will be a repeat of what has been said over and over again that should not take long. The court will then deliberate and hand down judgment."

"When—when should we hear?"

"A couple of days, three, four at the most."

"There can be little doubt that the verdict will be guilty?"

"I—" he began, then stopped, saying abruptly, "No."

"What will happen? To the others, I mean."

He sent her a swift look, as if surprised that she seemed not to doubt the fate of her father. "That is up to O'Reilly. The responsibility for the final sentencing is his."

"They say his orders are to hang them all, to make an example of the twelve he holds."

"It's possible. I can't say."

"Can't, or won't?" When he did not answer, she moved to stand beside him on the opposite side of the doorway. Clenching her fingers in the damask of the portieres, she whispered, "Why? Why?"

"Félicité," he began, an uncharacteristic hesitation in his voice.

"Oh, don't tell me! I know the reasons, but they don't matter. It's so senseless, so stupid to destroy people's lives in this way, to treat respectable men like common thieves and murderers. Having reasons doesn't make it right."

"No, and yet you don't condemn the smugglers and the corsairs in the gulf, simply because they have hard economic reasons for their misdeeds."

"I certainly don't condone what they do. And yet, if I were a man just now, the thought of striking a blow against some Spanish ship laden with booty stolen in the New World would be nigh irresistible."

"At least you are honest."

The ironic amusement in his tone encouraged her. "About the men on trial, don't you think King Carlos would listen if O'Reilly sent a report recommending leniency, saying how quiet the countryside is, how cooperative the attitude of the townspeople? Perhaps the orders could be changed?"

"Are you suggesting that I approach the governor-general with this recommendation?"

"I don't see why not."

"It will do no good," he said, his words blunt.

"How can you tell until you have tried?"

"I have tried, as have any number of weeping mothers and wives, staid merchants, and concerned priests. In every case, O'Reilly has refused to consider that course. It is not the place of a mere general, even one who once saved the life of the king in a Madrid street riot, to question the orders handed down to him by the crown. Royalty seldom changes its mind, even when an error is pointed out."

Félicité slanted him a glance tinged with wonder. What had caused this softening of his attitude? Could it be that his sympathy for the cause of the people of Louisiana had been brought about by the efforts of Ashanti and herself? It was ridiculous, considering the trouble she had been put to, that for some strange reason she hoped it was not so.

"Why do you say that?" she asked. "Why are you no longer defending your commander and his Spanish master?"

"A number of reasons," he answered, staring out over the balcony into the gathering dusk. "The men caught in this trap of international laws should have known better. Regardless, when you look around at how they lived, clinging to their pride and the customs of the land from which they came while barely scratching out a living, it's easy to see how the question of their nationality would be the cause of strong feeling. When you are here in this place, Europe with its pride and civilized posturing, its class structure, its haves and have-nots, pomp and squalor, seems so far away. Its laws seem more likely to strangle a colony, cutting off its life's blood, than to help it grow strong. Here, a title and the centuries of privilege that go with it are useless. What counts are a man's muscles and his brains, aided by the will to drive them and to rely upon himself. It isn't difficult to see how men with those qualities would band together, when the cause arises, for their own benefit. In a strange new country, almost another world like this, the craving for freedom and the urge to govern themselves for their own profit seems natural—just as it is natural for the Old World to prevent it. This small rebellion here may be over for now, but I can't help wondering how long it will be before the same impulse overtakes men again, here or in some other colony.''

''I see. As a future landowner you begin to recognize the problems we have dealt with here for years.''

''There may be some truth in that,'' he agreed. ''But I have also seen the trouble and pain the arrest of these men has brought to those who—who care for them. It sometimes seems, as the petitioners come and go at the governor's house, the wives, mothers, daughters, sons, uncles, aunts, cousins, nieces and nephews, grandparents, even godparents and godchildren, that the entire community is united in a terrible, spreading grief.''

''Morgan,'' she began, but he went on, the words falling relentlessly from his lips. ''We all feel it, every man from the arid and hungry provinces of Spain, every misbegotten mercenary from whatever corner of the earth spawned him, and the worst of it is, there is nothing we can do.''

She moved toward him then, reaching out to place her hand on his arm. He turned to pull her against him, holding her in a passionless embrace that offered only comfort, a refuge from her ceaseless fears. With her head resting against the firmness of his chest, Félicité closed her eyes, unresisting, oddly, disturbingly content in the strong circle of his arms.

Four days later, on the morning of October 24, 1769, the news raced through the town that the Spanish court on this day would hand down judgment. It would be pronounced and signed by O'Reilly, who would immediately thereafter read the sentences to be meted out, should any be necessary. The last was always added in a pathetic pretense that the Spanish tribunal was a just one.

Félicité spent the morning at the Church of St. Louis upon her knees. She was not alone. By the flickering light of votive candles there were many bowed heads to be seen, and the gentle clack and clatter of rosaries passing through trembling fingers was loud in the stillness. Above them, the carved figure of the Christ on the cross behind the altar gazed down with serene eyes from a face spent with torment.

It was not the first time Félicité had come, not the first time she had stayed until her knees were sore. It was, however, the first time it had given her no consolation. And though she was grateful for the kind blessing and the soft-spoken words of comfort given by Père Dagobert, neither seemed to penetrate the haze of dread in which she moved.

With her fair hair still covered by a scarf of lawn and lace and her prayer beads clutched in one hand, she moved homeward through the streets. The Spanish soldiers were much in evidence today. A patrol crossed an intersection in front of her, and a pair of officers, apparently out for an aimless stroll, though their watch around them was sharp, stepped aside for her passing. Glancing at them, Félicité thought of Juan Sebastian Unzaga and his offer of aid. She had not seen him since that time except at a distance, nor had she been troubled by the attention of any other Spanish soldier, officer or enlisted man. She had come slowly to understand that this was due to her unofficial position as mistress to Colonel McCormack. As O'Reilly's grip had tightened upon the town, and his influence, prodded by the progress of the trial, had grown, the importance of his second-in-command had also come gradually to the fore. No merchant and his wife, no planter, no lowly vendor of fruits and shellfish in the markets, now dared offend such a personage by insulting his woman. Her passage through the streets had not become much easier, however, for she was still bombarded by their cold hostility, cut off in her fears from the support and understanding of those who should have shared them. From all this Morgan could not protect her, though from the tenor of his words at times she thought he realized her loss and the distress it caused her.

Ashanti was in the kitchen when Félicité reached the Lafargue house. She could hear her scolding the cook, her way of releasing the tension of the waiting. With weighted footsteps, Félicité climbed the stairs. She pushed open the door, removing her scarf as she crossed the *salle* to her room. Folding it, she put it away in the armoire with her rosary, then tucked a few stray hairs into her high chignon in front of the polished steel mirror. With her head still bent, trying to catch a fine curl with an uncooperative pin, she turned toward the doorway. She would join the others in the kitchen. Perhaps if she kept busy, she would not have time to think.

Without warning, a man stepped from behind the door-frame to block her path. She halted, a startled gasp catching in her throat. An instant later, her eyes widened in recognition. "Valcour!"

"Oh, yes, it is I, your long-lost and unlamented brother. Not, regrettably, your lover." He threw at her the bunched-up shirt he held in his hand, one much larger than any he himself had ever worn. It struck her breast and spilled to the floor in a pile of crumpled linen.

Félicité stared at him for the space of a heartbeat, stared at the malevolent light in his yellow-brown eyes, and the smile that twisted his thin lips. For that length of time something undefined but ugly hung between them. She moistened her lips that were suddenly dry. "Where—did you come from, and—and what do you mean sneaking up on me like that?"

"Where I came from, I do not care to say. As to the rest, I was not anxious to meet Ashanti. I wouldn't put it past that black bitch to turn me in to the Spaniards. But enough. What I want to know, my darling sister, is why you have turned yourself into a strumpet."

"I am no such thing!"

"No? Deny if you can that you are living here out of wedlock with that turncoat son of an Irish bitch. Only think, I actually ran the first man to tell me of it through. Isn't that a fine jest? But it was not enough to keep you from being known all over town as McCormack's doxy."

He fondled the hilt of his rapier as a woman might handle a necklace she particularly enjoyed wearing. He was thinner than when last she had seen him, and he wore neither facial powder nor patches. His pockmarked skin, without such adornment, was brown with a yellowish undertone that made it near the color of his eyes, an indication that he had been much in the sun. His voice was sharper, if that were possible, with a more cutting edge of insult. But the changes did not stop there. Over a gray-white bagwig he wore a black hat with a plume encircling the crown and the brim fastened on one side by a jeweled pin. His coat was of green velvet of a sable darkness, heavy with silver braiding. It was worn over a shirt with lace-edged ruffles, though without either cravat or waistcoat. A gold sash bound his narrow waist, and his breeches were tucked into boots of soft cordovan leather dyed a discolored green.

"Before you heap more names upon me I don't deserve," Félicité said with a lift of her chin, "and before you injure other blameless men, perhaps I had better tell you that it is your doing I am in this position."

"Mine?" he snapped, his eyes narrowing. "How so?"

"If you had not been so stupid as to try to kill Morgan here at this very house, I would not have become embroiled in your ill-considered attack. Morgan would not, then, have considered me a part of the attempt, and for my apparent betrayal, forced his way into my house, my room, and my bed."

"You defend him?" Valcour queried in contempt.

"Never! Neither will I absolve you of the portion of the blame that is rightfully yours."

He ignored her words. "It seems to me the groundwork for what you call your position was laid down before I drew sword against the Irishman. I remember a bargain you made; your company for your father's life."

Félicité realized suddenly that for all the years that Olivier Lafargue had called Valcour his son, her adoptive brother had never given him the name of father, always speaking of him as Félicité's father alone, which of course he was. She brushed away the irritating insight. "What of it?"

"It is plain to me that your precious Morgan intended from the start to have you where you are now, his creature, his plaything between the sheets, his—daughter of joy."

His eyes roved over her, resting with indecent speculation on the curves of her breasts. Félicité was aware of the brush of crawling distaste. "That isn't true!"

"How can you deny it? It is perfectly plain that he never had the least intention of helping your father, that he meant to use your soft white body to slake his desire while he did nothing in return. For proof you have only to look at what has happened today. Have not all of the conspirators, all, been found guilty?''

"What?" she whispered.

"Had you not heard?" Valcour's tone was all innocence.

"And what of the sentences? What was given to my father?"

"I know not. Some were sentenced to be hanged, some given life imprisonment, others lesser punishments. My informant did not recall the names."

"My father will have one of the shorter prison terms, you will see," she said, desperation threading her voice.

"Such trust," he sneered. "To my mind it can mean only one thing. You are enamored of this hired soldier who deflowered you. How degrading. And how lost in the throes of passion you will be if your father has happened to draw the shorter term."

"That is so ludicrous, so insulting, that it doesn't deserve an answer! But at least Morgan has been man enough to keep his side of the bargain, at least he has tried to help my father. That is something you have certainly never done, Valcour Murat, with your running and hiding, your scraping up of money by the illegal sale of your manservant, and your cowardly theft in the night of my father's small hoard of gold. How dare you deny him the comfort that it might have bought as he rotted in his cell these many weeks while you, who should have shared his prison, slunk away to enjoy your freedom? Oh!''

He slapped her, reaching out with casual viciousness to crack his hand along the side of her face. She spun backward with tears starting from her eyes and the taste of blood in her mouth where her teeth had cut the inside of her cheek.

He stalked forward to stand over her, his voice hissing as he spoke. "Whore! I will make you sorry you ever said such words. I will make you weep with remorse that you ever spread your legs for Morgan McCormack, that you were born a woman, the daughter of your father. And one day I will make you curse yourself for ever feeling one shred of emotion for any other man!"

His footsteps retreated. The door crashed to behind him. Valcour was gone, and yet it was a long time before Félicité could drop the hands that covered her face, or shut out the frenzied shouts that rang in her ears with the sound of a vow.

Chapter 10

*F*élicité *had regained* some semblance of composure by the time Morgan returned later that evening. By then also, the names of the five men who were to die had been whispered from house to house, carried by the servants as well as their masters, until there was not a soul in New Orleans who could not have recited them.

Lafrénière, Noyan, Caresse, Marquis, Milhet the younger.

As Morgan entered, Félicité came to her feet, her velvet-brown eyes searching his face. She moved forward a few steps. Her voice was quiet, well controlled, as she spoke. "It's true, then?"

"I suppose it depends on what you mean. The verdict was guilty."

"The sentences?"

"Five are to be led to the public square on asses, there to be hanged. It might have been six, but the death of Villeré by apoplexy will be allowed to count for one."

"I thought he was bayoneted by his guards."

"The official version is apoplexy," he corrected with savage irony. "His memory, incidentally, has been officially condemned by the court to eternal infamy. You realize that this dead man, for the sake of the accusation impugning his honor, was represented during the trial by an attorney to his memory?''

Had that ludicrous provision been brought about by meticulous spite, or meticulous fairness? It was impossible to decide, and there were other, more important considerations than either the manner of his death or the treatment of it.

''And the others?''

His voice rough, unencouraging, he answered, ''Of the remaining seven, one received life imprisonment, two were given ten years, and four drew six years each, plus in every case confiscation of their property to the profit of the king, and perpetual banishment from the dominions of Spain. For all other inhabitants of the colony a blanket pardon has been issued, its purpose being to end this affair.''

''What—what of my father?''

''Six years at El Morro Fortress on the island of Cuba.''

She did not realize she had been holding her breath until she released it on a shuddering sigh. Six years. Could Olivier Lafargue with his uncertain health survive so long? ''El Morro? The place is little more than a dungeon.''

''It isn't pleasant, but prisons aren't supposed to be.'' He turned from her, shrugging from his coat. ''At least he will be alive long enough for appeals to be made for clemency. That is more than can be said for the five who will hang tomorrow.''

''Tomorrow! But why such haste?'' She moved after him as he walked into the bedchamber and flung his coat onto the bed.

''The sooner it's done, the sooner the thing will be over. It can be put behind us while the business of improving the colony is taken firmly in hand.''

''And O'Reilly will no longer have to listen to the supplications of the people of New Orleans.''

''That too.''

''Dear God!'' she exclaimed with suppressed violence. A few quick steps took her to the window, where she breathed deep of the evening air with one fist resting on the sill.

There was a quiet rustle of clothing as Morgan came to stand behind her. ''It isn't enough, is it? Nothing short of freedom for your father was ever going to be enough.''

"You have kept your part of the bargain," she said, her voice tight.

"The bargain be damned!" He caught her arm, swinging her to face him. "It's you I am concerned about."

"You needn't be. Like the others, I will survive."

"But how? With what damage to pride and spirit? Félicité—"

What he might have said then she could only guess, for Pepe appeared in the open doorway and the moment passed. Still, the residue of some soft and impulsive inclination lingered between them. It was enough so that later in the silence of the night as they lay side by side in bed, Félicité could stretch her hand across the space that separated them and spread her fingers over his chest in a caress that was also an invitation.

He went still. She could feel the jarring of his heart against her palm, though if he breathed she could not discern it. She allowed her touch to slide downward through the furring of hair on his chest, over the ridged hardness of his abdomen to the flatness of his belly. He inhaled then, slow and deep. Her daring was fueled by gratitude and the obligation of a debt of honor, and yet there ran beneath it a quickening of anticipation. She eased closer, raising to one elbow above him so that the honey-gold curtain of her hair, silken and scented, swung around them. She touched her lips to his mouth as her fingertips brushed the heated rigidity of his maleness.

He lifted a hand, twining his fingers in her hair. His other arm encircled her, his hand resting lightly on her hip. Sweet and throbbing languor suffused them as they pressed closer in the clouded blackness of the night. With mingled breaths and exquisite care, they explored blind sensation until their blood pulsed with the warmth and mystery of it. Holding her to him, he entered her, forging the bond of pleasure between them. Together they moved, reaching toward a dark and mindless rapture. Their thrusts became more frenzied, and his arms like corded steel grasping Félicité, he rolled over her, plunging deep, sending the rippling shock waves of piercing pleasure along her nerves.

She felt the gathering of somber forces, the dim surging of an opaque and turbulent ecstasy. It mounted higher, carrying her toward a shadowed explosion of being. It filled her, surrounded her, blotting out the trivial madness of the world, drawing her into its straining, night-black heart. She gripped his shoulders, spreading her hands over the scars that ridged the muscles of his back, and the one thing that made it supportable, that allowed her to pass through the fathomless depths unscathed, was the fact that she was not alone.

Afterward, they lay with their limbs entangled and their breathing rasping in labored gasps. With her eyes bleak and unseeing, Félicité felt the slow shift of dismay move through her. How simple she had pictured the joining of a man and woman. Perhaps it was for some. Perhaps under different circumstances, with another man, at another time, it would be for her. But for now and for her, with the Spanish-Irish mercenary Morgan McCormack, the desire of the flesh was a ravaging thing. It did not help to know that the taint which turned it from something to be enjoyed to a thing to be endured came from within herself. Excuse enough for it could be found and more. Resentment played its part, as did hate and fear. But what could change it? Would it ever change?

Sleep did not come easy. It had to be wooed with stillness and tight-lidded concentration. Even when it came, it was not restful, but was instead plagued with desolating and exhausting dreams. It was almost a relief when daylight began to seep into the room. That Morgan felt the same was proved by the irritable energy with which he wrenched out of bed and began to pull on his uniform.

It was unusual for him to put on his sword before breakfast. When he picked it up and began to buckle it about him, she said, "You are leaving so early?"

"I must. O'Reilly has ordered every man on duty for today. There will be extra patrols, and special details to be detached to the barracks prison and the Place d'Armes."

Félicité sat up, pulling the sheet up over her breasts.

"Surely he doesn't expect an uprising of townspeople?"

"It's always a possibility. Even the few Spanish officials left behind from Ulloa's brief tenure, Navarro, Gayarre, and Loyola, sympathize with the prisoners."

"This will be a—a public execution?" she asked, forcing hardness into her tones.

He adjusted the set of his sword and picked up his coat. "How else is the point, that of the unhealthiness of defying Spanish authority, to be made?"

"Of course. And the appointed time should, therefore, be when the greatest number of people can be present?"

"The time has not been set. The black man who usually performs the office of hangman has refused, and another will have to be found. You don't intend to be present?"

"Why not? These men were my father's friends."

"It will hardly be a pleasant spectacle for a lady."

The gaze she turned upon him was cold. "If I go, it will not be for the spectacle. It will be for the reason one sits beside the bed of a dying man, so he will not be alone."

"As you wish," he answered, reaching to take his tricorne from the back of the chair. He stood for a long moment turning it in his hands, his brooding gaze following its banding of gold braid.

If he had been debating a further warning, he thought better of it. Stepping to the bed, he pressed a hard kiss to her mouth, then turned his broad back and walked from the room.

The endless, racking hours of that day passed. More than once Félicité sent the maid, Marie, to the square before the church to see what was going forward. The report all through the morning and into the afternoon was the same: nothing, no activity. The delay in the proceedings was due to the search for a substitute hangman. None being found, it was decided just before noon that the sentence would be changed to death by firing squad, and O'Reilly so signed the proper orders.

The girl returned with another tidbit of information. It was being said that O'Reilly, pricked perhaps by conscience or else the need to prove himself humane, had let it be known that he would not be displeased if Noyan, the nephew of Bienville, should disappear from his cell. Heroically, Jean Baptiste Noyan had refused to cooperate with such a dishonorable release while his fellow countrymen remained behind; he would live or die with his friends.

It would have been difficult to remain ignorant of the

175

events when they were finally set in motion. The tramp of soldiers converging on the square, the shouting of orders, was enough to alert all but the deaf and blind. A short time later came the slow and regular thump of drums as the men were transferred from the old French barracks to the square. The sound grew louder, echoing through the streets of the town, rebounding from the stockade walls that surrounded it. There had not been much movement in the narrow thoroughfares all that long day. Now it ceased entirely as people went in and shut their doors. In the sullen quiet Félicité's footsteps, as with Ashanti beside her she hurried toward the Place d'Armes, had a hollow clatter that was unnaturally loud. She seemed to feel the contemptuous stares of hundreds of eyes watching her from behind closed shutters.

She was not entirely alone when she reached the open square. Though the crowd was sparse, two score or more of people stood in the warm autumn sun, their silence complete, their stillness absolute. Every eye was turned toward the five men being led, mounted on asses, toward them along the street. Their arms were pinioned behind their backs, and flanking them on either side was a heavy escort of grenadiers.

To one side stood O'Reilly, his bearing in his uniform glittering with braid and honors one of stiff attention. Near him, on his right hand, were the mayor of the town and a few other officials. On his left was Lieutenant Colonel Morgan McCormack, and behind them stood a military escort, two men of which bore the silver maces of the governor-general's office.

On the parade ground directly before the officials was a great body of Spanish troops some thousand strong. Drawn up in a square around the edges of the Place d'Armes, they had left a hollow opening in their center. Features wooden, stares impassive, they stood in a time-honored battle formation that was a bulwark against the townspeople as well as a living prison for the condemned men.

The prisoners came to a halt. They were assisted to dismount, and in single file were marched into the middle of the square. A court clerk came forward, and with his papers rattling gently in the warm breeze, read in Spanish the sentence that had been proclaimed. It was then repeated in French. That done, a copy was placed in the hands of a public crier, who, with a look both stern and self-important, carried it around, bellowing out the words to the troops and to the gathered crowd.

When the last syllable of his loud, clear voice had died away, a platoon of men were ordered forward. The prisoners were forced to kneel, facing away from the detail. The sword of the officer in command rasped from its scabbard. He called an order, and the men presented their muskets, already loaded with powder and patch, then lifted them to arm's length. The officer stretched out his sword arm, barked an order, then let the blade fall.

A fusillade of shots rang out. Dark stains bloomed with the sheen of blood on the clothing of the men. They toppled forward, twitched with the involuntary jerking of muscles, then lay still. They had spoken no word, had shown no sign of fear and trembling. Their quiet and unpretentious fortitude in the face of useless, inglorious death was a pitiable thing. And yet, it was also the single element that made the entire fiasco bearable.

Félicité did not expect Morgan to return to the house until late. Now, when the executions had been carried out, might be the time when the malcontents, the remnants of the men who had been a party to the original conspiracy, would feel compelled to retaliate, striking a final blow for their martyred friends. Orders had gone out that all places selling strong drink be closed, as well as all coffee houses, gaming halls, and other places of meeting or vice. Seeing that these instructions were met would be the responsibility of the military rather than the civilian government during this period of martial law, and therefore Morgan's responsibility. It was unthinkable that the colonel, even knowing her distress over the events of the day, should leave his post. It was, therefore, alarming to hear his footsteps on the stairs less than an hour after her own return.

She had been lying down, thinking of Cuba, wondering how she was to reach the island, if she could possibly arrange transportation at the same time as her father, and if there was any chance that Morgan might receive a transfer of duty to Havana that would allow him to take her with him. Now she slid from the bed, shaking the wrinkles from her skirt. Without bothering to search for the slippers she had kicked off when she lay down, she padded into the *salle*.

Morgan stood in the center of the room, a bundle in the curve of his arm. His face was drawn as he turned, and in his eyes was dull emerald finality.

She stopped, one hand on the back of a carved cypress chair. "What is it? Why have you come back?"

"Sit down, Félicité," he said, his voice carrying the expressionless strength of a command.

"Why?" she asked. Receiving no answer, finding none in his features, she allowed her gaze to drop to the parcel he carried. Of an awkward size and shape, it seemed to be several items wrapped in a coat. It was an instant before recognition came. She lifted her eyes to meet his once more, then with limbs grown heavy and clumsy, she moved to drop down upon the chair.

Morgan stepped toward her. Going to one knee, he laid the things he carried in her lap. The coat of snuff-brown velvet fell open to reveal a pair of shoes, a snuffbox with a cloisonné lid, a bound copy of Virgil, a book of poems, and a sword. The things, well worn, infinitely dear, were the belongings of Olivier Lafargue. She reached out to touch them with hesitant fingers.

"Félicité," Morgan said, his deep voice quiet, "though it gives me pain, I must tell you that your father is dead."

"Dead?" she asked, her voice dull. "But how? How can he be? His sentence was for six years only."

"He died by his own hand. Who can say why? Prison does strange things to the minds of men."

She raised her lashes, caught by a faint hint of evasion in his words. "How did it happen?"

"What do details matter?" he asked, drawing back. "It happened. That's all."

"No, it isn't," she said sharply. "I have to know." The thought that he might be keeping something from her, and of the form that omission could take, was like a goad.

"Don't do this, Félicité. Remember him as you saw him last and be content."

Her lips tightened. "Was he killed by his guards? Was he bayoneted like Villeré?"

"No. I told you, he killed himself during the night."

"That was convenient, wasn't it? Perhaps it was planned that way? Perhaps he even had help? That would make me a fine dupe, wouldn't it, trading my favors for my father's life while all the time you meant discreetly to do away with him? Was the idea yours, or was it O'Reilly's? Or did you ever speak to the governor-general at all?"

"Enough! You don't know what you are saying."

"Don't I? Last night while I slept in your bed my father died in his cell in some strange way. Nearly twenty-four hours have passed; in the meantime five of his friends have been shot, and only now am I told my father is not among the living. All this, and you won't explain. What else am I to think?"

"Think what you please, but these are the facts. Last night, Olivier Lafargue lost his grip on reason for a flicker of time and hanged himself with the cord used by someone to tie a parcel of clean linen. No one else touched him until they cut him down this morning and buried him in an unhallowed grave. No one."

"Buried? You mean—that has already been done?" She stared at him with loathing.

"It was, by my orders. Death by hanging is not an easy one. I thought to spare you the sight of it."

"You ordered the disposal of my father's body without consulting me, without giving me the chance to lay him out or dress him in funeral vestments, without allowing his neighbors and friends, to say nothing of me, to say their farewells? Without the blessing of a priest or a mass for his soul?"

"He was a suicide, Félicité. Religious rites would have been denied him, as would burial in consecrated ground."

"And so you threw him into a hole and shoveled the dirt over him as you would an animal!"

"Félicité, no," he said, trying to catch her hands. "Don't torment yourself like this. What happened was unavoidable, something to be accepted and done with as quietly and swiftly as possible.''

She struck out at him, knocking his fingers aside. "Leave me alone," she cried. "Get out. Get out and leave me alone!''

He rose to his feet, staring down at her a long moment before he said, "I'll send Ashanti to you.''

"I need no one," she said fiercely. "No one.''

"Nevertheless." His footsteps retreated to the doorway, where he stopped and turned back. "No matter what you think, Félicité, I am sorry.''

"I don't need your pity," she flung at him, his figure wavering with the film of tears that rose before her eyes. "And since my father is dead, I am free to tell you that I despise you. Never have I ever hated anyone as much as I hate you!''

"I know that," he said, his voice a rustle of sound. "I have always known that.''

"If that's so, then you will know not to come back here again, ever!''

He made no reply, but went out, closing the door quietly behind him.

The light was fading from the sky when Félicité, with Ashanti beside her carrying a massed bouquet of brilliant autumn leaves, found the place where Olivier Lafargue had been laid to rest. Located beyond the low palisade that enclosed the cemetery of St. Louis, it was unmarked except for a large barrel sitting on the heap of mud that mounded it. The rains of the last few weeks had raised the water table of the marshy ground to the point where it was necessary to weight the coffin to make it stay in the water-filled grave. From the splinters of wood that lay nearby she thought the barrel of iron ingots might not have been enough, that the gravediggers might have had to knock holes in the casket to keep it below ground. Even so, there was water puddled around the edges of the mound.

Despite the mud and wet, Félicité knelt and bowed her head to pray, with tears creeping down her face. She had already spoken to Père Dagobert, wringing from him a promise to say a mass for the repose of her father's soul in disregard of the irregularity. There was nothing more to be done.

With a soft murmur Ashanti dropped down beside Félicité. She passed the bright-colored leaves she held to her mistress, who placed them gently at the head of the grave. Time stretched. A dog barked somewhere, and an anxious mother called. Evening was fast approaching. Already one or two candles had been lit, their glow reaching yellow fingers into the gray twilight.

With stiff reluctance, Félicité came to her feet. Ignoring the stain on her gown, she stood staring down at the heaped, soggy earth. Her thoughts were chaotic, weighted with anger and despair. She was alone now. Tomorrow or the next day they would come to confiscate her belongings, to round up the servants and take them away in chains to be sold. The plans she had put off so long would have to be made. She would have to find somewhere to go, though where that might be, she could not think. As the former mistress of a Spanish officer, the daughter of a suicide and a criminal, there was no one who would take her in. So blackened was her character that the nuns of the Ursuline might even spurn her.

What was there for her, then? Must she walk the streets to fall prey to some soldier or drunken dandy, to have her skirts slung above her head in some dark side street? There was Juan Sebastian Unzaga, but would he want her now? And when he was through, would she return to the streets, coming finally to accepting coins for the one commodity she had to sell? Or would she decide in all cynical practicality that if such was to be her occupation she might as well have the comfort and protection of one of the brothels that sat discreetly on the narrow streets near the river, at least until she grew too old and diseased to earn her keep?

The single thing that might keep her from that course was her own self. When all was said, she was the only person on whom she could ever afford to depend. Women who lived with men, who leaned on them, looking to them for their lives and livelihood, whether fathers, brothers, husbands, or lovers, were deluded. Men died, they changed, they left or were forced to leave. Without meaning to, perhaps, they encouraged females to look to them for support, and when the dependence was complete, when the natural self-reliance of female childhood had been submerged in willing servitude, the support might be unthinkingly removed. The woman who could not stand alone was like a crippled beggar, dependent always on the indifferent kindness of men. Those who sought their security in such would never find it.

"Well met, my dear Félicité. I thought I might find you here."

Félicité whirled to face her brother, standing a few feet away. So engrossed had she been in her thoughts that she had not heard his approach. "You startled me."

"A habit of mine, it seems. My apologies, fair sister, it was not my intention. I wanted only to come close enough to speak, to have you hear me out before you turn your back as doubtless I deserve."

How could she berate him over her father's grave? She made a weary gesture. "There is no need."

"You are all that is most gracious and kind, Félicité, but I must speak. In my concern, and because of the harrowing events of the last months, I lost my temper. I would cut off my arm if it would serve to earn your forgiveness for striking you. I never meant to hurt you."

"Consider it forgotten."

"If the words you speak are from the heart rather than the mouthings of courtesy, then perhaps you will permit me to put forth a suggestion once again that I broached some time ago?"

Ashanti, standing close beside Félicité, stirred, sending her a warning glance. Félicité was mindful of it, and yet this Valcour, subdued, consciously gracious, was the one she remembered best, her companion from childhood who had never harmed her before, though he might visit sharp reprisals upon others.

"I can't remember a time when lack of my permission stopped you," she ventured, curious, though wary.

"I realize the hours are not long since your father's death, and you have not had time to consider what you mean to do, but I would like once again to beg you to come to France, with me.''

"To France? I thought you must have given up that idea long ago.''

"Never. I only waited, remaining not far away, until such time as you could come with me. That time is now. We can leave tonight if you will only agree.''

"Tonight? But why so quickly?''

"There is nothing to hold us here, either you or myself. It was a great misfortune that your father had to learn of what you had done to save him. Greater still was the tragedy of how he went about setting you free of your obligation to the turncoat colonel, but—''

"Wait! What did you say?''

"But *ma chère,* surely you knew?'' He lifted a brow, all frowning puzzlement.

"No. No, I wasn't told.''

"One sees why, of course, but I don't see how they could keep it from you. It was told me by the guard whom I questioned concerning your father's death. How he discovered your secret, no one knows, but last evening he was most despondent. He mentioned his daughter and the sacrifice she had made. And then this morning, he was dead.''

A great numbness beyond tears crept over Félicité. So deep was her feeling of unreality that she scarcely heard Ashanti as she whispered, "Don't listen to him, mam'selle. Don't listen.''

"What a great pity it would be if the action your father took to set you free was in vain,'' Valcour went on. "I am sure that with his great love of France he would say to you, 'Leave Spanish New Orleans, leave it and the past behind, go where you can forget and start anew.' ''

Morgan had known why her father had killed himself, he had known and would not tell her rather than pass to her the burden of guilt she had been bequeathed. He had accepted her insults, shouldering the entire blame himself. And in return he had had from her a hard and hateful dismissal. He had not objected. That being the case, it seemed he might well have been glad of it, glad to have her out of his life.

"But what would I do in France?" she asked, the look in her eyes dazed.

"You need not worry. I have money enough for our needs for several weeks, even months if necessary. After that, I have ideas in plenty. There will be no necessity for you to do anything except come. The days ahead will be filled with pleasure and gaiety."

"Pleasure?" she queried as if she had never heard the word. "I must go into mourning for my father."

"Of course," he said, his tone slightly impatient. "But when that time is past, there will be all the wonders of Paris to see. Together we shall storm the citadel of the court of Versailles, you with your beauty and I with my brains. And we will neither of us be—alone."

It was that unaccustomed descent into sentiment that decided her. This was Valcour, the man she had laughed and teased with and with whom she had played tricks upon the servants and neighbors. He wanted and needed her with him to start over in their mother country. He was offering her nothing less than a chance for a new life, and in addition that greatest of all boons, forgetfulness. She took a deep breath. "If we are to leave tonight, we must hurry."

"No, mam'selle, this is madness," Ashanti said, but Félicité did not hear.

Valcour insisted on returning with them to supervise Félicité's packing. To her protest that he would be arrested, he reminded her with cool irony of the pardon for all those not already caught in Spanish toils.

At the house, he took command. She could take no more than two gowns, and two sets of underclothing. Anything else would be unnecessary; they would buy what was needed when they reached Paris. In the meantime, it might well cause a hue and cry; she must remember that legally she was stealing from the Lafargue estate if she took so much as a handkerchief. So strict was he, when it came to decisions over what she could and could not take, that it was a relief when he asked what had been done with the remainder of his own wardrobe that had been left behind, and on being told, went away to search for it.

Her relief was short-lived. He returned almost at once carrying a pair of breeches and a shirt with a coat and waistcoat over his arm. The trip in an open boat would not be pleasant, as it wound its way 150 miles or more through the bayous to the ship waiting in a secluded bay near the mouth of the river, he said. There would hardly be room for her, much less her skirts and panniers. Moreover, the less attention they attracted when they went through the gates of the town, the better it would be. There was no time to stand arguing, or those self-same gates would be closed for the night. She must array herself as a young gentleman without argument.

A short time later, dressed in masculine attire, with her hair plaited into a queue topped by a tricorne, wearing her most somber pair of shoes and carrying a cane, she was ready. Valcour picked up her bundle, but she took it from him.

"A man does not carry a burden for another," she said.

"Quite right." Holding the door, he gave her a thin smile and bowed her through. "This," he said with a strange whimsy, "is the last token of respect you can expect from me."

Ashanti had disappeared toward her own room when they had reached the house. Now she stepped from the darkness at the foot of the stairs to accost them.

"Mam'selle," she said, "I must come with you."

A spasm of distress crossed Félicité's face. "But Ashanti, I thought you understood—"

"I do. I know that I have become a slave of the Spaniards to be sold at public auction, but if I am caught with you I will say I ran away, that in effect I stole myself. And if no one stops us, it will not matter."

"I wish you could come, really I do. But we must go through the gate. If two young men are seen with a servant girl it will look odd."

"Not so odd as you might think, mam'selle, especially if I giggle and press close to you. But if you would prefer, and if you would give me words in writing that say I have your leave to be on the roads at night and a purpose, then I will make my way through the gate alone and join you later."

Félicité glanced at Valcour. "Is there room in the boat?"

"Little enough," Valcour said, his narrow gaze on the maid.

"Please, could we take her? It would mean so much."

"I will not get in the way, M'sieu Valcour," Ashanti assured him, her black eyes meeting his squarely. "I will be most useful, and—valuable."

"Valuable," Valcour mused, then glanced at Félicité. "I suppose it could not hurt to have an extra piece of movable property."

Félicité frowned. Was he suggesting that they might sell Ashanti at some later date? She could never do that, not even if in dire need, not ever. "But Valcour," she began.

"A most wise thought," the maid murmured.

"Let us go, then," Valcour said. "We have wasted enough time already."

Despite the minutes they had spent teasing themselves over it, they were passed through the Tchoupitoulas gate without problems. The guard barely glanced at Ashanti. His problem this night was apparently not with those few leaving the city, but with those who wished to come in. He was there to prevent the gathering of large, angry groups, not to interfere with the homeward journey of planters who lived outside the wall of the town.

The small boat, little more than a canoe, that was to take them seaward was in its appointed place. The man guarding it stepped out of the dank and insect-infested darkness to guide them to it. Félicité and Ashanti stepped in. The guard, a gruff, bearded bear of a man with the accent of Marseilles, picked up a paddle in the prow, and Valcour, after pushing them off, settled into the stern. In silence, they began the long trip to the gulf.

The bayou on which they traveled wound past the scattered homes of planters, a few glowing like beacons with candlelight, though most were shuttered and still. A barking dog chased them, keeping pace along the bank for what seemed like miles, but was probably no more than a few yards. Cattle lowed. Frogs disturbed by their gliding passage plopped into the water with noisy alarm. A family of ducks startled at the

186

water's edge rose with the muffled flapping of wings. After a time, they ducked to glide beneath a bridge. Beyond that landmark, a wilderness of swampland closed in around them, smothering, concealing.

Félicité lay back against her bundle of clothing and what seemed to be a coil of rope covered by canvas. Above her she could see the drifting canopy of the trees, moss-hung, silhouetted by the night sky with the cool glitter of stars caught in their branches. She was glad of the coat she wore against the October night, and yet she felt, in all truth, neither comfort nor discomfort, gladness nor grief. She did not feel much of anything. This state of numbness could not persist, and yet for the moment it was welcome. Soon would come the time when she must think of all that had happened, of what she was doing, and had done. Soon she would think of Morgan, of the arrogant Irish mercenary in the pay of Spain, the man who had taken her innocence in anger, who had kept her with him by threat, and let her go with compassion.

He had not known she would leave. Would he have stopped her if he had? Would he have tried? She did not know.

That part of her life was over, done. The best thing she could do would be to forget it, to wipe Morgan McCormack from her mind. It should be easy; there was nothing of the long days she had spent with him to remember except anguish and humiliation, sorrow and self-contempt. Yes, to forget was by far the wisest course.

It was not her fault that memory, raw and unappeased, could not be forced to submit to reason.

Part Two

Chapter 11

❦

The river chuckled to itself, slurping mightily at the lugger that swung on its current, attached by hawsers to trees along the bank. In the baleful glow of the ship's stern lantern, Félicité climbed the rope ladder let down over the side, following Valcour and trailed by Ashanti and their guide, the last grunting with profane impatience. The masts draped with furled sails spiked upward from the deck. As they stepped aboard they could feel the planking moving underfoot with the calm regularity of a heartbeat. Beyond the range of the flickering light were dark humps of sleeping men, their snores a raucous chorus.

They did not remain long in the open waist of the ship. Valcour refused to wait for the captain to be awakened, sending word he would see him as soon as he had settled his passengers. Morning would be time enough for the amenities for them. Ignoring the stares and lewd growls of the dog-watch over Ashanti's presence, he bustled Félicité and her maid below.

The cabin to which Valcour led the way along dim corridors was small, being no more than a cubicle with a pair of bunks against one wall, a chest, and a washstand. Félicité was in no mood or position for complaint. After spending the better part of twenty-four hours in a cramped open boat, she wanted nothing more than to stretch out on a yielding surface and let the exhaustion nipping at her heels overtake her. She could muster no reply to Valcour's sardonic good wishes for her repose, nor could she bring herself to be overly concerned as to where her brother would find a berth. She was only glad when he left them alone.

Day had not broken through the enclosing fog when she was roused by movement in the dim cabin. Her eyes were sealed with fatigue as surely as with copper coins, and the effort to prise them open was too strenuous and chancy to venture. The shout of orders in nautical parlance and the sense of shuddering life through the hull beside her were an adequate explanation. They were sailing, heading out to sea; that much sifted through the gauze of her awareness. It was enough to send her burrowing once more into the deeper layers of sleep.

She could not remain with eyelids shut and mind shuttered forever. The noises of morning gathered beyond her, and she came awake with a sudden upsweep of lashes. Ashanti stirred in the bunk above her, but Valcour, swaying slack-jawed and unwigged in a hammock, slept on.

The puzzle of it knotted her brow as she stared at the squares of refracted sunlight glittering on the wall. Crowded ships were not unusual, especially on the sort of cargo vessel that plied between Louisiana and Europe. To make a voyage as profitable as possible, the maximum amount of space was given to merchandise; it was important, and the comfort of the people who transported it was not. In most cases, only the captain had a private cabin. The two highest-ranking ship's officers beneath him usually shared the only other available. When passengers were carried, they were strictly segregated regardless of marital status, the men and boys in one set of cramped quarters, the women and girls in another. In larger ships, there might be private cabins available for a price for high-ranking personages, but on smaller ships such as this, no such were to be expected.

What then were they doing with this small cubicle to themselves, she and Ashanti? And why had Valcour invaded their female domain?

The answer to at least a part of that question was obvious after a moment's consideration. She had come aboard dressed in men's clothing. Since he was now here, it followed that he had not seen fit to reveal the fact that she was a woman. The question, then, was why? And where did that leave Ashanti, who had, to all appearances, spent the night in this cabin with two men?

She sat up, swinging her feet off the bunk. Above her, Ashanti raised herself also, and with an expressive glance at Valcour, lifted a brow to Félicité. A long glance passed between them. When Félicité swung toward Valcour again, his eyes were open and there was sardonic amusement in their light-brown depths. His gaze drifted to where the open neckline of her shirt, heavy with ruffles, had fallen open when she removed her waistcoat. The soft, blue-veined curves of her breasts were revealed, though she had fallen into the bunk fully dressed otherwise. Never, in all the years she had known Valcour, had she been so aware of the lack of blood relationship between them.

She took a deep breath. Her brown eyes level, she asked, "What is this? Why are you here?"

"How fearless of you," he drawled. "Are you sure you want to know?"

"I did ask."

"Very well. This is my cabin, by right of ownership."

"Ownership?" she parroted.

"I have a—an interest in this—the ship. That being so, it is beneath my dignity to consort with the scum that serve as sailors for her."

"That may be," she snapped, "but what kind of privacy can we have cramped together here?"

"Privacy? Who needs it? Aren't we two cavaliers traveling together, and with a wench to wait upon us?"

"Be serious, Valcour! There is no reason to carry this masquerade further."

"There's every reason, *ma chère*, as you would realize if you had paid any heed to the gallows bait that is manning this ship. You, and Ashanti of course, are the only women on board, and it is a long way to France."

"You will be here to protect me."

Mirth surfaced in his eyes, before the yellow-brown irises turned bland. Ashanti made a small, abortive gesture, though

193

she did not speak. After a moment Valcour said, "I cannot watch fifty men at one time."

"Fifty? On this small ship? Why so many?"

He shrugged, shifting his gaze to the small high grate through which fell the only light in the room. "I suppose the captain likes company."

Félicité chewed on her bottom lip. "Is it—really necessary?"

"Unless you are enthralled by the thought of being hounded over this ship like a bitch in heat."

"That's all very well, but what of Ashanti?"

His gaze barely flicked over the maid. He folded his slim fingers over his chest. "Since she is attached to us, she should be safe enough—as long as she doesn't go wandering off into any dark corners. And if she isn't, what of it?"

It was Ashanti who answered. "You need not fear for me, mam'selle. I have with me a knife. Any man who touches me can expect to lose his fingers and then—whatever else he may press upon me."

"You see?" Valcour said. "That is settled, though I must not forget to warn the crew of their danger."

To Valcour it might be the end of it, but Félicité was undecided. She had played the part of a man for only a few hours at a time, the length of an evening at most. Could she actually hold to the pretense for the weeks it would take to reach the coast of France? She did not know.

The freedom of her nankeen breeches was welcome as she climbed the gangway to the upper decks, and yet in them she felt naked. The material molded itself to the curve of her hips and the length of her thighs. Only the long skirt of her coat, swinging as she walked, concealing the too refined femininity of her form, gave her the confidence to appear in public. Appear she must. Nothing could make her seem more suspicious, more an object of speculation, than remaining below while Ashanti, in common with the other deckhands, prepared their morning meal in the brick-lined firepit. It was strictly each man, or each pair of messmates, for themselves. There was no cook, and only the captain was singled out for special service, his food being brought by his cabinboy.

Even if that had not been the case, Félicité could not have

stayed below. On the deck was the lure of the fresh salt air and the wide expanse of rolling water. Sometime during the morning they had left the muddy waters of the Mississippi behind, and followed by persistent gulls irately screaming, were now heading through turquoise shallows toward the deeper-blue ocean depths.

It was not her first voyage; she had gone once to Mobile with her father. But on that occasion they had kept to the Mississippi Sound, sailing along the coast, never venturing far beyond the sight of land. This time it would be different. Would she be a good sailor? She did not know. On that other trip she had experienced no problems, spending hour after hour at the rail, staring at the horizon, scanning the water around her. The seas could not be depended on to be calm this time. Already they were on a tack that set them heeled over, the bow rising and falling, scattering sea spume on the wind.

The slanted sails thrummed, booming now and again above her while the masts creaked and taut-stretched rigging gave out a peculiar musical hum. From the masthead fluttered and snapped the captain's private flag, a black raven clutching a skull in his claws on a red ground. Beneath the bird of prey ran the legend *Garde le Corbeau*, which translated to ''Beware the Raven.''

Félicité exchanged greetings with one or two of the seamen who chanced to pass by. Several others eyed her. They were indeed a villainous-looking crew. French, Spanish, Irish, Swedes, Lascars, English, Africans; every nationality under the sun seemed to be represented. Their faces and arms were seamed with scars; many lacked teeth; one was missing an eye and another had only one horny hand. To a man they bristled with weapons, pistols and knives as well as swords. They watched Ashanti busy about the firepit with resentment and a certain cunning lust that stretched Félicité's nerves as taut as stay strings. It was a pity Valcour had not thought to outfit her with that indispensable item of a gentleman's attire, a sword.

''*Bon jour, mon ami!*''

At the cheerful greeting, Félicité turned to behold the most congenial-looking man she had yet seen among the ill-visaged crew, though that was in some sense a comment on the quality of those thus far brought to her notice. Dark-haired, rakish, he was a well-set-up man of perhaps forty-odd years with Latin brown eyes staring from a once-handsome face marked by dissipation and the effects of the rum bottle. The warmth of his greeting and his grin were unfeigned, though there was a flicker of shrewdness in his quick scrutiny. Regardless, the return Félicité made was noncommittal.

"Permit me to introduce myself. I am Capitaine Jacques Bonhomme, *à votre service.*"

The name was a common one, the most common, in fact, in all France, so common as to be definitely suspicious. For all that, it was more than she had thought to provide for herself in her masculine personification. She executed what she hoped was a passable bow to cover her confusion.

"How do you do? I am traveling with M'sieu Murat, as you must know. My name is Lafargue. Fé—François Lafargue."

"You are a trifle young, are you not, to be seeking adventure?"

She must remember to lower the timbre of her voice. "Sometimes, M'sieu le Capitaine, the position is reversed, and adventure seeks one out."

"Ah, a beardless philosopher. That should relieve the tedium." The merry light in his eyes robbed the words of offense.

"Do you make this voyage often?"

His *joie de vie* was abruptly quenched. "I do nothing else."

"You seem to have a great many men."

"*Certainement.* A fine cutthroat crew, are they not? And I their elected captain, heigh-ho."

"Elected?"

"For my sins and my *beaux yeux*, to say nothing of my skill at navigation. I am, in addition, thought to run a lucky ship, or at least a profitable one."

"I am sure your backers appreciate that."

"My backers? The *Raven* has none. What need of we for

such when we have a fair wind and the favor of Dame Fortune?''

The *Raven*. The name tugged at her memory, but she resisted that slight pull, following instead another tangent. ''None, M'sieu le Capitaine? I understood that Valcour Murat was one of their number.''

''You must have got it wrong. Murat has no greater or lesser share than any other officer on the ship. He has advanced far in the short time he has been with us, the reasons being his skill in hunting down quarry and his single-minded hatred of the Spanish which lets him smell one below any horizon. Authority he has as ship's quartermaster, except when the fever of malaria has me in its grip. Only rum will rout the chills and release the talons that this pestilence sinks into my bones. Someone else must lead my crew of corsairs then. Of late, it has been Murat.''

For a stark instant of remembrance Félicité stared, her gaze fastened on his mobile features as they twisted in a wry grimace. Gathering her wits, she leaned forward in a smooth bow. ''I would like to hear more, M'sieu le Capitaine, but I see the serving wench has breakfast ready. Perhaps I may speak with you another time?''

''Of a certainty,'' the Frenchman replied, amusement tracing through his dismissal as he leaned on the rail to watch Félicité walk away.

Her excuse was valid. She collected Ashanti along with the ship's biscuits the maid had toasted, the fried salt meat and dried fruit. They descended to the cabin. Allowing Ashanti to go before her, she stepped through the threshold and slammed the bulkhead door behind her. Valcour turned from the washstand, where he was shaving.

''What have you been up to?'' he inquired.

''I have been speaking to Captain Bonhomme. Tell me, Valcour, how does it come about that we have taken passage on a pirate lugger?''

He deliberately finished scraping the side of his face, put down the well-honed blade he was using, and with a length of toweling, wiped away the soap. ''It took less time than I expected for you to discover it.''

"Valcour, why—"

He lifted a brow. "It's a ship like any other. Why pay for passage when it can be had without?"

"And I suppose if we run across a likely prize your friends, or should I say your followers, will run up a black flag and seize her?" So intent was she on the extent of Valcour's duplicity that she scarcely noticed as Ashanti set down the breakfast tray, twitched a small packet from under the pillow in the bunk where she slept, and slipped from the cabin.

"Our good captain was garrulous, wasn't he? I never knew pretty boys had any appeal for him."

She ignored the gibes. "So it's true. This is where you have been, where you have spent your time, while my father was in prison. Here on one of the most notorious pirate ships to ever ply the gulf!"

"What can you know of it, *ma chère?*"

"So black is the record of this ship that tales of the deeds committed aboard her penetrated even to New Orleans!"

"Greatly exaggerated, I'm sure. The captain did tell you that I command only on the odd occasion when he is under the weather?"

"Are you trying to deny responsibility for the atrocities attached to this ship's name? I don't think you can, not so long as you stayed—"

"Very well," he grated, "I am of a most callous depravity, hungeringly cruel. Charge me also with incestuous lust, for I want you, my dear sister. I have longed for these many years to feel your soft body writhing under me, and I see no reason now to wait."

"What—what are you saying?" she breathed, a strangled sound. The blood drained from her face, leaving it white and still. She had meant to accuse him only of guilt by association, for staying with the *Raven* after he had discovered what she was, for returning to her. His words struck a savage double blow.

"How can you not understand? I have shown you in a thousand ways since we were children that you were mine."

She recognized the truth of what he said, realized also the

protection of her willful blindness. "You—you are my brother."

"No more am I, nor ever was!" He moved toward her with the springing steel of a swordsman in his step, and the expression rising slowly behind his eyes made the blood congeal in her veins.

"Valcour—" she breathed as she retreated.

"I am Valcour Murat, no brother of yours, no sibling, no safe relative. I am the man who watched you grow, watched you turn from a green girl into a woman ripe for plucking. You allowed another man to rob me of the first sweet fruit, a betrayal for which you must and shall feel the pain of punishment."

She moistened dry lips. "I told you I could not prevent it. If you had not—"

"Not that again," he cut viciously through her words. "The first folly was yours, my dear Félicité." He picked up her wooden-backed hairbrush from the washstand where she had left it without slowing his advance.

"This—this is madness." She flung a glance at the door, but he had maneuvered so that a quick lunge could cut her off the instant she made any movement toward it. She could scream, but if anyone came would they help, or would they be more likely to hold her spread-eagled while they waited their turn?

"But such a pleasurable insanity. How many times have I thought of this, of laying you across my knees face down, of throwing your skirts above your head, and while you squirm and cry for mercy, bringing the flat of my hand down upon the soft and tender whiteness of your *derriére*, leaving its imprint there like a brand? Instead of skirts, now you wear breeches to be pushed down around your ankles, but the final results will be the same."

With abrupt decision, he discarded the hairbrush, tossing it onto the bunk. As Félicité's attention was diverted by that movement, he swooped, jerking her toward him so that she stumbled and fell across him as he threw himself onto the bunk.

An exultant, uncontrolled laugh burst from his throat. His

fingers dug into her, gouging muscles, paralyzing nerves so that she gasped in pain, twisting and turning with all the wretched weakness of a gaffed fish. His hand came down in a stinging, stunning blow upon her backside. As she stiffened, he reached for the buttons that held her breeches.

Above the sound of the blood drumming in her ears and her own difficult gasping for breath as she kicked and struggled, she did not hear the door open. Without warning Ashanti was there carrying a tray from which rose scalding steam.

"Your chocolate, M'sieu Valcour," came her quiet voice that held within it the essence of a threat.

Valcour went still, poised under the sudden danger of scalding liquid held inches from his face. Félicité scrambled from his lap, crouching on her knees on the heaving floor. Ashanti swayed slightly with the movement of the ship, the steam from the open tin pot rising in white, wavering eddies. The strain of the moment lengthened with twanging tautness, then Valcour reached for the nearest of the cups beside the pot.

"How very enterprising of you," he said, snarling vindictiveness in his yellow-brown eyes as he watched the maid. "I won't forget."

Ashanti did not make the mistake of attempting an answer. Her movements deft, she poured chocolate into the cup he held, then filled one for Félicité and handed it to her. "There will be no chocolate tomorrow," she said, her voice prosaic. "They slaughtered the cow this morning. Will you have breakfast now, mam'selle, m'sieu?"

"We—may as well," Félicité agreed, recovering her aplomb with an effort.

"And then," Valcour said, watching with malevolent closeness as Ashanti parceled out the last of the chocolate into her own cup, "you can go while we bring our business to a—satisfactory conclusion."

Again Ashanti did not reply, only sending Valcour a long glance, her face smooth, dispassionate, as she watched him swallow a long draft of his chocolate in his anxiety to have done with it. She proffered a dry biscuit. He took it, bit into it, and drank once more.

Félicité grew slowly aware of an undercurrent of expectancy that had nothing to do with Valcour's threats. She ate her meal, sipping from her cup. She looked at Ashanti, sedately lifting her own chocolate to her lips. Valcour drained his and flung the cup down with a disdainful flip of his wrist. He glanced at Félicité, then turned his gaze to the maid.

Uneasiness washed over his face. The blood receded from under his skin, leaving it tinged with yellow. Globules of perspiration burst from his pores. He swallowed, then swallowed again. He started up, cracking his skull against the overhead bunk. Swaying, with blood starting from a cut on his brow, he raised a hand to his throat, tearing at his ruffles.

"For the love of God," he gasped, his wild gaze on Ashanti. "You've poisoned me!" He stumbled forward a step, then bolted for the door.

Valcour did not die. For the remainder of the day he hung from the after rail, giving up gall and bile into the sea, or else lay moaning, moistly pale, clutching his belly and muttering curses. The maid refused to help him. There was no antidote, she said with serene contempt.

Nor did the crew seem overly concerned. They eyed him now and then with a certain rude disdain, bawling obscenities at each other with leers and winks, and taking wagers on when they would be able to see his guts. The general consensus was that he would cast up a final accounting by eight bells of the afternoon watch, as night came down to buss the blue water.

Those who thought it was a sure thing lost their money. It was Captain Bonhomme who, with an offering of watered rum, effected the change. Moments after Valcour had drunk it down, he was up on his feet, staggering toward the head of the ship, bent over against the gripping in his bowels. There in that traditional shipboard ocean-wide latrine, perched precariously on the braces of the bowsprit where the ship's plunging into the waves would wash away the excrement, pawing at the forechains and screened by breast-high bulwarks, he stayed for the better part of the night.

The morning dawned red with a heavy swale. The wind

had swung around so that they ran free before it with all sails set and straining. Toward noon, a lug topsail, patched and yellowed, split with a crack like lightning. The pirate crew swarmed aloft to take it down and spread another, but when it was done, they stood on the deck, quartering the horizon with their eyes. A sage comment or two was passed about a falling glass, the dread word ''hurricane'' was whispered from lip to lip, and a dark, wild-eyed Portuguese in a stocking cap was seen to cross himself. A growling reference was made to the Negro wench; it was bad luck, they said, to have a woman of any color aboard. The best thing they could do would be stretch her out upon the deck, and when they were through with her, throw her overboard. There was some mention of Valcour's name, but as one wag pointed out, that mincing devil was in no shape to use her, or by God's blood, to object if they did. None seemed ready to act, however.

It seemed best for Ashanti to stay out of sight. Félicité, after she had carried the warning below, was inclined to do the same, though she also took up Valcour's sword from where he had left it the morning before, since he had not returned to the cabin, preferring to hang a hammock in the captain's quarters, well out of Ashanti's reach. Félicité strapped the blade around her, and felt if not better, at least better prepared.

At dusk of the third day out, the wind shifted once more, coming out of the southwest, blowing in an autumn gale. They shortened sail and rigged stormlines, swinging to skip before it. The ship pitched like a wild thing, flinging itself into the night-black maw of the storm. Lightning danced over the dark water with a terrible beauty. Thunder roared like the lions of hell, and the rain came down. It lashed them in wavering, wind-kicked shrouds, pouring across the decks, washing stench and noisome debris from the scuppers. The seas churned, rising to leviathan heights, spilling over the decks to add the tang of salt to the drubbing rain. It beat itself into valleys and mountains of water topped with foam. The hammering winds sent the scud flying, and seemed likely to bat the ship from the towering crests. League after league they ran with the tempest, holding the outer edge of its fury.

Off course, they plunged onward, driven and harried like a mouse before a tiger, praying for clear seas without reef or shoal.

The timbers of the ship groaned and snapped in torment. The single storm lantern in the cabin, turned low, swung in dizzying circles. Félicité and Ashanti were not greatly affected by seasickness, as many were, even the hardened sailors, most likely because of the herb they chewed. Still, they stayed strapped in their bunks. To wander about was to invite broken bones in the pitching dimness as the ship wallowed and dived like a bottle cork in the waves. Through the bulkhead they could hear Valcour groaning, but could not go to him even if he would have accepted their help. Whether the sailors realized Ashanti was responsible for his illness, or whether they were kept too busy by the storm, no more was heard of accosting her. From the strange looks the men had given her before the weather worsened, she thought they half expected the young gentleman sharing Ashanti's cabin to begin to share the same symptoms. They were admiring, intrigued, and perhaps consoled when she did not.

It occurred to Félicité as she lay staring at the swaying lantern to wonder why, if Ashanti could save her from Valcour, she had not performed the same service against Morgan. The answer was simple. Though she regretted the violence of Félicité's initiation, the maid had not been dissatisfied with the man who had accomplished it.

The gray light of morning brought no surcease. Vindictive and frustrated, the storm harassed them through the day and into the endless Stygian welter of the third night.

There came a day of heaving seas and close-huddled horizons. They had lost a topmast, were dragging a sheet anchor, and were taking on water in a thousand oozing, pitchless leaks that caused the pumps to be manned around the clock. But they were as jauntily afloat as the bung from a wine barrel. A fire was started in the brick-lined firepit that had been allowed to go out during the rough seas, and all hands gathered around for a hot meal and a tot of rum before setting to work in earnest on tangled cordage, open seams, and sodden sail.

Valcour, it was reported, was able to take a little boiled beef and broth. Nighttime brought a rift in the clouds that permitted pulsing starlight to shimmer down over the water. The captain hurried topside with his sextant. Taking a reading, he discovered they were not so far off their charted course as might be imagined, thanks to a graciously veering wind, and so they sailed on.

Félicité stood at the railing with her face turned to the warm and humid breeze. In waistcoat and shirtsleeves, she was still a little overheated. There was a trickle of perspiration between her shoulders and around her hairline, but it seemed best to go no further in her accommodation to the weather. She had just finished her turn at the pumps. As soon as she had rested from her exertions, she would be all right.

No one had ordered her to fall in and lend a hand. It had been the sidelong glances of sullen resentment that decided her. As the youth she appeared, fresh-faced, callow, and not above fifteen, little was actually expected of her, and yet it seemed best to appear willing.

"Wind-blown, rose-tinted of cheek, and in a pensive mood. Forgive me, young François, but you are too pretty to be a boy."

Félicité turned to face Captain Bonhomme. Drawing on a pretense of affront to keep the alarm from her features, she fingered the hilt of Valcour's sword. "I shall change, I'm sure."

"Don't, pray, draw steel against me! I meant no insult, and I am far too gone in fatigue from the last few days to fight you."

His words were accompanied by a penetrating glance that did nothing to allay her fears. She had caught him watching her more than once since the storm, and could not help wondering if Valcour, still sharing his quarters, had taken the man into his confidence, or else let fall something in delirium. She looked away over the ink-blue water. "I'm sure you are a fine swordsman, M'sieu le Capitaine. Doubtless you could give me pointers if it so pleased you."

The captain lifted his shoulders with Gallic eloquence. A

trace of derision was in his tone as he replied. "There may have been a time. No more."

"And yet you lead these men." She nodded over her shoulder at the men sprawled on deck, those not on the watch engaged in sleeping, fishing, splicing rope, or busily scraping at whale's teeth.

"Shall I tell you how I came to be a buccaneer, in the hope that you will confide the tale of why you are on the *Raven* clutching at the coattails of Valcour Murat? It is soon done. A younger son without a sou to my name, I became a *mousquetaire* at court through influence. There I caught the eye of the young wife of an old and rich nobleman. Merrily and often, I put the horns of a cuckold on his forehead, even to the point of making my bastard his heir. He noticed, finally, what was making his wife as happy as a singing cricket. Rather than trounce me in a public admission of his lackluster performance as a husband, something he was by no means certain he could manage, he arranged for a *lettre de cachet*. As you may know, such pieces of paper carry the authority of the king condemning the person named to be taken on sight and clapped into the darkest depths of the Bastille without hope of trial. I am not a man who craves to be forgotten, nor do I bear any resemblance to a mole. Warned by my mistress, I left Paris ahead of the gendarmes. The West Indies seemed a healthier section of the world. But having made my way here, I found myself cast onto these sandy shores without the means to sustain myself."

"A most romantic tale," Félicité commented.

He sent her a swift glance. "Isn't it? A bit more, and I am done. As a boy, I had spent a number of summers at my father's chateau on the coast of Normandy, where I went out with the fishing fleet. From those hardy men I learned the art of dead reckoning and something of sailing. I also met a man who had once been a prisoner of the Arabs, and learned the uses of the astrolabe and sextant. It sometimes seems these things are meant to be. I became a pirate."

Though the story was a bit glib and polished, there was still enough address in the captain's manner for there to be some chance of it being true. "So you became the leader of a band of escaped felons, deserters from half the navies and armies of Europe, and lately, the men turned off from both now that England, France, and Spain are no longer at war. Regardless, you insist it is not fear that makes these men obey you, but respect for your knowledge of navigation?''

''When any group of men gather, there must be rules to govern their conduct, else they will be forever robbing and killing each other with little hope of making anything of themselves as a coalition, and with less of sleeping safe at night. In the hundred years and more that there have been corsairs in these waters, the rules that govern their acts and actions have become barnacled with tradition. Shall I recite them for you?''

She had nothing else to do, and it was better than standing alone, collecting stares. She gave a nod.

''*Très bien.* These then are the articles of agreement signed by the men who come aboard the *Raven*. One, every man has a vote in affairs of the moment, has equal title to the fresh provisions and strong liquor at any time seized, and may use them unless a scarcity makes it necessary for the good of all to vote a retrenchment. Two, every man is to be called fairly in turn by list on board of prizes, because they are allowed a suit of clothes over and above their proper share. But if one defraud the company of the value of one dollar in plate, jewels, or money, the punishment is marooning. If robbery takes place between two crewmen, the guilty one shall have his nose and ears slit and be set ashore not on some inhabited place but where he shall surely suffer hardship. Three, no person shall game at cards or dice for money at sea. Four, the lights and candles shall be put out at eight o'clock at night. If any remain inclined for drinking, they shall do so on the open deck. Five, all shall keep their pistols and cutlasses clean and fit for service. Six, no women allowed. If any man be found carrying any of the sex to sea disguised, he is to suffer death—''

Félicité flung him a quick look. ''Where does that leave Ashanti, my—the Negro maid?''

''For the moment, she is listed as a passenger and, like you, a dependent of Murat. Later, who knows? Of course, she is also not in disguise. Where was I? Ah, yes, article number seven. Desertion of the ship or quitting quarters in battle is to be punished by death or marooning. Eight, no striking another on board ship. Every man's quarrel shall be ended on shore with sword and pistol, one or both. Nine, no man shall talk of breaking up their way of living unless each has shared a thousand pounds of goods. If any man shall lose a limb or become cripple in the common service, he shall have eight hundred dollars out of the public stock, and for lesser hurts proportionally. Number ten, the captain and quartermaster shall receive two shares in a prize; the sailing master, boatswain, and gunner, one share and one half; other officers, one share and one quarter; sailors, one. In these few laws there is a code of honor of sorts, however hard you must look for it."

"The quartermaster is Valcour, I know, but the *Raven* has the other officers you mentioned?"

"Most, yes, though I cannot blame you for not being able to pick them out from the others. As quartermaster, Murat is the voice of authority. He alone can order a flogging; according to Mosaic Law, forty lashes less one. And he is the first man to board a captured prize to make the decision of what will be set aside for the company's use. In theory, the captain should be the military leader of the ship, with absolute power in time of chase or battle, while the sailing master should be in charge of navigation as well as the setting of canvas. In practice, I share my leadership with Valcour while I handle the lesser post as well. Sometime soon the crew may decide I am not worthy of the command and replace me. I shall not repine. The days of the buccaneers are numbered. Every year there are fewer ports, fewer places where we are welcome, more ships of the Spanish *guarda de costas* to chase us down, and more and better guns on the prizes we seek to capture. I have been lucky; I am still a whole man, if sometimes put on the rack by fevers. I have my sight, and my sanity, and now and then I think I have tried the patience of *le bon Dieu* long enough, forcing him to protect my miserable hide. It is time to end it."

"And what will you do?" Félicité asked.

The captain smiled. "Who knows? But enough of me. You were going to tell me how you came to be aboard."

Félicité had an uncomfortable moment. As she sought for an answer, however, there came from above them the long-drawn-out cry, "Land ho! Land away to starboard!"

They swung to see a dark smudge on the horizon, like a low-lying storm cloud tinged with green. Félicité frowned. "What landfall is this? I expected none for days more on this route to France."

"France? What can you mean, François Lafargue? Ahead of us is our destination, the only one we have ever had from the moment we left the Mississippi River."

"But surely—" she began.

"I don't know what you expected, *mon petit ami*, or where you meant to go, but ahead of you is where the *Raven* drops anchor, one of the last refuges of those of the black flag, the island of Las Tortugas."

Chapter 12

*L*as Tortugas, *the* turtle islands. There were three bodies of land in the chain, none of any great size. The *Raven* dropped anchor in the curving shelter of the harbor of the largest. Called Grand Cayman for the Carib word describing the giant iguana lizards that made it their home, it stretched before them, a miniature paradise of waving palm trees, white sand beaches, and blue-green seas, like an emerald in a froth of lace worn on the background of a lady's turquoise gown. There was a village of sorts near the port, whose inhabitants were mainly British, but if it had a name, none could agree on what it was. From the huddled shacks pelted a stream of children of all ages, colors, and nationalities as the ship was sighted. They swam out to catch bow and stern lines from the lugger, taking the hawsers in and belaying them around the pilings of the rickety pier so that the ship could be winched up to it.

By the time this feat had been accomplished the wharf and the beach beyond were crowded with calling, laughing women, with vendors selling fresh oranges and limes and hot meat pies, with pitchmen from the taverns and gaming dens, with merchants calling out to the men on the forecastle, asking if they had taken prizes. The sailors at the creaking winches roared out a ribald chantey. Dogs barked, pouring from behind and inside of the tumbledown thatched huts and driftwood-and-canvas-covered hovels. Overhead, gulls whirled with piercing cries and frigate birds swept the blue with triangular black wings. And the gentle trades wafted the smells of decaying fish, rotting fruit, and open sewers upon the warm, somnolent air.

The instant the gangplank was laid, the crew leaped down it. They were met with open arms and smacking kisses, then towed away, the women who held their arms screaming like fishwives and scratching with talon fingers at any other vulture who tried to take their prey. The men, in varying states of unembarrassed tumescence, clutched at the breasts and hips of the dockside doxies.

Valcour did not leave the ship at once. Still somewhat weak from his ordeal, he watched the departure of the crew with malicious contempt. Afterward, he approached Félicité, inquiring if she intended to go ashore. He would, he said, see that a hut was constructed for use near the beach, set apart from the others. He was certain she was ready for solid ground beneath her feet.

Félicité declined. From what she had seen of this tropical port, she thought she preferred the saltwater cleanliness of the lugger. The amusements of the straggling town had no appeal, but perhaps she might promenade the beach in the cool of the afternoon. Possibly Captain Bonhomme would stroll with her if invited. He did not seem anxious for town pleasures either, and if Ashanti went with them, she could always hint that it was the maid who stood in need of an additional escort.

"As you wish." Valcour gave her a curt bow and turned away then, but not before Félicité had seen the stabbing look of malevolence he sent in the direction of the maid. Two hours later he was no longer on the vessel and was presumed to have walked into town.

The captain was accommodating. The three of them strolled along the white-sand shore, listening to the murmuring surf, watching the liquid aquamarine of the waves wash toward them to foam hungrily at their feet, and the packed sand of the waterline glistening pink and lavender with the fading light of the rose-red sun slipping into the cobalt sea. Thatch palms waved their wind-fretted leaves with a dry rattle. Shorebirds played catch-as-catch-can with the flowing tide. Broken wine bottles and breached casks, barrel staves and frayed rope ends, bits of bone and blackened coals littered the beach, while the enormous bleached carapaces of long-dead sea turtles lay half filled with sand like the discarded helmets of an ancient army of colossal warriors on a deserted battlefield.

"Turtles," the French captain declared, "are the cause of the piracy in the Indies."

"Why so?" Félicité queried, willing to be amused.

"A few hundred years ago, when the explorer Columbus hove over the horizon, they were so thick in these waters around the islands that they appeared like rocks along the beaches. There were then, and still are, several different kinds, most of gigantic size up to a ton in weight, among them the leatherback, the hawksbill or tortoiseshell turtle, and the green turtle. Great slow and clumsy beasts, they had no enemies except the Indians who lived here. They stayed most of the time in the sea, venturing landward on occasion. Every three months or so, they became greatly amorous, and as a result waded up on the beaches, where the female laid her eggs."

"Indians? I don't remember seeing any among the people who met the ship."

"No, you would not, by the mercy of the Spanish. They came two hundred years ago to begin the colonization of the islands of the Greater and Lesser Antilles. They rounded up the Indians, the Carib and Arawak. They saved their souls and put their bodies to use as slaves. Those they did not beat to death they killed with the diseases of Europe that were unknown to the islands until then. But before they did, they discovered the Indian way of catching turtles, using the remora or suckerfish. The fish survives by attaching himself to a host by suction in such a way he cannot be dislodged. If a line is attached to the tail of such a one and he is released again, he will swim at once to a larger fish or turtle, and when he is in place, both remora and host can be hauled in. Another way was to chase down a slow lumbering giant and use either several hands or a prising pole to turn him over onto his back. In that position they are entirely helpless and may be killed at leisure, as much as several weeks later.''

'But what has that, as interesting as it may be, to do with piracy?''

''Patience, *mon ami*, I come to that,'' Captain Bonhomme said, smiling. ''The Spanish, as you know, were a great success. Every spot on which they set their feet became a gold mine or silver mine, or else a cache of jewels. Spain grew rich and mighty, which made it a threat to the rest of Europe. The result was, as usual, war and more war. Privateers—that is, legal pirates, privately owned ships with letters of marque from their own governments entitling them to attack enemy shipping and keep the spoils—were sent out by the hundreds. When the hostilities were over, there were hundreds of men with no job to be done, men who had had a taste of easy riches. Harrying the plate fleet of the Spanish, wresting the silver and gold bullion, the jewels and ingots, from the dons had become a habit. And then there was the practice of France and England of sending their criminals to the islands, transporting them to be rid of their mischief.''

''And the turtles, M'sieu le Capitaine?'' Félicité reminded him once again when it seemed he had strayed hopelessly from the subject.

''Ah, François, you are as persistent of a point as a woman. Have you no interest in the grand story of an epoch that is passing before our eyes?''

"But of course," she answered, at once assuming a most serious mien.

"Yes, I am sure. Very well, the turtles. Privateers and pirates, beating the seas for days for a ship fit for the taking, cannot be forever scurrying back to port. In the damp heat of the tropics, salt pork and beef keep only ill, soon becoming so full of maggots and molds not even an iron-bellied veteran of the galleys will touch it. The Spanish, and to some extent the French and English, made a practice of putting beef cattle and hogs ashore on the islands to multiply, a great convenience when a ship is beached to repair rigging or scrape off the barnacles, but difficult to keep alive with the proper water and food on shipboard, even if you can keep the stupid beasts from breaking their legs in rough seas. Do you know, by the way, that the word for 'buccaneer,' the earliest sort of pirates, comes from their habit of chasing down these wild descendants of tame cows and pigs, cutting the flesh into strips, and drying them in a smoke-filled house? The house, you perceive, was called by the Indians a *buccan*."

He sent her a swift glance, his brown eyes flashing with laughter before he gave a mock sigh. "But the turtles. These beasts could be carried on a ship for weeks without food or water, without any problem at all except for the minor inconvenience of keeping them on their backs. The leatherback turtle is enormous, but unfortunately he dines entirely on shellfish, it being all one to him whether they be dead or alive, and so his meat is inedible. The tortoiseshell is much the same. On the other hand, the green turtle eats only sargossa grass and other green things, and *ma foi*, never have you tasted so delicious a soup as he makes. And so the well-fed pirate, sustained by turtle meat, palm wine, and cassava beer, can annoy the shipping of the world that sails into the Antilles down the Windward Passage by his front door. He need never return to land until his ship is so low in the water he is like to sink with the weight of his spoils."

"You still take on turtles?"

"*Certainement, mon ami.* We will load many tomorrow. But as fast as they are being eaten, they will one day be done. And what can a poor buccaneer do then but down sails and let the waves cast him up on land like a beached whale, until the crabs and gulls between them pick his bones and leave him forgotten, bleaching in the sun like the shells of the turtles?''

Despite the note of bathos with which their walk came to an end, it was necessary after that to taste a soup made with green turtles. Ashanti went down the gangplank to the town market for the ingredients, with Félicité at her side as escort. To find herself striding through the streets with her hand resting on Valcour's sword, which she had refused to relinquish, was a novel position. More than once she had to shake off clutching hands or shoulder past some determined damsel of the streets.

The aroma of the stewing turtle, heightened by a dash of herbs and a generous measure of sherry, brought Captain Bonhomme from his cabin. The three of them devoured the succulent dish with chunks of bread also bought in the market, a welcome change from the ship's fare.

It was sometime later, in the early hours of the morning, when Félicité was awakened by the sounds of shouts. They seemed to be coming from the captain's cabin. By the time she had struck a light from the tinderbox, Ashanti had climbed down from the upper bunk. She glided through the door, turning back only as Félicité called her name, asking where she was bound.

''I go to the captain, mam'selle.''

''What do you think is the matter? He isn't—that is, you didn't—''

''No, mam'selle,'' the maid said with the ghost of a smile. ''The captain is a good man, and though he may suspect what you try to hide, I think he will wait for you to reveal yourself.''

''What is it, then? You cannot go to his cabin this time of night. There may be others there.''

''I heard only his voice, no one else's. I saw this night in his eyes the fever coming on. It may be I can help him.''

Ashanti was right. Brought on perhaps by the chill wet of the storm followed by the heat of the port, the captain's ever recurring malaria had returned. He lay in his bunk alternating between chills and raging fever. His lips cracked. The look in his eyes grew wild, and he seemed ridden by nightmares of inhuman torture, of scourges, of smoking coal-red brands, and fantasies of a coward's death, of a man being tied to the muzzle of a cannon and blown to bits. He wanted rum, demanded it, and cursed in the languages of half a dozen countries when he did not get it. Ashanti brewed herb drinks and compelled him by strength of will to drink them. Félicité ordered his cabinboy here and there to see that he was kept clean and dry, and once or twice she sat to spoon broth between his flaccid lips, and think of the hidden pasts of men of the high seas such as the captain, and the charming tales they could concoct to hide the ugliness of reality.

One night his fever broke. By the next morning he was nearly himself again, though weak. And so the days passed and the tropical sun shone down and the trade winds never ceased to blow.

It was afternoon. Captain Bonhomme had left the ship to go into town and begin rounding up his men. It was time the *Raven* took wing, he said. The men had used up their last piastre, and as the rum haze wore off, were getting ugly, fighting among themselves, breaking into houses, raping anything female that walked on two legs. If he didn't make some kind of move, he would find half his crew hanged.

Ashanti approached Félicité where she stood at the railing, watching the captain stride briskly toward the center of town.

"Mam'selle?"

"Yes, Ashanti?" Félicité turned her head to smile.

"What are we to do now? If you go out with the ship again, you will surely be found out, and there will be trouble, or else M'sieu Valcour will find a way to separate us."

Never in the time they had been in the harbor had Ashanti harked back, reminding Félicité of her warning against this trip, against trusting Valcour. She did not do so now. There was nothing in her tone other than an acceptance of things as they were, and an anxious questioning about the future.

Félicité sighed. In the endless warm days made temperate by the breezes it seemed impossible to consider that things could change. The timeless sea surrounded them, lapping at the shores as it had through the ages. The sand sparkled like

ground crystal, dazzling the eyes, while the shadowed green-
ness of the underbrush that grew down to the beach promised
coolness for an afternoon, an evening, a lifetime of slumber.
That the promise was false she knew. Mosquitoes like small
demons sent for the punishment of man haunted the tropical
glades in clouds, along with five hundred other varieties of
insects, all of which stung or bit. And on that brooding
island, pitiless sun raised the passions of men and women to
such heat that they could destroy. There was no cool and staid
protection of laws. Regardless of its look of an Eden, no
defenseless lamb could venture there, for those who were not
rapacious and hungry lions were tigers or wolves, wolves of
the sea.

"I must confess, I don't know, Ashanti. It was stupid of
me to come with Valcour, to trust him. And I will admit it
would be worse still to go farther with him. But what else is
there?"

"I have been thinking, mam'selle. Where there are many
men and few women of respectability, there is always a need
for food, for dishes that are hot and hearty and filling. We
could open an eating house, you and I. You could remain a
man for safety, and act as host for our establishment, and
perhaps at times as the chef."

It was a good idea. Félicité felt the dawning of hope until
two major flaws presented themselves. "We have no money
to get started, to build a hut or to buy the meat and flour, the
vegetables and spices, or the utensils to cook them in. On top
of that, Valcour would never leave me behind willingly. He
would search the island from shore to shore."

"There might be some way we could arrange so that
M'sieu Valcour will not know we have left the ship until it is
well out to sea. As for the money, perhaps Captain Bonhomme
would allow you to borrow it if you ask."

The discussion did not end there. They went into it
exhaustively, but the conclusion was always the same; they
could do nothing without speaking to the captain.

The sun went down and the swift darkness of these latitudes descended. The glow of lights and sound of hilarity
came from the direction of the waterfront town. A few sailors

struggled back to the ship, flinging themselves down on their straw pallets that they called donkey's breakfasts on the open deck.

Félicité prepared for bed, washing as best she could in a butt of stale water. Ashanti picked up the chamber pot the two of them used in the privacy of their cabin rather than resorting to the head of the ship, preparing to take it topside to empty it over the rail. At the same time, she gathered up the scraps of their evening meal to fling to the gulls. Going out, she closed the door behind her.

Félicité climbed into her bunk. Lulled by the faint rock of the ship, she closed her eyes, dozing, waiting to let Ashanti in before she locked the door for the night. The maid was taking her own good time about returning. It didn't matter, of course; she was as entitled as anyone to stargaze. It was a little odd that she had never shown any tendency in that direction before. It was as if she had dedicated her life to serving Félicité at the expense of her own existence. It was disconcerting that it should be so. Félicité had done nothing to make herself worthy of such a sacrifice, and yet, what could she do to prevent it, especially now? She must be grateful, and vow to see that Ashanti did not go unrewarded.

An hour passed, and another. Was it possible that Ashanti had found someone to dally with in some dark corner? The idea was so unlikely that Félicité got up from the bunk, pulled on breeches and shirt, and stepped into her shoes. But though she walked the decks looking in every nook and cranny that she dared, even going so far as to descend the gangway and glance into the fetid hole of the forecastle where the crew slept in bad weather, Ashanti was not to be found. Had she gone ashore then on some errand of her own? Had she decided to look further into the possibilities of an eating house, or even a place they might use to conceal themselves from Valcour? Had she seen Captain Bonhomme from a distance, perhaps, and made up her mind to speak to him? Or had she felt the urge to walk along the beach?

Each idea seemed more fantastic than the last, though the fact remained that Ashanti was not aboard the lugger.

Félicité had almost made up her mind to venture into

the town on her own when she heard voices approaching and saw Captain Bonhomme nearing the gangplank with his boatswain. The second man had a crude jest for Félicité's concern and Ashanti's possible occupation at the moment, along with a warning that young François should have taken better care of her. The French captain questioned Félicité closely, however, then gathered up enough men for a search party and set out to look for the maid.

They combed the ship from stem to stern, from the mast-head to the bilges. They fanned out along the beach in both directions, and made a sweep through the town, peering into alleyways, huts, and unlocked warehouses, and scanning the faces of the women in the taverns. They upturned barrels and flung beached boats over backward, and at the end of it, found nothing except indignant iguanas and disgruntled crabs.

Milk-white dawn was reaching into the sky when they turned back toward the *Raven*. As they climbed the wobbling plank, they heard a curse and a cry.

It seemed one of the crew, too rum-sodden the night before to join in the search, had crawled from his pallet to relieve himself over the railing. He had seen the body of a woman being towed by a great turtle. It was Ashanti, quite dead. She had been brutally raped and torn, and finally killed by a gaping wound in her throat that ran from earlobe to earlobe.

The tall ship hove into view with white-bellied sails set and pennants flying. It ran free toward the harbor with the wind only a few points off her stern. She was French-designed and Spanish-rigged; so said the salts who lined the water's edge. A two-masted brigantine with fore and aft sails, she had black paint with a broad scarlet stripe bleeding backward from the bow, gilt-touched ornamentation, and a rearing horse as a figurehead. White sails shivered as she entered the lee of the harbor. Men like monkeys, dark with distance, swarmed into the sheets, slapping the sails, beating at them with their fists as they tugged, shortening sail. Onward she came, cleaving the water, the figurehead plunging over the waves, rising and falling, riding with a speed that made it seem impossible for her to stop without running aground. Nearer she drew, and

217

nearer still. The forms of men grew clearer, could be plainly seen.

Abruptly the anchor chain ran down with oiled precision. The ship pulled to a halt, her bow swinging so that the name in gold lettering could be spelled out for the first time. It was the *Black Stallion*, making port with a skill and panache that the onlookers saluted with a lusty cheer. Two things only kept the crew of the *Raven* from running pell-mell to man their own ship's guns to take the prize. The first was the *Raven's* lack of readiness, and the second was the black flag, solid sable and without insignia, ancient symbol of piracy, that flew at the *Black Stallion's* masthead.

They had buried Ashanti that morning, and Félicité was in no mood for empty, heroic gestures, but even she had to recognize the quality of daring and seamanship just displayed. She stood listening to the praises of the French captain while the *Black Stallion's* crew lowered a boat to the water. Since the *Raven* was already lying alongside the wharf, there was no room for the larger ship to tie up. Every man jack of her crew would have to pull for the dubious delights of the shore.

Not so her captain. He was entitled to be carted about with all the care of a nursemaid for a mewling babe. Félicité followed with her eyes the progress of a tall, broad-shouldered man as he descended from the quarterdeck, stepped to the side, and climbed with swift agility down the rope ladder to the boat. An odd *frisson* ran over her nerves. The boat pushed away from the side of the ship and started toward them in great surging bounds as the men bent to the oars.

Captain Bonhomme lifted a hand to his eyes, scowling seaward. "Name of a name, it can't be! I thought that man scuttled years ago, on the bottom with Davy Jones."

Félicité strained her eyes. The captain of the *Black Stallion* stood with one foot on the crossbrace of the longboat's prow. The ruffles at the open neck of his shirt and the gathered fullness of his sleeves fluttered in the wind. His breeches were black, tucked into the turned-down tops of jackboots, and banding his waist was a scarlet sash that held the wicked length of his sword. He was sun-bronzed and hard, this brigand, with a mane of mahogany-russet hair flowing backward in the wind, cropped short like that of a felon or a man ready for the executioner's block and blade.

"*Mon Dieu!* I knew I could not mistake. It's the devil's own, returned to haunt us. It's that cursed Irish corsair, Morgan McCormack!"

Whooping and hollering, the gathered hawkers, prostitutes, pitchmen, and beggars converged on the spot where the boat would land. The sailors were not far behind. Félicité, stunned into immobility, did not move. A hand fell on her arm, and Valcour was beside her, swinging her around, herding her in no gentle manner back toward the *Raven*.

She went without protest or backward glance. The last thing she wished at that moment was to face Morgan. The fact that he was here, in command of a pirate vessel, was more than she could grasp. How had it come about? How had he changed himself from a respected officer in the pay of Spain to a pirate captain overnight? And most important of all, why?

Chapter 13

The evening melted away and became night. Félicité lay on her bunk with her arm across her eyes. She was locked in; she had discovered that hours ago. From the sound, she thought the ship's officers and the majority of her crew had returned. Still, the *Raven* made no obvious preparations for departure with the morning tide. What was happening otherwise, she could not tell, though it seemed something was in the wind. From the quarters of the captain came the sound of raised voices with the timbre of disagreement. Footsteps came and went along the companionway to the cabin next door, from which she was certain she had heard Valcour's voice in a cutting rebuke.

That it concerned Morgan's arrival she had no doubt. Her adoptive brother would be ablaze with the need for revenge, and anxious to fall to it here, just beyond the reach of the lengthy arm of Spain. As for the others, hadn't she seen the greed for the other ship shining in their eyes? They were fully alive to the advantage of taking the brigantine, a much larger vessel with heavier guns. The question of honor would not arise; the captain who could not hold his ship did not deserve to keep her. The single argument for prudence might be the presence of Morgan's followers, and yet with such men, doubtless recruited in haste, how much would loyalty weigh?

Would Morgan recognize his danger? He must if he had followed on the heels of the *Raven,* if he knew Valcour's connection with the ship, knew the big island of Las Tortugas was one of her favorite ports of call. But did he?

Was it accident or design that he had arrived so close behind her? Had he, in fact, come in pursuit of her? Was he on the track of Ashanti, Spanish property now, that she might have been considered to have stolen? Or was it, could it possibly be, that his reasons were more personal?

It made no difference. Her hate for the man was a living thing. It had tentacles like those of some sea creature that were wrapped around her heart, squeezing out all gentle emotion. She cared not a whit what Valcour might do to him. More, she cared even less what happened to anyone else, herself included. The buffeting of the last weeks, her father's arrest, Valcour's defection, her own ravishment and position of degradation, the ostracism by former friends, the trial and deaths of the conspirators, her father's suicide, had left her drained. The murder of Ashanti in such a barbaric fashion, throwing her body to the fish and turtles like so much carrion, had been the final assault. Her feelings were too dulled with pain to accept anything more.

What was Morgan doing now? Was he cavorting with the island wenches, flinging his money away in the drinking houses? How long would it be before such amusement palled?

Not soon, she suspected. The women would flock to him, such a change from the rough-and-tumble sailors. And for him, such enthusiasm would be vividly different. His last bed partner had not been so responsive.

She slept finally, only to awaken within the hour to the racking shudder of sobs and the salty overflow of warm tears, tracking into her hair.

Day came. The ship was quiet, ominously quiet. A meal was brought to Félicité by the captain's cabinboy at mid-morning, and another in the afternoon. He professed ignorance of what was going on, though he did not quite meet Félicité's eyes. In the morning hours, he agreed to deliver a message from her to Valcour, requesting him to come to her. Later he told her that he had spoken to Murat and got a cuff for his pains. From now on, anything she wanted said to the mean-tempered bastard she could jolly well say herself.

The opportunity to do so did not come until near evening. Valcour unlocked the door, swung it wide, and stepped inside without so much as a pause for a knock. Pushing the panel to behind him, he sauntered toward her with a sardonic smile lighting his yellow-brown eyes. From his right hand hung what appeared to be a woman's velvet gown. "Good evening, *ma chère.*"

"Good evening," Félicité returned, her tone even. She swung her feet off the mattress and came slowly upright. She would have stood, but Valcour put a hand on her shoulder, forcing her back down before he moved to take a seat opposite her on the bound chest fastened to the floor. He draped the gown he carried to one side.

"I trust you have had everything you need? Meals? A relaxing rest?"

"Those two things, yes. Otherwise, my amusements have been somewhat—confined."

"Too bad. And you look as if you could use a hot perfumed bath, too."

She flung him a glance of acute dislike. "Could not everyone on this ship?"

"One of the drawbacks of going a-pirating. The lack of bathing facilities, I fear, accounts as much as the tropical sun

221

for the teak-colored swarthiness attributed to most of our calling. What say you to bathing in the ocean? So refreshing, this time of day."

"I wouldn't know. I haven't had the privacy to partake of such delights."

"We must remedy that."

"How—kind of you," she said, her voice taut, expressionless.

Reaching into his clothing, he withdrew his snuffbox with its cross-and-skullbones enameling. Flipping it open, he took a pinch, holding it ready between thumb and forefinger with a delicate gesture. "You mistrust me, I see. I wonder why?"

"Experience is a formidable teacher."

"You are right," he said, and snapped the snuffbox closed, inhaled, then tended his nose. "There is an unfinished reckoning between us, one that I shall enjoy pursuing. But for the moment, there are more important matters at hand."

Félicité came to her feet, shifting to rest her shoulder against the wall end of the bunk. "Of what nature?"

"I thought I told you," he said, his face bland. "You are going swimming—in this."

She caught the gown of rich golden velvet as he flung it at her. The folds hung in her hands, dragging, weighing her down with their great width even dry. "You must be mad. It's impossible."

"Nothing is impossible if you want it badly enough, and I want Morgan McCormack dead badly indeed."

Félicité looked up at him. "If I go into the water in this, it will be my death you will achieve, instead of his."

"I think not," he said, and slowly, carefully, began to explain what he meant for her to do.

When he had finished, she stared at him. She shook her head. "No."

"Yes."

"What if he knows I can swim?"

"You mentioned it to him?"

"I may have."

"In that case we must make the picture even more distressing."

"You presume too much, Valcour. He—may care not at all what happens to me. What then?"

"Think you I would allow you to perish?" he inquired with a narrow smile.

"Without a qualm."

"You underestimate your attractions—or my attachment."

"But I would be a party to murder!" she cried. She felt as if there were a noose being slowly tightened around her neck.

"You would also be very rich. I have been authorized to offer you a seaman's share of the *Black Stallion*. It seems Morgan and his men overtook an English vessel heading for Jamaica and captured for themselves a right valuable cargo of silks and satins, spices, jade, and ivory, plus a chest of bullion meant for the governor's pay chest."

"Blood money."

He lifted a brow in provocative misunderstanding of her scorn. "So far as I know, the English merchantman struck her colors after the first shot. Quarter was given upon request of the captain. Not a man was killed."

"You know very well what I mean!"

"Yes," he agreed, his voice taking on an edge, "and I warn you, I have listened to your parading of objections and scruples as long as I intend. Time grows short. You will take off your breeches and garb yourself in this gown, or I will be forced to perform that service for you. You will not enjoy it, I'm sure. But suffer though you may, my darling sister, you shall do as I say."

"Valcour, for the love of God—"

"God," he said, coming to his feet, stepping to where the sword she had removed, his own, leaned against the wash-stand and picking it up, "has nothing to do with my actions, nor ever has had."

"But I can't do this, I tell you. I can't!"

"Only think of what this man has done to you. Or did you, perhaps, come to like it after a time?"

"No, no, but—"

He unsheathed the sword and turned toward her, stretching out his arm until the point of the blade glittered before her eyes. "Or perhaps it is as I said once before. You are in love with him."

"No!"

"Prove it. Join with me in destroying him. Together we will wipe out the shame. Together, you and I, Félicité."

She watched him in fascinated horror as the tip of the sword dropped lower, coming to rest gently against her abdomen. He leaned slightly, increasing the pressure, the look on his face one of maniacal enjoyment. Félicité held her breath.

He tightened the muscles of his arm, twitching his wrist, and the blade sliced upward, cutting through the linen of her shirt until it met the ruffle-edged placket of the head opening. The material fell away, exposing the proud curves of her breasts. On her upper abdomen a small scratch oozed a drop of crimson against the whiteness of her skin. He studied the effect for a long moment, his head on one side.

"Valcour," she breathed.

His eyes glazed, he flashed her a smile. "You must permit me to congratulate you on your nerve, *ma chère*. Most men would have flinched, and quite spoiled the picture."

He dropped the sword edge to the buttons of her breeches, flicking away first one and then the other, so that the front flap fell open. Félicité grabbed for it with both hands, but he reached out left-handed to snatch one wrist. The length of a thigh was exposed from hip bone to knee. The sword point wavered, coming to rest on the back of her other clutching hand.

"The gown, Félicité," he suggested, his tone silken.

Refusal might gain a point of honor, but what use was it if she lost dignity and more in the process? This contest was unequal, weighted heavily in Valcour's favor. Later there might be a chance to even the odds.

She nodded. "All right, the gown."

Muscles stiff with reluctance, Valcour drew back the sword, and gave her a mocking salute with it before he rammed it into its scabbard. "Wise, as well as steady of nerve. What a pair we shall make, *ma chère*, as soon as you learn to obey the instant I command. That is something it will please me to teach you. I will return on the quarter hour. Do not fail me.''

She was ready, wearing the gown of golden velvet, captured no doubt from some Spanish ship's cabin. She had made no attempt to put up her hair without the help of Ashanti, but she had brushed it, pushing it behind her shoulders, where it hung like a honey-gold cape, blending with the shimmering velvet.

They left the cabin and climbed upward through the quiet ship. It appeared deserted of men except for the cabinboy kicking his feet on the edge of the wharf. He stared open-mouthed at Félicité as she came down the gangplank, his face in the light of the stern lantern both amazed and slightly knowing.

There was no moon. The night, wine-dark and impenetrable, lay on the gently heaving water, shot by shifting beams from the *Black Stallion*'s lanterns as it rose and fell on the swells. That light was the beacon toward which Valcour, in the stern of an island pirogue, directed his unwieldy craft, made of a hollowed-out log. At the snub-nosed bow, the waves that slapped beneath the hull threw spray upward. The droplets clung to Félicité's face and shoulders, jeweling her brows and lashes, as she sat forward. She blinked against their salt sting again and again, but could not wipe them away, for her hands were tied behind her back. Valcour had added that refinement to the plan he had outlined just before they had stepped into the boat.

Félicité scarcely thought of what she was doing. She should be happy, she told herself. In a way Valcour was right; retribution for what she had suffered at Morgan's hand should be a great satisfaction. The method of gaining it mattered little.

Or did it? Against her will, she thought of how Morgan had come to tell her of her father's death, of his attempts to prevent her from learning her father's motive for suicide. She thought back over her days with the former lieutenant colonel and of the nights, and the searching light of the lantern was reflected with a golden glow in the depths of her wide eyes.

The side of the ship rose above them. They could hear the creaking of the anchor cable as the ship swung against it, and soaring above that the long-drawn notes of a jew's harp. As a counterpoint to both came the drone of the voices of the watch. Valcour stopped paddling.

Félicité glanced back. Valcour was an odd figure in the stern. He wore a henna-red wig on which was perched a puffed cap with side lappets such as was worn by older women. He had a satin cloak flung over his lap to simulate skirts, and another swan's-down-edged capelet swung around his shoulders. Laying down his paddle, he picked up a slim dueling pistol, allowing Félicité to see it before he cocked it with a loud double click and concealed it under the cape. He sent her a narrow, probing stare, then, raising his voice, called out in a wavering falsetto.

"Ahoy, the ship! Ahoy, I say!"

A sailor's head appeared over the side. He took in the bobbing pirogue and its cargo in one brief, contemptuous glance. "What do ye want, you old whore?"

"I have a special cargo for the captain," Valcour whined.

"Our captain don't do business with such as you. Be gone with you!"

"This is a special one, she is," Valcour insisted. "One such as the captain has been looking for. You tell him his Félicité is here, and he can have her without charge if he will come and get her!"

"I don't believe a word of it, you sniveling harridan! Go!"

"You are making a mistake, one you will regret, my friend. You just whisper the name Félicité in your captain's ear and see how fast he comes running."

The man at the rail above them was joined by others, and others still, until they lined the side of the ship. They muttered among themselves, then one among them noticed Félicité's bound hands. They passed Rabelaisian remarks then that made her cheeks burn. How could such noise go unnoticed? she wondered. Perhaps Valcour's scheming would be for nothing, perhaps Morgan was not on board?

Abruptly he was there. "What is this, you scurrilous sons of Neptune?" he demanded. "The way you are gaping and gawping, a man would think you had spied a mermaid at the very least."

226

"There's an old brothel bitch down there, captain," the first man began.

Another broke in, "Got a female with her all right, even if she don't be one of them half-fish sirens. And the old lady's got her trussed up and right ready for plucking, you being the lucky man they got picked out for the job!"

"Name they gave for the piece was Félicité," a third chimed in. "They thought you might be interested."

Morgan's head and shoulders sprang into view. He gripped the rail, staring down at them.

"Ah, Captain McCormack," Valcour crooned. "I thought you might like to say goodbye to Félicité."

Even as her brother spoke, Félicité drew in her breath. "No, Morgan! It's a trap!"

Valcour shot his hand out in a vicious blow that made the pirogue roll. It caught her in the small of the back, sending her diving forward, toppling head first into the water. Even as she fell she heard the crashing explosion of the pistol as Valcour fired.

Down and down she went, with her breath, hastily caught, aching in her lungs and the burning of salt water in her nose. She struggled frantically to free her hands, wrenching against the bonds, twisting, jerking at them. The velvet skirts were clamped to her, muffling her kick, weighting her so she was carried deeper and deeper still. The sounds of shouts and cries, of heavy splashes and sodden thumps, radiated through the water, receding. She knew that high above her, on the opposite side of the brigantine, the men of the *Raven* were swarming upward on grappling nets thrown from a pair of longboats. Under the cover of darkness, with muffled oars, they had slipped from the shore, waiting for the diversion she had been forced to provide.

Such things had no reality for her as she swirled slowly in the water. To die in the darkness with the turquoise sea of the Caribbean filling her lungs for so mean a cause seemed a wretched and debasing absurdity.

How long it had been since she had sneaked away to dog-paddle in the river with Valcour and his friends! She had not forgotten how to swim, but she lacked the strength to try for long against such odds. She righted herself, pushing, straining upward against the drag of her skirts and the hampering awkwardness of her bound arms. But she could feel the tiredness of that tremendous effort pulling at her. It was as though there were stones fastened to her ankles and a steel hoop about her chest, pressing on the tight-held air, trying to force it from her body. The world was an infinite swirl of water, one she had been suspended in for eons of time. It seemed that if she would cease fighting, would let herself float free, after the first sharp pain she might breathe the sea and become one with it.

A long gliding shape brushed past her, roiling the water. She cringed as she felt a touch on her arm. An instant later, she was clamped in a hard, encompassing hold. She surged upward with dizzying speed, trailing the fine-jeweled air bubbles of the last of her pent breath.

Her head broke the surface. She gasped, choking, coughing. She nearly went under again, only to find the support of strong hands at her waist. She opened her eyes.

Morgan was beside her, his face no more than a blur with a trace of dark red running from the nicked lobe of one ear. He shifted his grip, reaching lower, and with a great upward heave somersaulted her into the empty boat floating beside them. For the merest flicker of time, he stared into her face. Reassured, if not overjoyed, he kicked away, the sweep of powerful arms taking him through the water to the rope ladder that dangled over the side. He went up it hand over hand, but even as he climbed there came the cry of "Quarter! Quarter!" The rattle of musket fire and the clatter of cutlasses faded, dying away. Morgan disappeared over the bulwark. A voice called, sharp with warning, and suddenly everything was quiet.

Félicité lay gazing with wide eyes at the stars, panting, unable to accept either the reprieve or the certain knowledge that ebbed through her brain. She was alive, but Morgan had saved her at the loss of his ship. Without their leader, his men had thrown down their weapons and given up the *Black Stallion* with the seaman's ancient cry for mercy. But would there be any mercy, any quarter, for the ship's captain?

It was Captain Bonhomme who came for her at last. With Gallic curses, he slit her bonds and pulled the boat nearer the ladder so she could gain a foothold. He steadied the swaying hemp for her ascent, then climbed up with careless agility. He gained the deck in time to step near, steadying her as she swayed.

It was over. A wounded man groaned here and there on the decks, but otherwise all was still. It would not have been difficult to tell who was the victor, even if she had not guessed. The men of the *Raven* held their weapons; the men of the *Black Stallion* had none. And the former master of the brigantine lay on the deck not far from Félicité's feet with his arms outstretched, his sword still in his hand, and his hair matted with blood at the base of his skull as if he had been struck from behind.

Valcour rose from his seat on the capstan and strolled forward. Flicking Félicité a look of malicious amusement, he drawled, "Now that the most important member of the audience has arrived, we may begin. Would someone be so good as to throw a bucket of water over our good Captain McCormack, the former lieutenant colonel under the Spanish dons, and let us see how bright shines the spark of life left to him?"

Félicité sat down suddenly on a great coil of rope. Seawater dripped, trickling from the seaweed fronds of her wet hair and oozing from her skirts, turning pink as it joined the trail of blood on the deck, Morgan's blood. Unconsciously, she began to massage her wrists, looking from the inert form of the man at her feet to her brother's pockmarked face.

A sailor dumped water over Morgan and then stood back. For long moments, nothing happened. Then as Valcour was on the point of commanding another drenching, Morgan made a low sound like a stifled groan.

Valcour stepped close to the prone man, prodding at him with his sword. "Up, dog, and face your punishment as best you can, like the *canaille* you are."

Félicité slanted a quick glance at Captain Bonhomme, a question in her eyes. The Frenchman allowed his dark gaze to slide away.

Morgan raised himself to one elbow, shaking his head in what appeared a vain effort to clear it. He looked to Valcour, and then beyond to the crews of the two ships drawn up around him. Finally, his green eyes came to rest on Félicité.

"Take him, men," Valcour screamed suddenly. "Tie him to the mast, and we will see how he answers to a touch of the cat!"

The cat, the dreaded cat-o'-nine-tails with its multiple ends to flay a man. It could leave no more than reddening stripes or cut to the bone, depending on the strength and skill and state of mind of the man who wielded it. Her eyes wide with horror, Félicité sprang to her feet as Valcour brought out a scourge with nine rawhide ribbons that were each loaded with bits of iron and glass at the tips to rip and tear the skin.

A squad of burly men jerked Morgan to his feet and hauled him stumbling to the mast. They wrapped his arms around it and tied them with tarred rope, then ripped his shirt asunder, exposing the scarred brown skin that covered his broad back.

"It seems this will not be his first encounter with a flogging. That he knows what to expect should make it more interesting!" Valcour dangled the whip from his hand, dragging it over the deck so it spread out, rattling on the boards as he moved closer to Morgan.

"No," Félicité whispered, taking a step toward him. "No!"

Valcour sent her a glittering smile. Drawing back his arm, he brought it down with a triumphant grunt, laying the cat-o'-nine-tails across Morgan's back.

The weighted thongs bit deep. Morgan stiffened, his head snapping back as gouts of blood appeared across his shoulders and ran downward in quickening streams.

"No! Wait!" Félicité screamed, and spun around to face Captain Bonhomme. "Is this your idea of fairness? What of your fine articles of agreement and your boast of justice on the seas? I heard the cry for quarter from the crew of the *Black Stallion*, and you must have granted it. Doesn't it extend to this man?"

"Murat is the quartermaster. To order a flogging is his right." The captain's face was pale. His dogged words were echoed by the whistle of another stroke of the whip.

"His right? For no reason except revenge? That's what this is, I swear it. That's all it is!"

"I don't know—" the captain began, his eyes troubled.

Félicité swept a glance at the crew, at Valcour carefully disentangling his bloodstained implement. An idea darted across her mind, and though it was a desperate chance, she seized it, words tumbling from her lips with fervid eloquence.

"You say you always offer a captured crew the chance to join you. No man here, I think, has been, or could be, so foolish as to refuse, least of all the captain, a man long familiar with the laws of the seas. Members of your crew, all, must settle their personal differences with sword and pistol on land, I believe the articles read. Isn't that so?"

"*Mais certainement.*"

"Then why not in this case? Why should the quartermaster be allowed to use his authority to gain an advantage denied to the rest? Why should he be any different?"

"You are right, mademoiselle, but—"

"You are the captain!" she cried as the whip rose and fell once more and she heard Morgan's short and sharp exhalation of near-unbearable pain. "Order this stopped. Enforce the articles of agreement!"

There was a stirring among the men, a murmur of concurrence as they cut their eyes toward Félicité, devouring the picture she made with the wet and heavy velvet dragging the low bodice lower still, until the pink aureoles of her breasts began to show. Murat was not a popular man with them, being ugly-tempered and finicking, and this François miraculously turned into a half-drowned mermaid, even saying she had no business being there, was a right telling advocate. The *Black Stallion*'s crew stood with grim faces and clenched fists, their attention on their captain. Among them Félicité registered with scant surprise the features of Juan Sebastian Unzaga.

Only Valcour, concentrating with moist lips and glazed eyes on the helpless man before him, did not appear to notice what she was saying.

"Stop!" Captain Bonhomme shouted, striding toward

Valcour. Lifting his hand, he caught the cat and tore it from the other man's fingers.

There came a soft breathed sigh from the men. Félicité looked down at her hands. They were trembling uncontrollably, and she clasped them together before her.

The French captain stood firm on the gently rocking vessel. "It is as Fran—the beautiful mademoiselle says. This is no way to satisfy a personal vendetta. It should be decided on shore in the usual manner."

"You fool!" Valcour snarled. "Why do you listen to her? What can she know of it? Return my cat and let me get on with it!"

The face of the French captain turned glacial. Softly he said, "You call me, Jacques Bonhomme, captain of the *Raven* and of this captured prize, a fool, m'sieu?"

"A—slip of the tongue made in the heat of the moment, one for which I apologize," Valcour, master of himself once more, said with smooth plausibility. "But for this McCormack, it is not worth the trouble of arranging a meeting of equals."

"Not worth the trouble? I disagree," the captain, unmollified, replied. "This is a man's life, m'sieu, and such a man! I knew him some years ago as a most glorious son of the seas, one successful at his trade of piracy. He would be a valuable addition to our company if the dispute between you, whatever its nature, could be settled." The captain cast a quick look from Morgan to Félicité before looking back to Valcour.

Valcour also flung a hard stare from Félicité to the man tied to the mast. His narrow yellow-brown eyes surveyed with disdain the bleeding shoulders, the wet, blood-clotted hair, the etching of pain and shock on features that were pale beneath the overlay of burnishing from the sun.

A low laugh broke from him. "I withdraw my objections," he drawled. "By all means let us continue this lesson with pistol and cutlass. Captain McCormack and I crossed swords once before in the dark. It is time and past that we meet again."

He had, of course, seen the advantage to himself in the proposed contest. Morgan had powder burns blazing on the side of his face and an injured ear; he had expended strength to raise Félicité from the sea's depths, sustained a cracked head that left him groggy, and steeled himself against the flaying of Valcour's devilish scourge. After so much strain, so much loss of blood from so many wounds, how could he match blades with the other man in a fair encounter? It might well be, Félicité saw, that she had condemned him to death as surely as if she had allowed the flogging to go on to its inevitable end.

The French captain saw it too. His brow creased in a frown. "There is no need to rush the matter. Morning will do as well as this midnight."

"There is nothing in the articles," Valcour pointed out as he drew a scented handkerchief from his sleeve to wipe Morgan's blood from his fingers, "about waiting. In fact, the sooner the discord is over, the better."

He was right; Félicité saw the answer in Captain Bonhomme's face before he gave the slow nod of agreement. Swinging hard around, the burly, once-handsome Frenchman bellowed the order to cut Morgan down.

The two men did not meet in complete darkness. A single lantern, shielded from the wind by a metal shade, sent its shimmering rays over the stretch of shore. Its yellow gleams turned the sand to gold dust and probed into the shadows that lurked at the palm forest's edge. The sea rolled in with crashing waves that hissed up onto the beach and sighed as they expired without quite reaching that burning glow.

They had come to this deserted length of sand by longboat. A seaman had sponged Morgan's injuries with salt water, pushed a ration of rum into his hands, and given him another shirt. His hair had dried on the pull to shore, sculpting his head in russet waves. His eyes as he stood to one side were jade-hard and alert, though there was a hint of gray about his firm mouth. Deliberately, or so it seemed, he refrained from glancing toward where Félicité waited.

Though the night wind against her damp velvet was cool, she did not feel it. There was an arrested sensation inside her, as if time had stopped. She was aware of Valcour taking snuff, of Captain Bonhomme on one knee before a pistol case

233

checking the priming of the matched weapons it contained, of the sputter of the lantern and its smell of hot whale oil, of the rustle of encroaching palms, the hollow slap of the waves against the hull of the longboat, and the mumbling undertone of the men who had manned the oars to bring them. Out on the dark sea-face was another boat, filled doubtless with men who had decided among themselves that this show was much too promising to miss.

The crewmen's disapproval of Félicité's presence was a palpable thing. They felt she had no right to be there, but she had insisted. Valcour, for his own dark reasons, had supported her. He surveyed her now with feline gratification and the slightest hint of impatience.

Captain Bonhomme did not wait for the remainder of the audience. With a brusque gesture, he motioned both men forward. Handing a chased silver pistol, butt first, to each in turn, he set them back to back. That each knew what was expected was plain. Holding their pistols pointed skyward, they stepped out as the French captain counted off the first pace.

In measured cadence, the men drew apart, their steps parallel to the water's edge. The wind snatched at the dry sand they dislodged, sending it blowing, whispering, across the beach. Six, seven, eight paces were counted off, doubling the distance as each man moved to twelve, fourteen, sixteen paces dividing them. Twenty paces. They stopped, dark statues with the lantern light fluttering over their backs. For the space of a heartbeat the wind died and it was still.

"Fire!"

They turned together, spinning, bringing the muzzles of their pistols level, squeezing the triggers with no time allowed for aiming on pain of having their weapons knocked from their hands. Valcour's pistol belched smoke and flame. The ball flew wide, singing away to clatter among the underbrush. Morgan's weapon struck sparks, but did not go off.

Captain Bonhomme swore softly. "A miss and a misfire! You will proceed to cutlasses, gentlemen!"

Cutlasses they were, with curving blades like sabers, sharp on one side and the tip, and fixed with rounded bell guards of brass at the hilts. They were the preferred cut-and-thrust sidearm of seamen instead of straight, double-edged swords. They flashed blue light as the two men saluted, then rasped together with a shower of orange sparks as Valcour lunged, snatching the first offensive.

Morgan parried, giving ground, meeting the wickedly darting blade in quinte, in sixte, swirling into a sudden riposte that sobered Valcour so that the grin drawing his thin lips back from his teeth faded. Cautiously, they circled, the blades tapping, chiming, singing together with the lick of fire.

The gleam of sweat appeared on Valcour's face. He watched his opponent with avid eyes, waiting for signs of weakness, feinting, testing. Morgan kept his guard, recoiling smoothly. His wrist was tempered, pliant, as he flicked Valcour's blade aside again and again, displaying a complete command of swordsman's tricks with which to defend himself.

Slow rage seeped into Valcour's face. He grew cunning, pressing and then withdrawing, so that they moved back and forth across the sand, their booted feet scuffling, their blades slipping, slithering, winking in the lanternlight. Both men were breathing hard, bellows-deep and gasping.

Abruptly, Valcour thrust forward with bent knee. Morgan twisted, leaping aside, parrying in seconde so nearly too late that the cutlasses scraped grittingly, their hand guards coming together with a bell-like clang. They strained body to body, their faces inches apart, their eyes clashing.

"What price vengeance?" Morgan queried, the words quiet and clear with the breathless mockery of a goad. He wrenched free, springing backward, recovering in form, but the red-brown splotches that stained the back of his shirt had darkened and spread, widening until they ran together.

Valcour's swordplay took on a vicious crackle. It was plain he meant to beat down the man who opposed him with sheer brilliance. Toward that end, he called upon every nuance and variation ever displayed by a New Orleans *maître d'armes*, those master swordsmen who were teachers of their art. A whirl of glittering, incipient death carried before him, he began his advance.

He could not sustain it. Five minutes passed. Ten. Morgan

was a wraith that could not be touched, could not be overborne. He countered every artifice, every rare ruse, with its companion defense stratagem, and though perspiration ran down his face and his breathing was a harsh rasp, he conserved his energy, watching for the next of Valcour's many devices. His concentration was narrowed to the shining point of the other man's sword. His brain, no less agile than muscle and sinew, directed his movements with an intensity that if he had been less impaired by injury might have been swiftly lethal. And yet, it almost seemed he was containing himself, deliberately refraining from the attack, waiting with close-gripped patience.

Félicité's eyes burned as without blinking she followed the dancing blades. She was suffocating, unable to expand her chest for air. She recognized in some detached part of her mind that she was watching a magnificent contest, but she could not appreciate it. Raw terror surrounded her, tearing at the cocoon of numbness in which she had encased herself, burrowing inward toward her heart. The snick and scream of the steel blades gave her a feeling of aching vulnerability in the center of her being.

Behind her, the oarsmen had not moved in a quarter of an hour, and the latecomers who had leaped from their boats were still standing hock deep in the washing surf.

Morgan stumbled. He was tiring, his pallor becoming more pronounced as his shirt grew wet with sweat and blood, and the waist of his breeches took on a soaked and scarlet sheen. His parries were less clean, scraping. He began, infinitesimally, to give ground.

Fiendish glee rose in Valcour's yellow-brown eyes. He redoubled his efforts, driving Morgan back step by step toward a goal chosen from the outset. It lay at the periphery of his vision, shining with brightwork varnish, the pistol case half hidden in the shadow of the longboat.

Félicité saw it and made a quick, abortive gesture, then dropped her hand. To distract Morgan's attention might be fatal. That a few among the crew had discovered Valcour's goal also was plain from the uneasy expressions that flitted across their weathered faces. To resort to trickery, abandoning honor and a corrupt society's rules of fair play, to defeat a troublesome opponent was no more than was to be expected. Any man nimble enough to keep his skin unpricked this long should know to look for such.

Did Morgan? He retreated before the clattering flurry of Valcour's sword like a blown leaf before a squall. He seemed to be hard-pressed, barely able to find the strength to hold the heavy cutlass steady. Failing, spent, he brought his heel down on the slippery surface of the wooden case and lurched, sprawling.

Valcour drew a hissing breath and extended himself, launching a yard of whistling death straight for Morgan's heart.

It was caught in prime on an arch of steel. Morgan, ready and fully expecting the ploy, braced on one arm and recoiled from the sand with his sword at a diagonal slant across his body. Edge to edge, the blades grated with a shower of fiery light. Morgan's circled, adhering with lightning speed and leverage, bending, binding, perfectly timed. Valcour's grip was broken. His cutlass sprang free, and flew like a comet to bury itself with quivering hilt in the damp salt and sand.

Lithe, renewed, Morgan pushed erect, pressing the point of his sword to Valcour's breastbone. Staring into the man's stunned, unbelieving eyes, he said, "My victory, I think. The penalty, my friend, for overestimation."

Valcour drew a retching breath, his eyes darting from Morgan to Félicité.

The French captain moved suddenly, as if unable to endure the cramped stillness. "I grant your victory, Captain Mc-Cormack, if he will not. Have done with it, *mon ami!*"

Morgan looked beyond the French captain, his gaze coming to rest on Félicité's pale face before he lowered his emerald eyes to Valcour once more.

"Will it be an end, Murat, or for the sake of your sister and a truce to quarreling, will you cry quarter?"

To accept his life from a man to whom he had denied the boon was an annihilating abasement, a black and bottomless retreat into cowardice. Valcour took it without hesitation.

"Quarter," he croaked.

Chapter 14

✦

The two longboats pulled back to the *Black Stallion.* Over one hung brooding silence, that carrying the captain, Félicité, and Valcour. From the other came lurid oaths in jocular tones as the pirate crewmen congratulated Morgan, who sat among them, and refought the passage at arms blow by blow, recalling other great bouts they had witnessed between men of prowess.

Félicité sat in frowning thought. They were nearly upon the brigantine when she realized there was no place for her upon it. Even if there had not been an article prohibiting her presence, she had no place to bunk except with Valcour, an impossible position now that he need not fear Ashanti's potions.

She turned in her seat. "Captain Bonhomme, I'm sorry. But I must ask you to turn about and put me ashore."

"At this time of night? Such a thing would be most ungallant; I cannot do it."

"But your articles concerning women—"

"We have bent them before, for short periods. It will not be a tragedy if we do so again."

"I have nowhere to stay," she protested.

"Considering what has happened, I can understand your reluctance to go on as before, most certainly. Do not worry your head. A berth will be found for you—somewhere."

The men at the sweeps would not turn about without a direct order. Already they were shipping the long oars to allow the boat to glide up to the looming bulwark of what had been Morgan's ship. She was more aware than she cared to be of the French captain's presence beside her on the forward seat, and of the soft huskiness of his voice as he addressed her.

"I—I suppose I must thank you," she said.

"*Mais non*. There is no need. We are—friends, are we not?" He reached to put an arm around her in a carelessly affectionate gesture.

"Yes, certainly," she replied, edging away.

"You are cold, *chérie*, and still damp in the self-same gown you had on when you went into the sea. What imbeciles we are, not to allow you to change! We can count ourselves lucky if some twice-cursed tropical fever doesn't take you off!"

"I will be fine. My hair is almost dry." He was chafing her arm, holding her tightly against him, ignoring her efforts to draw away.

"I saw a copper tub in the captain's cabin aboard the brigantine. I will order for you a hot soak and a dram of rum. That should help protect your health."

How could she refuse? The rum she could do without, but the tub of water! Pray God there was soap as well.

There was, though of the roughest kind, harsh with leached lye and with a smell she associated more with scrubbing floors than her own skin. It was, nonetheless, heavenly. She would worry about how she was to deflect the captain's ardor another time. For now, she meant to be clean.

In the privacy of the captain's cabin, she soaped herself, rubbing so hard her skin reddened and stung. She washed her hair, squeezing the lather through it again and again, rinsing until the last trace of soap was gone, then letting it dangle in wet strands over the side. She sat back then, with her knees drawn up and her eyes closed as she allowed the heat to seep into her bones, permitting muscles and nerves to relax that had not done so in weeks.

She had heard the sound of extraordinary activity ever since coming aboard. That the watch and the crew left behind had been busy was also evident. Several of the green turtles loaded on the lugger had been transferred to the larger vessel, and she had discovered in the second officer's cabin, while waiting for her bath to heat, the bundle containing her own clothing. The pirates, it seemed, could be efficient when they cared to be.

What would become of the *Raven*? She had served her purpose and would doubtless be sold. In times like these, a ship was too valuable a commodity to be abandoned.

How things changed. Who would have thought that Morgan, so staunch a defender of the Spanish regime, intent on becoming a landed proprietor and upstanding citizen in the newest colony of King Carlos, would turn again to a career on the high seas? What had taken place to bring it about? She would give much to know.

On a more personal level, who would have thought, only a day ago, that she would be affected by any injustice directed against the Irishman, no matter what form it took? Who could have predicted she would feel such overwhelming gladness that it was Morgan who had beaten Valcour to his knees, instead of the other way around?

Life was peculiar. People changed overnight; or was it just that the way others saw them changed?

The water in her tub dipped and rose with the movements of the ship at anchor. Overhead, there came a boom like a muffled explosion, and of a sudden the water surged in a miniature tidal wave, rising to Félicité's throat and spilling over the tub lip beside her before receding to splash over the edge beyond her knees. Félicité sat bolt upright. She knew enough to recognize that muffled explosion. It was the great mainsail of the brigantine filling with wind, stretching fat-bellied and wide. The *Black Stallion* was off and running. They had set sail.

Félicité stepped from the tub, and as the level of water dropped, it ceased its imitation of a cataract. Grimacing, she reached to pick up the glass the French captain had sent to her by his cabinboy. She drank down a mouthful of rum. She didn't want it, but he had acted as if he would be insulted if she allowed it to go to waste. She had no intention of becoming drunk, however; nothing so convenient, either for him or for herself.

Setting the glass back down, she dried herself on a length

of linen toweling laid for that purpose on the washstand. With it wrapped around her, she stood considering the contents of her bundle. She could put on the nightrail she desired above all things, don chemise, petticoats, and gown, or return to her breeches and shirt. The first would be entirely too provocative if the captain returned soon to allot her a sleeping space, and the last needed a good wash. That left her female attire, but the stays and petticoats it needed had been soaked in seawater along with the ruined velvet gown.

While she tried to make up her mind, she picked up her wooden comb, drawing it through the tangles of her hair. Her frowning glance fell on a sword that lay across a chair near the officer's desk in one corner of the cabin. By its military scabbard and insignia and its lines, she knew it at once. It was Morgan's uniform sword. It had been taken from him when he was unconscious after the attack. Since the meeting with Valcour required cutlasses, he had not needed it later. Had someone brought it here to his former quarters as a gesture of courtesy, or was it a part of the code that the sword of the deposed captain became the property of the victor?

It didn't matter. She swung away, moving to the chest against one wall. The lid lifted easily on well-oiled hinges. Inside was clothing—Morgan's shirts, cravats, discarded uniforms, and another set of breeches, coat, and waistcoat in shades of blue and buff.

That settled it. She would borrow a clean shirt from his store and return to her same breeches and her role as a young man. It would fool no one, but would be better suited to shipboard conditions—and to her newly formed, most acutely conscious, resolve.

No more would she play the part of helpless female, constrained by circumstances to accept her fate. From this moment she would gird herself to be her own protection. She was done with false positions. Alone, unfettered, she owed no duty, no loyalty, to anyone other than herself. Against all odds and the threat of superior strength, she would remain her own person, neither the chattel, the drudge, nor the plaything of any man.

There was a small steel mirror above the washstand for

shaving. In its dim surface, her face appeared touched with the tint of golden apricots by the sun, a delicate contrast to the pristine white linen of Morgan's shirt. Her hair as it dried seemed burnished with soft golden light, paling nearly to silver around her face. What she looked like mattered not, except perhaps as a handicap, she told herself. Swinging away, she pulled on her clothing, then, returning to the sea chest, bent to search for something with which to confine her long and troublesome tresses.

Behind her, the cabin door swung open. It was Valcour who stood there. She let fall the chest lid and turned to face him, every nerve alert. His eyes narrowed, shielding a rabid glitter as they ran over her. She was not the only one who had had a taste of rum, for she could smell the fumes that engulfed him from where she stood, see its effects in his loose-limbed stance and the precarious way he leaned to shut the door.

"I thought I would find you here," he said. "Trust you to run with the leader of the pack, whoever he may be. To the victor go the spoils."

There was more, in terms of sickening crudeness. She cut across it. "What do you want?"

"There is a matter of—importance that is unfinished between us, if you will remember?"

"That is over," she said, her voice cold. "You have befouled the memory of my childhood and made me regret that my father ever had the misfortune to cross your path. I never want to speak to you again. And if you touch me again, ever, for any reason, I will make you regret it."

"Mighty words, *ma chère*. Are you certain you can live up to them? I may have been bested by a superior swordsman, but you I can still turn over my knee at any time. That knowledge has sustained me for these long years."

She stared at him. "For years? What are you talking about?"

"Do you remember how when you were eight, *chère*, and I ten years older, you ran and hid from me in the armoire? I joined you there in the dark and—took delicious liberties while you squirmed and cried; nothing to harm you, but so very pleasurable. You told Ashanti's mother, and afterward she watched you closer, but I was enraptured.''

She did remember, abruptly. How could she ever have forgotten, unless it had been in some way a protection? The sting of that peculiar, shaming spanking was as hurtful now as it had been then, when she had not understood but had only been afraid.

''I am glad,'' she said distinctly, ''that Ashanti fed you poisoned herbs.''

''Even if it cost her her life?''

She stared at him, though less in shock, it seemed, than from the fact that he would admit it. ''You? It was you who did that unspeakable thing to her?''

''She had been asking for it for a long time.''

He was a monster, mentally deformed, wholly immoral. His wishes, his desires, what was best for him, these were his sole guide. It seemed suddenly a great pity that Morgan had withheld him from the death he so richly deserved.

''Get out,'' she whispered.

''Oh, no. No, indeed.'' He shook his head, moving toward her with the slow stalk of a hunting jackal scenting injured prey. ''You cheated me this evening when you pleaded for your lover, Morgan. You caused him to be set free, to have a chance at me with pistol and cutlass. Because of you, I was bested, I who have always prevailed in such encounters, my one source of pride.''

''What of the night Morgan sent you and two others running like whipped curs in the dark?'' She would not back away from him, not if he killed her.

''My own men got in my way, the stupid whoresons. One even mistook me for Morgan so that I had to prick him. That is not something I care to remember. We will not speak of it.''

''Why not?'' she jeered. ''Don't you want to admit that Morgan is a better man—''

Before she could finish, he lifted his arm and swung backhanded at her mouth. She turned her head at the last minute; still, she tasted blood as his knuckles grazed her lips. Rage surged to her brain, bringing a red haze before her eyes.

Without taking time to think, she drew back and struck her brother a ringing slap in the face.

He growled, reaching for her throat. She dodged and slipped under his arm, but he whirled to dive after her, catching her waist, bearing her down to the floor.

Gritting pain flared in her hip as she struck. It fueled the frenzy of the kick she drove into his legs. Her foot caught him a glancing blow in the crotch, and he grunted, releasing her. Twisting, scrambling away, getting her feet under her, she rose to one knee. He lunged after her, catching the fullness of her too-large shirt, dragging her slowly back.

She could not break his grip. She spun then to the attack, clawing for his face. Her nails raked across his eyes, and he gave a piercing yell. He brought his fist up in a stunning blow to her chest then, and followed it with another before he sent her flailing across the rim of the tub, skidding in the spilled water, crashing to the floor with him on top of her.

Anguish exploded inside her. It hurt to breathe or to move. Her answer was to curl her own fingers into a hard knot and slam them into his throat. He coughed with a gagging, gurgling sound, but managed to hold her, his hand fastening on her breast and squeezing until her nerves shrieked with the agony of it. He twined the other hand in her hair, pulling, wrenching her head backward on the stem of her neck. She saw behind her tightly closed eyes the first gray mists of merciful blackness.

With gritted teeth she heaved, shifting his weight that lay across her. Immediately she drew herself into a ball and kicked out. In protecting his crotch, he shifted, so both feet sank in his stomach. He doubled, his hold loosening. She dragged herself free, pushing, crawling out of his reach. Her elbow hit the chair, and Morgan's sword clattered to the floor. She pounced on it, drawing it slithering from the scabbard as she came to her feet.

Valcour, his eyes bloodshot, crazed with pain and distorted lust, shoved to a staggering crouch. He ignored the blade she leveled at him, plunging toward her.

She skipped back, panting. "Keep away. I am not Morgan, and I see no reason, in all honor, not to use this."

"Use it and be damned," came his hoarse shout as he lurched, grabbing for the naked blade with his hands.

It was his mistake. She drew back at his first touch, slicing his fingers and palm to the bone, then with rapier level and knee slightly bent, leaned delicately to skewer him in the heart.

It was not her fault that he saw his danger reflected in the midnight darkness of her eyes and straightened, trying to dance aside. Needle-sharp and deadly, the blade slid into his belly at an angle near the stomach and pierced through, emerging red on the other side.

Valcour stared down at the sword impaling him to the hilt, and then he screamed, the sound reverberating around the walls of the cabin.

"By Our Lady, she did it!"

Those words, low, stunned, almost reverent, were Félicité's first sign that she had an audience. Captain Bonhomme, who had spoken, stood in the doorway, while Morgan, with cutlass in hand, was halfway across the cabin.

The Irishman straightened from his swordsman's crouch. "Yes," he said, satisfaction rich in his tone. "She did."

Félicité dragged her sword free, and swept around to meet the newcomers. Morgan gave her a hard grin. Valcour ceased his screams and fell to his knees with both hands pressed to his side. The captain hesitated, then came slowly forward.

"I make you my compliments, mademoiselle. That was most handily done. There is, however, a prohibition against bloodletting on board this ship. I must ask you to surrender your sword."

It was pointless to refuse. Félicité bowed with the grace of a fencing master and, reversing the blade, presented her weapon hilt first over her arm.

"Admirable," Captain Bonhomme said, exchanging what had every appearance of a relieved glance with Morgan.

Valcour broke in then, cursing, demanding care for his wound. Morgan and the French captain picked him up bodily and laid him on a lower bunk. The entrance and exit wounds were plugged with wads of cotton swabbing soaked in rum, then a tight corset of bandaging was bound about his waist.

Sometime during this rough-and-ready treatment, Valcour's oaths and cries stopped as he swooned.

Leaving the patient under the watchful eye of the cabinboy, the two men with Félicité moved out into the companionway.

"Poor Murat," Captain Bonhomme said. "He does not fare well at the hands of his women. First the dead slave girl, your maid I presume, mademoiselle, doses him with a powerful purgative, and now you have carved a niche in his side."

"I am not his woman," Félicité said.

"I am delighted to hear it. I would hate to think the thing I just witnessed was a gesture of affection. Still, your skill with a rapier is likely to prove an inconvenience."

"How so?" She flung a quick glance at Morgan, who was watching the two of them with a careful lack of expression.

"Now that he is ensconced in my cabin, he will prove difficult to move. Sharing a cabin with you, *ma chère*, in addition to Murat and my cabinboy, was not what I had in mind."

"I was not aware that I was to share your cabin, captain."

"No? But it is obviously the only solution. You cannot sleep with the men in the forecastle or upon the open deck. Such would be to invite wholesale murder as each fought to claim you, or else a quick and uneasy death for you from overuse. Chafe how you will, you must put yourself under the protection of some man capable of defending the prize."

"You?" she snapped, her anger caused at least as much by the truth of his statement as by his audacity in settling her fate without consulting her in any way.

"Why not? I am the superior of most on board with a sword, and I am not so ill favored as some."

"You knew it would come to this when you refused to let me go ashore." She flung the accusation at him.

"That may be, but I assure you it would have been no different if you had ventured alone into that sinkhole of iniquity of a town. Come, *ma petite*, be reasonable. Be— resigned, if not happy. You know there is no other choice."

"But there is."

The words, deep and etched with challenge, came from

Morgan. Félicité and the French captain turned to face him, she in disbelief, he with stiff distress.

The captain spoke first. "What do you mean, *mon ami?*"

"Just now abovedecks, your men and mine in combination elected me to serve in the vacant post of sailing master, did they not?"

"They did," the other man admitted grudgingly, "though there were moments, as the tale of your swordsmanship circulated, when it occurred to me you might be their next captain."

Morgan shook his head. "I think not. You have the reputation of a captain who runs a lucky ship, one who is, besides, pistol-proof. Nevertheless, as an officer second only to you and the quartermaster, it is my right to occupy the cabin beside your own."

Captain Bonhomme's face turned a shade darker. "This is true."

"In that case, Mademoiselle Félicité can share it with me."

"No," Félicité cried.

The two men ignored her. The captain's brown Gallic eyes narrowed. "So it is Félicité, is it? The two of you are known to each other."

"I won't do it," Félicité said.

"Yes," Morgan answered, his green eyes holding those of the other man. "I know her—well."

The Frenchman sighed. "I feared as much. It should have been plain to me when you risked your ship to save her from drowning, when she begged me so eloquently to stop Murat's joyful maiming of you. I suppose you are prepared to defend your—your right of possession."

"Of course," Morgan said, the words clipped, uncompromising.

"Of course." The captain sighed. "I know my limitations. Against the cut and thrust of ordinary swordplay, I am the equal of any, but I have no desire to cross weapons with either a devil incarnate like Murat, or with you, *mon ami*, who fight as if St. Michael himself, the patron saint of warriors, directs your right hand. She is yours."

"No! You can't do this," Félicité cried.

The French captain turned to her. "It is done, *ma petite*, for the sake of your comfort and safety, and partially for my continued well-being. Do not repine. One man or the other, what difference does it make? Just as to men all cats are gray in the dark, I have little doubt for woman it is the same."

Félicité, thinking of Valcour, suppressed a shudder. "You know nothing about it."

"And I am destined, it seems, to know less. I leave you to McCormack while I seek what comfort can be found in a bottle of rum. It is a sovereign remedy, I do swear, for more than one kind of fever."

Captain Jacques Bonhomme gave them a mocking bow, then stepped back into the cabin they had left, closing the door behind him.

Félicité glanced at Morgan. He lifted a brow, then, moving a few steps down the companionway to the door of the second cabin, pushed it open and waited for her to enter. Félicité raised her chin. There was defiance in her brown eyes as she walked toward him.

Inside the cabin, she turned. "I hope you do not think that because you have arranged matters to suit yourself yet again, everything is going to be the way it was before."

"Isn't it?" he inquired, pulling the door to behind him so that the latch snapped with a sharp click.

"No, it isn't. This may be the best place for me to stay on this ship, but that does not mean that I am going to be your—bedmate as well as your messmate. You compelled me to accept that position once, but you don't have the means to do it now. My father is dead, and I have nothing more to fear." A taut quiet hung between them. Into it seeped the knowledge that brave though her words might be, they were false. There was force enough and more in the man before her, in the pliant strength of his swordsman's body, to compel her if he so chose.

He did not. Leaving her vain challenge unanswered, he said, "I never suggested that I would harm your father."

"Not in so many words, but the threat was there, the threat

248

that his continued good health depended on my conduct. Deny, if you can, that you took advantage of that dread.''

"I can't, nor do I intend to. How else could I come near you, after what had passed between us? Out of bloodlust and rage and disappointment that, as I thought, you had led me into a trap, showing yourself to be less the woman I had dreamed and more the treacherous, betraying jade, I forced myself upon you. Could I expect you to forgive me and accept my amends, I the enemy?''

"Why should it matter?'' she demanded. "Why should you care what I thought?''

"Oh, come, Félicité! What do you want? Declarations to fling back into my teeth? Never mind, it's over.''

"It isn't over, not so long as you are here, arranging my life for me once more.''

One corner of his mouth curved in a dry smile as he put his hands on his hips. "If it bothers you so much, this arranging of your life by men, why did you leave New Orleans? Whatever possessed you to go running like a hare before the hounds into this nest of oceanbound thieves and murderers?''

"If you really want to know, I will tell you,'' she said, and irritated by his amusement, launched into a concise account of Valcour's promise to take her to France, of their departure from the city with herself in the guise of a young man, the turbulent voyage, and finally the arrival of the ship at Grand Cayman.

"So you wanted to go to France, and wound up instead on the high seas. That must have been a shock.''

"It was, nearly as great a one as discovering you had taken the same path. How does it come about that you followed so quickly?''

"What makes you think I did?''

A frown drew her winged brows together. "I don't, but it seems stretching coincidence a bit far that you happened to arrive so soon.''

"I suppose it must. All right, I did follow you. There had been information concerning Valcour's activities, his flirtation with a pirate band, the name of the ship, her captain, her favorite port of call.''

"But isn't the outfitting of a ship under a pirate flag, the hiring of a crew, and the detailing of a highly valued officer a little extravagant, even for the Spanish, for the apprehending of a traitor's daughter and adopted son?"

He moved to stand leaning with one shoulder against the bunk. "You missed the point, my dear Félicité. I am no longer a Spanish officer, valued or otherwise."

She stared at him, unable to believe she had heard aright. "What are you saying?"

"It's true."

"But why?"

"Several reasons. To begin with, I was not happy with O'Reilly's decision to have your countrymen shot. While there was every justification for it, there was also ample justification for leniency. In addition, he and I had words concerning the land grant he had promised. He claimed it was to be awarded only after a year of service in the colony, while I maintained then, and still do, that he implied it would be parceled out immediately after the inhabitants of Louisiana had accepted Spanish rule. The end of the matter was that the governor-general hinted strongly there would be no land grant at all if I did not mend my ways. On top of that, when I requested permission to leave New Orleans, to take ship to find you, my request was denied. My duty, O'Reilly said, was to the army and the crown, not to some French girl who had left me, be she ever so beautiful."

"So you threw away everything you had worked for, your position as an officer, your hope of advancement, your plans for the future?"

"I did. And with Bast and a few other men of like mind I recruited, I stole a ship and reverted to my old habits."

"You chose well. The *Black Stallion* is a beautiful ship," Félicité said, lowering her lashes. "I am sorry that because of me you had to lose her."

"You were not, I think, a willing accomplice, not unless your brother has a strange idea of the way his confederates should be treated."

"That would not be an impossibility," she answered, her voice stiff, "but no, I was not willing."

EMBRACE AND CONQUER

His green eyes held a curious light as he stared at her. "Why not, if you knew I was the captain of the ship, and especially since I had accused you of something similar once before?"

"I prefer my revenge straightforward, and without trickery." It was as good an excuse as any, since she was uncertain just what exactly had made her so stubborn in her refusal to play the part Valcour had apointed for her.

"I will try," he said slowly, "to remember that. It should not be hard, especially if I bring to mind the way you stopped Valcour before he got started with his cat. I think that may have had something to do with your—disagreement with him just now."

"It did," she answered, her voice shaded with grimness, "though it was not the only one." She recounted for him the tale of how Valcour had attacked her aboard the *Raven*, and of how he had been prevented from repeating the experience by Ashanti, of the death of the maid and her brother's acknowledgment of guilt. Her voice tight, she told also of his attempt to intimidate her, and of the poisonous fancies and memories he had paraded before his final assault. As she spoke it was as if some old injury or neglected wound had been lanced, allowing the suppurating putrescence of years to drain away. With it went something of her bitterness also, and her grief.

There was a dull flush of rage under Morgan's skin when she finished. His voice was grating as he spoke. "If I had known," he said, "I would have spitted him like a pig for roasting."

"I did that myself," she said.

"So you did," he answered, and suddenly smiled.

Reluctantly, against her will, Félicité felt her own lips curving upward. Her brown eyes met his emerald gaze, and for a brief instant she felt the constriction around her heart ease. He pushed away from the bunk, stepping toward her, lifting the backs of his fingers to touch the purple shadow that lay along her cheekbone.

"It is getting late," he said, "and I will warrant this isn't the only bruise you have after this day's work. I will admit, too, that I am not as fit as I might be. We might as well go to bed.''

She jerked away from him. "We? I told you how it was going to be, and there has been nothing in what we have said to make me reconsider!''

"A slip of the tongue," he said, moving his broad shoulders in the hint of a shrug as he let his hand drop. "Don't upset yourself. I followed you, yes, out of conscience and compassion, and offered you the use of my cabin for the same reasons. But if you will recall, I have not asked you to change your mind. Nor, Félicité, have I asked you to share my bed.''

Chapter 15

His words were welcome, of course they were, Félicité told herself as she prepared for the night. Taking a rough coverlet from the chest, she spread it over the straw-stuffed bunk mattress with a frown on her face. She had no liking for being regarded as an object of pity; still, why should she complain as long as she was left undisturbed? She could sleep deeply and long for the first time in months. There would be little awkwardness in such confined closeness with Morgan; she and he had seen each other unclothed times without number, and were long past the stage of shrinking modesty. There would be no need to worry overmuch tonight about the bundle left behind this time in the captain's cabin.

While Morgan sat down to pull off his boots, Félicité stripped her shirt from her breeches and, crossing her arms, drew it off over her head. Naked to the waist, with her golden-blond hair swirling around her, now concealing, now revealing her firm breasts, she kicked off her shoes and began to unbutton her breeches. Becoming aware of Morgan's stillness, she looked up. He hastily dropped the boot he held suspended. Lowering his gaze, he bent to tug at the other.

The frown faded from her eyes, to be replaced by a considering expression. Perhaps Morgan was not so indifferent to her as he wanted to appear. It might have been male pride or some form of recompense for past sins that had made him deny his interest. Such a thing could be put to the test.

Turning her back, Félicité began with slow care to slip her breeches downward. The firm, slender curves of her hips were uncovered inch by inch, undulating gently as she swayed with the rise and fall of the ship. With one hand braced on the bulkhead wall to support herself, she eased the breeches from one finely turned calf and ankle, then swung half around, clinging with the other hand, to repeat the process. Completely nude, she straightened, flinging back her hair as she shook out her breeches and hung them with her shirt from a hook at the end of the bunk. Morgan's second boot crashed against the wall. He came to his feet with a rush, flung open the cabin door, and bellowed down the companionway, calling for the cabinboy to bring a hot bath.

Félicité dived into the bunk. She snatched at the coverlet, pulling it over herself. Anyone might be passing outside, she fumed. Turning her back, she closed her eyes. A moment later, she opened them again, smiled to herself, then let her lashes fall once more.

She might have slept if the commotion of the arrival of Morgan's bath had not roused her. When the cabinboy, grumbling about queer folks knicked in the knob over bathing all their parts, had gone, she turned with a pretense of restless shifting. Through slitted eyes, she watched as Morgan pulled off his blood-stiffened clothing and, lean, impressively male, stepped into the hot, steaming water.

He slipped downward until his knees were under his chin and a large portion of his broad back was submerged. He winced as the hot water reached the welts and cuts, then allowed a soft sigh to escape him. He had reason to be tired and sore, Félicité thought.

After a time, he sat up and began to rub soap through his cropped hair, a frown drawing his brows together as he touched the matted spot at the back of his head. He splashed water over it anyway until it ran in red streams down the back of his neck.

The tops of his shoulders where the whip had bitten deepest he could not get underwater because of the smallness of the tub. Dried ridges of caked blood still lay across them, slowly reddening as he scooped water over them. It was because of her, Félicité told herself, that he had those sickening gouges that would later turn to more scars. If she had not been used to distract him and his men, he might have noticed the attack of the crew from the *Raven*, might have repelled them, and thus would not have fallen into Valcour's hands.

Holding the coverlet to her, she slipped from the bed, then wrapped the length of material around her and tucked the end into the hollow between her breasts. She bunched the excess material into one hand as she moved to stand beside the tub.

"Shall I wash your back?"

He tilted his head to glance up at her, the look in his eyes wary. "Why?"

"It looks as if it is going to be a little difficult for you."

He stared at her a long moment, his emerald gaze flicking from the cascade of her hair to her draped costume just covering the swells of her breasts. Without a word, he surrendered the cloth he held.

She knelt beside the tub, soaking the linen cloth in the hot water, laying it across his shoulder. An involuntary shudder ran over him as the hot water seeped into the raw scourge marks, then he was still, uttering not a sound of either pain or protest.

Slowly the clotted wounds were uncovered. In one or two places they began to bleed again, turning the bath pink. The sight of his flayed flesh sent sickness over her. At the same time the feel of his warm skin with the muscles slipping under the wet surface gave her an odd sense of pleasure. With great reluctance but a knowledge of the necessity, Félicité used the soap then, cleansing thoroughly to prevent infection. While she was about it, she finished the job he had begun on his scalp, and for good measure, washed the blood from around the place where Valcour's musket ball had torn his ear. He would have a scar there also, an indentation in the lobe, but nothing more serious.

Done at last, she handed back the cloth and got to her feet, drying her hands on the coverlet. "You should have something to go on your back."

"Captain Bonhomme gave me a box of some sort of Far Eastern salve that he recommended, something used by the Lascar from his crew who tends the wounded. I'm not sure it wouldn't be just as well without."

While Félicité searched through his breeches for the salve, Morgan finished his bath, stepped from the tub, and dried himself. She turned with the box in her hand and, with lowered lashes, indicated that he sit on the only chair the cabin provided. Stepping behind him, she opened the salve. Since she had no place to put the lid, she handed it to him, then dipped her fingers into the salve, beginning to spread it over his back.

At first his muscles were tense, but slowly, as the pain receded and the strokes of her fingertips remained light and soothing, he relaxed. Almost beneath her eyes, the slow oozing of blood ceased and the fevered redness began to fade from the long stripes. She touched salve to his ear and scalp, then leaned across him to reach the lid he had placed on his knee. The rounded curve of one breast brushed against his shoulder.

He came erect as if she had touched him with hot iron, moving quickly out of reach. Startled, she sent him a wide glance, then bent to pick up the lid, which had clattered to the floor. With leisurely movement, she fitted the lid back on the box.

He stared at her for long moments, his green eyes narrowed. In the silence they could hear the sloshing of the water in the bath, the creaking of the ship as it drove over the seas, and the hissing of the waves that foamed against her hull.

"I wonder," Morgan said quietly, "if this magic salve would affect bruises."

"It's doubtful, I would say." She moved as if to turn away.

He stepped toward her then, stretching his hand to twitch the box from her hand. "It seems best to take no chances. It would be a pity if such a lovely face was marred, and then I noticed earlier that you have more marks at your waist and thighs."

"There's no need—" Félicité began.

"Oh, but there is," he interrupted. "How can I neglect you after you have taken such good care of me?"

She did not like the look in his eyes. She held out her hand for the jar. "I can do it myself."

"No, no, why should you? It will be an honor—and a pleasure—to tend you. I think it will be best, all things considered, if you lie down."

It seemed senseless to argue. Not only would it serve to make him more determined, but it would point up the fact that she was not as sanguine about their cabin arrangement as he appeared to be. She loosened the coverlet around her and, stepping in front of him, lay down, still wrapped in its folds. Leaning on one elbow, she presented one side of her face.

He knelt beside the bunk. Removing the lid, he rubbed hard fingers across the salve and applied it to her cheek, smoothing it carefully over the smooth curve and along the blue-veined fragility of her jawbone. With the tip of one finger, he tilted her chin, studying the other cheek, touching the ointment to a knuckle graze beside her lip. He shifted then, moving farther along the bunk. His long fingers flicked the coverlet aside, exposing the pale and slender length of her body. Apparently unmoved, he dipped once more into the salve.

Félicité drew in her breath as his warm touch found the scratch below her breasts, the turn of his wrist just grazing one mound as he bent to his work. He shifted then to her waist, kneading, massaging. His ministrations glided lower over the pearl-like sheen of the rounded curve of her hip and thigh. She knew the beginning of a perilous lassitude brought forth by the sureness of his hand upon her. Her eyelids felt heavy, and there was the stirring of almost forgotten sensation in the lower part of her body.

Abruptly his hand was still, resting on the tender turn of her hip. Félicité, with vast effort, brought her gaze to Morgan's face. He was staring at her in frozen concentration, as if locked in some violent inner struggle, unable to move. She felt her breathing cease, felt the clamoring surge in the beat of her heart, though she could no more stir than the man crouched over her.

From the deck above them came a roaring boom as the mainsail spilled wind and filled again. Morgan glanced up, then got stiffly to his feet. Moving toward the chest where his clothing had been transferred, he said, "It sounds as if the wind has veered, and for my sins I am now the sailing master of the ship. I had best go and order the sail reset."

He left the cabin moments later, and though Félicité lay staring into the lantern-lit dimness until the early morning hours, he did not return.

It was just as well. She needed the time alone to think, to worry at the edges of the unseen future. What could it hold for her as long as she plunged over the seas on a pirate ship commanded by a drunkard Frenchman while under the uncertain protection of a turncoat Irishman? What would happen to her if the *Black Stallion* was taken by stronger corsairs or crippled in the water by a prize with more fight in it than expected? In the first case she would doubtless be passed among the new crew, and in the second, she must hang with the others when the captured pirates reached land.

And what if the Spanish *guarda de costas*, some of O'Reilly's captains, or else ships from the other Spanish possessions sailing these waters to discourage piracy and smuggling should sight them? Would they blow them out of the water, sending them all to the bottom in splinter-torn death, or, failing that, have them shot like vermin?

For Morgan, a renegade mercenary who had stolen a Spanish ship from the port of New Orleans, there might well be an end of special ferocity. Could she share it? Would they permit that boon, if she claimed him then, if at no other time, as her own most faithless and dishonored beloved?

*   *   *

It was midmorning when Félicité came on deck. The brisk breeze that snapped the *Black Stallion*'s pennant molded the fullness of Morgan's overlarge linen shirt to the proud thrusts of her breasts and sent long, curling strands of honey-colored hair flying around her. She paused, ignoring the sly glances cast in her direction, searching with her eyes for Morgan. He stood at the railing on the poop in close conversation with Juan Sebastian Unzaga.

Seeing her, he broke off, then, with a curt aside, left the Spaniard and came toward her.

"If I remember correctly you threatened once to send Bast out chasing smugglers. This is something of a switch, isn't it?" As a greeting it was not bad, she thought—impersonal, safe, with possibilities for further conversation.

"As it happens, he was tired of the inaction, and of the cold shoulders, in New Orleans."

"He never seemed the kind to relinquish his role as a Spanish grandee's son adventuring in the army."

"People are capable of infinite shifts and surprises," he said, slanting her an emerald stare.

It was not so safe then, this topic. She tried again. "What of your manservant, Pepe? I haven't seen him on the ship."

"He is useless on the water, much to his mortification. The only thing that consoled him at being left behind was the letter of recommendation I gave him to present to O'Reilly, who was in need of a majordomo when I left."

"Pepe has moved up in the world, then," she commented.

The only reply she received was a short nod. She cast about for another subject. The French captain was far gone in rum, she had learned from the cabinboy, a defense against disappointment and the indignity of having his cabin turned into a sickroom. Valcour was feverish, but well enough to be profanely certain he was dying, and to demand as much attention as possible for his difficult demise. Félicité mentioned these two pieces of information.

Morgan nodded. "We could hear Valcour yelling from up here. I suppose you are glad that you didn't succeed in killing him?"

"I'm not so sure," she returned. "He murdered Ashanti, if you will remember, and mutilated her horribly."

"Don't think about it."

She shook her head. "There is so much to forget."

"There may be more yet," he said brusquely and turned to call out an order. The quiet crack of his voice sent men running to haul at the braces.

"Where are we bound?" she asked when he had turned back.

"I neither know nor care. The captain set our present course; I only hold to it."

"You must have some idea."

"In general, we trend toward the Windward Passage. More than likely we go to see what pickings can be had there."

He swung to see that the job he had ordered had been completed to his satisfaction, casting a hard eye over the set of the canvas above them. As he turned back to her the wind ruffled his hair with a thousand sun-shot red-brown gleams.

"Why did you cut your hair?" she asked without thinking.

"Convenience on a windy deck, since I am not fond of stocking caps or the tarred pigtails most seamen wear. And for the same reason the Macedonians under Alexander the Great were shorn, to give no handhold to an enemy in close fighting."

She tilted her head to one side. "It becomes you, for some reason. I wonder how I would look with short locks."

"Like a grubby street urchin," he answered, unsmiling.

"If by that you mean less female, then that might be a good thing."

He flicked a look over her. "I doubt anything would achieve that. In my opinion, to cut so much as a lovelock would be a sacrilege."

"What of my convenience—and safety in a close fight?" The memory of Valcour's hand wrenching at her hair the night before made her pugnacious.

He gazed down at her, his green eyes shadowed before he gave an abrupt nod. "Do whatever you will. The decision, like the hair, is yours."

When next he saw her, her hair no longer blew free but was close to her head. His face darkened to a scowl, then, as she came nearer, his mouth relaxed, curving to a slow smile. She had not cut it. Instead, she had plaited fat golden braids and wound them like a coronet around her head, fastening the ends with lengths of hemp pulled from a frayed rope. The effect was cooler and somewhat majestic, though not enough to discourage the stares that followed her wherever she went. There was nothing she could do about that, she realized without vanity, not so long as she remained the only woman on the seas.

The hot, blindingly bright days wore on. With little to do, Félicité wandered the ship, finally establishing a spot on the forecastle deck as her own where she could sit and watch the waves, the silver flash of flying fish, or the dorsal fins of the dolphins that sometimes raced ahead of their bow. She learned that Morgan had a supply of books in the captain's cabin and persuaded the cabinboy to bring them out to her. Thereafter, she was to be found in the shade of an awning rigged from a spare sail, trying to keep the constant wind from fluttering the pages as she read. Often she was aware that some member of the crew pretended to a task that would take him near enough to glance under her canvas protection. They devoured her slender form with their eyes, raking over its curves so finely outlined by her men's attire. In the main, she ignored them, though there was one hatchet-faced Britisher with close-set eyes and an oily, insinuating smile that disturbed her.

Morgan gave her no cause for complaint. He seldom came to bed before the early hours of the morning. If she addressed him, his reply was short and sharp-edged. The second time she offered to put salve on his back, he snapped at her and slammed out of the cabin to sleep the entire night on the open deck.

Usually he was gone by the time she awoke in the morning, though once or twice he overslept. On those occasions, she lay watching him as he splashed water over his face. Once she had stretched, lifting her arms, raising her breasts from the concealment of the coverlet. It had not been deliberate, not at first, not until she heard the swift intake of Morgan's breath. Then she had arched her back, sighing.

Before the mirror of the washstand, Morgan had exclaimed with a soft oath, then used the linen toweling to staunch the flow of blood from the cut on his chin. Ill-tempered and driven, he had flung down his silver-handled razor and wiped away the soap, leaving one side of his face still stubbled as he fled the cabin.

They were three days out when Félicité, catching sight of Bast lounging at ease, summoned him to her canvas shelter with a quiet hail.

"I vow you have been avoiding me," she accused him as he drew near. "Sit down and tell me why."

"Not so, Mademoiselle Félicité," he said, though he did not smile at her sally.

"Then why have you not spoken to me?"

"There is a certain etiquette in these matters."

"Surely we have passed the point of formality," she protested.

"Not so long as you share Morgan's cabin and he is still my commanding officer."

"The first, yes, that may be true. As for commanding, you are no longer in the army. Morgan is only the sailing master. He orders the set of the sails, nothing more. You are in all else his equal, are you not?" She studied him, at a loss to account for the constraint she sensed in the Spaniard.

He did not quite meet her eyes. "That—must be so, mademoiselle. I hadn't thought of it."

"Hadn't thought of it? I am persuaded that for most it would be the most important consideration, short of easy riches."

"I wouldn't know."

"Wouldn't you? Why did you turn to piracy, then? You need not say it was to come in search of me," she rallied him, "for I warn you I won't believe it."

"I have never been so happy as when I saw you alive and well; you must believe me when I say this, mademoiselle!"

"Very well, if I must, but that doesn't tell me why you

came." In discovering Bast's reasons she might also come nearer the truth about Morgan's.

"Who can say?" he answered, looking out over the waves. "Call it—an impulse, if you will. A—a necessity. You must excuse me, now. I have duties to perform."

She stared after him in perplexity. His strained manner and evasiveness were disturbing. Was he disappointed that she had fallen back under Morgan's protection so quickly? She doubted that was the reason, for the manner in which it had come about was not unknown to the crew, not on so small a vessel. If he was reasonable he could not blame her. Did her masculine dress upset him, then? His brief glance had held in its Latin depths the same glint of admiration she had seen in New Orleans. What then was there in her situation aboard the *Black Stallion*, or his own, to cause such a change in him?

As she spoke to Bast, she had glimpsed the British seaman loitering past. He returned now from the opposite direction, giving her a leer, his small eyes cunning as he slowed. It might have been a mistake, she recognized, for her to have personal contact with any of the men other than Morgan. It could so easily give rise to hopes that her favor was not fixed on one man.

A cold expression on her face, she lowered her gaze to the book in her lap. After a few minutes, the man moved on.

That was not the end of it. That evening as the sun slowly dipped below the stern and the lavender coolness of dusk settled over the ship, Félicité started along the companionway to the gangway leading to the deck. At the foot she paused, caught by the sound of men's voices raised in a rollicking chantey. It was being led by a French rogue, and concerned, in obliquely ribald rhyme, a pretty lame girl who carried her *beau petit pannier*, beauteous little basket, to market. There, the song went on, she met a sailor who led her along, taking the advantage to fill her "basket" for her.

"On a feather bed he made her anchor, and takes three reefs in her apron," the men sang between the repeating chorus. "Then he furls her petticoats, clewing up her lower sails—

"Then to get goin', this smart topman, sends up his main topmast!"

It seemed best not to put in an appearance until the ditty, rolling verse after bawdy verse overhead, had come to an end. She waited, caught between embarrassment and amusement.

A scuffling footstep sounded behind her. She swung around to see the hatchet-faced man appearing out of the gloom of the stern companionway. He looked her up and down, his smile unpleasant. "Well, look who we have here."

To stay where she was would not be wise, not now. Without speaking, Félicité turned to mount the steep gangway.

The sailor put out his hand, catching her arm. "What's ye hurry? Bide awhile. I can promise to entertain ye well; my topmast be fair aching to get to the job."

"Let me pass, or it will be the worst for you," she snapped, jerking her arm free, climbing upward.

"Not so fast," the man jeered, transferring his hold to the waist of her breeches. "I know of a place in the hold. There's a nice bale of silk there that will feel just fine against your back while I fill your pretty little basket for you."

"Let go!" She held to the sides of the gangway with both hands while she swung to plant her foot in the man's belly, giving him a shove.

His grip broke and she hurried upward, only to be stopped by a hand on her ankle. The seaman climbed the steps behind her, shifting his hold higher.

"Get away, you sniveling *canaille*," she cried, swinging the weight of her body so she slammed into him, forcing him against the side of the narrow way. He snarled in pain and frustrated rage, but would not be dislodged.

From above came the rasp of a sword sliding from its scabbard. The sailor jerked his head back, his face blanching as he looked up. Félicité swung to see Morgan standing above them, one hand braced on the door opening, one holding his rapier.

"Problems, my dear?" he drawled.

The events that followed, swift and terrible and relentlessly just, took on the aspect of a nightmare. The British seaman was hauled on the deck, dragged to the netting, and tied to it.

Morgan gave a hard order, and the burly sailor who acted as bosun stepped forward. A cat-o'-nine-tails, unloaded but still deadly, was brought out. The man's shirt was torn away, and to the droning count that would eventually reach thirty-nine, the blows began to fall.

Félicité stood it as long as she could, stood it until Valcour, weak, glassy-eyed, and bent over as he favored his wounded side, appeared on the deck to view the spectacle, until the Britisher began to jerk with hoarse screams tearing at his throat while the hands on deck grew silent. It was then she turned and with set face went below, not stopping until the door of her cabin had thudded to behind her.

Morgan joined her there within the hour. He paused on the threshold, meeting her dark-brown gaze as she turned to face him. Stepping inside, he closed the door.

"If you have come to serve me as you did that man, I warn you, you will have a fight on your hands!" She glared at him, stiff with defiance.

"What makes you think I have any such idea?" He unbuckled his sword and flung it to one side, then began to tug his shirt from his breeches.

"It is usual in a case like this to consider both parties equally guilty."

He lifted a brow. "Among the French, perhaps. As an Irishman, I fail to see the logic."

The answer loomed suddenly as an embarrassment. Her voice stifled, she gave it anyway. "In most cases, the woman is considered to have encouraged him, or driven him to desperate measures by—by her teasing."

"Oh, of that I acquit you without a moment's thought, my dear Félicité. Such measures you would, I'm sure, reserve for men you know well, those who for some reason have earned your hatred."

It was a blessing that he turned his back then. To gloss over that dangerous subject she said, "Then what are you here for?"

"To watch you."

"If you don't hold me to blame, why should you do that?" she demanded in sharp tones.

"I suppose I should have said to watch over you, to guard you. I have been somewhat remiss in that duty, especially as now, in the early evening."

"There's no need."

"Isn't there? Then a man has an aching back tonight for nothing." He turned then to face her, his green eyes dark.

She met his gaze squarely and risked a question that had been hovering at the base of her mind. "Why, Morgan? Why so severe a chastisement when you, yourself—"

"Severe? I should have hanged the dog! But what is this display of concern? I would have thought you would be happy to see him flogged."

She clenched her teeth against a shiver. "Never."

"Why? Can it be you feel yourself to blame, no matter what I think?"

"I—I don't know," she said, moistening her lips as he moved nearer. "I shouldn't be here."

"Granted. Situations like this are what the old taboo against women at sea is designed to prevent. But it was no fault of your own that you were brought on board, was it?"

She shook her head in wordless negation.

"As for the rest, is it the fault of the gold, bright-shining and infinitely pleasurable to hold, that men steal it? Is it the fault of the rum that men drink themselves blind and dumb? Why then should it be a woman's fault if a man throws away his self-control and succumbs to his most base desires? To hold it otherwise is no more than a feeble excuse for the crimes committed these centuries past against womankind. I say it is so, Félicité, and who should know better than I?"

She stared at him, lost in the jade-green certainty of his eyes, feeling his words seeping in quiet splendor through the tight-held turmoil of her mind. It was, she recognized, an unflinching apology for past offense. It was also a determination for the future, one she might test at will, with his compliments.

They prepared for bed then. Félicité sought her bunk first,

pulling the coverlet up to her chin. Morgan turned out the lantern and lifted himself into the upper bunk. And though the climb was laughably easy for someone of his strength, his breathing was hard for some time as they lay, together yet separate, staring into the dark.

Chapter 16

ail, ho! Sail away on the starboard bow!''
    The cry came from a man high on the foremast just after daybreak of near fourteen days of fruitless sailing. Morgan put his glass to his eye and pronounced the ship to be a Yankee merchantman from the English colonies of North America. Her cargo might not be rich, but the ship itself, a trim snow, would be worth the taking. They were sailing on a parallel course, but the brigantine, much the faster vessel, could overtake her in short order.

He stepped from the rail to go below, there to consult with the *Black Stallion*'s master. Though Captain Jacques Bonhomme had not yet been seen on this voyage, it was still his duty to order the brigantine into a fight and, drunk or sober, to command her during it.

While Morgan was away from the deck, Valcour mounted, sidling, to the poop. His face twisted with grim glee as he surveyed the snow, which could be made out now to be the *Prudence* from the port of Boston. His voice shrill, he called, "Crack on all sail! We will close in for the kill!"

The men, after a moment's hesitation, leaped to obey him. The *Black Stallion* swept forward like a spread-winged Pegasus.

Most broad-beamed merchant ships were designed to carry

the greatest amount of cargo with the least amount of crew. Speed took second place to stability, and there was virtually no provision for heavy armament that would take up precious space. The vessels were owned by men of wealth who took shares in the ships to finance their voyages, thereby spreading the risks as well as profits among themselves. The captains and crews shared little in the cargo, the seamen being paid a mean wage and the masters being given only a small space in the hold to carry goods for their own benefit. There was then no great incentive for them to protect either the ship on which they sailed or her cargo. For these reasons, the merchantmen were looked on as easy prey. Taking one was hardly sport at all, like gaffing fish in a seine.

The brigantine closed in, the men standing by with grappling hooks ready to swarm over the ratlines onto the smaller ship. The stretch of water between them narrowed until men could be seen scurrying about on the snow.

Without warning, smoke blossomed and a hail of shot rattled onto the brigantine's deck. The crew dived for cover, cursing. A man let out a shout. "Hell's bells! She's got murdering pieces!"

A less anxious captain would have noticed the light guns. At such close range their fire was murderous indeed. More than one man writhed with pain, his blood staining the holystoned planking. Valcour seemed not to notice. Intent on coming alongside he stood favoring his sore abdomen with his lips drawn back from his teeth. The helmsman at the whipstaff flung him a strained glance, but held the brigantine steady on the course.

Once more the falconets and minions spoke from the snow. Their missiles sang through the rigging. And then across the way, the merchant ship swung. From her bow a chase gun boomed, sending twelve-pound shot smoking through the topgallants. With slow grace, the white sails sagged, dangling from a broken yard, reaching toward the deck. The ship rolled with the glancing blow, and Valcour stumbled, falling to his knees.

"Hard aport! Helmsman, hard aport, for the love of God!" The order rang loud and clear with the edge of command.

Morgan, gaining the deck at a run, taking in the situation with a single hard glance, did not wait to see it obeyed.

"To your stations, men," he called. "Look lively!"

They took another blasting before they could come about, and fire, water, and oak splinters spouted in the air. Men screamed in agony. A gap appeared in the rail near the bow. Black smoke lay on the sea, drifting around them with an acrid stench that caught in the lungs.

The distance between the two ships widened. Orders were rapped out, and men scrambled aloft. The brigantine veered onto a parallel run with the snow, moving sluggishly, but answering to her helm.

"Fire!"

The guns boomed, splitting the fabric of the morning asunder, sending the sound rolling outward in slow waves of concussion as they recoiled to the limit of their hemp breeching ropes. The starboard rail of the brigantine began an upward climb as the ship reacted to the kick of her own guns. A single white geyser spewed upward in the water to one side of the snow, but every other shot smashed home.

Félicité saw the mainmast of the merchantman topple like a felled tree, taking with it a tangle of sailcloth and cordage. She heard the screams of injured men, and saw with a tremulous sigh the colors of the snow as they were struck, pulled down and waved by a lone seaman in token of surrender.

It was then that Morgan, turning to survey the damage to the brigantine, saw Félicité. His face whitened beneath the layer of soot that coated him, and his eyes blazed with green fire.

"God in heaven!" he ground out. "Why aren't you below where it's safe? Aren't you ever going to stay where you belong?"

The pirate crew fell over themselves boarding the snow. Any merchantman that went to such lengths to protect itself, they figured, must be laden with valuable cargo. They were disbelieving, then indignant, when they discovered the hold stuffed with barrel staves and salted cod, outward bound for Jamaica. But though they tore the ship apart searching, nothing else could they find.

The two ships floated side by side, rising and falling on the swells. Captain Bonhomme, finally sober enough to stand, consulted with Morgan over what should be done. Damage to both ships was not inconsiderable. It was doubtful that the snow would bring much as a prize in her present condition. It was necessary, however, to get something out of her if only to pay for the repairs to the brigantine.

Making port was advisable as soon as possible, prize or no. The *Black Stallion* would be a sitting duck until the ship's carpenter had given her the once-over; she not only had broken yards and spars, and a great hole in the starboard side, but the mizzenmast was cracked and would scarcely hold its sail in a zephyr, much less a gusting wind.

Valcour was for ignoring damage and attending first to matters at hand. He wanted to heat an iron spike and apply it to the soles of the bluff and bearded New England captain's feet. The purpose was ostensibly to persuade the man to reveal the hiding place of the supposed valuables. In reality, Valcour craved a vent for his rage at being summarily relieved of command. The crew credited Morgan with saving their ship and their miserable skins, no less, snatching victory from the sure defeat Murat had engineered. A diversion to turn their minds from their frustration might return their favor to him. Also, as if it would erase the error of judgment of which he had been guilty, he called for the scuttling of the snow with all hands on board, after the treasure had been discovered, of course.

The other two men ignored Valcour's ranting. If Captain Bonhomme had no objections, Morgan said, he knew a small island not too far distant where there was a sheltered cove. The place also had plenty of fresh water from a running stream, and a supply of pork, or did the last time he was there. They could put in for the ten days to two weeks it would take for repairs on both ships. While they were at it, they could also careen the *Black Stallion* and scrape the barnacles off her bottom. From the way she handled, it must have been a while since it was done. With everything in order, they could set sail without fear of being caught by a frigate or some other tall ship of superior firepower while they were too unhandy to outsail or outrun her.

It was agreed. They sewed the dead, two from the brigantine and four from the snow, into their pallets and slipped them overboard. Then they upped anchor, raised their jury-rigged sails, and moved off on a south-southwesterly course. Four days later they limped into the island harbor, and with a collective sigh of relief from all hands, ran down their anchor chains.

It had no name, this miniature paradise. Less than twelve miles long and six wide, it rose to a rocky bluff 140 feet in height at the west end, and sloped down until it ran flat at the east. The bluff was of limestone. It was honeycombed with fissures and caves, and from it ran the sweet springs that poured into the stream and made the island habitable. On the north side where the cove bit into the land there were signs, the foundations of houses and the rotting timbers of a rudimentary wharf, that people had lived there at one time. Now only gulls and terns greeted their arrival, wheeling against the brassy blue of the sky, their cries echoing over the sparkling sea with shrill loneliness.

They spent the remainder of the day unloading the ships, ferrying the boxes, barrels, and bundles to shore, with the longboats of both vessels plying back and forth. They spread out along the beach, the crews of the *Raven*, the *Black Stallion*, and the *Prudence* separating into groups. There was not overmuch mingling, even among the wounded tended by the Lascar from the *Raven*, men who might have been expected to commiserate with each other.

Tents were raised with spare sails and the trunks of saplings. The cooking pots and tin plates from the ships' galleys were parceled out, and a detail of men shouldering muskets went into the wood to look for wild boar. Within the hour, a pair of shots were heard. The men reappeared minutes later bearing a hog of over two hundred pounds hanging from a pole carried over their shoulders. There was more than enough meat to give the encampment of near a hundred men their fill of pork.

Toward the middle of the afternoon, Morgan detached two men and set them to clearing a space at the edge of the woods some distance along the curving beach from the others. When they were done, they started on a hut, building it with four walls and a conical roof striped with poles to which were tied the long and heavy fronds of thatch palms.

"Come try your new abode, Mademoiselle Lafargue," he invited when they were done.

He had given no sign until that moment it was for her, and Félicité had not dared hope. Flashing him a look of irritated gratitude, she moved to the open doorway and stepped inside.

It was not large, being less than four of her paces wide one way and three the other. At a squeeze there might be room enough for a small table and chair near the front door and a pallet in the back corner. Still, it was snug and private, and fresh with the scent of newly cut greenery. The breezes blew gently in at the door, and overhead the leaves of the arching palms made a soft and soothing rustling, while at the side a thorny bougainvillea had been left to trail its brilliant scarlet, paper-thin masses of flowers over the roof.

A shadow fell across the doorway. Morgan, with his arms full, ducked his head to step inside. He carried a small table that he sat on its legs before he turned to toss what looked like a pair of coverlets wrapped around a bundle of clothing over against one wall. There was no time to question him. Close upon his heels came a seaman with a pair of stools and a lantern, and following him was another with a collection of cooking implements and plates. They put down their burdens and then, at an easy word from Morgan, swung around to take themselves elsewhere.

"You seem," Félicité said, looking around her, "to have thought of everything."

"I tried."

"I could have made do with a sail tent like all the others. This wasn't really necessary, not just for me."

"It is not," he said deliberately, "just for you."

She swung to stare at him. "You mean—"

"I mean I will be staying here with you."

"*How* could I have ever thought otherwise?" she said, her smile brittle. "I must have my guard with me at all times."

"Yes."

"It was so nice of you to warn me in advance. I might have made only one pallet!"

"My mistake," he said, his green eyes holding hers for an interminable moment. Then, turning, he ducked through the door and strode away.

Félicité built a fire, and while it was burning down to coals on which to roast the shoulder of pork that was apportioned to Morgan and herself—the men who brought it being in no doubt about where he would sleep—sought to bring some order to the hut. She positioned the table and stools, found an empty crate to use to store the cooking utensils, and made pegs to hang their clothing. That done, she turned to the problem of the sleeping arrangement.

There was no way, short of putting the table in the center of the sand floor and angling a folded coverlet on either side, to place the bedding without having both pallets together. It crossed her mind that Morgan might have planned it that way, then she dismissed the idea. He was not so devious; if he meant to reestablish intimacy between them, he would have said so.

Or would he? Once he had used her concern for her father to force her to an appearance of friendliness with the Spanish, an appearance that might have become genuine if other events had not intruded.

No, she would not think such things. How could she be so ridiculous? Morgan McCormack wanted nothing from her. He might at times feel some stirring of desire, but nothing he could not suppress with a little effort, nothing that wasn't easily explained by their unnatural situation and his isolation from contact with other women. What did it matter, after all, if he was troubled by nearness? Let him be. She should be delighted to think that he might suffer some inconvenience. He deserved it, didn't he?

With stiff movements, she unrolled the coverlets against the back wall of the hut. Twitching them straight, smoothing out the wrinkles, she turned her back and vowed to think of it no more.

The roast pork was perfuming the air, the lantern was casting an oblong glow into the darkness, and the table was set with two plates, two daggers, and a clutch of small brown finger bananas when Morgan returned. Félicité sat not far from the doorway on the trunk of a palm tree blown down by some long-ago storm. She had been watching the dark sea, listening to the wash of the surf. She looked up as he appeared out of the blue-blackness, and without a word went before him into the hut.

She sliced the pork and filled the plates, placing one in front of Morgan. Even as she did so, she was acutely conscious of the implacable domesticity of the act. The damp darkness outside, the bright freshness and comforting aroma of food within were in stark contrast to the drunken revelries of the pirate crews on their sandy beach not so far away. The bed coverlets in the wall shadow invited, or so it seemed from the manner in which Morgan's green glances were drawn to them. For Félicité, his presence seemed to fill the hut, crowding out all else.

There was nothing to do when they had eaten except wipe out their plates with sand, rinse them, and put them away. It had been a long day and a tiring one. They might as well go to bed.

Morgan stepped outside to con the heavens. In his absence Félicité turned out the lantern and quickly undressed, then lay down, taking the pallet nearer the wall. Once she was still, it seemed as if the earth were moving, as if she were still on the ship. The effect was more pronounced when she closed her eyes, and she kept them wide with an effort. Beyond the doorway, the moon, soft and enormous, two-thirds full, was rising out of the sea. It shed its cool, burnished light over the sand, outlining Morgan where he stood, glinting silver on the linen of his shirt and catching dark copper gleams in his hair.

He glanced over his shoulder toward the unlighted hut, then walked off in the direction of the beach, where the men were beginning to whoop and yell as they swilled rum around a trio of salt-licked driftwood fires. After a few minutes, he returned, mug in hand. Taking a seat on the fallen palm, he drank, then drank again.

The moon was hidden behind the bluff when he came to bed. He stumbled over a stool and flung the crablike monster from him with an oath. He stripped off his clothes, dropping them on the floor, then threw himself down on the pallet.

Félicité, listening intently in the darkness, managed to roll out of his way. She came up against the back wall, and it shuddered, rattling under the impact. Morgan turned on his side, and one flailing arm fell across her waist. His grip tightened, drawing her to him, molding her to the curve of his body. Burying his face in her hair, he released a deep sigh. The next instant, stertorously, he slept.

Dawn, pale and opalescent, filtered into the thatched structure. Félicité stirred and opened her eyes. She lay in Morgan's arms, her limbs intertwined with his, her head resting on his arm. The warmth of his body encompassed her, a pleasant defense against the early-morning coolness of the wind that brushed into their shelter, rustling the drying fronds.

By raising her gaze, she could see his face as he slept. Strong, brown, firmly molded, it was shadowed with the stubble of his beard. His lashes made a thick line across his lids, and among the dark arches of his brows there were individual hairs with the wiry texture and color of copper. At the corners of his eyes were the fine, radiating lines of a man used to watching far horizons. Closed, invulnerable, there was nothing in the sculpted planes of his face to show what he felt or thought, or why he had turned to her again and again in the dark, drawing her to him when she sought to put distance between them.

It was not so much fear or even reluctance that made her wary. She did not trust the stir of her own emotions, the sense of quiescent desire, waiting for a certain moment, a certain timbre of voice, the silken slide of a certain touch. Félicité lowered her lashes, her considering brown gaze drifting over the turn of his shoulder, and the slack muscles of his arm that lay across her, and down the hard plane of his chest with its light furring of hair that narrowed to a dark line as it inched down his belly. What would happen, she wondered, if she allowed the tips of her fingers to take that same path, if she moved closer against him so that—

No. She was a fool even to think such a thing. Why should she invite the caresses of a man who cared nothing for her beyond the passion of the moment? A man who took her under duress, then let her go with scarce a backward glance when he tired of her? She could not bind him to her with chains of physical love. It was foolish of her to wish to try.

Slowly, so as not to wake him, Félicité turned to her back. She reached out with one foot to gain purchase, moving her shoulders, trying to slip from under the weight of his confining arm. As he stirred, she went still.

He brought his knee up, turning so it lay across her thigh. For a moment she thought he would raise his arm, but he shifted it instead so his hand lay between her breasts, the lax fingers lightly cupping one rose-tipped mound. When he was quiet once more, his lips were just brushing the smooth curve of her shoulder.

She drew a quiet breath, half of annoyance, half of disturbed senses, then let it out again. She allowed the dragging minutes to tick past until she thought he was settled in slumber. Carefully then, she eased her shoulders over the pallet. His hand trailed limply from one breast to the other. At that point he stirred once more, his fingers tightening, the muscles of his leg tensing until she was held immobile.

She turned her head sharply in suspicion, and was in time to see his eyelids quiver, as if just snapping shut. She lay still, sorely tempted to let matters rest as they were to see how he would proceed. The thought was so insidious, so entrancing, that she caught her breath.

In a sudden decision, her fingers flew up to snatch his hand from her, flinging it off. She rolled from his grasp in a fluid movement that brought her up on her knees. Reaching for the coverlet, she jerked it from under him to haul across her lap.

"Wake up, you vile, grinning jackanapes!"

He gave a heartrending groan. "Be still, woman. My head feels as if it had the devil's own smithy inside it."

"Good! That's what you deserve for soaking yourself in rum before you come to bed!"

"That I did is something for which you should be grateful. I don't think you would have liked it if I had come sober." Catching the edge of the other coverlet, he rolled, wrapping it around him as he faced the wall.

She glared at his back in frustration. "That's something you'll never know, isn't it?"

He whipped back to face her, his emerald eyes dark. "Take care, Félicité. I am sober enough now, and more, to venture any gale."

She shook back her hair in cold rage. "Take care yourself, Morgan McCormack. Lay one finger on me in the bright light of this day, and I'll cut it off for you!"

"It might be worth the loss," he said, uncoiling from the coverlet, coming to a sitting position, "to see if you are as I remember."

His intention was reflected in stark pain in his eyes. As he lunged, she hurled herself backward, scrambling for the crate that held the knives. He caught her waist just as her forearm hit the edge of the box, turning it over with a muffled jangle onto the sand of the floor. The point of her shoulder struck the shifting grittiness, then Morgan loomed above her, his shoulders blotting out the light, his mouth coming down upon hers with bruising strength. Above her head, her groping fingers closed around the handle of a dagger.

And then his lips were warm and sweet, their pressure ravishingly gentle. He tasted the honey of her own, exploring the moist corners, and as they parted in languorous acceptance, sank deeper. Her senses expanded, and she knew a soft and glowing lassitude. She lifted a hand to place it on his shoulder and felt the weight of the knife lying forgotten in her grasp.

She stiffened. His mouth clung to hers a moment longer before he raised his head. His eyes were jade-dark as he stared down at her, and from their depths welled derision that was directed as much at himself as at her. Félicité's grip tightened on the knife, and with painful deliberation she pressed the point to the brown column of his throat.

"Release me," she said, her voice a husk of sound.

He smiled with a slow and tantalizing curving of his lips, but neither moved nor spoke.

She increased the pressure until the point indented the skin. Realizing that her left hand lay against his back, she lifted it, spreading the fingers, holding them wide. Still, he did not let her go, but hovered, an overpowering, intensely masculine presence above her.

Suddenly a drop of bright scarlet formed at the point of the dagger, hanging like a jewel from the tip. Revulsion gripped Félicité, and with a small cry, she jerked the knife away, sending it flying to clatter among the pots.

"Sweet Félicité," Morgan said on a ragged laugh. "You are going to have to make up your mind what you want."

Without waiting for an answer, with no sign of expecting one soon, he flexed the long muscles of his arms and pushed away from her. He caught up his breeches, and with them in one hand, surged to his feet in a plunge for the doorway and the beach beyond.

Like a released spring, she came to her knees, calling after him in taut rage, "And what about you?"

He halted, turning back, magnificently naked in the orange-red glow of the rising sun, with the look of an Adam cast in bronze. He smiled with twin red sparks like devil gleams in his green eyes. "Oh," he said, "I have already decided!"

Félicité would like to have stayed alone in the hut, lying on her pallet, staring at the thatched underside of the roof, mulling over her wayward feelings. She was allowed no such respite. Morgan returned from his sea-swim looking vital, virile, and self-satisfied, and with a raging appetite. While he rummaged for leftover pork and sea biscuits, he spoke over his shoulder, his eyes averted from the pallet. They needed to quarter the palm forest for fresh fruits and vegetables. It would be better if they went early, before the others arose. By the middle of the morning, he wanted to be back to set the men to work. If he didn't, there was no telling when they would get started, or how much trouble the hungover, short-tempered, ill-humored sons of Satan would stir up if they weren't driven to more productive labor.

There was more reason for haste. The longer the ships sat out of water for repairs and careening, the greater the odds of being spotted either by another corsair or by the frigates of the ever-patrolling Spanish *guarda de costas* whose job it was to make pirating unprofitable, if not downright dangerous.

Félicité tried to insist that she could manage the foraging alone; Morgan would not hear of it. To begin with, she wasn't familiar with many of the tropical fruits and vegetables. Then there was the possibility she might meet some member of the three crews on an isolated trail. For the moment they were enough in awe of Morgan not to approach, as long as he was near. If she was alone, the tale might be different. Since her bout with Valcour, she had become in some sense a challenge to the manhood of the seamen, as well as an object of desire. That there was an element of danger in pursuing her, far from making them sheer off, only added to her luster. There was not a sailor among them who did not ache to tame her, even if he had to shut her mouth permanently when it was done to avoid Morgan's certain revenge.

Carrying a pot each, and Morgan with a wooden bucket dangling by its rope handle from his fingers, they ventured into the tangled growth of the forest. They crossed and re-crossed the meandering stream, little more than a creek, that came out on the east side of the cove. Palm trees leaned over them, and the fronds of great tree ferns brushed their faces. Thick vines with splotches of yellow on their virulent green leaves twisted up the trees, looking like strangling snakes. There were flowers everywhere, the brilliant red and soft fuchsia of hibiscus, the pink and white of oleander, and the bright, flaring orange of flame trees. Low bushes of unnamed varieties, covered with yellow and white blossoms, sprawled everywhere, while blooming vines soared to the tops of trees. Even the limbs of the branches that met overhead were laden with strange-looking leathery leaves from which grew flowers of exotic beauty that filled the air with intoxicating perfume.

As gaudy as the flowers were the birds, great squawking parrots and smaller birds with beaks as big as they were, and tiny darting hummingbirds as contrary as they were delicate. Pigeons, the remnants of some long-ago colony established by the former tenants of the island, roosted in the trees, making standing under one a danger, and here and there scuttled a small chicken that Morgan called a *pintada*.

Once a wild hog, frightened out of a shaded hollow, charged them. Before they could react, a litter of ten or more piglets burst from the other side of the thicket, squealing in dudgeon as they went. If it had been a boar, they could have been in danger. As it was, between relief and sympathy, they did not have the heart to chase down the sow and her family.

They found a damp gully thick with plantains, their dark-green leaves like enormous arrowheads shining in the sun. Nearby was manioc, also called cassava. Improper preparation of either could lead to digestive disaster, Félicité knew, but Morgan seemed to have no qualms about showing her how to go about it. For more in the way of vegetables, they robbed the centers of cabbage palms and from others took their meaty hearts. Fruits they discovered in abundance, ripening, falling on the ground. So easy was it to fill their baskets that it soon became plain they could live there for a lifetime without danger of starvation.

Félicité glanced once at Morgan striding along beside her, carrying the heaviest of their burdens, standing aside to hold a tree branch as she passed. The thought occurred to her that this was the way Eden must have been before the fall. If they had been alone, she and the man with her, without danger of invasion from the outside world, would they take off their clothes and disport themselves like Adam and Eve, free and untrammeled by past sins and misdeeds?

She looked quickly away, and saw before her the limestone outcropping of the bluff. Morgan stopped, searching the towering face of the rise with its gullies and vegetation-choked draws. An animal path led upward like a well-trodden road, becoming lost as it crossed the blinding-white calcareous rock.

"Come, there's something I want to show you."

He led her over the animal path, then diverged to drop down onto a track like a series of descending terraces to the narrow shingle of beach that fronted the clifflike face of the bluff. Standing back at the water's edge, he pointed upward. "Look up there. See it?"

She squinted against the sun's glare. Halfway up was a dark shadow, an indentation in the rock. Above the sound of the surf that boomed behind them, foaming at the foot of the bluff not far away, she called, "Is it a cave?"

He nodded. "It can also be your bathing chamber, Mademoiselle Lafargue, if you don't mind sharing it with a few bats."

"What?" she cried.

"There is a pool of fresh water, a natural cistern, inside."

She turned to him, her eyes shining. "When can we try it?"

"Not now," he answered without commenting on her choice of pronoun, though a smile tugged at the corner of his mouth. "We need to get back. Perhaps this evening, though, after our work is done."

It was a long day. The men toiled in the tropical glare, their skin shining with perspiration. They snarled and they cursed, but they performed prodigious feats of labor under Morgan's lashing tongue. Captain Bonhomme, nursing an aching head, fell to with the rest, and was soon roaring out a chantey to make the work go easier as with the others he hauled and pulled, pushed and shoved. Only the wounded were exempt, among them Valcour. He lay brooding under a sail awning, watching the bent brown backs of the others with a sneer on his thin lips and ordering the cabinboy, every time he passed with the bucket of rum and water, to refill his glass.

By the time the sun started coasting down the sky, Félicité had prepared boiled cabbage palm, steamed plantains, and flat cakes made from the sawdustlike flour of the manioc baked on a flat stone before the fire. Served with a few slices of the roast pig left from the day before, it made a meal she was not ashamed of.

Morgan seemed to find it more than adequate. He wolfed down his portion and looked around hopefully for more. It was not surprising. He had worked as hard as any and harder than most. Several times during the day Félicité had glanced toward the ships drawn up in the cove, picking out his broad-shouldered form with his scarred back from the rest.

She had noticed in the last days on the ship, and here on the island also, that Morgan enjoyed physical labor, doing something with his hands. In many ways he seemed more in his proper element here, freed of the constraint of a uniform and the endless niggling details and petty restrictions that were the lot of a Spanish officer. It was a pity, she thought, that he had been unable to turn such thrusting energy into some worthwhile endeavor. For instance, the estate he had envisioned on the grant of land promised to him. O'Reilly had made a mistake in not keeping to his promise. Such men as Morgan McCormack would do much to make Louisiana the productive colony that it needed to be, should be.

What use was it to repine? Morgan had lost his land, and she had lost her home. There was nothing for them but this island and the sea and an uncertain future. She looked up to find Morgan watching her, a serious light in his green eyes.

"What are you thinking?" he asked.

"I was wondering what you mean to do—later, I mean, when you are finished with all this." She waved a hand at the ships in the harbor.

"Do? Why should I do anything?"

"You can't go on like this forever."

"Why not?"

"Because you aren't likely to live that long!" she snapped, irritated by his deliberate obtuseness.

"Why should I not make my fortune by sacking English capitals? Like Iberville, who nearly bankrupted the Hudson Bay Trading Company by destroying Port Nelson and Fort William Henry, to say nothing of dozens of other English fishing villages in North America, before he became the respected founder of the fair city of New Orleans. If he can live so exciting and honored a life, and die in his bed, why not I?"

"He may have died in his bed, but he was put there by a tropical fever before he reached thirty-five, not something you would wish to emulate, I hope. But at least he had his country to back him and to accept his allegiance. To my knowledge, you have none. From whence, then, will come your honors?"

"Most likely the first country I tender a bribe," he answered with easy cynicism. "What piques my curiosity, my sweet, is why you are so concerned."

"That must be obvious," she countered. "For the moment my future is linked with yours."

"So it is. You are my messmate, my bedmate, my woman—as far as the other men know or can tell. If you are unhappy with the arrangement, there is Bast over there proudly grieving. Or perhaps you would prefer the good captain? He has the undoubted advantage of being one of your countrymen."

"No," Félicité said, then spoke louder, trying to see past the mask of his features. "No."

"Why? Because I am undemanding? I cannot promise always to be so."

Félicité lowered her lashes. "If you mean to make me regret asking you questions, you are doing a fair job of it."

His silence was intense, arrested. She glanced up to see him rubbing a hand over his face in an old familiar gesture, running the fingers back through his hair. His green eyes were dark as he said, "I think maybe it's time we went to see about that bath."

They reached the cave along the beach, climbing to it using handholds and ledges that had been cut decades ago. Their ascent flushed a colony of terns, which circled, crying, above them, the undersides of their wings pink with the glow of the setting sun.

Inside, the cave widened, growing higher. Tunnels and passageways opened from it, winding away into darkness. Their slightest word echoed in the hollow emptiness, and the sound stirred the furry brown bats that hung from the ceiling, speeding their evening flight. They darted here and there, swooping out the front opening, emitting thin, high-pitched shrieks, but seemed harmless enough. After the first one brushed past her so that she jumped, Félicité, catching the amusement on Morgan's face, stood still and let them go.

The bathing pool was a dark and mysterious shimmer at the back of the cave. Félicité moved toward it over the sandy floor as if drawn. It looked bottomless, a catch basin perhaps eight feet wide and the same in length with red-brown stone on its sides. It caught and reflected small glimmers of light, and also the white of the overhead limestone, so that it appeared like a giant moonstone, luminous and uncomforting.

Morgan fished a small piece of soap from his pocket. "You go first. I'll watch."

"Yes, all right," she said, and could not keep the dubiousness from her voice.

He laughed down at her. "Don't worry. It's only about five feet deep, or less, and the bottom is solid rock."

He walked away, back toward the entrance, his tall form silhouetted by the light. Félicité removed her clothes and gingerly put her foot into the water. It was cool, marvelously so, and she was hot and sticky after the long day and their brisk walk to get here. Sitting down on the edge, she slid carefully into the depths, holding the side as she tested them. It was as Morgan had said; the water did not come quite to her neck. In one spot it shelved to a mere six inches or less, forming a bench, hollowed, perfectly smooth, on which she could sit to soap her hair.

It was lovely, a luxury beyond anything she had known. Water and more to rinse her hair again and again, water to sweep away the lather from her body, water to surround her and buoy her up, to relax in and upon. In carefree, sybaritic abandon, with her eyes closed and her hair suspended like a silken web around her, she floated. Below on the beach, the tide was coming in, and the thundering surf that frothed at the base of the bluff caused vibrations to ripple through the pool. It gave her a sense of being a part of the elements, magically in and of the water.

There was a splash beside her, and a wave dashed into her face. She went under and came up spluttering, wiping water from her eyes. Morgan was beside her, naked, chest-deep in the pool.

"Sorry," he said, without sounding the least repentant. "You made it look entirely too inviting."

"You are supposed to be keeping watch!"

"I was." His gaze swept over her, striking through the clear water to the wavering shape of her body that gleamed white in the dimness.

"For the others, not on me!"

"There was nothing happening out there."

"Nor is anything happening in here!" She plunged away from him then, reaching for the shelving end of the pool. He caught her from behind, one sinewy arm wrapping around her waist. He hauled her back against him, and as she felt the heated rigidity of him in the coolness of the water, she was still. Her hair, streaming water, flowed over his hand clamped to her abdomen, clinging wetly to his fingers.

As if drawn, she turned her head to stare up at him. His face was closed in, and yet pensive with yearning. She could feel the throb of his heartbeat against her, sense the pounding of her own. Her strength seemed to drain from her, leaving her too weak to move, too passive to protest as his lips, warm and firm, touched hers.

From somewhere inside her there came a surge of desire as white-hot as the tropical sunlight that fueled it. Her mouth clung, her tongue sought his recklessly, without hesitation. Of her own volition she turned in his arms, pressing the peaks of her breasts into him, flattening the firm globes against the broad hardness of his chest. His hands smoothed over her back, drawing her against the lower part of his body as with deep-drawn breath he tasted the sweet headiness of her surrender. She lifted her arms, sliding her hands over his shoulders, locking them behind his head. She wanted to be held close and closer still. There was racing pleasure in being crushed against him, a burgeoning excitement that suffused her skin with glowing heat. Locked together, they swayed with the moving water, feeling the shattering roar of the surf in their blood.

Holding her still, Morgan moved to put one knee on the sloping shelf just beneath the surface of the water. He lowered her beside him on that marble-smooth surface, cushioning her head on his arm at the pool's edge. The water sheeting them to the waist like a glassy coverlet was warm now and pulsing, a living thing. Under it, Morgan's hand, callused, slightly rough at the fingertips, glided over the firm mound of her breast, sliding into the hollow of her waist, slipping lower. Félicité trailed her nails along Morgan's chest and down his belly, dipping into the water, lost in pure sensation, her mind barred to thought.

They came together then like the clashing of storm waves, with driven fury and flowing force. Their mouths slanted, bruising, burning with sensuous sensitivity. Their bodies merged, blending in smooth-sliding entry. With slow-gathering power, the tide of the pool grew more tempestuous, flooding to comber-beaten swells.

It was a maelstrom, a hurricane, a heart-wrenching upheaval of the senses of such immense power the world lurched off course, plunging out of control. There was no time or place, or identity, nothing except the violent magic that welded them each to the other. With expanding senses Félicité rose against him in wild, wanton acceptance of his thrusts. She held nothing back. Shadows fled from the darkness of her eyes as she gave herself without stint, and in return she felt him pierce to the deepest recess of her being, filling the aching emptiness until she was replete, whole and fearless, once more.

The water in the pool grew still. Morgan shifted from her, leaning to gaze into her eyes, his own dark with spent yet unslaked desire. He did not speak, but after a long moment, gathered her close, holding her, rocking her gently in his arms. His lips brushed her temple, the shell-like curve of her ear, then pressed with fierce possessiveness to the tender curve of her neck. His grip tightened. She could feel the thudding of his heart.

"Morgan," she whispered, spreading her hand over his scarred back, assailed by the sudden conviction that he was afraid, not for himself, but for her.

He drew back. "Are you all right?"

She nodded, searching his face.

Summoning a smile, he said, "As pleasant as this is, I am neglecting my duty. I'll keep watch while you dress."

He surged from the water, and gathering up his clothes, padded to the entrance while he pulled them on. Félicité followed his example more slowly. As she pushed her shirt into her breeches, there was a thoughtful look in her brown eyes.

They climbed down the face of the bluff and walked back toward the cove along the beach. After a few steps, Morgan caught Félicité's hand, holding it tightly in his. She glanced at him in a half-smiling inquiry, but though his lips curved in a brief reply, he turned from her, his emerald gaze searching the face of the heaving turquoise sea.

Chapter 17

❦

They *had been* on the island nearly a week when a sail hove over the horizon. Pandemonium broke out among the seamen on shore. The masts of the *Prudence* and *Black Stallion* were bare of sail. The larger ship was missing a mizzenmast altogether, though it lay trimmed and ready to be stepped into place as soon as the green wood was a bit drier. Fires smoldered in the sand, and over them hung great pots of water with curling steam rising from them, ready to be used to curve the timbers to replace the bow section that had been blown away. They were as helpless as ants in a disturbed hill, running this way and that with no one certain whether they wanted to come to grips with the intruder or escape him.

A man with a spyglass in hand shinnied up a wine palm. From that vantage point he called down that the ship was a brigantine, and like the *Black Stallion* was French-built and Spanish-rigged. She flew no flag, but the pennant at the mast was of black and silver, and unless the lookout was bedazzled by the sun, her figurehead was a great damned dove.

She came closer, skimming like a bird indeed over the waves, the sails spread like white wings. She was black and silver with gilt ornamentation that shone like gold, brass cannon, and decks of sepulchral whiteness. As she neared, she broke out a rippling of pennants in red, blue, yellow, green, purple, and brightest orange. Beneath them on the deck stood creatures dressed in those same shadings, feminine and fair, with their hair streaming in the wind. More females clung to the rigging in breeches and shirts, competent seawomen with not a man among them. On the forecastle in place of a captain stood a woman in black, wearing over her gown a gauzy cape that flowed out behind her, revealing folds of pale gray running into purest white.

For Félicité, drawn by the commotion to the door of her hut, shielding her eyes with her hand against the glare, it did not need the dancing letters on the bow to spell out the ship's name. Without question she knew, long before the words became clear, that the brigantine would be the dove indeed, *La Paloma*. What she did not know, what she could not decide until the full-throated roaring and jubilant shouts of the men capering on the sand told her, was the purpose of the vessel and its women. And when she knew, when she understood, she still could not believe it. Greeted with joy and ribald anticipation, with crowing lechery and boundless lust, the *La Paloma* was no less than a floating brothel, carrying a cargo of whores.

The men were not allowed to rush at the women. Isabella de Herrara came ashore first quite alone, reclining in her longboat like Cleopatra on her barge. Her hair was drawn back with combs and set with feathers on either side of her head, echoing the winged streaks of soft white at her temples. She stepped upon the sand as if it were the finest carpet, and gave her hand to Morgan, who was there to help her alight. The Spanish-Irish noblewoman leaned to press a light kiss to his bronze jaw, greeting him in low tones, her voice musical.

By the time Félicité reached the beach, Morgan had made his answer and Isabella was speaking again.

"My dear Morgan, it is a profound relief to see you looking so—well."

"You expected otherwise?" His smile was easy, though her hand still lay in his.

"One heard of the capture of your ship. I should have known you would make a place for yourself. You have a great facility for it."

"You also, Isabella, if you will permit me to say so." Morgan nodded in the direction of the graceful ship at anchor in the cove beyond the two stripped-down vessels.

"You may say anything to me you like, as you well know," the woman replied before she turned away. Her black gaze came to rest with coolness upon Félicité in her breeches and Morgan's shirt.

Morgan turned. "Félicité, there you are. I don't believe you have been formally presented to the Marquesa de Talavera. Isabella, this is Mademoiselle Félicité Lafargue."

"Ah, yes, the young woman from New Orleans. So you did find her. How pleasant for you," the other woman said when she had returned Félicité's polite greeting.

"Yes, most," Morgan agreed.

But the attention of La Paloma had already wandered, coming to rest on Captain Bonhomme striding toward them. "And who is this?"

As the introductions were made, the French captain bowed with the remnants of a cavalier's grace. "Madame, you do us great honor," he murmured. "What brings you here to this godforsaken island?"

"A fair wind, I think," the woman answered, her smile whimsical. She glanced at Morgan. "And a knowledge of my old friend's haunts."

"Curse you, Morgan," Captain Bonhomme growled. "Have you a previous acquaintance with every beautiful woman we are like to meet?"

"Not all," he said with a laugh, his gaze flicking to Félicité.

She gave him a cold stare.

Isabella was speaking again, suggesting a meal for the ladies with whom she was traveling, a collation of food and wine served alfresco. Regardless of the fact that the men had been dining in no other fashion for some days, this was greeted as a novel idea. Afterward there would be entertainment, the best rough seamen could provide, and then might the ladies not feel that much more amorous, especially since the moon was full?

They might. They would need time to prepare, however. Isabella would return, and her ladies with her, at sunset.

It was as well the men had been given extra hours. As it was, the afternoon scarcely sufficed to accommodate all their speculation as to the quality, expected to be high, of the goods being offered, or to spread out the meat for the feast—the roast piglets, boiled crab and conch, baked snapper and grouper, and as an afterthought, a plate of salt cod. To go with it there would be stewed palm cabbage, manioc cakes, roasted plantains, and a great salmagundi of palm hearts, boiled turtle eggs, chopped pork, and wild garlic and onion, all stirred together with herbs and oil. For dessert there was fruit, the ever-present bananas and oranges. To wash all this down were palm wine aged the entire week, a watered-down ale the pirates called "belly vengeance," the great delicacy known as "bumboo" consisting of rum, water, and sugar flavored with nutmeg, and finally, the crowning achievement, a punch. This last concoction, made with rum, palm wine, brandy, herb tea, and lime juice, sweetened with sugar and flavored with spice, was guaranteed to put any man in a concupiscent mood. If he wasn't careful, it would also put consummation quite beyond him.

They piled driftwood high for a pair of enormous fires, one at either end of the long bolt of sailcloth laid on the sand for a table. Plates and knives and antimony mugs were scoured with sand, rinsed, and piled artistically in an empty water butt.

When all was in readiness, and for some long before, there was a great trimming of beards and slicking of hair. The best shirts and waistcoats were brought out. One man doused himself with a most vile perfume, and before the scent had polluted the air for more than a yard, his bottle had been pounced on and passed around, down to the last drop.

There came then the time for parceling out to the men a fair division of the spoils of the *Black Stallion*. The assembled crew watched with anxious, avid eyes as Valcour directed the barrels and chests and bales to be brought forth. On this dealing out their night's pleasure depended. How else were they to afford the favors of such high-class beauties?

Félicité retreated to the hut. She had no interest in the spoils, but the advent of the women was just as disturbing to her. She was not immune to the prospect of competition, or the general air of refurbishing. She took out her bundle and unwrapped her feminine attire. The gowns were hopelessly crushed after all this time, and there was no chance of pressing them. They were, in any case, serviceable day gowns such as she had thought she might need for wearing on the streets of Paris. Compared to La Paloma and the other women, in them she would be quite extinguished. Not a man on the island would be aware she was even present, so dowdy and rumpled would she appear.

Morgan, finding her with her gowns spread over the coverlets, was unsympathetic. She would be beautiful in anything, he said. There was no need to upset herself.

She was in the process of telling him, most vehemently, that she was not upset when a man stepped into the open doorway, blocking the light.

"Forgive me if I intrude," Valcour said, his smile belying the politeness of his words.

"What do you want?" Morgan turned to face the other man squarely, his features hard.

Valcour still was forced to stand slightly bent at the waist in spite of the healing of his wound. He turned to indicate the man carrying a chest who trailed him. "I regret to disturb your quarreling, but since neither you, Sailing Master McCormack, nor Félicité was present just now, I thought it best to deliver your three shares to you before they were lost in the confusion."

"Our shares?" Félicité inquired, a frown drawing her brows together.

"But of course. As odd as it may seem, as an officer of the pirate crew of Captain Bonhomme, Morgan is due two shares of the *Black Stallion*'s captured English prize—taken before she reached Las Tortugas."

"And the third share?" Morgan asked.

"Belongs to Félicité, hers by right for her indispensable aid in the taking of your brigantine," came Valcour's answer.

She had forgotten. She might have known Valcour would not, especially if there was the least chance of causing trouble. She ran her tongue over her lips, sending a quick glance to Morgan's unyielding face, before she turned back to her brother. "I told you then, and I tell you again; I don't want it."

"Want it or not, it's yours, *ma chère*. You earned it."
Valcour made an imperative gesture, and the man behind him
stepped forward to up-end the chest in the middle of the sand
floor. An ivory chess set spilled out, the pieces tumbling from
a box of inlaid teak and gold. There was a shower of gold
coins, a cascade of cloth, a gleam of green jade. And there
was also the slither and slide of a gown of cream satin
brocade. It lay shining in the slanting rays of the dying sun, a
glistening pool of decadent, beckoning luxury.

Félicité stabbed a look of hate at Valcour. He had always
been too clever in matters of women's dress, and also women's
weaknesses, much too spitefully clever.

He bowed, his smile baleful. "I trust I will see you both
later."

His footsteps retreated with those of the seaman, crunching
in the sand. Félicité clasped her fingers together as Morgan
moved slowly to take up the shimmering satin gown. His
fingers crushed the fabric as they closed on it.

"You have something new to wear now," he said, his
voice quiet.

"I—I swear by the Virgin, I did not help take your ship for
gain, or willingly."

"Don't repine. There is a certain justice in it. I was well
served." His face was averted, without expression.

"But I tell you—"

"Don't! Don't tell me." He cut across her words with the
command, dropping the gown as if it were hot.

"I would have died if you had not saved me. Don't you
remember?"

He turned his head to stare at her, dark-jade grief mirrored
in his eyes. "It might have been best if I had not."

Her mind closed tight against the pain, leaving her nothing
to say. She watched him swing from her and stride from the
hut. When he was gone, she sat down on the coverlets,
stacked together, doubled now. Stretching full-length, she
buried her face in her arms. A shiver ran over her, and then
another. Despair, black and blighting, crept in upon her.

Here she and Morgan had lain and loved in the week past.
Here she had found deep pleasure. Held through the night in

Morgan's arms, she had felt safe, content, secure. Gradually she had allowed herself to hope, to dream, to trust.

It had been a mistake. The certainty of it was like a swordthrust to the heart, one from which she could not flinch, had no protection. In this contest she had been for some time disarmed.

Was that true?

She sat up, resting her back against a pole support. With narrowed eyes, she considered Morgan's undeniable passion for her, the way he turned to her in the darkness with soft words and gentle caresses, seeking the solace of her body again and again as if his thirst for her could not be slaked. Was it possible, could it be that this aspect of their alliance could be forged into a weapon?

Her brown eyes intent, Félicité uncoiled from the coverlet and gently picked up the satin gown, shaking it out, holding it against her.

La Paloma's tactics were admirable. After a day of careful preparation the pirate crew and common seamen alike were as diffident as schoolboys promised a treat. Men who would have bedded a trollop with gusto and scant notice, or tossed any unsuspecting, chance-met maid and gone on without a backward glance, were after a day of waiting nigh sick with expectation. They crowded the shore peering toward the new brigantine long before there was any sign of departure from her.

The women came at last, boatload after boatload, to the number of near a hundred, few enough in all events for the combined crews of the *Raven*, the *Black Stallion*, and the *Prudence*. Except for Isabella in her usual black, they were dressed in bright-colored gowns of fine floating silk, and with silken flowers in their hair. They laughed, they chattered, fluttering here and there, exclaiming over everything in clear voices to rival the calls of the birds in the trees. Not the usual waterfront trulls, they were still females without the impediment of virtue, and so there were roguish glances, sly innuendos, and the air of availability even as pinches and clutching hands were avoided.

Wearing the gown of satin brocade, Félicité left the hut to join the others. It felt strange to be trussed up in stays and panniers again, and to have the swirl of skirts at her feet. She looked well enough, as far as she could tell in the steel shaving mirror Morgan had tacked to a tree outside their cramped quarters. The gown was a trifle large in the waist, but was a fair fit otherwise. The cream color was a perfect foil for the golden tint of her skin and the sun-bleached fairness of her hair. Without pins, it was difficult to do anything with her long tresses, but she had drawn them back from the temples on either side of her face, and tied the mass with the ribbon from her chemise so that it cascaded in waves and curls down the back of her head.

She came to a halt near the fire at the upper end of the spread sailcloth. Its flickering orange glow, edged with the blue-green of salt-soaked driftwood, played over her, reflecting on the shining fabric of her gown with a strange, unearthly light. Morgan was standing with Captain Bonhomme and Isabella. He turned, then went still, as if transfixed. The seconds passed. His face masklike, he did not move, gave no indication that she was welcome to join their group.

Unhurriedly, Félicité looked away. Juan Sebastian lounged against an oaken barrel of pitch. Forcing a smile to her lips, she strolled toward him.

He came to his feet as she drew near. Inclining his head in a bow, he sent Morgan a quick glance before he spoke. "Good evening, Mademoiselle Félicité."

She returned his greeting, asking, "Why are you here alone when there is other company to be enjoyed?"

"The other company is not to my taste." His dark, admiring gaze brushed over her, implying the direction his taste might run. "May I ask why you are not in the company of my friend Morgan?"

"A difference of opinion," she said, looking away toward the other fire at the opposite end of the sailcloth before she gave him a brilliant smile.

"I trust it is not—serious."

She moved one shoulder in a weary gesture. "I fear so."

"One man's misfortune can be another's happiness. If you

are truly at odds, perhaps you will sit beside me at supper.''
The expression in his eyes grew warmer.

"I would be delighted," Félicité answered without hesitation.

Captain Bonhomme, a short distance away, stepped forth
then. "What are we waiting for, men?" he shouted. "To the
table!"

The glassy-eyed seamen were no less anxious to get the
preliminaries out of the way. They urged the women toward
the spread cloth, plying them with food, then falling to
themselves. The wine and punch and ubiquitous bumboo
were passed up and down the table. Faces grew flushed in the
firelight. Voices trilled or guffawed in an ever-rising crescendo.
More frequent slaps and laughing protests rang out, as hands
groped in the semidarkness.

The French captain sat at the head of the cloth, with
Isabella at his right as guest of honor, and Morgan beside her.
Félicité and Bast were seated halfway down on the opposite
side. It was a trial to watch Morgan and Captain Bonhomme
vying with one other for the woman's attention. Though Bast
piled her plate with food, Félicité had little appetite. She
sipped from her cup of punch, and promptly choked on the
breath-snatching mixture. Bast pounded her on the back then
until, laughing, with tears streaming from her eyes, she begged
him to stop.

The sense of constraint between them was eased after that.
Bast felt it too, for he caught her hand, gazing at her with
something near adoration in his eyes. "Mademoiselle—Félicité,
you are beyond compare in loveliness tonight."

"Thank you, Bast. It is kind of you to say so." Her smile
was perhaps more confiding than it might have been under other
circumstances.

"You grow more beautiful every day. I have watched you
and marveled, when you did not know I was there."

"Bast—" she began uneasily.

"Does it trouble you to know that I keep you in my sight?
It has become a habit with me, watching you from a distance,
when you are with Morgan. It gives me pleasure only to be
able to see the place where I know you rest, though it also
brings pain to think of you with another."

How could she be unaffected by such a declaration? "Oh, Bast, I didn't know."

"How should you, if in my pride and despair I hide it, at times even from myself. Ah, Félicité, I must speak to you, later, when we may be private."

His voice was low and hurried. He flicked a look at Morgan. The other man sent them a hard stare, then leaned close to hear Isabella as she spoke over the increasing noise.

"I don't know," she began.

"Please, the time grows short."

Her lips curved in a smile of determined gaiety. "But the night has only begun."

"I wasn't speaking of this night only—" He stopped, closing his mouth in a tight line, though the look of pleading did not fade from his eyes.

How uncomplicated he was, and how faithful. Did he fear that she and Morgan would be reconciled before he could make his declaration? He need not. The possibility was remote. But why should she not allow him to speak? There could be no harm in it.

"Very well," she said, "later."

Before a half hour had passed, the food was gone, down to the last crisp curl of pork skin. While the rum punch made another round, a jew's harp, a squeeze box, and a fiddle were brought out. A man from the *Prudence* danced a hornpipe as his shipmates bellowed the words. A jig followed, and then a quadrille and a gavotte. The seamen pulled the women to their feet and whirled them over the sand. Dipping and swaying, laughing, staggering, they kept time to the music.

The inky waves pounded on the shore as the tide came in, sending salt spray toward them in a fine mist. The stars sifted down, hanging just above the sea as if caught in a netting of cloud. The fires burned down to red embers over which small devil flames played. The shadows of the palm forest darkened, becoming impenetrable, and the dark crowned heads of the trees rearing toward the sky were silhouetted, blackness upon blackness. Gradually, the crowd about the table grew thinner as men and women drifted into the woods. The sound of muttered voices and small panting cries echoed on the wind.

Then from the sea rose the glittering edge of a silver disc. The water took on a lighter, more turquoise tint, and the sky softened to gray. By small jerks visible to the naked eye, the great, round, full moon leaped upward. It threw down a glaring track along which waves rolled, and silvered the world with brightness so hard and blazing that the dimmest printed folio could be read with ease.

There were only a few couples left at the table. They gazed at each other with drunken ardor, or else were locked together with cohesive mouths hungrily agape. Turning toward the head of the table, Félicité saw with a small sense of shock that Captain Bonhomme sat alone, nursing a mug of rum and staring with brooding eyes at the rising moon. Morgan and Isabella were gone.

Félicité drew her feet under her, preparing to rise. Bast came quickly erect, putting a hand under her elbow to help her. "Where are you going?" he asked.

"I—I don't know. Shall we walk?"

"If you like."

He fell into step beside her, retaining a light grasp on her arm. Under the circumstances, the beach seemed to offer the least chance of embarrassing encounters. By common consent, they turned in that direction. Bast shifted to walk nearer the water's edge, touching his fingers to her arm once more. The wind ruffled his hair, fluttering the ribbon of his queue, and slapped his shirt collar against his cheek. It sent the ends of Félicité's hair flying and billowed her skirts so that she was forced to keep one hand on them to hold them down.

The cove where the ships were hove to had a shape like a sickle. On the two curving points at either end, the palm forest grew almost to the water's edge, blocking the view of the beach farther along the island. The thatched hut shared by Félicité and Morgan was near the western end of the half circle. Almost by instinct, Félicité glanced toward it as they passed, but it sat dark and still and, to all appearances, empty. They took a narrow path that cut across the westernmost point of the cove, passing under the bent and twisted shape of sea pine. Before them lay the long stretch of open beach, shining pale gold with the light of the moon.

In the shadow of that thin band of forest, Bast halted, his fingers tightening on Félicité's arm so that she stopped beside him. "*Querida*, my dearest one," he said. "Once I asked you to come to me unwed. That was a grievous mistake, perhaps the most terrible I have made in my life. I should have offered you my heart, my life, my lands that will come to me from my father, in short, everything that I am, I have, or ever hope to own, and with it, my name. I beg you to forgive me for the omission, and to accept it now."

What had she expected? A declaration of love to soothe her shattered vanity? An expression of desire that she could not answer in kind, but might, if he were gentle and caring, have agreed to assuage on this night with Morgan and Isabella somewhere on the island together? She should have known it would not be so simple.

"Oh, Bast," she said. "It's impossible."

"Nothing is impossible. When we leave here we can return to New Orleans—"

"Return to New Orleans! It cannot be."

"Why? Is it because you fear how people will behave toward you? I assure you they understand now, since you left so soon after your father's death, that what you had done, your association with a Spanish officer, was for his sake. They honor you for your sacrifice, even if it was in vain."

She stared at him, wishing she could see his features more clearly there in the moving shadows. "If that is true, I can only be thankful, and indebted to you for telling me of it. But soon enough they will learn that I am with this band of pirates, a corsair's woman. What will they say then? And what will they say of Juan Sebastian Unzaga, a Spanish officer turned renegade? If you return you will be arrested on sight."

It was a long moment before he spoke, and then his voice held a tone of reluctance, as though there were arguments to be presented for his case if he cared to use them. "Yes—I suppose you are right. We could go to Havana then, and from there take ship for Spain."

"But surely even there you will be a wanted man?"

"My father is not without influence at court." He made a

careless gesture with one hand. "Something may be done to clear my name."

A frown drew Félicité's brows together. He was taking a most cavalier attitude toward his career as a buccaneer. "Bast," she said slowly, "I don't think you realize—"

"But I do. I realize I love you, Félicité, that I want you as my wife. Whatever it takes to have you, to pluck you from this damnable coil in which you are caught, I am ready to do."

It seemed so remote, this future that he was suggesting, like a dream that could not possibly come true. The only reality was the island and the sea and the ships that waited. What more was there? What more could there ever be?

She turned from him, walking once more so that he had either to hold her by force, release her, or walk with her. He chose the latter course, falling into step beside her.

"I don't know," she said, shaking her head so that her hair streamed like a gold curtain behind her.

"I do," he said. "Only put yourself in my hands and I will arrange everything."

"What of Morgan?"

"What of him? You owe him nothing, since he has not even seen fit to tell you—"

"To tell me what?" she demanded, her voice taut. "The things you have said? He did offer marriage once, and I refused."

He caught her arm, swinging her to face him there on the empty stretch of moon-silvered sand. "And what of love, Félicité? Has he offered you love, as I do?"

She shook her head, and the anguish was plain to see in her velvet-brown eyes there in the warm white light of the moon. He caught her close with a soft groan, holding her against him.

"Ah, Félicité, forgive me."

There was comfort in his arms, but nothing more. "That, yes," she whispered, "but I cannot marry you. You deserve better."

"Better? Such a thing cannot be."

"It can. You deserve someone who can love you in return."

"And you, Félicité, what do you deserve?"

He kissed her then, a passionless caress, a reverent touch of his firm lips accompanied by the brush of his mustache.

He drew back, his eyes bright, his mouth curving in a smile. "So long have I wanted to do that—" He stiffened, swinging his head to stare along the shore.

A man and a woman were just stepping from the shadows of the forest's edge perhaps a hundred yards away. The woman was a dark wraith in colorless clothing, marked by the pale gleam of her shoulders and face; the man's shirt shone with refracted light, while his hair that ruffled in the wind gleamed like old copper coins.

Morgan came toward them over the sands, while Isabella stood where he had left her. After a moment La Paloma picked up her skirts and followed behind him. The urge to run swept in upon Félicité, though it was not caused by fear of what he would do so much as it was by the transparency of her pain at his defection. Hard upon that knowledge came anger that she would let herself be so bemused, so dependent upon his continued attention, whatever form it took.

Morgan's strides were long and quick; by the time Bast had turned, squaring his shoulders, he was upon them.

"Hold on," Bast began with an uplifted hand.

"Hold on and be damned! What is the meaning of this?" Morgan set his hands on his hips as he demanded an answer.

"I resent both your tone and your attitude," the Spaniard said with a proud lift of his head.

"Do you?" Morgan said sarcastically. "I thought you, Bast, of all the men on this island, could be trusted!"

"Trusted? To what end? To hold your place for you?"

"Trusted to treat Félicité as the lady she is, instead of like a common—"

"Take care!" Bast exclaimed. "You are on no very firm ground there yourself. Any treatment she receives from me must be better than she has had from you."

As Morgan stared at him, Isabella glided to where they stood then, taking Morgan's arm, curling her fingers around it as though she would restrain him. The Spanish-Irish noble-woman glanced from one tó the other, her brows lifted in inquiry. "What is the matter?"

When no one answered, she looked to Félicité, saying with great directness, "Are they quarreling over you?"

It was Bast who answered. "It would seem so, yes. Morgan objects to my being here with her, and with reason, since I have taken the opportunity to ask her to be my wife."

"You what?" Morgan demanded.

"You heard me."

"So I did," Morgan ground out. "Tell me, when will the nuptials be held? Who will perform them, and where, since there is neither priest nor chapel on this island?"

"I explained—"

"I can just imagine," Morgan snapped, cutting across his words.

Bast frowned. "No, I didn't mean that the way you think."

"Then how did you mean it? I think you had better tell me."

"Of course," Bast said, and inclined his head as if the suggestion had been an order.

"If you will excuse us, ladies," Morgan said, and with a curt nod toward the deserted beach behind him, swung from them. Bast fell into step beside him, and they moved away, their words drifting back, indistinguishable, blown on the wind.

Félicité lifted a brow, her considering gaze on Morgan's broad back. There was something here she did not understand, something perhaps she was not meant to understand.

"Well," Isabella said, "congratulations."

Félicité turned to the other woman. "I don't know what you mean."

"To have two such men fighting over you is quite an honor."

"To some, possibly; not to me."

"Ah, you have a preference then. Why could you not have said so and saved ill feeling between them?"

"How do you know I did not?" Félicité said, her tone tart.

"When a woman has been firm enough in her answer, a

suitor no longer clings to hope. Unless a woman is promiscuous, enjoying the personal attentions of two men at once, this is the wisest course."

"You speak from the height of great experience with keeping lovers apart, I suppose?"

"As it happens, yes."

The woman's air of superiority was unendurable. "I would not have thought, in your present occupation, that many occasions for disappointing the men whose attention you attract would arise."

La Paloma's eyes gleamed more like those of a hawk than of a dove. "Let me give you a bit of advice, my dear young woman. It is never intelligent to judge from appearances."

"You do mean something by that, I expect?"

"Oh, yes, several things."

Félicité's nerves were so tightly stretched she wanted to scream. Instead, she retreated into frozen politeness. "Tell me about them."

"To begin with, my position aboard the ship in the harbor is not what you think. It is an amusement only, this voyage, because of a friend whom I knew when I was younger. In a fit of whimsy, she named her ship of women after me, and it pleased me to make her—if you will excuse the expression— maiden journey with her."

"How—interesting," Félicité commented, her disbelief patent.

Isabella's lips tightened. "Then there is the matter of Morgan. It was naive of you to concoct this little drama for his delectation. You will find he despises such subterfuges."

"You think I planned that he should see me with Bast? Nothing was further from my mind! I did not even know you and he were there!"

"Come," Isabella mocked, "you can do better than that."

"I would most certainly not have interrupted your pleasure if I had had the least idea you were there groping in the dark."

"My pleasure, in such a place? Allow me to inform you," Isabella said with swelling chest, "that I am above such plebeian delights as rutting in the sand!"

Driven by a rage of jealousy, Félicité laughed. "You should try it sometime—you might be surprised. But if what you say is true, you were enticing Morgan in the wrong direction entirely, were you not? The nearest thing to a bed the island affords must be on your friend's ship."

"That was not my purpose, I tell you!"

"Then you should have come forward more quickly just now. You looked for all the world as though a promised treat had been snatched from your hand."

An imprecation fell from the woman's lips that no Spanish noblewoman should have known. "What a foul-minded little trollop you are."

"I would not descend to calling names if I were you," Félicité said with a lift of her chin. "Knowing something of your history, I would say there is every chance that if I began I might hit on one or two that were true."

"Before God, why Morgan has jeopardized so much to find such a one as you, I cannot imagine, such a stupid little bitch as you are!"

"Stupid I may be about some things," Félicité declared. "But even I understand his reasons, as should a mistress of the whores like you!"

With catlike quickness, Isabella reached out and slapped her. Félicité's reaction was instant, automatic. The dark-haired woman's head snapped back under the strength of her blow.

With a hand to her cheek, Isabella straightened. Her eyes like slits, she said, "I understand you have some facility with a sword?"

"A little," Félicité agreed.

Isabella flung a quick look along the beach to where the figures of the two men were small with distance. "Good. It is my belief that you could profit from a salutary lesson in manners."

"It is necessary for the person who wishes to teach a subject to have a superior command of it!"

"Are you speaking of swordplay, or manners?"

"Whichever you choose," Félicité answered, her brown gaze level, her smile cold.

"We shall see then."

"Yes," Félicité said, "we shall see."

Without a word more, they turned and moved in the direction of the encampment.

Chapter 18

W*here to find* swords loomed as a problem. Every man on the island went armed at all times, not only with cutlass but most with pistols thrust into a belt at a diagonal across their chest. Still, would any with a blade fit to have give it up to them, even if the seamen could be persuaded from the palm forest?

Félicité thought of Captain Bonhomme, but he was gone from his place at the table and was nowhere in sight. There were, however, a score or so others wandering in from the woods, making for the bucket of rum punch. They greeted the idea of a meeting with swords between women with raucous, disbelieving glee, a comic distraction rather than a serious event. Chortling drunkenly, they began to compare blades to find two of the same approximate weight and length.

It was Valcour who served them best. Because of his wounds, he had spent the afternoon gambling with the other convalescing seamen. During that time he had acquired by dint of careful play a pair of matched rapiers, a part of the captured prizes. Slender, deadly, less cumbersome than the cutlasses offered by the others, they were more suited for women. With a polished bow, he offered the first of the two to Isabella, giving her a smile reminiscent of his old fastidious charm. The other, with less grace, he gave to Félicité.

A space was cleared by the simple expedient of bundling up the sailcloth with the plates, food scraps, pots and platters inside and dragging it some distance away. More wood was piled on the fires, so they leaped high. Like spectators at an arena, the few unoccupied men gathered around, seating themselves on the ground. A hilarious expectancy, punctuated by the murmur of bets, gripped the audience.

Félicité in white and Isabella in black, the two women saluted each other. The blades flashed silver and gold light from moon and fires as they swept up, then down again. The swords held in slim white hands crossed, and then, with fluid, stunning grace, the contest began.

Like fog and smoke, swirling, unfurling, blending, they came together. The blades clicked and tapped, sliding upon each other with a sighing whine. The wind caught their hair, sending it flying around them, and whipped their skirts that dragged over the sand as they danced with airy grace; advancing, retreating, brown eyes and blue clashing with icy intent.

The men quieted, grew still. It was then, with gossamer lightness, that Isabella began her attack. Félicité parried in tierce with a melting, bell-like chime of blades, and the strife began in earnest.

In the swordplay of the women there was none of the gritty power that there had been between Morgan and Valcour. Still, it was no less deadly for its lightness. Isabella fought with speed and textbook precision. Félicité brought an excellence to the meeting that, combined with a certain intuitive knowledge, Isabella clearly had to take into account again and again as her follow-through and feints were prevented. Less than five minutes after the Spanish-Irish noblewoman had moved in upon Félicité, the blades clashed with a shower of yellow-gold sparks, Félicité, parried, circled, and her rapier slashed through the black lace of Isabella's sleeve.

La Paloma's eyes blazed, then narrowed. "There may be more to you than I thought," she said.

"Thinking can be dangerous," Félicité answered.

Her words were nearly lost in the yelling of the pirates, and then the fighting began in earnest. They slid and scuffled in the sand, turning, dipping, reaching in and out of sword's length, the glittering reflection twinkling over the sand, shifting in blue-white lozenges across the skirts of their gowns. For the two women there was nothing except the incessant clanging blades, the beating jar running up from wrist to elbow, and the precious drawing of breath. Parries, ripostes, contes, froissées; each trying and failing, failing and trying, to free their blades for the damaging lunge.

Blood, the men wanted blood. Though their audience had grown quieter once more, there was a sense of avidness in their breathless attention. Félicité was tiring, her anger evaporating as if it had never been. She saw in the face of the other woman something of her own regret. Their fatigue was as much from the encumbrance of their heavy skirts as from the weight of ringing steel in their hands. Their breasts heaved with the deep drawing of breaths that strained their stays, and perspiration dampened their hair. And yet they could not, would not stop. It was a thing of pride and skill, a refusal to accept the humiliation of defeat, or to allow the other victory. Brilliant female fiends, they drove each other toward a precipice of inescapable injury, or else the ultimate horror of soft and feminine death.

At the edge of her vision, Félicité caught a flicker of movement, saw beyond Isabella the stealthy approach of the French captain, saw in the other woman's eyes the ghost of her own fleeting disquiet, and caught a hazardous flashing glance beyond Félicité's own shoulder.

"Now!"

With that ringing masculine command, there were four blades in the arena, four glittering metallic instruments of slicing destruction. Félicité felt a blow to her rapier that numbed her arm to the shoulder, heard the squealing scrape of metal on metal. Caught on the thickness of a corsair's heavy cutlass, her own blade was swept upward. Less than six feet away, Isabella stood similarly disengaged by the force of a cutlass in the hand of Captain Jacques Bonhomme. Turning her head, Félicité, with arm held high and sword hilt still in her grasp, stared into the emerald eyes of Morgan McCormack.

Once more Félicité glanced to Isabella. The woman lifted a brow, and moving in concert, as if the maneuver had been practiced times without number, they snatched their swords free and whirled to stand shoulder to shoulder, presenting their weapons point first toward the two men who had dared to interfere.

It would have been difficult to say which man, whether Morgan or Captain Bonhomme, was most disconcerted. By reflex action, they brought their blades up in defense, but the will to do more was absent from their blank faces.

"Shall we spit them before they regain their senses?" Isabella asked, her lips curving in real amusement. "Or shall we show mercy?"

"They—meant well," Félicité said. "That much is in their favor."

Around them the pirates were howling in protest, or else vociferous in their preference for the order of battle, urging that the clash continue.

It was Morgan who decided the outcome. He whipped his sword down, withdrawing, resting the point upon the sand. "I entreat mercy from you, Félicité, now and in the future."

With a gusting sigh of relief, the French captain followed Morgan's lead, withdrawing likewise. His gaze was filled with admiring concern as he watched for Isabella's next move.

"Too bad," Valcour said, strolling forward, his drawl breaking the silence. "Seldom have I seen anything more exciting. I will relieve you of my sword, marquesa, if it pleases you, and then perhaps you will allow me to lead you to a glass of punch."

Isabella, her face slightly haggard, turned from Valcour. Her right arm trembled, but stepping back, she lifted it once more in salute to Félicité. "Mademoiselle, that was most excellently done. I congratulate you."

"Not at all," Félicité replied, "it was, I think, a fine lesson."

"You are too generous," the Spanish woman said, "but then I expect I am not the first one to discover that."

Isabella de Herrara passed her sword to Valcour then, before she turned to the French captain. A smile curved her lips as she gazed into his Latin brown eyes. "I wonder, sir, if I could prevail upon you to show me to the punch bowl?"

"It would be an honor beyond my deserts." The captain covered her fingers with his own where they rested on his arm. He leaned down, his head close to her dark hair, as he led her away.

Félicité lowered her sword arm, pushing the point into the sand, watching her brother as he glared after the couple, slowly bending the sword he held between his two hands. Releasing the hilt as her own rapier stood alone, she swung away. The seamen closed in around her, congratulating her, speaking with admiring voices of her prowess, of the grandeur of the fight and the shame of its early end. They proposed a toast to her health, but she did not heed them. Pushing through, she moved with quickening footsteps and blind eyes toward the hut.

At the last moment, she veered, heading toward the point of the cove and the stretch of the beach beyond. She crossed the narrow, forested spit of land with breathless haste, ducking under the gnarled sea pine. The deep, loose sand slipped under her feet, slowing her, then she was on the hard-packed water's edge. Lifting her skirts higher, unseen and unseeing, she ran faster and faster. Her breath sobbed in her throat, and the scalding tears that streamed from her eyes were dried in salt-crusted tracks by the wind.

Fleeing from the pain of lost closeness, the distress of Morgan's suspicions, the reminders of a way of life gone beyond reclaim and the confusion of dead anger, she did not hear the pursuit until it was nearly upon her. It came on with the quick thud of booted feet. To look would be more terrible than not knowing. Who else could it be except some seaman wandering in the woods who had lost his lady love and blundered out of the palm forest on the wrong side of the cove? To give chase to a running female would be as natural as for a hound coursing a deer. If he knew from her gown she was not of the cargo of the *La Paloma*, if she turned to tell him, what hope was there it would make a difference?

The pounding footfalls came nearer. Félicité's breathing was so labored after the exertions of swordplay that she knew she could not outstrip him. Most sailors could not swim, however. Without a second's hesitation, she splashed into the water. A great wave of the incoming moontide staggered her. At the same time she was caught from behind. Thrown off balance, she and her assailant fell, and the creaming surf washed over them, wetting them to the shoulders. Félicité struggled, but Morgan pinned her to the washing sand. He leaned over her, his eyes burning into hers.

"Dear God, Félicité," he said, the words a rasp of strain, "what more will it come to you to do to flay my soul?"

His mouth tasted of salt and rum and the warm, honeyed sweetness of remorse. Did he believe she had not been a party to the capture of his ship, or did he not? What could it matter so long as he held her, and with his sure and gentle touch, brought the surging of the restless sea to mingle with her blood?

They stripped away their clothing and flung it in sodden rags onto the shore. The flowing, melted turquoise water was warm against their skin, and if the sand gritted and clung, they did not feel it. With fast-cleaving mouths and entwined limbs, they disported themselves, primitive and beatific, nude and without lewdness. Félicité could feel the pounding of his heart, the pressing of his thighs against her, and the pounding shocks of pleasure that had the same ceaseless rhythm as the tide. Faint but fiery with desire, she took him deep inside her, and heard in the stillness of her own mind the explosive rush of the blood in her veins. Drowning in sensation, awash with joy, she saw the brightness of the moonlight behind her eyelids, felt its white-hot shining along the wet and lustrous surface of her skin. The luminous night surrounded her. The water sparkled and the sand shone like sifted yellow diamond dust. But deep in her eyes as she gazed into the face of the man above her was tangible ecstasy, scintillating and shimmering, the most radiant thing of all.

*   *   *

The morning was half gone when the women came straggling from the woods, doing up catches and laces and picking bits of trash from their hair. The men followed behind them. A few moaned in self-pity, declaring themselves barely able to walk; others were morose and foul-tempered if spoken to, but most seemed in charity with the world and ready for their breakfasts.

Disheveled women and rumpled, scratching men, they scrounged for food, mixing manioc cakes and slicing smoked meat while the gray smoke of freshly made fires curled into the sky. Every plate on the island being thick with congealed grease, they did without, tossing the hot cakes and meat from hand to hand until it was cool enough to hold. They washed the food down with palm wine and rum, and daintily or wolfishly, according to their personal habits, licked their fingers.

Done, the women rose and stretched, then began to look toward the *La Paloma* swinging at anchor in the cove.

Though the men tried, the female crew of the ship could not be dissuaded from leaving. They must not overstay their welcome, they said, or strain the hospitality of such a fine group of men. Isabella, sitting in the curve of the French captain's arm, seemed reluctant to make a move. But she too insisted, in spite of the soft whispers of Captain Bonhomme in her ear, that they must leave. Still protesting and pleading, the pirate crew ferried the women out to the ship, though so slow was the sweep of their oars that all were agreed it would have been much faster if the ladies had rowed themselves.

Isabella was among the last to leave. She stepped to where Morgan and Félicité stood to one side with Captain Bonhomme. A smile tinged with melancholy lighting the severe lines of her face, she gave her hand to Morgan.

"I take my leave of this island with regret," she said. "The world expects a great deal of people, does it not, my old friend? I had never realized until now just how much."

"Duty," Morgan said, his gaze direct, unfathomable, "is a four-letter word. Perhaps you should follow my example and forswear it."

"The temptation is strong, but I must resist, though perhaps some way can be found to be dutiful only in part,'' Isabella agreed, her eyes bright.

Their words were plain, and yet they carried an undercurrent of hidden meaning Félicité could sense, but not comprehend. Her stare was puzzled; then, as Isabella turned to her, all speculation fled.

''I give you my thanks,'' the Spanish-Irish noblewoman said. ''Making one's bed in the sand has much to recommend it. I am indebted to you for the suggestion.''

Félicité found suddenly that she liked this woman with her forthright manner and independent reserve. Given the circumstances and time, they might have been friends. For the moment, she was too aware of the interested gaze of the two men beside them for comment. Smiling, she said, ''It may be that we will meet again.''

''Yes, I pray it will be so,'' La Paloma replied, and moved on, finally, to the French captain. ''Farewell,'' she said, laying her hand in his.

''It is only *au revoir*,'' he answered. ''I refuse to say goodbye; there is no sea wide enough to keep me from finding you again.''

''Perhaps,'' she said, her smile arch, faintly challenging. ''If the rum doesn't make your track too weaving ever to cross mine.''

''From this day, I am a sober man.'' Captain Jacques Bonhomme said the words with all the reverence of a vow.

''A fine boast, but can you sustain it?''

''We shall see.''

''Yes,'' Isabella said, ''it may be we shall.''

They drew apart from the others then, and the French pirate captain held the noblewoman with loving closeness, pressing his lips to hers. She broke from him then and hurried to the longboat drawn up upon the sand. Stepping in, taking her place in the bow, she lifted her hand in a final wave, then turned her face toward the ship that waited.

They watched her go, watched the *La Paloma* weigh anchor, raise sail, and beat slowly out of the cove. The men dispersed, going about their business. Still Morgan and Félicité stood staring out to sea. Captain Bonhomme stood not far away, his hands on his hips and feet widespread as he stared after the grim and graceful brigantine.

"Why now?" he queried, his voice ragged. "Why after all these years, when I am no more than a rotting hull, should I meet the woman who could make life worth living?"

"A very good question, my friend," Morgan said, though his brooding green gaze was on Félicité's face.

With the departure of the women, the work on the two ships resumed. The *Black Stallion* was maneuvered closer to shore and farther along the cove where the trees came down to the water. The ship was then careened. Blocks and tackles were hitched from the bases of the masts to the trees, and the hull was pulled over until almost on beam ends, flat on its side. Floating about it in boats, the seamen scraped the incrustation of barnacles and other shell creatures from the hull thus drawn from below the water line. That done, they caulked and pitched the seams of the planking, daubed them with sulfur as a deterrent to burrowing sea life, and coated them with tallow. They left that side for a day to dry, then turned the brigantine around and repeated the process on the other.

When this enormously taxing undertaking was done, they stepped the new mizzenmast, reattached the topmasts, bent on new sails, and spliced and restrung her rigging. They touched up her paint, brightwork varnish, and gilt, polished her brass, and holystoned her decks. There was some discussion between Captain Bonhomme, the bluff captain of the *Prudence*, and Morgan of changing the name of the ship, christening her the *Raven II* in spite of her stallion figurehead. The deciding vote was against it. Still the French captain ran his personal flag brought from the lugger, the black raven on a red ground, to the topmast before pronouncing the ship ready to sail.

They could not leave yet. There was still the *Prudence* to be put in order. Spurred by rum and curses and a belaying pin in the hands of the *Black Stallion*'s bosun, the men turned their attention toward the smaller vessel.

The days continued hot and dry, with the trades becoming no more than a warm breeze that did nothing to alleviate the heat. The rustling of the palms became a dusty clatter, hordes of flies gathered, stinging the bare, sweaty backs of the working men, and gnats danced around their heads, clogging their nostrils as they breathed. One day the men, tiring of pork and fish, chased down one of the big, ungainly iguanas. They roasted the meat, basting it with pork drippings. Some few of the men declared it to be good, a great delicacy, while laughing at the disgusted looks of their fellows, but most of the carcass was thrown back into the forest to make fodder for the ants and maggot-worms.

At night the men drank sitting around the fires. They told tales of roaring fights, of beautiful ladies and ugly bawds and the strange customs of exotic ports. Sometimes they sang or made up impromptu theatricals, and once on a night of particular creativity, they got up a mock court.

The captain of *Prudence* was drafted as the judge, and the bosun was named as the criminal; the ship's carpenter served as attorney general, while twelve men tried and true took their oaths as the jury, and a man armed with a marlin spike had the honor of being the bailiff.

The judge slung a muddy, much-tarred tarpaulin around his shoulders, stuck a woman's wig upon his head and settled a pair of spectacles upon his nose. Thus attired in dignity, he swung himself upon the limb of a tree. The sailors, armed with crowbars, hand spikes, and oars, gathered below him, and the criminal was brought out with the long face of an innocent man falsely accused.

The attorney general, with his waistcoat properly buttoned for once in his life, assumed an air of great knowledge. Clutching his lapels, he called out the charges.

Drawn by the general hilarity, Félicité and Morgan stepped from their hut, walking closer to the fires to watch the proceedings.

"And it pleases your lordship and the gentlemen of the jury," the attorney general intoned, "here is a fellow before you who is a sad dog, a sad and sorry sea dog. It is my most earnest hope that your lordship will order him to be hanged out of hand, forthwith!"

"Why, what has the man done?" the judge asked, bending a sour look on the bosun.

"He has committed piracy upon the high seas, and it is my purpose to prove, and it please your lordship, that this base criminal, this sad sea dog brought up before you, has run before a thousand storms, escaping them entire, and yea, has got himself safe ashore when the ship he rode was completely cast away and lost. This, as all men know, is a positive sign he was not born to be drowned! And still, not having the fear of hanging before his eyes, he went on ravishing and robbing, man, woman, and child, plundering the cargoes of ships fore and aft, burning and sinking schooner and sloop, barque and boat, as if the devil himself lived inside him. And this is not all, my lord. He has even worse vices and villainies to his name, for we shall prove that he has been guilty of drinking belly vengeance, thin and sour stuff, and your lordship knows that never was there a sober fellow but was a dangerous rogue!"

At this a great rumble of laughter went out from the men before they quieted enough to hear again.

"My lord," the attorney general went on, "I'm sure I could have spoken much finer than I have, but as your worship knows, the rum is running low, and how should a man remember to spout the law that has not sipped his dram? That aside, I hope your lordship will order this pesky rascal to be hanged!"

The judge looked over his spectacles at the criminal, who was trying valiantly not to laugh. "Hark ye to me, sir! You are a lice-ridden, pitiful, and ugly-visaged dog; what can you say for yourself that will persuade us not to string you up immediately and set you adrying in the sun like a skeleton on a gibbet? How do you plead, guilty, or not?"

"Not guilty, and it please your lordship," the prisoner sighed.

"Not guilty! Dare to repeat those words, sir, and I will have you hanged forthwith, trial or no."

The bosun hung his head. "And it please your honor, my fine sir, I am but a poor honest seaman, as good a man as ever went between stem and stern of a ship. I can hand, reef, steer, and clap two ends of a rope together as well as any man that ever crossed salt water, but I was taken by one bastard of a pirate, the most notorious gentleman-thief that ever was unhung, the captain of the fair ship *Prudence*, and it was he who forced me to become a pirate myself, your honor, all against my will.''

The judge, the self-same captain of the *Prudence*, bent a terrible stare upon the bosun. "Answer me, sir. How will you be tried?''

"By God and my country!''

"The devil you will! Why, then, gentlemen of the jury, I think we have nothing to do but to deliberate and pass judgment.''

The attorney general gave a firm nod. "My thoughts exactly, my lord, for if this dastardly fellow be allowed to speak, he may clear himself, and that would, without a doubt, be an insult to the court!''

"But kind sirs, gentlemen, all of ye,'' the prisoner pleaded, "I hope you will consider—''

"Consider?'' the judge demanded with great affront. "How dare you talk of considering, sir? I never considered in all my life, if that be the same as taking thought. Why, I'll make it a hanging offense to consider!''

"But I hope your lordship will listen to reason.''

"Listen to the scoundrel! What have we to do with reason? I'll have you know there is nothing here that smacks of reason, we having instead the law!''

This sally too found favor with the pirates, perhaps because it so nearly coincided with their own thoughts and experiences with judgments handed down by the legal communities of the world.

The judge signaled for silence, demanding to know if dinner was ready.

"Yes, my lord,'' the attorney general answered.

"Then hark ye to me, ye scoundrel at the bar. It is the decision of this court, sir, that you must suffer the most extreme penalty. For this there are three reasons. First, because it is not fit that I should sit here as judge and nobody be hanged. Second, you must swing because you have a damned swinging look. And third, you must be hanged because I am hungry, and because as you know, sir, it is the custom of the court that whenever the judge's dinner is ready before the trial is done we cut short the proceedings with a hanging. There is the law of the land for you, ye sad dog. Nay, stay! I have a better decree. You shall eat at my right hand. By the time you fill your stomach with the belly timber we have had of late, you will wish, by damn, you had been hanged!''

There were a great many truths to be found in the play-acting of the men; too many, Félicité found, thinking of her father and the other men condemned as traitors in New Orleans, and of the judgments so summarily handed down against them.

Another truth concerned the rum. They were running low of this necessary commodity. If they were to have enough to see them through the repairs to the *Prudence* and the days of sailing it would take them to reach a port where the supply might be replenished, they must ration it.

This decision did not sit well with men used to swilling all they could hold, men who needed forgetfulness, who worked all day in the broiling sun and had need of liquid to put back their lost fluids and who refused to drink water unless it was laced liberally with alcohol. As everyone knew, it was bad water that gave men fluxes and fevers.

Tempers grew short. So important loomed the possibility of being without rum that when a man was discovered trying to steal more than his share one night, he was beaten senseless and would have been kicked to death if Morgan had not put a stop to it.

Captain Bonhomme, once able to rally his men with a jest and his presence, kept to himself after the sailing of *La Paloma*. Though he touched not a drop of liquor, he was a changed man, brooding and silent, fighting his need in private as he walked the beaches.

Deprived of much of their greatest solace, smarting under the authority of Morgan, a man who should have had no more than they, after long hours of hard work with little hope of reward in the shares to be had from the cargo of the *Prudence*, perhaps it was not surprising that the men began to

315

mutter among themselves, gathering in small groups. As the days followed one after the other, turning into a week, then two, Valcour was often seen in a circle of men, speaking earnestly, keeping his voice low and a watchful eye out for Morgan's or Bonhomme's approach. The men from the *Prudence* and the *Black Stallion* kept clear of him for the most part, but he found a ready audience in the motley crew from the old *Raven*.

What with their hard work and the toil in the sun, Félicité and Morgan visited the bathing pool in the cave at the end of every evening. It was, for Félicité, her favorite time of the day, when she and Morgan could be alone, away from the encampment and the constant brawling, cursing, and stares of the sailors. It was a time of quiet and serenity, when the last of the sun's slanting rays played over the green slopes of the island and coolness crept from the fern-edge forest glades, when the waves sighed onto the shore and the sea birds quartered the sky one last time before making for their roosts. It was a time of repose, a time when she and Morgan, afterward, could retreat to their hut, leaving the world and its problems outside, and seek in each other the surcease that kept them sane.

One evening as they left the cave, climbing down its limestone face to start back along the beach, there was a different feeling in the air. Though the pink afterglow of the sunset lit the western sky, to the northeast a gray haze lay upon the sea and the waves breaking at their feet seemed heavy, washing back and forth with an oily surge. The air was hushed and still, so that their footsteps in the sand grated and crunched. Overhead a blue heron winged inland, though the rest of the sky was empty of life.

"It looks like we may get some rain," Félicité said.

"It does that," Morgan agreed, a frown between his eyes.

"Is it going to storm?"

"Who can say? It's always possible in these latitudes, though it's late in the season now for a big blow."

They walked a few yards in silence. Driven by the sullen oppression around her, so similar to the atmosphere among the seamen these days, she moistened her lips. "Morgan?"

He turned his head to stare down at her, his expression attentive.

"Have you—have you noticed the men lately?"

"What about them?"

"They seem more surly than usual, as if they might resort to mutiny at any moment."

"When was a pirate crew not a hair's breadth from mutiny? It's a natural state for them."

"Possibly—I wouldn't know. But it seems dangerous, especially for you."

His mouth tugged in a wry smile. "I am flattered at your concern, but why for me?"

"I have seen Valcour talking to the others, and I don't think it is Captain Bonhomme who has earned his hate."

"You have done him more damage than I thus far. Maybe you should look to yourself." His green eyes were watchful as he smiled down at her.

"Even if what you say is true," she pointed out, "you are the one who stands between him and me now."

"So I am," he said, his tone thoughtful as he turned his gaze seaward once more.

"Perhaps if you didn't drive the men quite so hard," Félicité began.

"Someone has to do it, if we don't want to be caught here, and there doesn't seem to be anyone else inclined to take on the job."

It was true; Félicité could see that, and yet she could not help being afraid.

Morgan reached out, taking her hand. "We had better hurry if we want to get back to the hut before the rain begins."

They could see it coming toward them, marching across the sea on long gray stilts of water. Thunder rolled like the sound of guns, and the silver fire of lightning streaked from the gray bank of clouds into the water. The atmosphere took on a yellowish tint, and the smell of ozone was strong in the air. The wind began to rise, carrying salt mist and spraying sand before it, and swaying the feather-decked heads of the palms, moving the trunks in a graceful and limber dance. They could breathe the dampness, feel it on their skins. The first drops of rain, huge and wet, splattered warmly on their upturned faces, and then the hut was before them.

They flung themselves inside and dived panting on their pallet. From that uncertain shelter, rustling dryly with the strength of the wind and the first raindrops, they watched the descent of the dragging curtain of rain as it closed over them, rattling, splashing, beating the water of the cove into a froth.

Darkness closed in, accompanied by the growl and roar of thunder and lit by the flare of lightning. Abruptly Félicité was reminded of the night after the masquerade, of the clash of Morgan with Valcour and the two others in the darkness, and the violent aftermath marked by the passage of the storm. She glanced at the man beside her, and found him staring down at her in the dimness.

"Félicité," he whispered, reaching out to touch her cheek, sliding his warm fingers through her hair to cup her neck. "Don't look at me so, for I can't bear it."

Lowering his head, he touched his mouth to hers, his lips a firm and heady antidote to memory. With soft and searing kisses, he outlined the curve of her cheek, the tender angle of her jaw, moving down the turn of her neck to where a pulse throbbed in the hollow of her throat. His strength limitless, controlled, he eased her down on the pallet then, resting on one elbow above her. His hands smoothed over her, exciting, arousing. He tugged her shirt from her breeches, pushing it upward, pausing to snatch a kiss from each rose-tipped peak of her breasts as he bared them before drawing the shirt off over her head. He pushed her breeches down, following their slow slide over the flatness of her abdomen as he had before, moving lower, and lower still.

When she lay naked, he removed his own clothing, rolling toward her once more, pulling her against the hard length of his long body. He traced the curves and hollows of her form with exquisite care, setting his own pleasure aside for the moment as he assured hers. There was sensuous enjoyment of his task in his lingering caresses.

She touched the thick vitality of his hair, and felt the dissolving of her being, the liquid flow of longing rising to a floodtide of wanton desire. On its crest, he entered her, the firm power of his body a sensual delight, the quiver of the sculpted steel of his muscles a gauge of his stringent restraint. Moving together in a rhythm measureless and wild as the elements around them, they strove with panting breaths to thunderous heights of pleasure, and found at the summit, in oblivion and peaceful exhaustion, the perfect panacea for remembrance.

"Morgan—" Félicité whispered when they were still at last, lying side by side once more.

He reached across her to ease the taut pull on her hair where it was caught beneath her shoulders, then gathered her to him. "I am here," he said against the top of her head. "Go to sleep now."

There was much she wanted to say, needed to say. Despite the press of it against her throat, she closed her eyes, and to her own astonishment, slept.

The rain died away in the night, leaving the world wet but unbowed. The trades blew cool once more; parrots called with raucous joy as if trying to rouse the sleepers in their rain-drenched tents. The tracks of shorebirds crocheted the wet sand, running in and out of the sea wrack; the twists of seaweed and rotted driftwood and broken shells thrown up by the storm tide. The sun rose bright-edged and golden out of the sea, its light dazzling on the water, silvery on the wings of the gulls that circled overhead, heading out over the water to where three ships crawled like giant spiders over the sea, a pair of frigates and a slender brigantine with sails set, bearing down on the island with the morning light reflecting in a blinding glare from their spread canvas.

Chapter 19

❧❧❧

A *shout of warning* went up. Men came to their feet, rubbing their eyes, their curses for the man who woke them dying away as they gazed out over the water. The Spanish lines of the ships could not be mistaken, even at that distance, nor could the menace of the rows of gun ports along their sides. This was the *guarda de costas*, the dreaded Spanish fleet whose job it was to hunt down pirates in their lairs or on the water, and their presence in the delicate freshness of the morning did not denote a picnic or a roll in the sand.

With panic-stricken yells, the seamen kicked friends and comrades still sleeping from their bedding, snatched up cutlasses and pistols, and began to throw their belongings together.

Captain Bonhomme, on his feet, staring seaward, turned with decision. "Belay that! There's no time! Head for the boats as you stand up. We have to make the brigantine or we are all dead men!"

The reason for the French captain's words was plain to see. There was a chance, if they could reach the *Black Stallion* and make ready to sail in time, that they could slip from the cove before the frigates could get within range. If they were so fortunate, the pirate brigantine would be able to outdistance the heavier, less wieldy vessels, showing them a clean pair of heels. If they could not, if they were caught inside the sheltering arms of the cove, they would be trapped like a fly in a bottle. There would be no escape.

Félicité, drawn from her pallet by the cries, flung a quick

look at Morgan, who stood just outside the doorway of their hut. His face was grim as he took in the situation.

"Morgan!" Captain Bonhomme shouted, waving an arm at them. "For the love of God, make haste!"

Still Morgan hesitated, frowning as if weighing alternatives, though as far as Félicité could see, there were none. At last he swung to her.

"Félicité, I want you to take food and water and go to the cove."

"No!" she protested. "I—couldn't run and hide, not knowing what is happening, waiting to be found."

"Even if it is the best and safest course for you?"

"Is that what you plan to do?" she asked, her gaze direct.

"The case is different with me."

"I don't care!"

He clenched a fist. "If we get away safely, we can return for you. If not, the men on the frigates will not expect anyone to have stayed behind."

"I would rather face what is going to take place with my eyes open, I thank you, and with a fighting chance." She did not add, but could have, that she preferred to face it with him.

He gave a reluctant nod. "All right then. Let's go."

As they reached the French captain, he ceased his lurid laments over the length of time they had tarried and the slowness of his men and turned toward the longboats. From all directions, as if at some given signal, men converged, determined to be the first aboard the brigantine, terrified suddenly of being left behind.

Then a group of some thirty men with pistols at the ready flung themselves between the beached boats and the surging mass of seamen. Valcour, a pistol in one hand and drawn sword in the other, was at their head.

"Hold!" he called, his voice ringing with shrill virulence. "That's as far as you go!"

"What is the meaning of this?" Captain Bonhomme growled, coming to a halt in a flurry of sand.

"My men and I," Valcour shouted, "have first call on the boats! Or perhaps I should say, the only call."

"Name of a name, you treacherous dog! This is mutiny!"

"Why, so it is, my good captain. How intelligent of you to recognize it. You will be so kind, all of you, to lay down your weapons."

"The devil we will! Look you, man. Can't you see our only chance is to get to the ship? The Spanish dons will hang us all, men and woman, if you leave us marooned here!"

"Yes, with one exception. I wish I could remain to see it, but my men and I must depart."

"You can't get away with this," Morgan said, pushing forward with Félicité at his side. "There are more of us than there are of you. We can surround you."

"The first man who moves," Valcour cut across the words, "is dead."

At that moment, a sailor at the end of the line shifted, reaching for his pistol. Without the flicker of an eyelid, Valcour fired. The seaman screamed, falling writhing to the ground. In seconds he was still.

"I did warn him. Death now or later, it's all one to me." There was emptiness behind Valcour's yellow-brown eyes as he dropped his now useless pistol. "But as I was saying, only the men shall hang."

Before she could move, before anyone saw his intent, her brother lunged toward Félicité and clamped a hand on her wrist, dragging her across the stretch of beach that lay between the two groups. As Morgan jumped after them, Valcour whirled with leveled sword. Morgan came up short, his green eyes blazing.

"That's right, back down," Valcour said on an exultant laugh. "As much as I would enjoy running you through, I think it would be too easy an end. I prefer you to be tried and hanged by your Spanish masters. So fitting, don't you agree, and so amusing for Félicité."

Valcour spun her wrist, twisting it behind her back so she was brought up, white-faced with pain, against him. One of the mutineers growled something, and Valcour nodded in agreement.

"As my friend here pointed out, we waste time. Gentlemen,

your weapons? Carefully now. What a shame it would be if anything went off and hit my dear sister.''

It seemed at a glance that most of the men who had thrown in their lot with Valcour were, as might have been expected, from the *Raven*, the most villainous and hardened of the lot, the ones most likely to act without compunction if the order that had been given was not soon obeyed. Bast, his brown eyes fastened on Félicité, was the first man to bend and put down his primed pistol, placing it with care so the weapon would not discharge accidentally, then laying his sword on top.

"Valcour, you can't do this," Félicité said, finding her voice, forcing the words through the tightness in her throat.

"Can't I?" he sneered. "I would have thought you would thank me for the invitation to join us, instead of objecting to our methods. I am sorry I have to use you as a hostage for the good behavior of the others, particularly Morgan, but that is the fortune of war."

"You can't leave so many to die!"

"Why not? I have done worse, my dear, believe me." Narrowly he watched the men before him.

"Then I beg you to leave me here, too. Please, Valcour, I ask in the name of my father."

"Your father? Why should you think I would be moved by a plea in his name, *ma chère?* I had no reverence for the man who adopted me; more than that, I despised him. But I paid him back in the end for his years of patronizing me, of reminding me at every turn of my dependence on his charity, and of how far I fell below his expectations of what I should be. On the day he died, he regretted his slights more bitterly, I do assure you."

"What—what do you mean?" she asked, watching with sickness as Captain Bonhomme, his Latin eyes dark, dropped his cutlass and pistol along with the others.

"Why, Félicité, haven't you guessed? I was so certain you must have! It was I who told Olivier Lafargue of your cohabitation with the former Lieutenant Colonel McCormack, of the way you were spreading your legs, ruining yourself so that he might live. What else could he do, being your father, except take his own life to wipe out the dishonor and free you from such base servitude?''

Anguish shafted in her as she thought of her father alone in prison, faced with such grievous knowledge, such a loss of regard for her. What shame and despair he must have felt, what impotence as he sought to find a way to help her, before he had taken his final decision! "How could you, Valcour? How could you?'' she whispered.

"It was easy. A few words in a note, a coin to the guard, and it was done. It was I, in reality, who set you free. You should be grateful. I cut the cord that held you to New Orleans, sliced away the encumbrances so we could start a new life. We can still have it, too, in France, when we have money enough to take our rightful position at court."

"You are mad!" Félicité said. Morgan was putting down his arms now, with the same care as Bast, the last man to do so. There was a white line about his mouth under the brown of his skin as he watched Félicité and the man who held her. As he came slowly erect again, she saw his pistol lay butt first, toward her. She met his emerald gaze, saw his almost imperceptible nod, and realized she alone could help herself. The others dared not for fear of the danger to her. Moreover, of them all, she was the only one Valcour and his men might hesitate to kill.

"Mad, am I?" Valcour laughed, and paused to indicate with a wave of his sword for his men to begin gathering up the weapons. "Mad? Hardly. I was sane enough to trade what I knew of the conspiracy and the men who indulged in it for my own freedom. Sane enough to escape the net that caught them, just as I will escape this one."

"You speak as if you were innocent, but you weren't. You were as guilty as the men who died, maybe more so!" His grip was looser as he began to move backward toward the longboat, pulling her with him, as he explained his cleverness. If she could only keep him talking, act as a drag upon him as she stumbled, barely moving; anything to delay him. There were as yet a few pistols left on the ground amid the confused movement of the mutineers as they picked up dropped weapons.

"Was I? It doesn't matter. I wasn't stupid enough to stay

around, and I fooled the Spanish, got away clean even though I was the most wanted, most hunted man in the colony. They couldn't touch me then, and they won't touch me now.''

She jerked her arm free then, driving the point of her elbow into her brother's wounded side. He gasped, yelping with pain as he released her. She dived, rolling, coming up with Morgan's pistol. As she leveled it at Valcour's chest, he stopped abruptly in his rush after her, spreading his arms wide, easing back.

If he had had a pistol he might have killed her, so violent was the rage in his eyes. As it was, the reach of his sword was not enough.

''Now,'' she said on a deep breath, speaking into the abrupt stillness, ''drop your sword.''

Valcour smiled, a curling of the lips that did not reach his eyes. ''I can do that, but it won't make a difference. My men care nothing for my death, and you have only one shot. They have no choice now but to carry through with the plan. To be hanged by the Spanish, or hanged by the captain there as mutineers—those are their only options otherwise.''

''They can go without you then.'' At her words, there was a rumble of agreement among his followers, and they began to back slowly toward the boats once more. A few were close enough to fling the awkward extra weapons they carried inside and, grasping the gunwales, drag the longboats into the water.

''You won't shoot me, Félicité; not in cold blood, not without the goad of a fight beforehand. That's not your way, heaven be praised. Put down that pistol and come with me. Choose life instead of hanging. I never meant that for you, truly. Know you now, Félicité, *ma chère*, that I do care for you in my own manner, as much as I am capable of caring for anyone or anything. If I did not, I would never have troubled myself to try to rescue you from Morgan that night in New Orleans, would never have bothered to return for you. If I tricked you into coming with me, or forced you by threat of degrading pain to help deceive your lover and take his ship, it was because you would not have done so, otherwise. And if I have hurt you it is because it is necessary for me, for without it I can never bring myself to possess any woman.''

His tone made it sound as if he considered his reasons for what he had done valid, as if they should make a difference. They did not.

She would not allow them to penetrate her hard resolve, though they sent a shiver of something like revulsion through her that was mirrored on her face. ''If you believe I won't shoot, try coming nearer.''

''Before God, Félicité, be reasonable,'' he cried. ''There is no time for this. Come!''

''Never!''

''Then die with your renegade lover and be damned!''

He spun around, leaping for the last of the longboats as his men pushed it into the water. Anger, cold and implacable, rose in Félicité. Holding the heavy pistol with both hands, she sighted in on Valcour and squeezed the trigger.

The weapon exploded with a mighty blast, kicking upward in recoil, but it was already pointing skyward, the barrel swept up by Morgan's hand. The ball whistled harmlessly over Valcour's head. Swinging around, his face black with rage, her brother cursed her.

''Let him go,'' Morgan said, kneeling beside her. ''You don't want his blood on your hands.''

Perhaps he was right, perhaps she didn't, and yet it would have been a satisfaction, some recompense for the losses she had sustained because of Valcour Murat.

Around her, the men left on the beach snatched up the one or two remaining pistols, firing after the fast-rowing pirates as they drew away. Splashing into the water, they shouted, yelled, cursed, flung sticks of wood and sea shells, all to no effect. The men in the boats pulled farther and farther out to sea, taking the weapons, the hopes, the chance of survival of the men on the island, leaving them marooned with nothing except the specter of harsh Spanish justice.

The babble of rage and blame, despair and fruitless plans died away. The *Prudence* lay with bare poles; there was no chance of getting her ready in under six hours of hard labor at least. She was useless then, and her boat had been on shore

EMBRACE AND CONQUER

and was now gone. They had nothing with which to defend
themselves other than a few knives and daggers, carpenter's
tools and hand spikes that would be useless against well-
armed soldiery. The only thing left was to take to the woods,
going into hiding, though the island was so small it would be
only a matter of time before they were found and dragged one
by one from their dens.

A few took the chance, sidling away, disappearing into the
green shadows of the palm forests, but most stood where they
were.

The bluff captain of the *Prudence* could be heard counsel-
ing his men, drawing them apart. Most of them, he said, were
English by birth and recently taken by the pirates to boot. It
should go easy with them, even the dons being able to
understand the oaths men swear when the devil drives. They
had only to tell the same tale, and like as not their ship with
her cargo, the salted cod left uneaten by the pirates, would be
returned to them, Spain and England being, for once, not at
war with each other.

There was no such comfort for the others as they watched
the mutineers swarm aboard the *Black Stallion*. With the
frigates growing larger on the horizon, they could hear the
shout of orders and squeal of the winches of the brigantine
drawing her anchor free of the blue water. They saw the
white sails unfurl beneath the yardarms, dropping downward
until the trades bellied them and the great fore and aft sail on
the mainmast filled, the boom swinging wide. Sleekly, without apparent effort, the ship began to move out of the cove,
leaving them behind with a fine kick of froth at her stern.

"He's going to make it," Captain Bonhomme said. "That
whoreson is going to make it."

But Morgan was watching the trees at the points of the
cove, a frown drawing his thick brows together. "I think
not."

From around the curves of the cove, coming from opposite
directions, their masts mingling with the tree trunks, were
two war vessels, great ships of the line mounting more than
two hundred guns between them.

"*Sacre bleu!*" the other man breathed, though it was difficult to tell whether in sorrow or gladness, as his gaze swung to follow Morgan's sighting, then returned to the slender lines of the brigantine. Though the men on board were mutineers, they had also been his crew for many a long day and longer leagues of sea travel. That the men aboard the *Black Stallion* had seen them was plain from the scurrying to and fro and the angling of guns.

Félicité drew in her breath as she recognized the danger.

"It may be they can still get away," Bonhomme said, "if only they can clear this deathtrap of a harbor."

"He's going to try for it," Morgan said, his voice quiet.

"He may as well. The brigantine has a shallower draft, right enough, and he could run back into the cove where the frigates and heavier ships could not follow, but the cannon of the Spanish are longer, with greater weight and range. The dons can stand out to sea and smash him to flinders. Nay, he has to try for it, or else choose the rope."

The Spanish ships converged, coming nearer and nearer the pirate vessel, until, squinting against the sun, it seemed to Félicité that a stone thrown from one deck could easily have hit the other. "Maybe," she said slowly, "the Spaniards are not going to fire on him."

Captain Bonhomme shielded his eyes, staring at the nearer vessels, casting a long doubtful glance at the frigates farther out. Then as his gaze lighted on the more distant brigantine, a great oath was torn from him.

"What is it?" Félicité asked.

"Ah, that I should live to see the day," the man groaned. "*Mon Dieu*, what have I done to deserve this betrayal? What did I ever do?"

Félicité turned her eyes toward the lighter-weight ship traveling under the protective convoy of the frigates. Her voice soft with puzzled amazement, she said, "Why, it's *La Paloma!*"

"Of a certainty. It is the ship of that beautiful whoring bitch Isabella. She has sold us out to the dons."

"You must be wrong," Félicité said, slanting a quick look at Morgan, waiting for his denial. He said nothing, his face bleak as he stared out to sea.

"No, I am not wrong," the other man said, "and well our friend Morgan knows it!"

It was then that the *Black Stallion* opened fire, all her starboard guns speaking at once with a single, deep-thudding boom. At such point-blank range, every shot struck the westward-gliding war vessel. Sails flapped and splinters flew. Shrieks of agony drifted over the water, but the Spanish ship glided onward for the space of several breaths without retaliation. Then from her decks there blossomed smoke and flame, and she heeled with the recoil of a thunderous broadside. The smoking cannon balls exploded across the deck of the *Black Stallion*, leaving tearing havoc in their wake. She veered then in ponderous grace, taking herself from the line of fire of her sister ship bearing down upon the now crippled brigantine.

Like a wounded minnow, the *Black Stallion* zigzagged, trying to bring her port guns to bear despite shattered bulwarks and tattered sails. But there must have been damage to her helm, for she could not come about completely. One or two of her guns roared from near the stern, but the range was faulty. The round shot fell short and to the right, sending brine splashing skyward.

It was the last shot fired from her, for the second war vessel with its high, ornate Spanish poop opened fire then with bellowing destruction. The cannonade reverberated against the sky and echoed from the hollow limestone bluff of the island. The men gathered on shore gave a collective grunt as the hurled shot brought down newly stepped mast and fresh sails.

The cries of the dying sent a shiver along Félicité's nerves. The brigantine, caught in the rays of the rising sun, seemed to glow, and then she realized that the bright shimmer amidships was licking tongues of fire. In hot greed they ran upward into the tangled and broken rigging and along the railing, feeding on tar and tallow and combustible pitch. Within minutes the ship was an inferno. Men with clothing ablaze leaped screaming into the water. One man climbed out upon the bowsprit to escape the rampaging heat and lost his grip, falling with a despairing wail to disappear beneath the waves. Great clouds of steam rose hissing to the heavens as the ship began to settle. Fearful of floating sparks of fire and windblown flame, the Spanish vessel stood off.

"My God," Morgan muttered, "aren't they going to pick up survivors?"

As if in answer, one tall ship began with leisurely motions to launch a longboat, but though it swept back and forth around the dying ship, by the time it reached the scene, there was no one left alive to rescue.

The *Black Stallion* burned to the waterline, took on water, and sank stern first into the waves. Long before the final bubble of air had floated upward from the hulk, the war vessels rendezvoused with the frigates out on the sea and anchor cables were run down. There was a great breaking out of signal flags as complimentary messages were relayed back and forth and orders dispatched. Then, as if with one accord, the attention of the men on the Spanish vessels was directed toward the island.

Valcour was dead, and with him more than a score of men. Félicité had seen them die, could even now see the dark turn of corpses and charred timbers in the waves, could smell the smoke and see it dissipating over the sea. Still, she could not believe it, did not want to believe that life could cease so easily in the soft light of morning. That such a thing could happen, suddenly, without appeal, seemed more a crime against nature than the justice she knew it to be. That her own life could be nearing its run, the seconds fleeing with every passing breath, was something she understood, but could not accept.

Her fears, as with anguished brown eyes she watched the longboats filled with red uniforms put out from the Spanish vessels, were not entirely for herself. They were also for the man at her side. How would Morgan, a turncoat Irish mercenary and former officer, fare with the Spanish? What would they do to him? What special death would they reserve for one who had betrayed them so publicly and was now caught in their snare?

The boats swept nearer, cresting the waves, the gathering brilliance of the sun touching gold braid, flashing on scarlet, and glinting silver-blue along musket barrels. In the prow of one sat a dark-haired woman with white-streaked hair. Seeing her, the French captain moved with dragging footsteps farther down the beach, where with hands propped on his hips and the wind ruffling the brown curls of his hair he stood waiting.

The other men gathered in groups. Bast, some distance away with several other members of the *Black Stallion*'s original crew, stared in Félicité's direction. The depths of his dark eyes seemed to hold a silent farewell, but he made no attempt to approach. Félicité smiled, a small gesture of contrition from the aching fullness of her heart, then, lifting her head, she turned from him toward Morgan.

Reaching out, she laid her cool fingers upon the muscled hardness of his forearm. Her voice low and clear, she spoke his name.

He turned his head to stare down at her, his mouth curved in the ghost of a smile and the look in his green eyes dark. "Yes, Félicité?"

"There is something I must tell you."

He put his fingers over hers, his touch warm, but oddly tentative. "I too," he said in low tones, "but perhaps it would be better if we wait."

She shook her head, refusing in the urgency of the moment to listen to him. "For what? Soon it may be too late, and I must tell you that—that I love you."

"Félicité," he breathed, the word a whisper of pain. "It is a fine gift for a man about to die, but—"

"I didn't tell you for that reason," she said, searching his face, her velvet-brown eyes wide, "but because I wanted you to know, and there may not be another chance. I have known it these many weeks, long before Valcour asked me to help him take your ship. I have known it and would not speak, because—" She faltered and could not go on.

"Because you could not trust me," he finished for her, his voice dull. "Why then is now any different?"

"If there is no future, trust is no longer important. Nothing matters except this moment."

He drew her into his arms then, holding her close, rocking her gently. "No matter how long I live, or what happens hereafter," he said, his breath warm against her temple. "I will never forget this day, nor will I forget you, Félicité, in your shirt and breeches with the wind and the sea in your hair. And the words you have spoken will be engraved on my heart when I quit this life."

He pressed his lips to hers then in a warm, caressing salute that might almost have been a renouncement, then, cradling her in the circle of his arms, held her brown eyes with his own emerald gaze.

Behind Félicité, there came the scrape and thud of longboats landing at the water's edge. The time had run out. For her, from Morgan McCormack, there had not been, would not be, a single word of love.

Chapter 20

Isabella de Herrara was the first to step from a Spanish boat. The French captain gave her his hand, helping her down to the sand. She smiled with great warmth, her fingers resting in his grasp for long moments. She spoke then a few quiet words that left an arrested look on his features, and turned away. Captain Jacques Bonhomme bowed, retreating a few steps, though his gaze did not leave the Spanish noblewoman.

With orderly precision and little sign of haste, a pair of Spanish officers disembarked. After them came the soldiers in red who formed ranks with shouldered muskets and stood stolid and incurious, awaiting orders.

"Morgan!" Isabella cried, as, looking around her, she discovered him with Félicité. Her smile was luminous with relief as she advanced. "I cannot tell you how marvelous it is to see you alive and whole. I so feared you would do something rash, such as attempting to fly with Félicité."

"The thought crossed my mind," he answered, taking the hand the woman stretched out to him.

Isabella nodded to Félicité and smiled before turning back. "Through the glass, I could not see you aboard your ship, nor could any other. Still, it was impossible to be certain. Of course, when the *Black Stallion* fired on us our captains had to assume either that you were not, or else you had gone mad! They had no choice except to destroy the vessel."

"I understand perfectly," Morgan answered.

It was more than Félicité did, and yet she was beginning to entertain a surmise so sweeping that it left her with a hollow feeling in the pit of her stomach.

"You are safe, that is all that matters. The rest can be—adjusted," Isabella said hurriedly, then stepped aside as one of the Spanish officers drew near.

"Ah, Colonel McCormack," the man said, bowing with a hand resting on his sword. "I am sure the marquesa has expressed our relief at finding you here on the island, and our regrets for the destruction of your ship. It is only left for me to extend congratulations for the successful conclusion of a most difficult mission."

Morgan returned the bow. "Thank you, Captain Ortega. The end of the affair would have been quite different but for your timely arrival."

With a murmured excuse and a thoughtful look in her eyes, La Paloma slipped away then. The captain watched her go with a trace of admiration in his face before he turned back to Morgan.

"For our prompt arrival," the man said, "much credit is owed to the Marquesa de Talavera. It was she who located your position for us. With the change of your status after the pirates took your ship, and the whole of the Caribbean in which to search for you, it would have been a harder and more time-consuming task without her and the unusual vessel she commandeered. I will admit I was skeptical of the usefulness of the offer when she first expressed an interest in being

333

of aid while cruising in the area, but I have since been much chastened by her accomplishments. As she put it to me, there are many places *La Paloma*—the ship I am speaking of, you understand—can go without causing alarm that a fleet of ships of the line cannot.''

''Quite true, I would imagine,'' Morgan answered, his tone dry.

Isabella had reached Captain Bonhomme, and was speaking to him in low tones once more. To one side stood the captain of the *Prudence* waiting impatiently to have his say, while beyond him, Bast, his shoulders assuming their military straightness once more, was standing at ease in laughing conversation with the other ship's officer. Félicité watched them all with a sense of grim unreality. The friendliness and respect being shown Morgan was not mere civilized behavior. With certainty, she saw that Morgan was not, had never been, a renegade. He had, in fact, never ceased to receive the pay of Spain. His presence in the Caribbean, far from being his own preference, had been carefully arranged, its purpose no doubt directed against the pirate activity in the area that threatened the success of the Spanish takeover of Louisiana.

The Spanish captain was speaking once more. ''This operation, and the way it has ended, should give the sea bandits plaguing our shipping pause. They will be looking over their shoulders from now on! Governor-General O'Reilly will be pleased, I'm sure.''

''It's only a beginning.''

''But a salutary lesson, a statement of our position that had to be made.''

''Yes,'' Morgan agreed without enthusiasm.

The officer nodded, then, dismissing the subject, asked, ''What of this Murat you were bound to catch? Where is he? And what of the other vessel in the cove and the man here with you? What is their position? Also, I believe a few of the pirates were seen making for the wooded area. Should men be detailed to round up the stragglers. Just what do you suggest, colonel? My men are at your disposal.''

Morgan glanced at Félicité, not quite meeting her eyes. ''I will explain about Murat later. The men who took to the woods were understandably nervous of your arrival, having no idea of just what you intended toward any of us. Most are either from the snow in the harbor, or else were recruited by me for this expedition. The captain of the snow is waiting to be introduced, but first let me repair my bad manners by making you known, Captain Ortega, to Mademoiselle Lafargue.''

"Mademoiselle," the Spaniard said when the introduction had been completed. As he executed his bow, there was a knowing look in his dark eyes that said plainly it was not the first time he had heard her name. The gaze flicking over her costume of shirt and breeches was disapproving.

"I would be grateful, captain," Morgan went on, "if you would send this lady under escort to your ship."

"Of course," the officer replied, his face hardening.

Félicité swung sharply to stare at Morgan. He met her gaze for an instant only before turning back to the other man.

"You will oblige me by showing her to whatever quarters may be provided for me, and by—seeing she is granted every comfort and expression of respect."

The officer inclined his head with slightly pursed lips before he turned to give the necessary orders.

"I—I must get a few things from the hut," she said over the constriction in her throat. Was she a prisoner, or was she not? Though Morgan's position was changed, the same could not be said of her own. She had gone on board the *Raven* willingly enough, had aided in the capture of the *Black Stallion*. Nothing she had done or said since could alter these facts, no excuse mitigated against the offense. In the eyes of the Spanish, then, she must be considered a female pirate and subject to the extreme penalties meted out for the crime.

As she moved away, she thought Morgan looked after her, but he did not speak.

Once in the hut, she gathered up her scant belongings, piling them together, rolling them up any which way, avoiding the sight of the rumpled pallet against the wall. With the bundle in her arms, she stood for a moment in the center of the floor, looking up at the rough thatched walls and conical roof, then out through the doorway to the heaving blue breast of the sea. She took a deep breath then, and, lifting her head, left the hut. Her footsteps were firm as she walked over the sand to the detail drawn up waiting for her.

The pull to the frigate was not a long one. She went up the rope ladder thrown over the side with practiced ease. It was as she reached the deck that she noticed another longboat sweeping from the shore, making for the brigantine, *La Paloma*. Even as she watched, it gained the smaller ship. Isabella negotiated the ladder, followed closely by a man. With a sudden shock of gladness, Félicité recognized Captain Jacques Bonhomme, saw too that the ship's anchor was being drawn up and the female sailors of the floating brothel had leaped to the rigging, preparing the ship to sail. Isabella and the French captain moved to the bow, standing close together.

On impulse, Félicité raised her hand in a wave, a gesture that was returned with vigor, and then the great white sails of the brigantine filled, and she was away with the white dove of the figurehead lifting its wings as if in flight, taking Isabella and her pirate lover swiftly away from too impartial justice, far over the seas.

There was not a ship in the harbor that could catch the fast brigantine. Smiling a little at this small "adjustment" of circumstance, this moment of quiet joy, Félicité watched the longboat that Isabella, in her own inimitable way, had purloined, race back to the island.

She turned to her own escort, finally. The men around her had been as interested in what was happening as she, but now they returned to duty. A Spanish lieutenant stepped forward, and with imposing courtesy led her below.

The cabin of the frigate was larger than any she had yet seen. Due primarily to the high poop, it had a wide expanse of windows giving ample light and air to a space provided with a single commodious bunk of carved mahogany spread with a down mattress, fine linen, and a velvet coverlet. A washstand of teak stood in one corner, and a desk of the same wood was set about with armchairs fitted with velvet cushions. There were gimbaled lanterns of brass hanging on the paneled walls, and an expanse of Turkey carpet on the floor. It was all in all a most luxurious prison.

Standing in the center of the room with his hands clasped behind his back, the lieutenant averted his gaze from her masculine attire and asked if there was anything she needed. When she signified that there was nothing, he paused, his gaze on the rumpled roll of clothing she held. Then, saying he would send the captain's personal manservant to her, he bowed himself out.

It was no more than a quarter hour later that a knock fell on the door. Moving to open it, Félicité found it was not locked. Her movements slow, she swung the panel wide.

Outside was a small, dapper man clad in the height of the Parisian mode. Inclining his head, the manservant said in perfect French, "I was told you might have need of my services, mademoiselle, in making yourself presentable."

For a brief flicker of time, anger gripped Félicité. Then, as she realized how true was that none too delicate hint concerning her appearance, a laugh was forced from her.

"Yes," she agreed, ushering the small man in. Why should she not make herself as attractive as possible for her jailer, if and when he decided to appear?

Félicité had time and more to attend to half-forgotten beauty rituals, to bathe and wash her hair with fine-milled soap scented with attar of roses, to smooth pure white goose grease into her roughened skin, to use a pumice stone to remove calluses, and also to shape her nails before she buffed them to a gloss. There was even time for a nap in the afternoon while her freshly laundered underclothing, her chemise and stays and petticoats, dried in the sun.

Clean from head to toe, with the scent of roses surrounding her, she donned the trappings of a woman once more. Her gown, pressed by the manservant, André, was of chocolate brown with ivory lace, the nearest she could come to the long-deferred mourning for her father. Thus attired, she let André into her cabin, where with casual skill he put up her hair in a mass of curls, allowing a soft, fat ringlet to fall over one shoulder. The pins for the task he produced from the same store, known only to him, whence had come the sweet-smelling soap and other accouterments of the feminine toilette.

She had thought that in her state of anxiety, with little more to do than wait for Morgan, she must know when he boarded the frigate. It did not turn out that way. Evening was drawing in and the ship was preparing to sail when he came to her. He had availed himself of the opportunity to freshen his appearance and change into his dress uniform. As he stood just inside the door with his fingers still on the handle, a tall, broad-shouldered figure with sun-bronzed features filling the cabin, Félicité's gaze rested on the familiar scarlet trimmed with gold braid he wore. She remembered seeing it aboard the *Black Stallion*, and later in a sea chest on the island that had been unloaded from the brigantine while she was careened. She should have known then that a true renegade would not have kept such a reminder of past loyalties.

He moved then, coming toward her with easy strides. "You look lovely, Félicité, though I'm not sure I didn't prefer you as a grubby urchin."

"And I you as the sailing master." The look in her eyes, as well as her tone, was cool.

He stopped, the smile fading from his expression. After a moment, he said, "Are you hungry? I have ordered supper for the two of us to be served here."

"Perfect," she said with irony. "I had no wish to intrude upon the officers' mess. And what other arrangements for my pleasure have you made to beguile the journey back to New Orleans? Surely you have thought of something to prevent me from brooding overmuch on what it feels like to be hanged? Or perhaps I should not worry. There is always the more honorable alternative, if no hangman can be found, of being shot!"

His eyes turned to green ice. "What are you saying?"

"Don't look so amazed. That is usually the fate of the pirates unlucky enough to fall into the hands of Spanish officialdom."

"You think I am actually returning you to New Orleans to stand trial as a pirate?"

"Oh, with every attention to my comfort and the greatest show of respect! But yes, what else?"

He stepped closer, his hands on his hips. "This passes all

bounds of what I will endure! Have you no idea what you mean to me?''

"Why should I have? How can I begin to guess what a man like you will do, a man who would make use of me for the sake of duty, who would hold my father's fate over my head? A man who could tell so plausible a collection of lies concerning his venture on the high seas while hiding a most secret and vital purpose?''

He dropped his hands, turning from her, moving to the window with its abnormally thick and wavy green glass. Taking a deep breath, he let it out slowly. "If you must hark back to the beginning for examples of my perfidy, then by all means let us rake through them and have done. For my treatment of you, there is no excuse, and I make none. Concerning your father, the bargain I made I kept. If it could have been bettered, I would have done so. It could not, and I don't believe I gave you reason to hope or expect otherwise. As for his tragic death, I had nothing to do with it. I was as shocked as you were."

"I know that," she answered his last words in strangled tones. "I also know, though I didn't understand at the time, why you tried to keep his reasons for taking his life from me. Valcour told me."

He rubbed his hand over his face, raking his fingers back through his hair. "Your brother had much to answer for, but we were speaking of my faults."

There was in his reaction to her misjudgment, her suggestion that he meant to see her hanged, enough anger to make her doubt that had been his purpose. With the easing of her tight-held fear came a disinclination to force him to this examination. It might well be that in his self-flagellating honesty, he would tell her something she would prefer not to know.

"Morgan, don't—"

"No, it's time and more that you understood. At that straggling, nameless port on Grand Cayman, when I saw you in the boat with Valcour, saw what he was doing to you, I lost my head, and so lost my ship also. That knowledge, with the ruin it could mean to so many plans, was unacceptable.

The brigantine I commanded, you see, was supposed to be an instrument of chastisement, preying on pirate ships. How mortifying it was to have it taken from me by a moment's inattention over a woman! Once, following Valcour's lead, I let myself believe that a portion of the blame might be yours. It wasn't long before I remembered your attempt to warn me, and knew I had been a fool. As for the lies—''

''You don't need to tell me. I have had a great deal of experience with your notions of duty.''

''There is that, of course. But if you think I was ordered to take command of the *Black Stallion*, then you are mistaken. O'Reilly considered I would be of more use to him in New Orleans. It was I who pointed out to him the value of my previous experience in the Caribbean among the corsairs. The rest happened just as I told you before; he let me take the mission because otherwise I would have gone in defiance of his orders.''

''To bring back Valcour, since you knew of his connection with the *Raven* and its atrocities?'' she suggested, her lashes shielding the perversity of her expression.

''No, my simpleton. What interest did I have in a mincing rogue like him, be he ever so vile and deserving of the rope? It was you I wanted, you who haunted my dreams so that I came awake night after night in a cold sweat of terror that I would not find you, ever again, so that I hired seamen and drove them to have the *Black Stallion* made ready so I could set out after you in the shortest length of time. I had sympathies of sorts with the pirates and smugglers, men trying to make their fortunes despite Spain's edicts, and I also understood O'Reilly's determination to follow the orders he was given. Despite the first, I was bound to try to carry out the latter. But my main purpose in beating the seas was for a golden-haired woman, and everything else could go to hell until I had her safe again.''

His voice rang as he turned to face her. ''Can you think, Félicité, that having risked so much, I would meekly give you over now to the hangman's noose?''

''Perhaps not,'' she said, meeting the blaze of his emerald

eyes, unconsciously according him her belief, "but if Spanish law decrees my guilt, can you do otherwise?"

"There will be no trial," he declared. "There are enough witnesses, and more, who heard Valcour say you were tricked aboard the *Raven* and were an unwilling accomplice to the capture of my ship to clear your name. And if that is not enough, why then I will fling O'Reilly's land grant in his face and take you with me back to sea. We will become pirates indeed, as I so nearly decided to do this morning rather than risk even the slightest chance of danger to you."

"Land grant?" she repeated. "I thought you said the governor-general had rescinded his promise of free land."

"I had to say something to account for my break with him."

"Another lie," she said softly.

He swung on her then, coming slowly back to her. "And what of you, Félicité, with your keeping score of words spoken of necessity and under the most stringent duress? Haven't you lived a lie these many weeks, pretending to despise me? Or was it told this morning? Did you perjure yourself with words of love, and offering of the paradise I was losing, one last tender blow between the eyes, before, as you thought, I was led away to a pirate's fate?"

"Morgan, no," she whispered. "How could you think so?"

"How could I not, when you have never by word or deed hinted at such a thing before, when you have lived in discontent with me, barely tolerating my touch, when time and time again I have found you with Bast? You may think you would be better suited with that spawn of a Spanish grandee, but I can tell you that you would not!"

"I know that. He asked me to marry him, to go with him to Spain when we got off the island, but I refused."

He stopped. "Is there no proposal to your liking? Why would you not agree to be the wife of the heir to one of the greatest fortunes in Spain?"

"Because," she said distinctly, "I did not love him."

Even as she spoke, she realized that Bast's proposal had been based on the fact that he had known of Morgan's mission and the imminent arrival, once *La Paloma* left the island, of the Spanish *guarda de costas*. Thinking back, she saw that he had come very near to giving away the secret then, if she had only known how to listen.

Morgan reached to pick up the love lock that lay across her shoulders, holding its shining softness carefully in his hand. "You did not answer my question in its entirety. Perhaps I can put it another way. If I were to ask you now, for the second time, to be my wife, would you say yes?"

Tension that bordered on trembling ran along her nerves. She stared at the gold buttons on his waistcoat. Her voice a whisper of sound, she said, "No."

He caught her forearms, his fingers biting into her flesh as he dragged her against him. "Before God, Félicité, you will drive me mad! Why?"

"It is true that I love you," she began, then pressed her hands to his chest, as he would have pulled her closer. Her velvet-brown eyes were soft with glistening tears of anguish as she went on. "But you were right; I would not have told you if I had not thought—that everything was over for us. For one to love while the other feels no more than desire, be it ever so consuming, is not enough. I could not bear to be your wedded wife on such terms, to have no more than your passion and your sufferance for the sake of a past wrong. I could not!"

His brows drew slowly together, and emerald fire danced in his eyes. "Because—dearest heaven, Félicité, how can you think I do not love you? Have I not told you so in a thousand ways? You are the breath of my body and the beat of my heart. The thought of you is a constant flow in my mind, and has been since the first moment I saw you with the contents of that damnable chamber pot perfuming the air! If I had not been obsessed with you to the point of sickness, the thought of your plotting my death with Valcour would not have been so enraging, and you might be a virgin still. If the look and feel and taste of you were not the only solace of my soul, why else would I have bartered for the command of my own private hunting expedition? I love you beyond the conception of sober and lucid men or the shrouded visions of yearning women, and if you will not agree to come with me and be the wife I would cherish in sanctified pleasure, then torment me how you may, I will forswear the part of a civilized man and become a pirate again, shackling you to me by force!''

The tears shivered on the ends of her lashes as her lips curved into a slow smile. ''And if I will?''

''Then no man, no court, no set of laws, will ever take you from me as long as we both have breath.''

She went into his arms then, clasping her hands behind his bent head. Their lips met with passion and power, sweetly savored, tenderly possessed.

Morgan held her close then, his chin against the silk of her hair, his senses reeling with the fragrance of roses. ''We can say our wedding lines before the captain this night, if you like.''

''Yes, eventually.'' By slow degrees, she freed herself, drawing him with her toward the beckoning comfort of the velvet-covered bunk.

Much later, she stirred, cushioning her cheek more comfortably against Morgan's arm as she spread her fingers over the sculpted planes of his bare chest. ''You knew,'' she said softly, ''that Captain Bonhomme went away with Isabella, did you not?''

''Yes, I saw,'' he answered, his voice deep with lazy satiation, the sound vibrating against her palm.

''I wonder if they can possibly be as happy as we are?''

''No.'' The answer was simple, positive, and required, of course, a reward. After a moment, he said, ''I expect Bonhomme will make a fine marqués when he has grown used to the new identity Isabella will provide for him.''

''Perhaps he will use his own rightful name, left behind when he became a corsair?''

''Perhaps.'' He turned, brushing the silken strands of her hair from her shoulder, leaning to press his lips to the curve he had uncovered.

''André, the captain's manservant, will be furious about my hair, and about having to press my gown again.''

''It doesn't matter,'' Morgan murmured.

Félicité's voice grew drowsy as he seared a path from her shoulder to the peak of her breast. "Doesn't it?"

"His services will not be required again."

"Not even for the wedding," she mused, running her fingers through the hair over his ear and along the nape of his neck. He turned his head to smile at her, a promise in his green eyes.

"Well," he conceded, his tone a fine blend of reluctance and anticipation, "perhaps once more."

About the Author

Jennifer Blake was born near Goldonna, Louisiana, in her grandparents' 120-year-old hand-built cottage. It was her grandmother, a local midwife, who delivered her. She grew up on an 80-acre farm in the rolling hills of North Louisiana and got married at the age of fifteen. Five years and three children later, she had become a voracious reader, consuming seven or eight books a week. Disillusioned with the books she was reading, she set out to write one of her own. It was a gothic—SECRET OF MIRROR HOUSE—and Fawcett was the publisher. Since that time she has written twenty-three books, with more than four million copies in print, and has become one of the bestselling romance writers of our time. Her recent Fawcett books are THE STORM AND THE SPLENDOR, GOLDEN FANCY, and ROYAL SEDUCTION. Jennifer, her husband, and their four children are currently enjoying the completion of their new home near Jonesboro, Louisiana—styled after the old Southern planters' cottage.